STEPHANIE FAZIO

OPAL SLAYER

OPAL CONTAGION BOOK 2

Syafant Press

New York, New York

Copyright © 2020 Stephanie Fazio.

Cover designed by Keith Tarrier

This book is a work of fiction. Names, characters, places, and incidents either are the product of the author's imagination or are used fictionally, and any resemblance to actual persons, living or dead, business establishments, events, or locales is entirely coincidental.

Stephanie Fazio

Visit www.StephanieFazio.com

Printed in the United States of America
First Printing: July 2020

Library of Congress Control Number: 2020907467

ISBN 978-1-951572-07-5

PROLOGUE

The councilman's widow kept adjusting the hood of her cloak to hide her face. Her dragonhide boots clipped along the cobbles as she hurried down the road. It was early morning, so Lagonia's roads were empty and quiet. Even if there had been others around, no one would have taken any notice of Kelsleigh. Now that her family's reputation was shattered, she might as well be a ghost.

For months, Kelsleigh had suffered the gossip, whispers, and cruelty generated in the Lagonia court. She'd been forced to stay silent, when all she'd wanted to do was scream at the top of her lungs, *My husband was framed!*

Kelsleigh climbed over the stone wall that surrounded the overgrown training field. The earthy scents of moss and wet leaves filled the air as she tramped through the grass. It was so easy to forget the rest of the continent was covered in ice and snow at this time of year. Lagonia's balmy temperatures were partly a result of its mountain and ocean enclosure, and partly from a gift from the Insorsil queen to the former emperor.

Her late husband's sword thumped against her leg with every step. Its clunky weight was a comfort…a reminder.

Be brave, my darling.

Those were her husband's last words to her before he was led to the executioner's platform.

Kelsleigh stiffened her spine and went to meet the soldiers who were already gathered. There were close to fifty of them standing on the field, although Kelsleigh knew it was only a small fraction of the ones who supported her cause.

At least, that was what the captains Wilsean and Ciago had told her.

It was a shame the men weren't at the meeting now. Alas, they were out supervising tax collection…again. It was the third time the Emperor had sent them this week.

Kelsleigh rested her hand on the pommel of her husband's sword and cleared her throat.

"I've called this meeting because I think we can all agree that Emperor Jaikon, Jr. is no longer fit to be our sovereign."

She looked around at the soldiers. Not a single one of them fidgeted.

"Before we wage war against our own," one soldier said, "we need to know who we will instate as the new emperor."

A dark-skinned woman who had been instrumental in organizing this meeting stepped forward.

Her name was Dannica, Kelsleigh recalled.

Dannica said, "There's no question who the new emperor should be." She turned so she was facing the rest of the group. "Rhett."

A murmur of approval went through the crowd. Some of the soldiers stood taller, like the mere mention of the now-disgraced former Chief Assassin gave them strength.

"If we can find him," Aliamu, a high-ranking soldier, cautioned.

"He'll come back," Dannica assured the crowd. "And when he does, we're going to have his throne waiting for him."

All at once, the shadows in the treeline began to move. That's when Kelsleigh saw the gleam of weapons. Cloaked men, camouflaged to blend in perfectly with their surroundings, peeled away from the trees. They threw off their cloaks to reveal the black and gold armor of the Lagonia guard.

Kelsleigh's blood turned to ice.

The rebel soldiers surrounding Kelsleigh reacted immediately. They drew their own weapons and spread out, forming even lines that stretched out across the field. Their expressions remained calm and focused as the Lagonia guards parted to make room for a looming figure.

The silence got heavier as Emperor Jaikon strode onto the field.

Kelsleigh forced her trembling arm to still. This was the man who had ordered her husband's execution. This was the man who had destroyed her entire world.

She drew her own sword and anchored her stance, grasping for the steadiness the soldiers around her seemed to come by naturally.

The new Chief Assassin stood beside Emperor Jaikon. Elouicia—as hated by the soldiers as Rhetteman was loved—grinned. His smile revealed teeth that had been filed into canine points. There was a mad twinkle in the assassin's eyes.

"Well, well, well. What have we here?" The Emperor's voice matched the ice blue of his eyes.

Kelsleigh looked up and met the frigid gaze of her husband's killer.

None of the soldiers spoke. They stood shoulder-to-shoulder as they gripped their weapons.

Dannica was the first to speak.

"Rhett is our true leader. He always has been."

"Rhetteman is a traitor." The Emperor spat on the ground. "He is a coward. He is nothing."

Hatred twisted the Emperor's face into an ugly sneer.

"Rhett will be this empire's savior," Aliamu said.

"Enough." The Emperor raised his hand for silence.

A hush fell as everyone on the field made the same observation at once. The Emperor's right hand was crippled. His thick glove couldn't disguise the unnatural bend of his wrist and the way his fingers curled in on themselves.

There had been rumors, but Lagonian gossip did tend to take on a life of its own. It was clear this story, at least, was grounded in truth.

The palace gossip wasn't clear on how the Emperor's hand had been shattered. Some said it had been a parting gift from Rhetteman before he escaped the torture cage. Others said it had been his lover.

Kelsleigh hoped the injury caused him excruciating pain.

The Emperor knew what had drawn everyone's attention. His sneer turned into something dark. Elouicia was running his tongue over his jagged teeth, like he was looking forward to devouring every one of them. She'd heard stories….

"I will allow the first person who begs for his life to walk off this field unharmed," the Emperor said in a soft voice. He gave them a benevolent smile that raised the hairs on Kelsleigh's arms.

No one spoke. The soldiers gathered in this clearing had been trained by Rhetteman Loniger himself. They didn't flinch.

A guttural cry tore from Kelsleigh's throat. She lunged.

With one hard thrust, she sent the Emperor's weapon flying out of his clumsy left hand. His face flashed surprise as the point of her sword struck home.

Or, it should have struck home.

Instead, a blue light began to pulse around the Emperor. Kelsleigh's sword quivered as she tried to drive it through the Emperor. The blue light barrier resisted. The harder she pushed, the brighter the light became.

With a sound that set Kelsleigh's teeth on edge, the sword's blade shattered. She was thrown backward. Her sword hilt, which was all that remained of the weapon, thumped onto the grass beside her.

Jaikon stepped forward and bent to pick up the hilt. He tossed it in the air and caught it.

Too dazed to do anything but stare, Kelsleigh watched as the pulsing blue light retracted. It was absorbed into a small pin on the Emperor's chest.

"Now," the Emperor said. "Who wishes to beg for his life?"

The Emperor ignored Kelsleigh, who lay stunned on the ground. His gaze roved over the crowd of soldiers.

"Rhett will defeat you," Aliamu said.

Kelsleigh's pulse sped up at the sound of those words. The Emperor would be defeated, and then her husband would be avenged.

Two long strides brought the Emperor before Aliamu.

"I am Lagonia's Emperor." Jaikon regarded the other man. "And I am invincible."

Jaikon slammed the hilt against Aliamu's head. The soldier went down.

The Emperor struck again. And again. Blood and bone flew into the air until the man on the ground was no longer recognizable.

Kelsleigh was the only one whose cry carried across the otherwise-silent field.

Jaikon gave the barest nod to his guards. The men didn't hesitate to attack.

Kelsleigh's soldiers were stronger, better, and more numerous, but it didn't matter. Time and time again, their blades struck against barriers of glowing blue light. Whatever was making the Emperor immune to death also protected his guards.

The rebels' swords shattered on impact or ricocheted off with a force that threw them from their owners' hands. Either way, Kelsleigh's soldiers were left weaponless and exposed. One by one, they fell.

Their blood soaked into the grass.

Five…ten…twelve…. Kelsleigh had to stop counting the bodies when her stomach lurched. She turned to the side and vomited onto the bloodstained grass.

"Majesty!"

The crash of weapons paused as the Master Interrogator stalked onto the field. The man's face betrayed no hint of emotion as he took in the carnage.

"What is it, Stone?" The Emperor raised one golden eyebrow.

"Majesty, these traitors are beneath your notice," the Master Interrogator said in a cold, merciless voice that sent chills down Kelsleigh's spine. "Besides, killing soldiers when there is so much unrest isn't wise. You risk alienating the rest of your army—"

"I am Lagonia's Emperor!" Jaikon roared.

"Indeed, you are," Stone agreed. "And these soldiers have born witness to your invincibility. Let them spread the message of your strength to the edges of the empire. That will put any other murmurs of dissension to rest."

Jaikon thrust his sword into a corpse at his feet. Kelsleigh flinched, even though the already-dead body did not. The Emperor stroked his left hand along his beard as he considered the Master Interrogator's words.

"There are none who can stop me now," Jaikon mused.

Stone gave his emperor a nod. "You have proven to these soldiers that you are invulnerable. They will not hesitate to bow to you again."

Jaikon nodded. "But their actions cannot go unpunished."

"Majesty, think about how your other soldiers—"

"I won't execute them."

The Emperor strode up to Dannica, who was either too brave or too foolish to back away.

"You will renew your loyalty to this empire by completing a mission," Jaikon announced. "You will conquer the Giant Realm in the name of Jaikon Horowicken II, the eternal emperor of Lagonia."

Kelsleigh pressed a hand to her mouth to stifle her gasp. The Giant War, which ended two years earlier, had claimed the lives of thousands. And that conflict had been over only a small island in the middle of the Brookgar Sea.

It was a well-known fact that the giant lord only permitted those with giants' blood to set foot on his shores. If these soldiers sailed all the way to the Giant Realm, they'd be slaughtered before their ships moored.

"Oh," the Emperor said, as if as an afterthought. "And if you return before you have successfully completed your mission, my Chief Assassin will personally execute every person you hold dear."

Elouicia bared his canines in a fierce grin. The Emperor casually made his way among the soldiers standing stock-still on the field.

"Like your brother and elderly father," the Emperor said to Dannica. "And your mistress," he told another soldier, whose lips went bloodless. "Your infant daughter," Emperor Jaikon continued, flicking his hand at another soldier.

Kelsleigh understood the Emperor's cruel brilliance. He wasn't killing the traitors outright, but he was sending them to their deaths.

Not a single one of these soldiers would return.

Jaikon turned to Stone. "Gather every other soldier who was on duty the day Rhetteman and Opal Smoke escaped. Send them with the others."

Stone bowed without uttering another word.

The rebel soldiers stepped over their fallen comrades as they marched off the field in orderly columns. Not a single one of them cried or begged, even though they must have known their assignment was a death sentence.

Kelsleigh was pushing herself up on unsteady legs, when the Emperor's quiet voice made her go still.

"Someone must be made an example of. I cannot allow my subjects to think me weak."

"Majesty, I think you've already made your point." Stone indicated the dead on the ground.

Jaikon, who hadn't once looked toward Kelsleigh, pinned her with a glance. The widow felt cold sweat slither down her back.

Be brave, my darling.

"A man who makes false accusations doesn't deserve to be emperor," she said. "Our rebellion will succeed, and then you will be forced to answer for your crimes."

Kelsleigh's voice didn't waver, even when the new Chief Assassin came closer. Stone hovered behind them.

The Emperor's lip curled back in a sneer as he stood in front of her. "Here is to the end of your rebellion."

The Emperor's sword cut into the lovely silk dress Kelsleigh had selected for today. The blade slid through her skin until it hit bone.

The pain was intolerable for only a few seconds before it began to fade away. Wetness and heat spread across her midsection. The ivory silk turned crimson.

"Find Rhetteman and Opal Smoke," the Emperor said to the guards clustered around him. "Bring them to me alive."

His voice had a faraway quality, like Kelsleigh was underwater. The image of him was blurred, too.

"Alive?" Elouicia asked, bearing his sharpened teeth.

The men's voices were getting farther away, even though no one had moved.

"For some, there are worse punishments than death," the Emperor replied.

His voice was so distant Kelsleigh could barely hear him anymore. She could no longer see him through the dark curtain that was being pulled over her eyes. Still, she strained to hear. This kind of gossip was too good to allow to slip through her fingers. The court ladies would sit at her feet and lap up every word....

"By the time I'm finished with them, death will be a mercy."

Yes, it was, Kelsleigh thought as a calmness came over her. As the last breath left her body, she knew the ones the Emperor was hunting wouldn't be so lucky.

CHAPTER 1

L iss tipped the final drop of potion into Rhett's mouth. She waited with baited breath.

Nothing happened.

Her disappointment was crushing enough that, for several seconds, her heart stilled.

"Maybe it takes longer to work," Spence suggested, peering at Rhett's unmoving form.

"It's been two weeks." Liss heard the desperation in her own voice.

Two weeks since the golden dragon deposited them in the Insorsiled forest. Two weeks they'd been holed up in a small recess built into the side of the rocks, which barely protected them from the wind and prying eyes. Two weeks she'd been administering the potions Samara had given her.

Liss had slept in fits and spurts, since she hadn't wanted to miss even a single dose of Rhett's medicines.

His broken bones had mended back together. His fever was gone, and he no longer cried out and thrashed in his sleep. His mortal wounds had healed, but his skin was still mottled with bruises.

Liss turned to the large bag of flowers she guarded more carefully than she would a newborn baby. She unzipped the bag, and opal-hued light spilled out. The color danced across the snowy ground. Rainbows glinted off the tiny facets of ice particles.

Liss took out a single dried flower. The blossom fit in the palm of her hand. Its petals looked like they'd been dipped in opal-colored oil. If Liss stared at them for too long, she began to see rainbow-colored spots across her vision.

Liss poured some water into a cup. As soon as she added the blossom, it disintegrated. It turned into a fine, white powder. And then even that dissolved, until it looked like there was nothing left but water.

She hated how fragile the flowers were. It was a daily reminder of how the flowers were all that kept her very essence from being a deadly poison to Rhett.

Samara's sister had been clear in her instructions. Rhett needed precisely one flower a day to stay immune to the opal contagion. Liss gave it to him at the same time each day so there was never any underlap. It was common knowledge that the virus was potent enough to infect a person within minutes of an encounter.

Liss couldn't stand the idea of Rhett's skin breaking out in those awful, festering pustules that were the first symptom of opal contagion.

Liss tipped Rhett's head up and poured the water down his unresisting throat. She wanted to shake him and demand that he wake up. Instead, she replaced the cap on the water bottle and zipped up the bag of flowers.

She stared into his soul again. There were emotions floating in the depths, but they were too fuzzy for her to make sense of. It was so different from when he was awake. Usually, his soul was filled to bursting with all of his contradicting emotions. Now that he was unconscious, she kept turning to her Extension to reassure herself that he was still with her.

He was so still.

Rhett felt more than anyone she'd ever met. It was what had drawn her to him before she'd even laid eyes on him.

"You need to eat something," Spence said, pushing back his mop of burnt orange hair. "I got some rolls and a bag of apples. I even managed to steal an entire hock of ham."

While Liss sat and worried over Rhett, Spence had snuck into Insorsil to steal basic necessities—blankets, food, and water. It would have been easier if they could have flown the golden dragon all the way back to the hideout where the rest of their caravan had gathered. But the stolen dragon had lost patience with its cargo shortly into the flight. They'd barely managed to land and scramble off before the dragon could burn them to a crisp. The dragon had taken back off, and now they were stuck in this little hideaway until Rhett woke up.

Liss listened with half an ear as Spence told her how he'd stolen the ham.

"I didn't even have to put the shopkeeper to sleep," Spence added. "The dope was so busy collecting the basket of oranges I knocked over, he didn't even notice I had an entire ham."

"I couldn't be prouder of my protégé," Liss said. "You're going to have me out of a job."

It was easy to forget Spence was still just a kid. He'd sprung up like a weed in the months Liss had been away in Lagonia, and she still hadn't gotten used to his newly-deepened voice.

Spence pffed. "Like you could get anywhere near Insorsil without getting arrested. Your faces are plastered on every building."

Liss nodded absently. She was staring up at the sky. It looked like it was going to snow again.

Fall had turned to winter in a blink. Already, the earth was coated in a layer of frost. Dead leaves crackled as the wind sent their icy remains scattering across the ground. The air was so cold it stung her nose and numbed her toes.

There was nothing else Liss could do to keep Rhett warm aside from piling blankets on top of him.

Wake up, she silently begged him. She reached out to touch his cheek. Insorsiled quick-heal had taken care of the deep gashes there, but three scars remained.

Jaikon. Jaikon had done this to him.

If Rhett didn't kill his half-brother, Liss would do it herself.

"So, what are you going to do with Opal Slayer once he wakes up?" Spence asked.

Liss winced. Spence had been operating under the assumption they'd rescued Rhett to use him for leverage against the Lagonians, and she hadn't exactly done much to divest him of that misconception.

"Um, yeah, about that—"

A bone-rattling thud shook the forest.

Liss was on her feet in an instant. She had Rhett's dagger, which Stone had given her along with the dried immunity flowers.

Another bone-rattling thud shook the ground.

"Get behind me," Liss whispered to Spence.

She stood protectively in front of Rhett. Liss didn't really believe the dagger in her hand would save them from whatever was making that noise, but she would be damned if she went down without a fight.

"Holy—"

Liss's curse stuck in her throat as an enormous, hairy foot slammed into the ground at the edge of the trees.

Liss followed the foot up to an even hairier leg. If she stood on her tiptoes, she might be able to reach up to touch the giant's waist. Not that she would try.

The dagger quivered in her unsteady grip.

Liss didn't have time to wonder why a giant was on this side of the sea.

Deal with today's problems now, and tomorrow's problems later. The mystery of the giant's presence was a tomorrow problem.

"Get out of here," Liss whispered to Spence. "I'll keep the giant's attention, and—"

"Hungry!"

The giant's voice sent a colony of bats shrieking out from whatever tree they'd been nesting in. Liss jumped back, knocking into Spence, who *oofed* as his back hit the ground.

"We did *not* survive every soldier in Lagonia just to get eaten by a giant," Spence whispered.

Did giants eat people? Liss didn't think she'd heard anything to that effect, but the giants were known for their brutality.

Her heart skipped a beat when she looked up at the hideous creature. At the same moment, the giant looked down.

Don't scream. Don't scream. Don't—

"Yummy."

The giant stalked closer, his beady eyes fixed on Liss.

Regardless of what she had or hadn't heard about giants' dietary preferences, there was no question what kind of food this one was craving.

Her.

Liss tightened her hold on the dagger. Maybe she'd get lucky and hit an artery....

"What do we do?" Spence asked in a panicked whisper.

"Run," Liss ordered him. "I'll distract it."

Liss looked down at Rhett once more, desperately hoping the giant's stomping had woken him.

Rhett was as unmoving as he'd been for the last two weeks.

A blur of opal skin and orange hair passed by her. Liss looked up in time to see Spence sprinting for the giant.

"Spence!"

Her friend slid across the frozen ground and slapped his hand on the giant's hairy foot.

Any human would have fallen dead asleep at the contact, but the giant was no human.

"Huh?" the giant scratched his matted beard. His eyelids drooped.

Liss realized if the giant passed out, he would crush all three of them.

"Oh shit," Spence said, having come to the same realization.

Luckily—maybe—the giant didn't fall asleep. He took a stumbling step backward, shook his head, and blinked again. The giant yawned. His mouth was cavernous enough to swallow her whole. A wretched, rotting garbage smell wafted toward her.

Liss tried not to gag.

"Spence, please," she said, as the giant wavered on his feet.

She wasn't going anywhere without Rhett, and she couldn't carry him. But Spence could save himself.

"I'm not leaving you behind." Spence's orange-rimmed eyes blazed with defiance.

The giant grunted. He took another step toward them.

Liss raised the dagger. She tried not to think about how her weapon was the length of the giant's index finger.

"No wear furs?"

Liss blinked.

"Um...what?"

The giant was close enough for her to stab his foot, but she was afraid that would only infuriate him.

"No one wants furs no more." The giant shook his head sadly.

Liss took hold of her fear long enough to sort the giant's emotions. She had never been this close to a giant before, much less glimpsed into one's soul. Apparently, they worked the same way as humans in that regard.

The giant's soul was simple. She could tell he was a little dim, but his soul didn't feel evil the way she'd expected. There was desperation and fear, although Liss couldn't guess what the giant was afraid of.

"Hungry," the giant said again.

He kneeled. Liss prepared to strike.

Instead of reaching out to grasp her as one might a juicy drumstick, the giant pointed.

Liss followed the line of the giant's enormous, dirt-encrusted finger.

The giant was pointing at the small pile of supplies Spence had gathered.

"Oh!" Liss's legs wobbled only a little as she backtracked to the food. She grasped the ham hock and offered it up to the giant. "Is this what you want?"

The giant gave Liss an uncertain look. When she peered into his soul, she saw hope and yearning.

"It's alright," she told the giant in what she hoped was a soothing voice. "You can have it."

The giant reached out and plucked the ham out of Liss's hand. She tried not to wince when the giant tossed the entire thing into his mouth and chewed. Bones crunched between the giant's teeth, but he didn't seem bothered. He smacked his lips, burping loudly enough to make the ground underfoot tremble. The smell was almost enough to make her pass out.

"*Nasty,*" Spence breathed.

"Good," the giant announced as he licked each of his fingers.

The desperation and fear in his soul were calmer than they'd been. Liss looked more closely at the giant. Now that she wasn't as afraid of being devoured, she craned her neck to get a good look him.

His face was covered in dirt. His tangled beard frizzed and extended outward in the world's largest rat nest.

The giant was wearing a fur cloak. Liss felt a moment of sympathy for the sheer number of animals that had must have been needed to make the garment.

Liss realized that, for as big as he was, the giant was too thin. In the gaps between his fur cloak, Liss could see enormous ribs protruding through his dirt-streaked skin.

Liss knew starvation when she saw it.

"Here." She tossed an apple to the giant.

Instead of reaching out his hand, the giant bent and caught the fruit in his mouth. He chewed once and then swallowed.

"Good!"

"Cool." Spence grabbed another apple and tossed it at the giant.

Spence threw one apple after another until Liss wasn't sure if he or the giant was having more fun.

The giant was giggling—a sound that scared off what little wildlife remained. Spence's orange eyes were bright with mischief as he juggled the remaining apples before popping them off his elbow and into the giant's open mouth.

Boys, Liss thought, rolling her eyes.

They gave the giant every bite of food they had in the camp. When all of it was gone, Liss started to worry the giant would come for them next.

There was no violence on the giant's soul, though. For as savage as these creatures were known to be, this one seemed downright placid. The desperation and fear she'd sensed were weaker than they'd been before the giant's meal.

"Grub," the giant said, pointing to himself.

For a confused moment, Liss thought the giant was demanding more food. Spence caught on faster.

"I'm Spence, and this is Liss," he said.

"That's his name?" Liss whispered.

Spence shrugged.

"For you." The giant lowered a satchel that had been strapped across his chest.

The satchel thudded to the ground.

Spence opened the leather tie while Liss stood with Rhett's dagger still gripped in her hand. Just because the giant wasn't evil, it didn't mean he wasn't going to devour them.

Human-sized fur blankets, fur cloaks, and fur hats spilled out of the bag. She and Spence exchanged a puzzled look.

A merchant giant? This encounter was getting weirder by the second.

She tried not to let her confusion show on her face. Furs were the giants' greatest—their only—commodity, as far as Liss knew. On this side of the sea, the only animals with hides worth turning into clothes were the dragons bred for that very purpose.

There were many varieties of soft-pelted animals that made their homes in the Giant Realm. Clothes made from their hides had become the height of Lagonia fashion several years back, despite Lagonians having no need for such warm clothes. Normally, though, the furs arrived by boat, and the Insorsiled traders were the intermediaries between the giants and those who wished to purchase the pelts.

In general, when a giant was on this side of the Brookgar Sea, it meant trouble for everyone.

"Thank you," Liss told Grub, "but we don't have any jewels to pay for them."

"No jewels," Grub said. Slight offense filtered into his soul, and Liss realized the furs were meant to be a gift.

"Thank you." She took out a cloak and wrapped it around herself to show her gratitude. It was slightly too large, but she was immediately cocooned in warmth.

"Goodbye, friends," Grub said, waving at them. "Go to find new giant home."

The giant lumbered off before Liss could think of something to say.

A new giant home?

Nothing the giant said made any sense. Of course, giants weren't known for their scintillating intellect.

Still shaking a little, Liss let the dagger drop to the ground before she accidentally cut herself.

"Phew, that was a close one." Spence plopped back onto a soft fur blanket he'd pulled out of the sack.

Grub's footsteps crashed back through the forest.

Liss stared after him. With the damage done to the trees, she now had a clear view to the open road. They weren't as far into the woods as she'd originally thought. The recess that shielded them from the wind wasn't deep enough to hide them completely. Now, all the soldiers who were searching for them would be able to see them.

The thought had barely entered her mind when something came whipping through the air.

"Look out!" Liss shouted.

They both dove to avoid the silver lasso. Liss could tell it was Insorsiled by the way it locked onto Spence and ensnared him, even though it should have passed right over him.

Spence's eyes bulged. Liss threw herself at him, desperately grabbing at the slippery rope to loosen it.

The lasso tightened. It pinned Spence's arms to his body so he wouldn't be able to use his Extension.

Liss fumbled at the knots that re-tied themselves the moment they were loosened. She growled in frustration.

She almost had Spence free when a rope lashed across her legs. Her ankles locked together. She hit the ground. Before she could get up, a second rope looped over her neck and squeezed.

Liss struggled, but it only made the noose tighten.

She fought like a caged beast, writhing on the ground as she tried to loosen the rope's hold.

Even without anyone on the other end of the rope, Liss's lasso began to drag her across the ground. She could either follow the rope's tug, or let it snap her neck. With no other choice, she crawled along with the rope's pressure. Spence was beside her. He wrestled against the noose around his neck, but he didn't make any more progress than she did.

"I'll kill you!" Liss shouted, her voice raspy from the pressure of the rope around her neck.

They were deep into the trees by the time the ropes stopped yanking them forward. Liss and Spence collapsed in a small clearing. They huddled together as their numb, bloodied fingers continued to fumble with the knots that refused to release them.

Someone stomped into the clearing, whistling as he came up behind Liss. She smelled sour beer and felt long nails scrape against the back of her neck. She didn't need to be a Soul Sorter to know the man was evil, but when she looked at his emotions, she couldn't help the shudder that went through her.

There was only one kind of person with a soul this rotten. Slavers.

Except, now that the immunity flowers were almost gone, there was no longer any demand for Extended slaves….

"Little flies caught in a web." The slaver chuckled. "It's a good day to be a spider."

Liss screamed.

CHAPTER 2

Rhett woke to the sound of Liss's scream.

Save her.

Nothing else mattered, even though he knew he was too close to death to be useful. He felt no pain, but he remembered the damage that had been done to his body. He braced himself for one final fight…one more attempt at saving Liss. Unless he was already dead.

He opened his eyes and sat up.

He wasn't in the torture cage like he should be. There were no shackles on his wrists and ankles. His body ached, but it was the kind of ache from overuse. One of his eyes was swollen and tender to the touch, but Rhett could tell it was nothing more severe than deep bruising. He didn't feel the burn of torn flesh or the lightning-hot sear of broken bones. And yet, the lack of pain wasn't because he was so close to death pain had ceased to exist.

Rhett was healed.

The crisp air and pine needle smell told him that, somehow, he was in the Insorsiled forest. He glanced down and found his dagger beside him, like it had been waiting for him to wake up.

Rhett grabbed his weapon and got to his feet.

It took a second to find his balance. He was weak with hunger and his muscles protested with every movement, but since he'd been seconds from death the last time he was awake, he wasn't complaining.

He also wasn't interested in anything that wasn't related to finding Liss.

Where was she?

Rhett took two steps before he caught sight of the deep depression in the frozen ground. It was a giant's footprint. *What the hell was a giant doing in Insorsil?*

His gaze tracked the path of ruin the giant had left in its wake. Young trees had been broken in half. The giant had gone back the way he'd come, but Rhett saw no evidence of a struggle. There were no drops of blood on the frost-covered ground.

Where was Liss?

A cry, this one male, had Rhett turning away from the giant's footprints.

He forced his stiff and aching muscles into a jog. He slipped through the trees, keeping to the shadows.

When he caught sight of Liss, his anxiety turned to white-hot rage.

She was lying on the ground. There was an Insorsiled rope around her neck and another around her ankles. The Extended boy Rhett vaguely remembered was tied in his own Insorsiled rope, but Rhett barely spared the kid a glance. It was the slaver looming over Liss that captured all of his attention.

It took every ounce of willpower he possessed not to go charging straight for the man. He didn't fully trust his newly-healed body, and he couldn't risk the slaver getting a weapon into Liss before Rhett separated the man's head from his body.

Besides, Rhett needed the man. The only way to unknot an Insorsiled rope was for its owner to complete the task.

"The posters all over Insorsil didn't lie," the slaver said. "You are *fine*."

"Your soul is as ugly as your face," Liss retorted.

Rhett's heart expanded at the sound of her voice. He moved as quickly and silently as he could, using the trees for cover so he could approach the slaver from behind.

"Brave words from a fly stuck in a web," the slaver taunted.

The man was crouched beside Liss. He wore a thick, yellow anti-contagion suit that covered him from head to toe. Rhett hadn't seen those suits in almost two years, since the immunity had made them unnecessary.

The slaver's voice was muffled through the transparent lining that covered his face. One of his gloved hands was on the rope and the other was on Liss's neck.

Rhett's pulse crashed in his ears.

"The Emperor wants you *bad*," the slaver told Liss. "The reward is enough to make it worth running around in this suit. Worth having to smell your filthy Extended blood all the way back to Lagonia."

The man was so intent on Liss that he didn't sense Rhett behind him. Rhett grabbed the man's yellow hood and jerked his head back. He sliced his dagger across the fabric of the anti-contagion suit. Then, Rhett fitted the blade of his dagger against the slaver's bare throat.

"Release her," Rhett commanded.

"Rhett!" Liss gasped, even though she couldn't see him.

"Whoever you are, this isn't your business," the man snarled.

"You made it my business when you touched her. Let her go."

Rhett dug the blade of his dagger deep enough to draw blood.

"I'll get opal contagion," the slaver whined as began unknotting the rope around Liss's neck and ankles. "All the jewels in the empire won't be worth shit if I'm dead."

Rhett moved his dagger back just enough that he wouldn't accidentally kill the man before Liss was free.

"Now the boy," Rhett ordered, keeping his blade steady against the slaver's throat.

The man turned to look at Rhett. His eyes widened.

"You're Lagonia's Chief Assassin."

Rhett's all-consuming rage at the man was tempered by those words. That had been his title for the last two years. Before that, he'd been a Lagonia soldier. Now, he was neither.

Rhett shook off the disturbing thought as he watched the slaver unbind the Extended boy.

Spence, Liss had called him.

"You and this pretty lady are the empire's greatest enemies," the slaver told Rhett, clearly emboldened by the thought of the reward he'd gain for reporting the fugitives' location. "Every soldier in Lagonia is looking for you."

"Then, I better not make it easier for them to find us."

Rhett slashed his dagger across the man's throat. The slaver was dead before his body hit the ground.

The death was too painless and quick for this monster, but Rhett knew Liss wouldn't want him torturing the man.

Liss threw off the tattered coils and ran to him. He dropped his dagger to lift her up. His legs might have forgotten how to run, but his arms remembered how to hold her.

Her whole body shook as she cried against his neck. Her words were too muffled to make sense of, but Rhett understood the tenor of what she was trying to say. He held her tighter.

Part of him was still bewildered that he was here at all, when he had known he was about to die. The other part of him didn't care about anything beyond the feel of Liss's body pressed against his own.

He hadn't thought he'd ever have the chance to touch her again. He'd tried to hold onto the memory of her as death took him. Now, he was alive, and she wasn't just a figment of his imagination. She was really here.

Liss lifted her head and smiled at him, displaying the dimple in her left cheek. His heart felt huge enough to burst at the sight of her beautiful face.

She was alright. They were together.

He lowered his head, and their lips met.

"*Liss.*"

They broke the kiss to see Spence was staring at them. His orange-rimmed eyes were ablaze with fury.

"Spence, listen," Liss began, disentangling herself from Rhett.

"No." The kid backed away. "One of *his* soldiers killed my mom. Did you forget?"

Rhett's stomach lurched. He had no idea what the circumstances of the Extended woman's death had been, but he didn't doubt Spence was telling the truth.

He should say something, but he knew there was no apology he could make that would undo this kind of pain.

"I should have left him to rot in that cage," Spence shouted as he stormed off.

After giving Rhett a glance that told him not to follow, Liss hurried after Spence.

A cold wind blew through the clearing, bringing other memories with it. Rhett's last days in the torture cage had been a haze of pain, but now, he remembered the wound that had cut deepest of all.

Liss was Opal Smoke.

She'd lied to him. The Insorsiled Empty he'd fallen in love with wasn't an Empty at all. She was Extended.

No, Rhett corrected himself. She was half-Extended. It was why she looked Lagonian but had an Extension.

Soul Sorter. The awful truth came back to him in a rush. He stumbled back until he was leaning against a tree.

Liss had used him to find the source of Lagonia's immunity to opal contagion. She'd stolen the emotions from his soul. His thoughts—the only possession that had ever truly been his own—had been laid bare at her feet. She'd used him.

She also saved your life, a silent voice argued. *She came back, when she could have escaped.*

Rhett didn't know what to think.

Liss reappeared a few minutes later. There was a hesitant smile on her face.

"How long have we been here?" he asked, reverting to the clipped tone he used when he questioned suspected criminals.

Liss's smile faltered.

"You've been unconscious for two weeks."

Rhett's head spun. Two weeks was interminable. What had happened in Lagonia during that time?

"Ciago and Wilsean," he said. "Where are they? What happened to the rest of my soldiers?"

What had they…what had she…done?

"They pretended like Spence put them to sleep just like the Emperor," Liss said. "Jaikon won't know who helped me get you out."

Rhett was shaking his head. He knew Jaikon. The Emperor wouldn't let Rhett's escape go unpunished. Someone would have to pay. And Rhett wasn't there to answer for his choices.

"I have to get back."

"I know." Liss came closer and took his hands in hers. "But not yet. You almost—" she cut herself off, like she couldn't say the word *died* out loud. "I need to go back to Lagonia, too. But getting you better is the priority."

"I'm fine."

It was the truth. He could feel bruises all over his body, and he was stiff. But that was as far as his injuries went. Whatever Liss had been doing to him over the last two weeks had made him almost as good as he'd been before he was tortured.

He didn't thank her for it. All of the anger and betrayal he'd felt before were coming back to him now.

He'd been foolish enough to fall in love with Opal Smoke. And now, his friends would pay the price for his choices.

Rhett had abandoned all of his rules for Liss. He'd given himself to her, body and soul. He'd been ready to throw away his duty, his friends...his life...for her.

Now, he was an outcast from the only home he'd ever known. Worse than an outcast. He was a traitor. He'd betrayed his soldiers and the people he was supposed to protect. Because of him, Lagonia was no longer safe from opal contagion.

All his life, Rhett had sworn he'd never give Jaikon something to use against him. He'd sworn he'd never be owned.

"Rhett—"

"Are you doing it right now?" The tight leash he always kept on his emotions abandoned him. The hurt was too raw and deep. "Are you rifling through my soul?"

A pained expression crossed Liss's face. Rhett hated himself for being the one to put it there. In spite of all the lies she'd told him, his feelings for her hadn't changed. And that frustrated him most of all.

Liss opened her mouth to reply, but before she could, Spence returned. Rhett wanted to curse the kid's bad timing.

Steel doesn't know love or despair. It can't be bent or broken. It needs no heart or warmth. I am steel.

Stone's mantra, the one Rhett had used to bury his emotions all his life, didn't hold the same meaning it once did. He'd never be able to go back to the way he'd been before, but the words' familiar rhythm helped a little.

"What have you got there?" Liss asked Spence.

The way Liss tensed put Rhett on his guard. He bent to pick up his dagger.

"I retraced the slaver's steps to see if he had any supplies with him," Spence said. "I found this, but it smells terrible."

Spence was dragging a cloth sack behind him. Rhett noticed the rust stains on the bottom of the sack.

"Don't—" Rhett began.

It was too late.

Liss and Spence cried out, confirming his suspicions. The sack tipped to the side. Severed human heads rolled out.

There were five of them.

Orange hair matted with blood. Opal skin, the rainbow sheen dull in death. Expressions frozen in terror and agony.

They were all Extended.

Liss and Spence were staring at the heads, their expressions full of horror. Spence's hands covered his mouth to stifle a scream. A tear slid down Liss's cheek.

Rhett took a step toward them and then stopped. His need to comfort and protect Liss was overwhelming. But he could tell from her closed-off expression that she didn't want his comfort.

No one spoke as they stared down at the gruesome scene.

Rhett understood what the Emperor was doing, and it sickened him. Jaikon had recruited the degenerates who used to collect Extended slaves to exterminate the carriers of opal contagion, instead.

Now that the source of immunity to opal contagion was destroyed, it wouldn't be much longer before Lagonia's stash of dried flowers ran out. Once that happened, every Lagonian would be at risk.

These Extended heads were the proof that would have been needed for the slaver to collect his jewels.

Rhett bent to the ground. As carefully as he could, he gathered the heads back into the sack. At least he could prevent Liss and Spence from having to look at the mangled and rotting heads of their people.

It was difficult to be respectful when the heads kept rolling out of his grasp. The rotting flesh stunk to high hell, and he had to bury his nose in his collar to keep from gagging.

"I have to get my people out of Lagonia before they're all killed," Liss said, her words choked with the tears still spilling down her cheeks.

Rhett understood her desperation. He felt it himself.

But with every slaver and Lagonia soldier searching for him and Liss, he had no idea how they'd manage to do anything besides wind up back in the torture cage.

CHAPTER 3

Liss had known the Lagonians would start killing the Extended once the immunity ran low. She just hadn't expected it to happen so soon.

"We always kept at least a month's worth of dried flowers in the palace," Rhett told her as they walked. "We still have time before—"

...before all the Extended slaves are slaughtered.

"How do you know they won't kill everyone now just to be safe?" Liss challenged.

"Because." Rhett's expression was grim. "The Lagonian elite who own Extended slaves won't want to give up their property."

Property.

The thought made Liss want to throw up. She could sense the disgust in Rhett's soul and knew he felt the same way. It didn't make her feel any better.

If Liss didn't rescue those slaves, no one would. She had to do something.

Spence, his soul a storm of angry emotions, stomped ahead. When she called out to him not to go too far, he ignored her and picked up his pace. He was angry at her, but he was also driven by the same desperation Liss now felt.

They needed to get back to the caravan's hideout.

Unfortunately, the weather was refusing to cooperate. Fat flakes of snow had begun falling, and they still had miles to go before they reached the Extended hideout. Already, the last rays of sunlight were seeping away. The moon's blue glow was hidden beneath a layer of clouds.

The fur cloak she's wrapped around herself—courtesy of Grub—kept the snow from seeping into her clothes, but it didn't help with the visibility. The snow was coming down so fast she couldn't see more than a few feet in front of her.

After telling Rhett about Grub's strange presence in the Insorsiled forest, and his even stranger behavior, no one spoke. Rhett was as puzzled by the giant's presence on this side of the sea as she'd been, and he didn't have any explanation for what it might mean.

"We have to stop for the night," Rhett said, sounding as unhappy about the idea as she felt.

Spence, his shaggy orange hair weighed down by the snow, scowled up at the sky.

They stopped when they came across a tree with thick branches that shielded the ground beneath from the worst of the blizzard. Rhett knelt and began piling up the snow to create a makeshift barrier to keep any more snow from blowing in.

Liss marveled at the combination of Insorsiled medicines and Rhett's seemingly endless strength. He had been unconscious for two weeks. Today, he had killed a slaver and walked ten miles without a second thought.

Unzipping the bag she carried, Liss handed one of the immunity flowers to Rhett. It looked even smaller and more insignificant grasped between his long fingers.

That tiny flower was all that kept him from succumbing to the virus that lived in Liss's blood.

Seeing that slaver's yellow anti-contagion suit was a stark reminder that, if they didn't find a way to get more immunity, Rhett would have to wear one of those suits to even be near her.

They'd never be able to touch each other.

If only Liss hadn't unwitting led Burk to the cliff that overlooked the flower fields. If only his Flamer hadn't burned them all. If only she could have made the deal she'd intended, which would have kept the Lagonians she cared for safe while giving her people a chance at salvation.

Now, because of all of her failures, there was no stopping the evil emperor who was orchestrating her people's slaughter.

Because Jaikon couldn't be killed.

Liss had heard the rumors but hadn't believed them. Then, she'd tried to kill the Emperor herself. Instead of drawing Jaikon's blood, her weapon had shattered.

"What do you know about Jaikon's invincibility?" Liss asked Rhett.

When she looked at him, he flinched back.

Liss bit the inside of her cheek in an effort not to react. He felt disgusted and betrayed. She could feel the emotions pulsing from his soul along with half a dozen others.

She turned away so Rhett wouldn't be able to see the look on her face. She didn't want him knowing how much his reaction stung.

"It has to be something Insorsiled," Rhett said. "But I've never heard of magic that strong."

"Well, we're going to need to figure out a way around that little problem before we can go back to Lagonia," Liss replied.

Rhett finished with the snow barrier and motioned for Spence to go inside the little enclave.

Spence gave Rhett a death glare and spat on the ground. He announced, "I'm not sleeping anywhere near the Viper." His orange eyes glowed as he turned his accusing gaze on Liss.

Spence had every reason to be angry. Liss had deceived him, recruiting his help to break Rhett out of the torture cage without telling him the truth.

She's fallen in love with Lagonia's Chief Assassin.

It had been so long since Liss had thought of Rhett as the man responsible for killing dozens of her people. She had to keep reminding herself that, until a few months ago, she had shared Spence's hatred for all Lagonians.

"We need to stay together," she told Spence.

"And I'm not Lagonia's Chief Assassin anymore," Rhett said.

There was a note of bitterness in his voice, but when Liss glanced at his eyes, his expression just seemed lost.

"I can't believe you're letting *him* into the hideout," Spence muttered under his breath.

He had a point, although not for the reason Spence meant. Liss knew Rhett wouldn't hurt any of the Extended in the hideout, but she and Rhett were being hunted by every slaver and soldier in Lagonia. They'd be putting her people at risk by going to the only safe place her people had.

Deal with today's problems now, and tomorrow's problems later.

Those words had always helped her to organize her thoughts in the past. Except these days, everything seemed like a *today* problem. Bringing her people's greatest enemy into their camp was a today problem. Getting all of the Extended slaves out of the empire was a today problem. Immunity flowers…Jaikon's invincibility….

Just thinking about it was enough to give Liss an ulcer.

She ignored Spence's grumbling as she tucked him into the fur blanket Grub had gifted them, making sure there were no gaps where the cold could seep in. She sat on the hard ground beside Spence, hoping her presence would help keep away the nightmares she knew would come as soon as he closed his eyes.

Seeing those Extended heads was bound to drudge up memories about how Spence's own mother had died. Not to mention sleeping within throwing distance of Lagonia's ex-Chief Assassin….

Spence was at that awkward age of fourteen when he thought showing any emotion, or accepting any comfort, was a weakness. Still, as he drifted off, he didn't argue against Liss gently stroking his mop of orange hair. He rarely let anyone touch it, since his mother had always been the one to brush and cut it.

By the time Spence fell asleep, Rhett was bundled up in his own fur cloak.

With all of her worries about the Extended slaves stuck in Lagonia, and Rhett being so close and yet so distant, she knew she'd never be able to sleep. She took her cloak and laid it on top of Spence's other blanket, making sure he wouldn't be cold during the night. She had just finished tucking it around him when Rhett's low voice cut through the silence.

"You'll freeze without that cloak."

He sat up so he was facing her. His face was blank of any expression. She longed to sort his soul, but she resisted. She'd felt enough of his betrayal. She didn't want to be reminded of all the ways she'd failed him.

It was unnatural to ignore the pull of her Extension. Most of her people would never even consider suppressing their natural abilities, but Liss had taught herself how *not* to use her Extension when she was a child. It had been her only escape from her mother's debilitating sadness.

"I'll be fine," she said.

"No, you won't. Take mine."

Rhett started to get up, but she put out a hand to stop him.

"You're still healing," she said. "You need it more than I do."

Purple bruises still ringed Rhett's eyes. His right eye was so swollen he couldn't open it all the way. Liss's gaze moved to the three newly-healed scars along his cheek.

They didn't detract from his good looks. In fact, they somehow made him even more attractive. They were a mark of what he'd endured and survived. They were also a painful reminder of what he'd been willing to sacrifice for her sake.

Rhett was silent for several seconds. Liss could tell he was wrestling with a decision. Her impulse to look into his soul was almost too painful to resist, but she left him to whatever private thoughts he was having. Instinct told her she didn't want to know what he was thinking, anyway.

"Then, come here." Rhett held up a corner of his cloak in invitation.

There was nothing she wanted more than to curl up against him and pretend like everything between them hadn't changed.

But everything had changed.

Liss shook her head. "I don't want your pity cuddles."

"Pity cuddles?" He raised an eyebrow at her. His lip twitched, like he was trying not to smile.

"Yes." She felt her temper spring to life. "You can forgive me if I don't come begging for the scraps of your affection."

She swallowed the lump in her throat and sat down against the tree. She tried to convince herself it would be a comfortable place to wait out the night as cold seeped through her clothes.

She didn't look up as Rhett's footsteps came closer. He sat down next to her and drew the cloak over both of them.

"You're freezing," he murmured, wrapping an arm around her and fitting her body against his.

She should pull away, but her soul reached out to him with a strength that was impossible to resist. She could tell his soul felt the same draw toward hers. He sighed and drew her closer so his chin was nestled against her hair. The closeness sent a shiver through her that had nothing to do with the cold.

"Liss, I—"

A twig snapped.

They both tensed. Slowly, silently, they got to their feet. Liss peered into the darkness but saw no sign of danger.

An animal, maybe?

As soon as the hopeful thought crossed her mind, Liss heard a very non-animal sound. It was the twang of a bowstring.

CHAPTER 4

R hett yanked Liss to the side. The arrow missed her by inches, embedding itself in a nearby tree.

"Get behind that fallen log," Rhett ordered Liss, who was already going to wake up Spence.

He ducked behind a tree just before the next shot sliced through his throat. The archer had excellent aim and wasn't wasting time with warning shots.

Rhett stepped out from behind the tree just long enough to coax the archer to let another arrow fly. This time, he tracked the direction it came from. Rhett ran forward, keeping low to the ground and swerving to avoid the next shot.

He collided with his would-be killer, who was dressed all in white. He tackled the woman before she could release her next arrow.

Rhett wrenched the weapon out of the archer's hands, noting the black diamonds embedded in the bow's limb. He pressed his dagger to her throat.

A pair of furious, hazel eyes stared up at him.

Rhett's grip on his dagger didn't falter, but his mind splintered into a hundred different directions. He knew this soldier.

Gwendylina.

She had been in the Lagonia army for two years. Rhett had trained her himself.

She had a better work ethic than most, and she was one of the best spear-throwers in Lagonia. Rhett had fought side-by-side with her during the Giant War. She had a wicked sense of humor and had once drunk Ciago under the table.

"How could you?" Gwendylina howled as she struggled against Rhett.

She was all muscle, but she was weaponless and smaller than Rhett. He kept her pinned with his dagger to her throat, even though he had no desire to hurt her.

"It's not what you think," Rhett said, even though he wasn't sure that was true.

Stone had tried to warn him, but Rhett hadn't listened. He'd been so certain of his choices…so certain he had everything under control.

He had fallen in love with Opal Smoke and chosen her over everything. He had left his people vulnerable and defenseless. He'd put everyone who cared about him in an impossible position.

His soldiers had been forced to choose between their duty and his life. And now, he'd as good as abandoned them.

"Traitor." Gwendylina's eyes blazed.

Guilt sliced through Rhett, but he didn't let her up.

"You'll have to come with us," Rhett told her.

He couldn't risk Gwendylina giving away his location, since they were only a few hours' walk from the Extended hideout.

"I'm not going anywhere with you!"

"Rhett?"

He turned at the sound of Liss's voice. She stood behind him, a jagged stone clutched in her hand and raised like a weapon.

"She's one of mine," Rhett told Liss.

Gwendylina snarled and struggled like a rabid beast. Rhett had to concentrate to keep from slicing her neck by accident.

"You need to come with us," Rhett said again. The only other alternative wasn't one he wanted to consider.

Killing a slaver or one of Jaikon's new recruits was one thing. Killing a soldier he'd trained and fought beside was another.

"Kill me or slit your own traitorous throat," Gwendylina ordered. "Because if you let me up, I'm going to kill you."

Rhett looked at Liss, who was glaring down at the woman pinned beneath Rhett.

"I'm not asking you," Rhett said, letting his voice go cold and commanding. "This is an order, soldier."

Gwendylina barked out a laugh. "I'm not your soldier anymore. Traitor. Traitor. Traitor!"

The word rattled around in Rhett's brain until he could barely think. It was only when he felt Liss's gentle hand on his back that his mind cleared.

"Do you want me to do it?" she asked in a quiet voice.

Rhett saw pity in her eyes. She understood what Rhett didn't want to. He shook his head and turned back to Gwendylina.

"Don't make me do this." *Please.*

Gwendylina thrust her elbow into Rhett's ribs. He let go of her, moving away before she could hit him again. She attacked, letting out a war cry as she came at him. They rolled over twice until Rhett got a grip on her dragonhide jacket. He pulled her close. And then he slashed his dagger across her throat.

Her blood sprayed across his cheek.

Gwendylina's eyes widened. She went limp as a final breath huffed out of her body. Rhett gently lowered her head to the ground. He watched her blood soak into the trampled snow.

Rhett couldn't look away.

He'd killed a soldier he'd sworn to protect. He'd murdered one of his own.

Liss knelt beside him. She didn't say anything as she leaned against him.

Rhett had no idea how long he stayed kneeling beside Gwendylina's corpse before he found the strength to stand. Spence, who was hovering behind them, gave Liss a questioning look. She shook her head at him and slipped her hand into Rhett's.

His hand was cracked with dried blood, but she didn't let go. Without a word, they left the soldier in the snow.

✳ ✳ ✳

The snow stopped falling, and since no one was getting any sleep after what had happened, they forged ahead.

They weren't dressed for the weather, but none of them complained. Not even Spence, even though his shoes were much too thin for traipsing around in snow. If Rhett's boots wouldn't have drowned the kid, he would have tried to give them to Spence.

Not that the stubborn Extended boy was likely to accept anything from him.

"You did what you had to do," Liss murmured, giving Rhett a sympathetic look.

Rhett didn't say anything. Gwendylina had just been following orders. *Just like he used to.*

Once again, he'd chosen to betray one of his own in favor of protecting Liss.

What the hell was wrong with him?

He'd chosen Lagonia's enemy over one of his own countrymen. He'd chosen Liss over one of his soldiers. And still, he wouldn't hesitate to make the same decision again. The realization made him simultaneously furious with her and himself.

Just as quickly, his anger vanished as the memory of Jaikon's hand wrapped around Liss's throat filled his mind. He couldn't forget the Emperor's promises about what he would do to Liss to break Rhett's mind before his body was thrown over the cliffs.

Rhett's powerlessness to help her had consumed his unconscious thoughts since he'd nearly died in the torture cage. He'd swum in and out of a nightmare he couldn't escape, where Jaikon was torturing Liss and Rhett could do nothing to stop it.

He couldn't suppress the chill that went through him.

"We'll go back to the hideout and figure this out," Liss told him.

By silent agreement, they all picked up their pace.

Rhett blew out a frustrated breath. His friends and soldiers had been stuck dealing with Jaikon without him for two weeks.

Rhett's only consolation was that Jaikon wouldn't dare kill Ciago or Wilsean. His best friends were the sons of the two richest families in all of Lagonia. Not even the Emperor could punish them without facing the nobility's wrath.

But Stone, Dannica, and all the others who had been on duty that day were a different story. Their loyalty to Rhett was well-known. The thought of them needing to answer for Rhett's choices was more than he could bear.

He glanced at Liss, who was cradling the bag of immunity flowers to her chest. Rhett grimly wondered if there was a woman in all the world who was more poisonous for him than Liss.

She was the spy who had stolen his empire's greatest secret. As if that wasn't enough, her mere existence could kill him if he ever failed to take his flower.

Every Lagonian knew the symptoms of opal contagion, which could begin within minutes of exposure.

The pustules came first. They oozed and bled, and caused the patient so much pain Rhett had heard of people clawing their own skin off to be rid of them. Next came the fevers and muscle spasms. The final stage was the bleeding....

All told, it took victims anywhere from a few days to a week to succumb to the grotesque disease.

"Do you think you'll ever forgive me for lying to you?" Liss asked, startling him out of his thoughts.

"You saved my life, *again*," he said. "There's nothing to forgive."

The first time they'd met, it had been when Rhett was dying of poison. Liss had stopped to help him—a complete stranger.

He didn't want to think about that. He wanted to remember how she was the reason why he was now a fugitive. He wanted to be angry with her.

He just couldn't muster the energy. All he could manage to feel was a heavy, bone-deep tiredness.

"But you don't trust me anymore," Liss said.

Rhett tried to find the right words to explain. He'd grown up in the Lagonia palace, where subterfuge was the rule and trust an illusion.

"Just give me some time to get used to all of this," Rhett said.

"I understand." She looked away.

It wasn't a question of wanting her. He did. But she'd lied to him. She'd stolen his emotions.

Was she listening to his soul right now? The thought stopped him in his tracks.

"Tell me how it works," he said. The gruffness in his voice made it come out sounding more like an order.

Her brow furrowed.

"How what works?"

"Your Extension. How can I block you out?"

Hurt flashed in Liss's blue eyes. He hurried to explain.

"I don't have a problem with you being Extended. At least, I don't think I do. It's your Extension."

"Lovely," Liss said, sarcasm dripping from the word. "Thanks so much for clearing that up."

Rhett cursed under his breath. While he wrestled with the right words to explain, Spence stalked past them.

"You know, I could just put him to sleep and we could leave him here," the kid muttered.

Rhett waited until they had some distance from Spence. He wasn't interested in having an audience for this particular conversation. He also wasn't eager to get too close to an angsty teenager who could knock him out cold with a mere touch.

"That wasn't what I meant," Rhett said in a low voice.

"Then how did you mean it?" Liss gave him a furious look, but she stayed by his side.

Vulnerable wasn't an emotion Rhett had much experience with, and it went against every instinct he had to tell her the truth. But he didn't want Liss to think he was just another bigoted Lagonian. Besides, Rhett didn't want to play games with her.

"The only thing in my life that's ever truly belonged to me are my thoughts."

The extent of Jaikon's cunning was inexplicable to anyone who hadn't experienced it themselves. Liss had seen some of what the Emperor was capable of, but it was impossible to explain the pleasure he took in discovering people's weak spots and exploiting them.

"I don't want anyone to be able to take my thoughts and emotions at will."

Not even you.

Liss nodded, but Rhett could see she was still hurt by what he'd said. He wanted to take back everything. Instead, he stayed silent and waited for her reply.

"You can't block out my Extension," she said finally, "but I can stop myself from seeing into your soul."

Anger flashed through Rhett.

Then why didn't you? he wanted to demand.

Instead, he asked, "You can do that?"

Liss hesitated, and then she nodded.

"Will you give me your word you won't sort my soul?"

Rhett had never put much faith in spoken oaths, but he didn't see any way around taking Liss at her word.

He heard Stone's rebuke in his head.

What kind of fool trusts someone who already lied to him?

"I promise I won't look at your soul," she said.

There was an expression on her face Rhett couldn't interpret.

"Are you serious right now?" Spence, who had doubled back, was staring at Liss with a mixture of incredulity and disgust.

"Mind your business, Spence," Liss said with an exaggerated sigh.

To Rhett, she said, "Now that you know I'm not sorting your soul, I want you to stop flinching every time I look at you."

Rhett started. Had he really been doing that?

One glance at Liss, and he knew it was true. She was biting her lip, like she was trying not to cry.

Again, he'd hurt her. Rhett's anger softened. In spite of everything she'd done, he wanted to take her into his arms. He wanted to kiss her.

"Stupid Lagonian prick," Spence muttered.

Liss waited until Spence was out of earshot before turning to him.

"Do we have a deal?" she asked.

Rhett met Liss's gaze. "We have a deal."

CHAPTER 5

Before she left to rescue Rhett, Liss had convinced her mom to buy warding charms from Insorsil. The expense had wiped out all of the jewels Liss and the kids had stolen, but it was worth it.

The large, abandoned field and the path through the Insorsiled forest that led to it were now protected. The ward hid the smoke from their fires and blocked out all sounds. Anyone who came near the ward would feel a subtle compulsion to go in a different direction. Still, the ward couldn't actually stop anyone from getting inside the hideout if they really wanted to. And now, the two most wanted people on the continent were here.

We'll be gone again soon, Liss told herself.

As soon as they had weapons and a plan, they'd be heading back to Lagonia.

Liss stopped walking before they reached the ward.

"Spence," Liss said in a quiet voice.

"Yeah, yeah, I know," Spence muttered, glaring at Rhett. "I won't tell anyone the Caravan Butcher is *in our caravan.*"

"Thank you." She let out the pent-up breath she'd been holding.

Spence stalked over to Rhett and glared up at him. "If I so much as see your dagger while you're in our camp, I'll get my friend's brothers to crush you like a bug."

Liss tried to hide a smile. Rhett was the most dangerous man on the continent, and Spence was threatening him.

Rhett's face betrayed no emotion as he gave Spence a curt nod.

Liss almost looked into his soul before remembering her promise and clamping down on her Extension. A slight tremor went through her from the effort. For some reason, blocking out her soul sorting was harder with Rhett than it ever had been with her mom.

Liss glanced at Rhett, but his expression was guarded as he rubbed a smear of dried blood off his hand.

Liss knew how seriously Rhett took his responsibility to protect the men and women in the Lagonia army. She couldn't imagine what it must have done to him to kill one of them. It would be like her killing an Extended. With the one exception of Burk, she couldn't imagine anything that could drive her to kill one of her own people.

"With any luck, my mom will already have a team of Extended armed and ready to go," Liss said, trying to make all of them feel better. "We can go into Insorsil in the morning, grab some illusion potions, and storm Lagonia by the afternoon."

Rhett chuckled darkly. "Just like that?"

She managed a small smile. "Well, there might be a few other details to work out."

The ward rippled as they stepped across the barrier and into…pandemonium.

"What the—" Spence began.

Rhett's dagger whispered out of its sheath.

For several seconds, the three of them just stood and stared. The quiet, organized hideout Liss and Spence had left was no longer. Everyone was running around and shouting. Supplies were strewn everywhere. The air was filled with swarming tree fairies, who were buzzing around and screeching in their high-pitched voices. The Extended were attempting to do…something…but there were too many of the creatures.

One of the fairies streaked past Liss's ear, shrieking because it was on fire. Another one hit the side of the cottage. The tip of the arrow that pierced it was wider than the fairy's entire body.

Some of the Extended were wielding frying pans. Others were tossing handfuls of dried oatmeal or small rocks at the fairies to try to stun them. Mari's four Fighter brothers were trying to use blankets to capture a whole group of them at once, but the little devils kept flying out before the men could pin them down.

"Don't let them leave!" one of Liss's people shouted as he raced past, tossing snowballs at the fairies.

Another Extended trailed him, collecting all the stunned fairies and stuffing them into a lidded jar.

Everyone was yelling. The fairies' high-pitched squeaks made Liss's head feel like it was going to explode. They swarmed around with swords the size of needles, going for her people's eyes.

A chattering fairy buzzed in front of Liss's face, waving a tiny, bloodied fist.

"Will tell everyone," it jabbered. "Will get our reward. Will get all the nasty Infected killed. Fun, fun, fun."

Liss smacked the fairy with her palm. She grabbed the unconscious creature out of the air and tossed it to her caravan member with the lidded jar.

"They're going to tell Jaikon where the hideout is," Liss said as she began to comprehend the emergency. "We need to contain them."

Another woman raced by carrying a length of cheesecloth crammed full of squirming fairies.

Liss was about to join the fray, when Rhett put a hand on her arm.

"Get some honey."

She must have misheard him. She thought he'd just said—

"Liss, do it. Trust me."

While Rhett swiped the flat of his blade across a column of fairies, felling a dozen of them at once, Liss ran off in search of...honey.

The wagons were all in disarray. Liss almost broke her neck when she tripped over a can of coffee beans rolling across a wagon floor. She rummaged through cabinets, heedless of the mess she made as she searched.

She found a small pot sticky with honey in the fourth wagon she searched. Snatching it off the shelf, she raced back to the bedlam outside.

"Keep them in the ward! Keep them—" Liss's mom shouted as she loosed arrow after arrow at the ones who got close to flying out of the hideout.

"Rhett!"

He didn't look her way as he struck out at another group of fairies with the flat of his blade. He caught the pot of honey one-handed behind his back.

Rhett took the lid off and raised the pot of honey in the air.

To Liss's amazement, the fairies went still. They stopped chattering. The only sound was their fluttering wings as they hovered in place.

"There!" one of them squeaked, pointing at Rhett's hand.

Liss had a moment of legitimate fear for Rhett when the hundreds of fairies buzzed toward him at full fairy speed.

Rhett put the honey behind his back.

"Line up," he called in a clear and commanding voice.

Whimpering, the fairies did. Their tiny nostrils flared. They tried to twist their bodies to catch sight of Rhett's hidden hand from their position in line.

Liss was beginning to think maybe she had gotten knocked on the head without realizing it. Spence and the other Extended looked as bewildered as she was.

"It's like a drug for them," Rhett explained without taking his eyes off the orderly column of fairies.

The little creatures were salivating as they hovered at the height of Rhett's hidden hand.

"There's a reward out for any who can locate Extended caravans," Liss's mom said. She had an arrow nocked and was aiming it at the column of fairies. "We have to kill them before they give us away."

"Wait," Rhett said.

That one word carried so much authority that even Liss's mom, the leader of their caravan, lowered her bow.

"Honey is more of a reward to them than the jewels being offered in Lagonia," Rhett explained.

To the fairies, he said, "You will never give up this hideout or the location of a single wagon if you want more honey. Is that understood?"

Yes yes yes yes yes.

The fairies laced their tiny fingers together and held them out toward Rhett. Liss wouldn't have believed any of this if she wasn't witnessing it with her own eyes.

"They'll agree to anything you want," Rhett told Liss's mom.

"I haven't been able to send any messengers to the other caravans because the slavers are everywhere," she replied.

Liss's anxiety rose. They needed those other caravans. She needed a group of Extended who would be able to help her get back into Lagonia. They would be needing more Fighters than just Mari's four brothers…more Energizers….

"Do you hear that?" Rhett asked the salivating fairies. "You will split up and track down every single caravan and tell them to come to this place. You will tell *only* the caravan leaders about this location. If anyone else asks, you'll stay silent under pain of never receiving another bite of honey."

Whimpers and muffled wails came from the line of fairies.

"I don't think the other caravans will come," Liss's mom said, her shoulders drooping in defeat. "I did manage to send Burk's old phoenix to one caravan, and the message I got back was that all the wagons were trying to get as far from Lagonia and the slavers as they could."

"Write this down," Rhett ordered the fairies.

To Liss's shocked amusement, the fairies began whipping tiny booklets out of their pockets and clutching even tinier charcoal pencils in their hands.

"The Extended hideout is fortified with a barrier, specifically designed to protect against the slavers and soldiers—"

"We don't have that," Liss's mom said, aghast.

"You will," Rhett said.

The fairies' charcoal pencils were poised for the rest of Rhett's message.

He continued, "We have a store of weapons and can keep their caravans safer than anywhere else they could go."

"Unless you count frying pans and cooking knives as weapons, we don't have anything besides my arrows," Liss's mom said, frowning. "Our people are banned from purchasing weapons."

"I can get you weapons," Rhett said.

Rhett's focus and command of this entire situation made Liss's heart beat faster. It was equal parts intimidating and sexy.

"Why are you doing this for us?" one of the Extended asked.

"I'm not doing it for you," came Rhett's simple reply.

He looked at Liss. She felt her cheeks warm. Even without sorting his soul, his meaning was clear. He was doing it for her.

"Tell the caravans they need to get here as fast as possible," Rhett told the fairies.

A sigh went up from the fairies as Rhett brought the pot of honey back around to where they could see it.

"One bite, and then go straight to deliver our message," Rhett told the fairies. "When you return, you'll get more so long as you haven't revealed this location to anyone except the caravan leaders."

The fairies pushed and shoved as they tried to get to the pot. Rhett had to pull one fairy out by his wings because he'd dive-bombed into the pot. Liss swatted at another, who was moaning and licking Rhett's finger where a drop of honey had fallen.

Rhett raised his eyebrows and gave Liss a suggestive grin. She narrowed her eyes at him.

Everyone in the caravan heaved a collective breath when the fairies were all gone.

"Why hasn't anyone else used honey to control the tree fairies before?" Liss asked Rhett.

She felt a little badly about using the creatures' vulnerability against them, but when it came to protecting her own people, she was willing to do just about anything.

"Most people just see the tree fairies as a nuisance," he replied. "As far as I'm aware, the only one on the continent who has ever bothered to learn about them is Stone."

Liss crossed her arms, bristling at the mere mention of Rhett's mentor.

"If Stone knew about the tree fairies' addiction, then why didn't he use them to serve the empire?" she asked.

Rhett held her gaze. "Stone is more complicated than he seems."

Liss humphed. She still didn't trust the man, even though he had helped her get Rhett out of Lagonia. While he might have made an exception to his obsession with duty for Rhett, Liss didn't think he'd changed so much that he'd actively be helping their cause from inside Lagonia.

"Liss, sweetheart. I'm so grateful you're back safely."

Her mom hurried over to her, wrapping her in a fierce hug. "I was losing my mind with worry the whole time you were gone." She kissed the top of Liss's head. "The next time you go anywhere, you're taking a corresponder so I don't have to wonder what's happened to you."

Liss laughed. "Like we have any of those just lying around the hideout."

Corresponders were exorbitantly expensive, and some of the most sought-after magical items from Insorsil.

Liss's mom pulled back to look at her. "I found a set of corresponders hidden in Burk's wagon. I don't know how he got them, but they're ours now."

Liss felt a flash of bitter resentment. During Burk's tenure as caravan leader, the caravan's wealth flowed from Liss to Burk. If Burk had bought a set of corresponders, he'd done so with wealth Liss and the kids had stolen. To make matters worse, he'd probably wanted the corresponders so he could betray the Extended by communicating with the Emperor.

Forcing herself to swallow her anger…for now…she let her mother continue to fuss over her. When they separated, her mom gave Rhett an appraising look.

"I'll meet you in my new wagon after I speak with Mari's brothers," Liss's mom said, giving her a smile before sliding another curious glance at Rhett. "I'd like to learn more about the man my daughter risked everything to save."

CHAPTER 6

L iss tried not to become discouraged as they walked through the camp. She'd been hoping more Extended would already be here. Instead, she counted only the twenty-four wagons from her own caravan. She didn't see a single unfamiliar face in the crowd of people cleaning up scattered supplies from the field.

Liss felt strangely removed from her own people as she strode through the camp with Rhett by her side. She caught the accusatory emotions passing across their souls.

She couldn't blame them. Months ago, she would have given Rhett the same death glare and muttered the same furious oaths under her breath.

Her people hated Rhett on sight, and they didn't even know he was Opal Slayer. It had been so long since she'd thought of him that way herself. Liss had to remind herself that just because she'd come to terms with who he was, it didn't mean her people would accept him.

"What are you doing with one of *them*?"

Liss tensed at the voice of Dolo, their caravan's Flooder. He was one half of a set of twins whom Liss could never tell apart by sight. Dolo's brother Romile was a Flamer, and he had a far better attitude. Liss made a point of avoiding both whenever possible, since she never knew if she was going to get a respectful nod or a biting remark. Unfortunately, it wasn't easy to avoid the men who lit all their fires and brought in every drop of water the caravan used.

Dolo had hit on Liss for an entire summer a couple of years back. When she'd finally convinced him it was never going to happen, he'd gone from annoyingly solicitous to downright nasty.

"Rhett is being hunted by the Lagonians just like we are," Liss said.

She tried to go past the Flooder, but he stepped in front of them, blocking their path. She felt Rhett stiffen beside her. His arm twitched, like it wanted to reach for his dagger.

"Want some opal contagion, Lagonian?" Dolo taunted. He blew out a puff of air in Rhett's direction.

Rhett didn't so much as blink. Liss was shaking with fury. She held the bag of Rhett's immunity flowers more tightly against her chest.

"I wouldn't stand that close to him if I were you," Liss told Dolo, keeping her voice light.

"Why?" Dolo retorted. "You think the Lagonian's gonna try something when he's surrounded by all of us?"

"No." Liss shrugged. "It's just that you look so small when you stand next to him. It might make people start to wonder what else of yours is tiny." She held up her thumb and forefinger an inch apart to emphasize her point.

Rhett's mouth twitched. Dolo's opal cheeks brightened as his soul filled with furious embarrassment.

Spence narrowed his eyes. "Were you just making a joke about his—" Liss slapped a hand over his mouth before he could finish his sentence.

Rhett's deep, husky laugh replaced her irritation with warmth.

"You always thought you were too good for the rest of us, didn't you?" Dolo hissed. "Strutting around with your Lagonian good looks and acting superior, all because your mom slept with the enemy."

Before Liss could say anything, Dolo added, "Us opal-skinned men were always beneath your notice."

"It has nothing to do with your skin and everything to do with the fact that your soul is rotten," Liss said, annoyed.

Dolo's eyes blazed. He opened his mouth, and Liss braced herself for his retort.

"Choose your next words carefully," Rhett told Dolo in a chilling tone, "or you'll find your tongue lying on the ground."

If there was one thing Liss knew about Rhett, it was that he didn't make idle threats.

"If you attack me here, no one will condemn me for killing you," Dolo retorted. "Don't think that little trick with the tree fairies will save you."

They'd gained an audience. The souls around them were full of the same loathing and distrust as Dolo's.

"No one's attacking anyone," Liss said.

She hurried to get in between the men. She put a hand on Rhett's chest and gave him a pleading look. He pinned Dolo with a gaze that left no room for debate about what would happen if Dolo crossed him.

Spence split off from their group to go find Mari and Jema, the two youngest members of Liss's old thieving crew. Liss took Rhett's hand and pulled him away from the crowd and toward her mom's wagon. She clenched her fists as she wrestled down her anger. Normally, she wouldn't have been affected by Dolo's insults, but his words had struck home in a way the Flooder never could have guessed.

Did the others in her caravan think she believed herself above the rest of them because she looked Uninfected?

The thought had never occurred to her before. If anything, it was the opposite. She had spent most of her childhood longing for the beautiful opal skin and orange hair that every other member of her caravan shared. She had been embarrassed by her Lagonian appearance and had often wished her father had been *normal* like the rest of her caravan.

"Are you okay?" Rhett asked, all of his attention fixed on her.

Liss took a deep breath. "Fine."

Mercifully, no one else stopped to taunt Rhett before they got to the wagon. It was the one Burk had occupied until recently, and which Liss's mom had taken over as the new caravan leader.

The wagons were all sized differently to accommodate the number of family members who lived inside. They all had more or less the same layout, with a tiny common area, even tinier kitchen, and tiny bedrooms. Families used paint and sparse decorations to make the space more unique and inhabitable.

Burk's—now her mom's—wagon was painted gold. Flecks of color had chipped off, revealing the gray-brown wood beneath. Liss knocked once and then pushed open the wooden door.

Her mom turned off the flame underneath the pot of oatmeal heating on the small stove. She filled two bowls to the top. She added a light dusting of an Insorsil spice that hid the bland flavor beneath a tongue-scorching heat.

"I'm sure you must be famished," Liss's mom said, gesturing for them to follow her through the tiny kitchen into the slightly-less-tiny living room.

Liss still wasn't used to seeing her mom on her feet rather than shivering underneath layers of blankets. Her opal skin was brighter, and there were no tears trickling down her cheeks. Liss couldn't believe her mom had almost completely weaned herself off the potion that had been her lifeline for as long as Liss was alive.

Before Liss was born, a witchdoctor had helped her mom transfer her strength to her Lagonian husband. The spell had left her mom permanently weakened. Unfortunately, the spell had only kept Liss's father immune to her mother. Despite their attempts to isolate themselves, they'd crossed paths with other Extended. That was how Liss's father had contracted the contagion. He'd died, and Liss's mom was left weakened and debilitated for the rest of her life.

Except, Liss's mom didn't seem weak anymore. When Liss had needed her most, her mom had overcome her decades-long illness through sheer force of will.

When Nya discovered Burk's plan to betray Liss to the Lagonians, she'd taken charge of the caravan and become the Extended Huntress Liss had heard about but never seen.

Rhett squeezed into one of the two velvet chairs, ducking his head to avoid a stained-glass lantern dangling from the ceiling. Rhett was too big for the chair. He was too big for the whole wagon, really.

With the bookshelves, two chairs, and Burk's stupid collection of trinkets, the three of them barely fit. If one more person tried to come into this wagon, the whole thing was liable to explode.

"Are you the one who looked after my daughter when she was in Lagonia?" Liss's mom asked Rhett.

He glanced at Liss before returning his attention to her mom. "Liss took care of herself."

Liss couldn't tell for sure without looking at his soul, but she thought she could sense an air of animosity radiating off Rhett in the direction of her mom. She wondered why.

"This is Rhett," Liss said, interrupting the stare-down the two were having.

She didn't give his full name. There weren't many outside of Lagonia who knew the Chief Assassin's name, since Rhett had always made a point of keeping a low profile, but she didn't want to take any chances that someone would put the pieces together. Since the Extended didn't have surnames, it wasn't weird not to give one.

"I'm Nya." Liss's mom held out her hand.

Rhett hesitated only a moment before shaking it.

Rhett didn't seem at all put off by the simple meal, even though Lagonia's food was nothing short of extravagant. When he finished his bowl, Liss handed him hers.

Rhett gave her a questioning look.

"I'm not hungry," she said with a shrug.

Rhett's brow furrowed. "We haven't eaten in days."

It was true. Under normal circumstances, Liss would be ravenous. Her appetite was always good, even when there was nothing more exciting on the menu than oatmeal. Except, right now, the thought of eating anything had her insides rebelling. She had a pounding headache, which was making her feel unbalanced and queasy.

"I'll be fine." She pushed the bowl into Rhett's hands. It had been more than two weeks since he'd consumed anything besides the healing herbs and grainy nutrition potions she'd forced down his unconscious throat.

Rhett's frown deepened. "Is there something wrong?"

To save herself from having to answer, Liss asked her mom, "So, none of the other caravans you contacted were willing to come?" She tried not to make it sound like an accusation.

Nya blew out a breath. "I tried, Liss. I really did. But slavers and soldiers are everywhere. Your Runner friend hasn't come back since he returned to his own caravan, and there isn't anyone else here who has the skills to track the other caravans."

"That wouldn't by any chance be the Runner who miraculously escaped from the torture cage, would it?" Rhett asked in a voice low enough that only Liss could hear.

She smiled at him without apology.

"Hm." Rhett looked more amused than angry.

"Thank you again for your help with the tree fairies," Nya told Rhett. "If you hadn't shown up when you did, I'm not sure what we would have done."

Rhett gave her a curt nod.

"I'll send the kids into Insorsil for more honey tonight," she continued.

"I can get it," Liss said.

"No," Rhett and her mom said at the same time.

She glared at them. "I am this caravan's resident thief."

"Not anymore," her mom said.

"A spy and a thief?" Rhett asked, putting down his spoon.

Liss stiffened. "Don't you dare judge me. You have no idea—"

"I wasn't judging you." Rhett looked at her in that way of his that made it seem like he put the rest of the world on hold while he gave her his full attention. "It's just something else I hadn't known about you."

"We don't have jewels just lying around, and we obviously don't have our own farms or any way of providing for ourselves," Liss said, feeling defensive on behalf of herself and her people. "Stealing is the only way to survive."

"I know." Rhett put a hand over hers. "I understand about surviving, remember?"

She gave him a terse nod as her righteous indignation retreated back inside her.

"The kids have been doing a fine job while you've been away, and they'll continue to do the thieving until we can make other arrangements," Liss's mom said.

Guilt further curdled Liss's already-queasy stomach. Jema was only nine, and even though she'd been on Liss's thieving crew for the last two years, Liss hated the idea of the kids going into Insorsil to steal without her to protect them.

"You two need to rest and get your strength back. It looks like you could use it." Nya gestured at Rhett's bruised eyes.

She started for the door to the wagon and then, having another thought, turned back to them. "Rhett can sleep in the abandoned cottage. I'll send along Dolo and Romile to fill a bath and start a fire, and Mari will bring you a blanket. I'm sure we have one we could spare."

Liss's mom wandered out of the small room, still talking to herself about everything that needed to be done.

"What do you think?" Liss asked Rhett, once they were alone.

"I think the last thing I want to do is wait around for these caravans to decide if they want to help us, but I don't see any other choice." He stared off into the fire crackling in the potbelly stove.

"The problem isn't getting into Lagonia unseen," Liss pointed out. There were Insorsiled illusion potions that could help them with that. "The problem is getting hundreds of people out of the empire, especially when we've got an invincible enemy."

Rhett's expression darkened. "We'll go into Insorsil tomorrow and do some digging…find out if there's any way to reverse the magic of that pin."

Liss didn't like the idea of waiting around any more than Rhett did, but she didn't see any other choice.

"Come on," Liss said, getting to her feet. "I'll get you settled in."

Rhett's lip curved up just a fraction. "Are you escorting me for my protection or theirs?"

"Yours," she said, leading him out of the wagon. "I know you wouldn't attack one of my people."

"I wouldn't," Rhett said, and she heard the promise in his voice.

While they'd been inside her mom's wagon, it had grown dark. Liss was grateful the night shielded them from any more glares or unkind remarks.

They got to the cottage without incident.

"Cozy," Rhett murmured.

The cottage was anything but. The wooden walls were old and rotting, and gaps between the boards let in frigid air from outside. The inside was dark and dank.

It was warm, though, thanks to the fire in the center of the room. And at least no one would try to bother him in here.

Liss went over and peered into the cast iron tub, making sure Dolo hadn't filled it with something else or done anything to the water that would hurt Rhett. She didn't trust the Flooder not to do something vindictive like that.

"There are rumors about this cottage being haunted by the Insorsiled couple that died in it," Liss said cheerfully as Rhett started pulling off his layers.

Rhett's lips twitched, but he quickly schooled his expression.

Liss was annoyed. They had been through too much together to pretend like the fire between them had dimmed. Rhett might be angry with her, but she knew his deeper feelings toward her hadn't changed. Hers certainly hadn't changed toward him.

Maybe he just needed a little reminder of where things stood between them.

Liss bent down to shift one of the logs closer to the fire, giving Rhett an eyeful of her cleavage. After all, what was the point of having assets if she didn't use them?

Liss felt a heady rush of satisfaction at the way Rhett froze with his jacket half-off to stare at her. She moved past him, accidentally-on-purpose brushing her hip against the front of his pants.

His reaction was instantaneous.

"You don't fight fair," he accused, his voice a low growl.

"I never said I did."

Liss turned and hit him with something she knew he couldn't resist. Her smile.

"Sweet dreams," she told him, heading for the door.

Before she'd made it a step, Rhett caught her hand and tugged her back.

"You can't leave me now," he said in his gruff voice. "The ghosts might haunt me without your protection."

He drew her closer until his warmth surrounded her. Being this near to him made her forget about giving Rhett space. It made her forget about her own aching heart.

She reached up and traced a finger along the scars on his cheek.

"You could stay in my wagon if you want," she said in a whisper. "You know, to avoid the ghosts."

Rhett went very still in the way he did when his soul was bursting with emotions. Her soul reached for his, her Extension demanding to know what he was feeling. She had to bite her lip until she tasted blood to keep from breaking her promise not to sort Rhett's soul.

Rhett took her face in his hands. His callused fingers were impossibly gentle as he cupped her cheek, his thumb resting on the spot where her dimple always appeared.

She angled her head to bring her lips to his.

Everything else fell away. So much had happened between them, and yet, none of it had dimmed the desperate passion that neither of them had ever been able to resist.

Rhett's arms came around her, locking her body against his. Liss deepened the kiss, exploring the satin heat of his tongue with her own. Rhett made a deep, rumbling sound of pleasure that sent fire racing through her veins.

A knock came at the cottage door. They sprang apart.

"Come in," Liss called, breathless.

Jema, barely visible with the blanket she was half-holding and half-dragging, skipped inside. Mari was behind her, carrying a pillow and a folded stack of clothes.

Jema tipped her head back to look up at Rhett. She caught sight of the dagger in his hand, which must have looked even bigger and more menacing to her than it did to Liss, and squeaked.

"It's okay," Liss hurried to say, as Rhett re-sheathed his weapon. "He's not going to hurt you."

"Lissy!"

Forgetting to be afraid, Jema dropped the blanket on the floor and ran to her. She threw her arms around Liss's waist.

"Missed you," Jema said, her words muffled from where her face was pressed against Liss's shirt.

"Missed you too, nugget." Liss leaned down to kiss the top of Jema's hair.

Liss held out an arm for Mari, who dropped everything she was carrying and ran over to hug Liss. Both girls held onto Liss as they peeked up at Rhett, who was watching their reunion with a bemused expression on his face.

"Mari and Jema, meet Rhett," Liss said. "Rhett, meet Mari and Jema."

"It's um, nice to meet you," Rhett said, looking uncomfortable.

Liss hid a snort of laughter.

"The big scary Lagonian is afraid of two little girls," she teased.

"We won't hurt you," Jema assured Rhett with wide-eyed sincerity. "We're not Fighters."

The idea of these two tiny girls being Fighters was laughable, but to his credit, Rhett gave them a solemn nod.

"I appreciate that," he told them.

"Are you half-Extended like Liss?" Mari asked, emboldened by Jema's fearlessness.

Rhett shook his head. "I'm all Lagonian."

"He's a nice Lagonian," Liss clarified. "Even though he looks grumpy."

Rhett glared at her, reinforcing her point. Liss smirked in satisfaction. She had almost forgotten how much fun it was to tease him.

"How come you're here?" Mari asked Rhett.

Rhett looked at Liss.

"It's a long story," she told the girls.

Jema peered up at Rhett.

"Do you like Lissy?" she asked.

Rhett nodded. He looked so serious that Liss couldn't keep herself from chuckling.

Jema considered that for a moment. Then, she asked, "Do you love her?"

"Isn't it time for you to go to bed?" Liss asked the girls, shooing them toward the door.

"He does, I can tell," Jema whispered loudly enough for everyone to hear as Mari took her by the hand and started dragging her away. Jema squirmed and tried to pull free, undoubtedly scheming about new ways to make Rhett blush. It was more than a little endearing.

"Spence, Mari, and I are going to Insorsil to steal honey so we can make the tree fairies drunk," Jema boasted to Rhett.

Guilt made Liss's stomach turn over. Providing the food and supplies for the caravan was her responsibility. Now, because her face was on the posters scattered throughout Insorsil, it wasn't safe for her to visit any of her usual haunts. Still, the thought of that responsibility falling on the kids made her feel even worse about all the danger she'd put her people in.

"Don't worry," Mari told Liss, wrapping an arm around Liss's waist. "We're careful, and no one pays an attention to us, anyway."

"As soon as Rhett and I get everything straightened out, I'll start helping you again," Liss promised.

"We don't need your help anymore," Jema informed her, as tactless as always.

Making sure Rhett was watching, Jema lowered her head and wrapped her arms around herself as her Extension began to take over.

Within seconds, the little girl was gone. In her place was a small, round sphere that rolled across the floor of the cottage.

"Good night," Liss told the little ball that was Jema as it nudged against her foot.

Jema rolled herself to the door, which Mari opened, and out into the night.

Mari closed the door after Jema, and then, giving Rhett a shy glance of her own, stepped right through the wall of the cottage.

Rhett blinked. "That's useful."

Liss chuckled. "I think you have yourself a fan club."

She was expecting him to come back with one of his dryly humorous remarks…or maybe even something flirtatious. Instead, he gave her a fleeting smile before turning away from her.

"I'll see you in the morning," he said, his attention fixed on the pile of clothes Mari had left.

His dismissal stung. He didn't mention anything about their kiss or her offer to spend the night with him. He was bending down on the ground, adjusting the damn blanket.

All at once, his words from earlier came back to her.

I don't have a problem with you being Extended.... It's your Extension.

Indignation, followed by hurt, filled Liss's soul.

"See you tomorrow," Liss said, infusing just the right amount of brightness into her voice to keep him from noticing how deep his curtness had sliced.

He didn't even look up as she crossed the room and let herself out of the cottage.

CHAPTER 7

s soon as Liss was gone, Rhett let out the breath he'd been holding. He hadn't spoken or even let himself look at her. If he had, he would have taken her in his arms and refused to let her go until sunlight poured through the missing slats in the cottage walls.

Her kiss alone was enough to make him senseless. If he had asked her to stay like he wanted to, sleep would have been the last thing on either of their minds. But he didn't want to go down that road until things were right between them. Besides, they both needed rest before figuring out how to deal with all of their urgent and equally unsolvable problems.

Rhett peeled off his clothes and tossed them onto the fire. He didn't look at the rust-colored stains from Gwendylina's dried blood.

He kept seeing her shocked, betrayed expression. He kept hearing that word. *Traitor.*

He got into the bath, welcoming the freezing temperature as it banished every other thought from his mind. He used the rough sliver of soap to scrape away the dirt and dried blood coating his skin. He scrubbed himself raw. He got out only when he was certain every droplet of blood was gone, and he was cold enough that he risked hypothermia.

He dried himself by the fire and then put on one of the threadbare outfits Liss's friend had brought.

Rhett lay down on top of the borrowed blanket. He made sure his bag of flowers was nestled against his side in the place where he wished Liss was, and held his dagger loosely in his other hand. He lay on his back and stared at the fire.

It wasn't the first time Rhett had been an outsider on someone else's land. The difference with all those other times was that he'd been surrounded by his soldiers, and he had been the one in charge.

When he walked into this camp, he'd found himself in a sea of people with opal skin and burnt orange hair. No one knew his true identity, and yet, every one of the Extended had looked at him with judgment in their orange-rimmed eyes.

He'd never felt more exposed in his life.

Rhett had a new appreciation for what it must have been like for Liss when she first set foot on Lagonia soil. She had looked like she belonged, but she had been as much of an outsider as he was now.

He had thought her brave before when he believed she was an Insorsiled Empty forced to flee her home. Now that he knew the truth, he thought she was the most fearless person he'd ever met.

His thoughts turned to the problem that had brought them here in the first place.

Killing Jaikon was the most logical solution, but with the Emperor's newfound invincibility magic, that wasn't possible. Rhett wracked his brain, trying to recall if Jaikon had ever let slip how the pin's magic worked.

He couldn't remember anything that would give him a clue about how to divest Jaikon of this new power.

Rhett ground his teeth. He could be on the other side of the world for all the good he was doing right now. He was useless to the ones who needed him most.

At the same time, his presence here was putting Liss's people in incalculable danger. The sooner he and Liss got what they needed and left this hideout, the safer her caravan would be.

Shame crept under Rhett's skin until he was filled with it. He'd heard fragments of a conversation about the Viper earlier. He'd seen the fear on the Extended people's faces as they discussed…him.

Of course, their fear was merited. Rhett had killed dozens of Extended. He hadn't been happy about it, but he had been following orders and upholding his sworn duty to protect the citizens of Lagonia.

Rhett glanced around at the shabby cabin. He had seen some of Lagonia's outer villages, where the soil was poor and the farmers barely eked out a living. Rhett had thought that was poverty. Only now did he realize he had never truly understood the meaning of the word.

This hideout was the opposite of Lagonia's excess. He had seen no stores of food, because there weren't any. Opal-skinned families huddled around fires because they had no coats. And the only way to keep them alive was to send children into Insorsil to thieve for scraps.

Rhett's mind circled back to his newest revelation about Liss, that she'd been her caravan's thief.

In Lagonia, Rhett had thought he knew Liss inside and out. Now, he realized he hadn't even scratched the surface.

As he discovered the new layers of her, he found his respect for her determination only grew, even though he was still wary.

Absently, he touched the fresh scars on his cheek. He hadn't had the opportunity or the inclination to look at his reflection, but he could only imagine how he looked with his swollen eyes and the scars from Jaikon's black diamond-studded brass knuckles.

He wondered what Liss thought about his altered appearance.

Rhett still wasn't sure what to think where Liss was concerned. She had deceived him, but she'd also proved she cared for him in a hundred different ways.

When he'd been in the torture cage and Samara snuck her sister down to heal him, she'd told Rhett that Liss's feelings for him were real. And yet, there was so much about her that he didn't know.

Was she even the woman he'd fallen for?

It was a stupid question. He knew the answer, just like he knew he needed water and oxygen to survive.

Rhett woke on a silent scream with his dagger slicing through a throat that wasn't there.

His dream was the same one he'd had over and over again during his two weeks of unconsciousness. He saw Jaikon smile as he loomed over Liss. He heard Liss's screams. He felt the iron cuffs around his wrists that kept him from reaching her. He saw her blood coating the stone floor.

Gasping and shaking, Rhett blinked until the interior of the cottage came back into focus.

Not real, he told himself, as his heart continued to race. *It was just a dream.*

He was drenched in sweat, even though the fire had died down and he knew the temperature in the room was freezing. His hand was bone white where it clutched his dagger.

Steel doesn't know love or despair. It can't be bent or broken. It needs no heart or warmth. I am steel.

Rhett repeated the mantra over and over in his head. It had never failed to bring him comfort in the past when he'd been afraid or lonely. Now, it did nothing to ease the panic that was hovering just beneath the surface.

Just a dream, he told himself. *It was just a dream.*

Except, it wasn't, really. It was exactly what would have happened to Liss if Spence had shown up only a few minutes later. It was what would happen to her if Jaikon ever got his hands on her again.

CHAPTER 8

Jaikon slammed his hand down on the golden armrest of his throne.

The soldiers standing below the dais cringed.

"I have thousands of men and women in my employ," Jaikon raged. "How is it possible you aren't able to find Rhetteman and his whore?"

The soldiers lowered their head in a combination of fear and shame.

"Majesty." Stone strode into the throne room.

The Master Interrogator's expression was as cold and unrevealing as Rhetteman's, which wasn't surprising, given that the man had been Rhett's guardian.

"We need to begin the process of closing up the empire," Stone said. "Our immunity flowers will only last until the end of the month. We need to ensure all our old protocols are in place before then."

"Why should we have to hide, when the Extended are the ones who are a blight on all of society?" Jaikon retorted.

He earned a round of applause from the courtiers assembled in the gold velvet chairs below the dais.

Stone opened his mouth to reply, but Jaikon cut him off.

"I have a better idea. Have the anti-contagion suits distributed among the mercenaries. Tell them to track down every last caravan and kill the Infected within."

The idea pleased Jaikon as much as it did the courtiers, who had been grousing about trade already slowing with the fear of opal contagion returning.

Not only would it be good for morale, but this new solution would enhance the empire's coffers. The mercenaries loved gathering opal heads in sacks almost as much as they loved spending their payment in Lagonia's own bars and brothels. Jaikon thought the empire's wealth might actually grow from this edict rather than diminish.

Stone stood stock-still for several moments, and Jaikon wondered if the man would argue with him in front of his entire court. The interrogator had to know he was living on borrowed time. Jaikon had kept Stone in Lagonia rather than sending him along with the other suspected traitors because his skills were unmatched. Still, Jaikon was no fool. He knew Stone and Rhetteman had a twisted kind of familial bond.

Remembering his place at last, Stone bowed.

"I will see it done, Your Majesty." He hesitated. "And might I also suggest rethinking sending those soldiers abroad?"

"Those men and women have the chance to make history. They should be honored by this assignment."

The glittering, bejeweled sycophants in his court voiced their agreement.

A thrill went through Jaikon at seeing Stone fold himself into yet another bow. But his pleasure was tempered by a nagging unease.

He briefly wondered if he was making a mistake in sending nearly a thousand of his best soldiers across the sea.

The ships wouldn't be leaving until this afternoon. He still had time to change his mind.

No, he'd done right, he assured himself.

Even though all of those soldiers would perish, they were certain to weaken the giants before they were slaughtered. Every dead giant would only make Jaikon's job easier when he got around to taking control of the lands across the sea.

His ally in Insorsil had already delivered a handful of the pins. Once Jaikon had enough to make the entirety of his army invincible, he would lead them to the Giant Realm. They would obliterate the giants and claim the sea routes as property of Lagonia. Then, Jaikon's subjects would know how much they needed their emperor.

They would remember who their true sovereign was.

Jaikon had been incensed to discover that arresting all those soldiers hadn't silenced the whispered talk about Rhetteman returning to Lagonia. Councilmen…court ladies…servants….

It seemed every Lagonian had a soft spot for the traitor.

One advisor had been foolish enough to mention that the bastard might be able to drum up the support needed to steal the throne. Jaikon had cut the man down where he stood for the mere suggestion.

Jaikon returned his attention to the line of soldiers waiting to deliver their reports. The next soldier stepped forward.

"Your Majesty." The woman flinched when Jaikon raised his hand to adjust his cuff. "We believe Opal Smoke may be using her Extension to make them both disappear."

It was possible. The truth was that he knew next to nothing about the spy who shared his former Chief Assassin's bed. That fact had Jaikon's temper flaring hotter.

Jaikon glanced at his right hand, which he'd stuffed into a thick glove. His mangled fingers gave him terrible pain, but to admit as much to the court physicians would be as good as standing on the Sapphire Bridge and announcing to the entire empire that he was weak. That he was vulnerable.

"We don't even know if they're still travelling together," another soldier said, keeping his eyes fixed on the floor.

"Of course, they're still together," Jaikon snapped.

The unflappable, arrogant Rhetteman Loniger had begged for her life. He'd been ready to die for her.

Jaikon thumped his left fist down on the armrest again as his fury churned and sparked within him. He'd finally found Rhetteman's weakness, and Jaikon hadn't been able to use it. *Her.*

Jaikon laughed out loud. The soldiers and advisors stopped their squabbling and looked at him.

Jaikon, you're a fool, he thought to himself, still chuckling.

He'd been going about this all wrong. He was searching for the two elusive traitors, when all this time, he had everything he needed to bring both of them to him. All he needed to do was lure Opal Smoke out. She'd set her own lover's trap.

"Elouicia, get some handkerchiefs. We're going to visit our guest."

* * *

With Elouicia keeping pace beside him, the Emperor descended the stone steps that led down into the palace's underbelly.

The *drip drip drip* of water along the stone walls tapped out a pleasant rhythm as the stairs carried them deeper and deeper underground. At the first whiff of the noxious odor that came from the adjoining sewer, Jaikon held out his hand for one of the handkerchiefs.

Elouicia shoved a balled-up cloth over his own mouth and nose as he choked on the stench of raw sewage. Apparently, Jaikon's new Chief Assassin wasn't immune to this place, in spite of his penchant for unpleasant things.

The observation pleased Jaikon. If Rhetteman was here now, Jaikon was certain the insufferable man would be as stoic and unphased as ever. The Emperor had only ever seen Rhetteman Loniger lose control of himself once.

It was an experience Jaikon promised himself would be repeated. Soon.

Jaikon made sure his Insorsiled pin was fastened to his shirt over his heart before he turned down the next corridor. The pin protected him against anything that could kill him, including opal contagion. Against the advice of the court physicians, he'd stopped taking his daily immunity flower in order to save them for his subjects who weren't so fortunate as to be invincible.

Jaikon smiled to himself at his own magnanimity.

He and Elouicia stopped outside a narrow metal door. There was no lock on the door, but he knew the room's occupant would be home. After all, he had nowhere else to go.

"How's my head of the newly-formed Council of Sewer Management?" Jaikon crowed.

When Jaikon received no response, he opened the door and let himself inside. Even with the handkerchief pressed to his mouth, the smell was only a hair's breadth away from intolerable.

It was cold, although not unbearably so. The room was small. There was a pallet on one side and a rickety wooden chair on the other. A tiny washroom adjoined the sleeping quarters. As Jaikon had pointed out to the room's occupant with some humor, the washroom was superfluous. The tunnels down here were really one big toilet.

"Emperor Jaikon," a voice whispered from the corner.

Greasy strands of shoulder-length orange hair hung across the Extended man's face. Even the gloom couldn't hide his eerie opal skin and orange eyes.

"Speak up, Burk," Jaikon said, deliberately raising his own voice in a way he knew caused the hearing-enhanced man pain.

"Emperor Jaikon," Burk repeated, in a slightly louder whisper. "I require new accommodations." He let out a dry cough that sounded fake.

"The contract you wrote, and we both signed, specified accommodations in the palace and a position on my council in return for all your knowledge on the Extended," Jaikon said. "You were the one who failed to specify the details of the accommodations or the particular council to which you wanted access."

Burk looked up at Jaikon. Those glowing orange eyes blazed with hatred.

"You'll have to learn to be clearer when you dabble with Insorsiled ink in the future," he told the Extended man.

"But the stench," Burk whined.

"If you despise the smell down here, then do something about it." Jaikon looked around at the moisture dripping down the concrete walls. "That does fall right within your jurisdiction, after all."

Burk got to his feet, stumbling a little in the process. The man was as thin as a cadaver, even though Jaikon ensured food was brought three times a day out of the goodness of his heart. Perhaps the smell had put Burk off his appetite.

"You don't care about the sewers," Burk whispered. "You only created that damned council to torture me."

"How right you are," Jaikon agreed amiably.

"You did destroy my fields of immunity flowers," he reminded the Extended man, although he wasn't really angry.

Oh, he had been at first. But afterward, when everyone in the empire had discovered that only a month's worth of immunity remained, his subjects' fear of the contagion had roared to life. It had brought about a competition for his favor in hopes of winning additional flowers. Jaikon was rather enjoying the whole experience.

Really, Jaikon owed Burk for destroying the fields.

"While I'd love to discuss your comfort and well-being, that's not why I'm here," Jaikon said. He waved a hand to interrupt Burk's rant about Lagonian riches and unmet expectations. "I need information."

"I've already told you the caravan's route," Burk sulked. "If they aren't there, I don't know where they might be."

"Talk to me about Liss," Jaikon said, repeating the name Rhett had cried out as he bled to death in the torture cage. "Who are the people who matter most to her, and where do they spend their time when they aren't rolling around in their little wagons?"

Burks's chapped lips twisted into a petulant expression. "Her mother never leaves the wagon, and she has no other family."

"And what about her friends?" Jaikon prompted, sensing the other man wasn't telling him everything he knew.

Jaikon knew he'd asked the right question when perspiration began streaming down the Extended man's face.

Burk was attempting to avoid answering the question, but he wouldn't keep quiet for long. Their contract required that Burk tell Jaikon everything he knew. If the Extended man held out, he would die. Insorsiled ink was that unforgiving.

Jaikon smiled and waited while Burk writhed and babbled to himself.

Elouicia chuckled as the opal-skinned man sank down onto his filthy cot, clutching at his sunken chest.

"The children," Burk wheezed. "There are three children on her thieving crew. They get jewels and supplies wherever the caravan stops. If the caravan isn't on its usual route, they're probably hiding out in the outskirts of Insorsil where it's easier to steal."

"Very good." Jaikon nodded in approval as the pathetic man quaked and hugged himself.

"Majesty."

Jaikon turned to see his Master Interrogator standing in the doorway.

"What is it, Stone?" Jaikon asked.

"The peasants are unable to meet the new tax demands. The soldiers have taken everything they have, but it isn't close to the amount you were hoping for."

"Well then, send them back out for more," Jaikon replied, barely glancing at the man.

"The peasants are on the verge of revolting," Stone said, his words measured and his face betraying no hint of emotion. "I suggest you allow the famers to focus on their crops before you have a rebellion on your hands and insufficient soldiers to put it down."

Jaikon snapped his fingers at Elouicia. "Give the peasants a demonstration of your invincibility. Tell them whichever of them most impresses you with their loyalty to the crown will be rewarded with an invincibility pin of their own." To Stone, he said, "And get my damned citizens to pay their taxes."

More money would procure more pins, and then a few rebelling bumpkins would be the least of his concerns.

"Bring my dragon," Jaikon added as an afterthought. "It'll give the peasants a little extra motivation."

His mood soured at the reminder of how Rhetteman had used the Emperor's own dragon to escape from justice. The beast had returned the same day looking for food, since it wasn't likely to find a trough full of gold nuggets out in the wild. But the useless creature hadn't been of any help in leading Jaikon's soldiers to the disgraced assassin's whereabouts.

Both of his men bowed.

Before they could leave to carry out their orders, Jaikon said, "Organize the fifty strongest fighters we have. Prepare them to go to Insorsil."

When dealing with Rhetteman and his opal whore, Jaikon would prefer to send his invincible soldiers. He and his ally weren't ready for the Insorsil queen to know about the pins just yet. He had to wait just a little longer.

Jaikon ran his hand over the circlet of metal fastened to his shirt. With the magic contained in this pin, and the alliance he'd established in Insorsil under Queen Gatria's nose, it wouldn't be long before he controlled both the Giant Realm and Insorsil. He'd triple the amount of land belonging to Lagonia and expand their assets infinitely. They would be untouchable, and everyone would know Jaikon was the one responsible for the conquests.

In a matter of months, no one in the empire would even remember Rhetteman Loniger. He would be a ghost, as significant as…well, smoke.

Jaikon chuckled at his own cleverness.

A muffled whimper of pain brought his attention back to the confines of this filthy room. Elouicia was kneeling beside Burk. He was using his Insorsil-enhanced fingernails to carve into Burk's opal skin.

"Don't kill him," Jaikon reminded Elouicia. "The man is under my protection, after all."

Jaikon's Insorsiled ally had warned him the pin wouldn't protect against a bargain made with Insorsiled ink.

Jaikon turned to Burk. "Now, tell me how to lay my trap for these thieving children."

CHAPTER 9

Rhett's stomach growled as he stepped into the tiny kitchen that smelled like gruel and smoked bacon.

"She isn't awake yet," Nya said, noticing the way Rhett's eyes scanned the rest of the wagon. "She's staying in our old wagon, but I'm sure she'll be over soon."

Rhett nodded in thanks as Nya slid a bowl of porridge and steaming mug of coffee over to him.

"We have no Insorsiled syrups, I'm afraid, but there is sugar," Nya offered.

"This is fine," he replied. "Thank you."

He glanced at Nya, looking for some similarity to her daughter. As far as he could tell, there wasn't a single one.

Beyond the obvious difference in skin, hair, and eye color, they were as different as two strangers. Where Liss was petite and shaped like an hourglass, Nya was tall and board-thin. Nya's eyes sagged at the corners and were somehow dull even with their orange glow. Liss's, in contrast, were bright and full of the emotions she never tried to conceal.

Nya hunched in her chair and seemed to take up less space than her frame should require. She looked as frail as Liss was strong.

He remembered Liss telling him about her mother ailing over the death of Liss's father. That, at least, seemed to be the truth.

Rhett's pulse stuttered. He hated not knowing which of Liss's stories had been true and which were lies she'd made up to hide her true identity.

"I'll admit, I didn't want Liss going back to Lagonia to save you," Nya said, staring at Rhett over the rim of her coffee mug.

"You should have stopped her," Rhett said. "You never should have let her come to Lagonia in the first place."

She had come so close to torture…so close to death….

Rhett knew he should be trying to win over Liss's mother, but he couldn't help the intense dislike he felt for the woman who had forced Liss to grow up caring for her mother instead of the other way around.

Because Liss's mother was too depressed and sickly to care for her own family, Liss had needed to become a thief. She'd needed to risk everything to become a spy in Lagonia.

Nya gave Rhett a look that was a bit too knowing for his taste, and for the first time, he saw the glimmer of resemblance between this woman and Liss.

"You care for my daughter, don't you?" Nya asked.

Rhett didn't see any point in lying.

"I do."

"Are you in love with her?"

The question threw him off guard. Long years of practice allowed him not to show even a hint of the turmoil that those words awoke inside him.

Rhett wasn't in the habit of lying when he was asked a direct question, but he also didn't discuss his feelings.

"It's—"

"—complicated?" Nya finished, giving him a small smile.

Rhett nodded.

"People always say that about love, but they're wrong." Nya took a sip of her coffee. "Love is the simplest thing in the world. Either you truly love another, and you'd sacrifice anything for their sake, or you don't."

Rhett bristled. He didn't know why he felt the need to defend himself to this woman. He rarely felt the need to prove himself to anyone.

He looked at Nya through his still-swollen eye, and said, "I understand about that kind of sacrifice."

Nya studied him for a long moment. He stared back.

"I can see that you do," she said after a long pause.

Nya got up from the table and pulled a small vial from a shelf. Uncorking it, she took a sip of the swirling pink liquid.

"Did Liss tell you I nearly died trying to make my husband immune from the contagion?" she asked, putting the vial back in the cupboard.

Rhett felt relief wash through him at the confirmation that Liss hadn't lied about that.

"It made you weak, but it didn't protect your husband," Rhett said.

"He was protected from me, just not from any other Extended." Nya turned away, but not before Rhett saw tears glistening at the corners of her eyes. "I get illnesses that don't affect other Extended, and my heart was permanently weakened from the spell. I'm getting stronger, but it's…difficult."

"Do you regret it?" Rhett asked.

"Never." Nya's answer was immediate. "I only had one year with my husband before he was taken from me, and yet, it was the happiest year of my life. My only regret is that we didn't have more time together."

She gripped the corner of the narrow counter and hunched over it, like her grief was too much for her to bear standing up.

This was what Liss was afraid of, Rhett knew. This was the reason why Liss had never been with anyone before Rhett…why she'd hesitated to give herself to him.

Well, that wasn't the only reason, he reminded himself. The other, of course, was that they were supposed to be enemies.

"So, your illness was the reason why you couldn't take care of your daughter?" Rhett asked, his tone more confrontational than he'd meant it.

Nya turned back to him, her orange-rimmed eyes brighter from the tears.

"He was everything to me," she whispered.

Rhett wanted to feel disgust for this woman who had been too weak to meet the barest of her responsibilities. Instead, his thoughts turned to his dream from the night before, and his memory of the terror he'd felt when he saw Liss standing outside his torture cage.

Nya frowned to herself as she placed a mug of coffee in front of the empty chair at the table.

"I can never remember if she takes it black or sweetened," Nya murmured to herself.

Feeling another burst of resentment that Liss's own mother hadn't bothered to learn her daughter's likes and dislikes, Rhett took the narrow canister of sugar off the counter. Ignoring the dainty spoon resting beside it, he poured most of its contents into the steaming mug.

He took a sip, grimaced at the cloying sweetness, and added a little more. *Just how Liss liked it…with more sugar than coffee.*

"You just put two months' worth of sugar into that mug," Nya said, bemused, as he swirled the cup to dissolve the sugar.

Rhett felt a small pulse of guilt. He'd seen how little the Extended people had to spare. But it had been for Liss.

The door opened and Liss stepped inside.

Rhett jerked to his feet, forgetting about the low ceiling and hitting his head.

Blood was streaming down her neck and onto her chest. She was reaching out to him for help…she was dying….

"Rhett?"

Rhett blinked, and the bloody, dying woman before him disappeared. She was looking at him, her brow furrowed in concern.

Rhett released a pent-up breath. "Nothing."

What the hell was wrong with him?

He was grateful Liss wasn't looking into his soul. He was pretty sure if she did, she'd see the hints of madness.

Liss gave her mother a kiss on the cheek as she navigated the narrow kitchen with ease. She gave him another questioning look before sitting down at the table.

"How did you sleep, darling?" her mother asked.

"Great." Liss smiled.

Rhett frowned. Her smile was too bright, and she didn't look either of them in the eye. *She was lying.*

As he studied Liss, he noticed there were bruise-like circles underneath her eyes. There was a hollow look to her face that wasn't usually there.

"I went hunting last night," Nya told her daughter. "There's smoked boar in the porridge, and even a little butter."

Rhett, who hadn't taken his eyes off Liss, saw her grimace. Her cheeks actually turned a light shade of green as she backed away from the stove.

"Just coffee for me, thanks," she said, still looking repulsed.as she rubbed the back of her neck.

"What's going on with you?" Rhett asked. He tried to keep his voice low, knowing that Nya was watching them.

This meal might not be the golden cake of Lagonia that Liss loved so much, but he'd never seen her turn her nose up at perfectly good food.

"I'm just not hungry." Liss sat down and took a sip from her mug.

She smiled, and Rhett forgot his anger at the sight of her dimple.

"Wow, you made it just how I like it," Liss told her mom.

Nya gave Liss a weak smile in return. She excused herself from the table, saying something about feeding the phoenix.

Rhett waited until she had disappeared behind the bird cage in the other room.

"You have to eat," he told Liss.

Her beautiful smile turned to a scowl. "I'm not one of your soldiers. You can't just order me around."

"I'm not—"

"Good," she snapped.

Rhett didn't have a temper, but at that moment, he had a fierce desire to throw something.

"So, what are we doing about this barrier and the weapons you're promising the other caravans?" Nya asked as she returned from the other room.

Still distracted by Liss's strange behavior, Rhett took a minute to process the question.

"There's a stockpile of weapons and jewels hidden in a cave about ten miles from here." He passed Nya the map he'd drawn the night before. "And I wrote down all the materials you'll need to construct a barricade strong enough to keep the Lagonians out. You should be able to get everything from Insorsil with the jewels from the cave without too much trouble."

Traitor. Traitor. Traitor. Gwendylina's voice echoed in his mind. Her blood slicked across his hands.

Those weapons and jewels were there for his soldiers. They were a fail-safe in case trouble ever arose in Insorsil and more weapons were needed.

"I'll have one of our Energizers take us there this morning," Nya said, examining the crude map Rhett had drawn.

"I'll go with you," Liss said. "It's not like we can do anything else until the other caravans arrive."

The wagon door flew open without warning. Rhett had his dagger in his hand before he saw there was no one outside the door. At least, there didn't appear to be anyone. Liss pushed him over, making room for her by his side.

Movement drew his attention down to the ground, where a small, brown ball rolled across the wooden porch. As he watched, the ball transformed itself into a small child.

Jema, Rhett recalled from the night before.

Except the smiling, giggling child was gone. In her place was a bloody, soot- and tear-stained girl who looked on the verge of collapse.

Rhett blinked several times, convinced he was hallucinating again. But unlike his vision from a few minutes ago, this one didn't disappear.

Liss reached Jema first. Rhett pulled out a chair, and Liss helped Jema into it. The little girl was trying to speak, but she was crying too hard to get the words out.

Rhett assessed the child, leaving Liss to deal with her emotions as he pieced together what must have happened.

The sleeve of her threadbare jacket was torn, like she'd yanked it free from something or someone. The cut on her cheek was shallow and clean, which meant it had come from a sharp blade.

Few of the Insorsiled knew how to wield a blade, and the ones who did didn't bother keeping them sharp.

Rhett's small breakfast rose up into his throat. He felt as sick as Liss had looked earlier. He knew, before Jema spoke the words in her trembling little voice, who her attackers had been.

Lagonia soldiers.

CHAPTER 10

Liss knelt down until she was facing Jema. Fear and guilt were radiating off the little girl's soul.

"What happened?" Liss asked.

"We went to Toil and Trouble like we always do." Jema paused to wipe her running nose on her sleeve. "Mari found a diamond earring that had just fallen on the floor, and Spence picked up a purse someone had dropped."

Liss cringed. A lost diamond earring *and* a lost purse didn't just happen by accident. The whole thing screamed as a set-up. She looked at Rhett, who nodded at her in confirmation.

Liss felt nauseous. If she had been with the kids, she would have known something was wrong and gotten them out before—

"The soldiers just started appearing. We tried to run, but they surrounded us. They were waiting for us." Jema let out a sniffle that ended on a hiccup.

"Spence and Mari?" Liss was almost too scared to ask.

"The soldiers got them," Jema whispered. "I tried to help. Really, I did. I tried to think about what you would do, and so I stole one of the soldier's swords." She looked up at Liss through watery eyes. "But it was too heavy, and I dropped it."

Jema's hold on her fear broke, and she began to sob. Liss cradled the little girl in her arms.

"I know I shouldn't have left them, but I couldn't fight the soldiers. So, I used my Extension and got away."

Jema cried harder as she buried her face against Liss's stomach.

Liss was too full of grief and fury to speak. She took the cloth her mom handed her to wipe the trickle of blood from Jema's lip.

"I'm sorry," Jema said. She turned her mournful gaze on Rhett and Liss's mom. "Lissy would have been able to save them."

To Liss's surprise, it was Rhett who spoke. He knelt down in front of Jema. Even on his knees, he dwarfed her.

"You're as brave as any soldier I've ever met," Rhett told her. "You should be proud, not sorry."

Liss didn't think she had ever loved him more than she did in that moment.

Rhett got to his feet and turned his gaze on Liss's mother.

"Get any Extended who can help us and all the weapons you have in the camp. We're leaving for Insorsil in five minutes."

Liss's heart expanded in gratitude and anticipation, but she couldn't ignore the growing unease in her own soul. As soon as her mom had left to return Jema to her parents and round up the Extended, Liss turned to Rhett.

"You know Jaikon planned this to lure both of us out, right?"

Rhett's expression was one of grim acceptance. "I know."

* * *

Five minutes later, Liss found herself stuffed into a narrow wagon with her mom, Rhett, Romile, Jema's parents, and Mari's three oldest brothers.

Mari's youngest brother was staying behind to guard the Extended hideout. They'd left Rhett's flowers with him, too. The thought of letting Rhett's lifeline out of their sight for even a minute made Liss sick with worry, but they'd both need their hands to fight, and they couldn't risk the flowers being destroyed or taken by their enemies.

Jema's parents were Energizers, which meant they had the ability to animate the inanimate. They were making the wagon hurtle across the open field that would bring them to Insorsil. With the Energizers' Extension, it would take less than an hour to reach northwest Insorsil. It would have taken almost an entire day to walk from their hideout to Toil and Trouble.

Romile, their caravan's Flamer, would be useful for as long as his strength lasted. He wasn't as strong as his Flooder brother, and he was already straining himself to keep everyone in the caravan warm now that winter had come.

Mari's brothers would be far more useful. Liss had never seen them in action before, but Fighters were some of the most feared Extended for good reason.

The men cracked their knuckles and bounced their legs as they waited for the opportunity to pounce on the soldiers who had their sister.

No one else in the caravan had been willing to come with them. They'd all been too afraid to venture away from the hideout.

Liss was disgusted with all of them.

"Small steps, sweetheart," Nya told her as the wagon jostled and creaked as it shot across the uneven ground. "Convincing everyone to even stay in one place for more than a few days is extraordinary progress. We can't expect our people to change overnight."

When it came to saving two innocent kids from their own caravan, Liss certainly could.

As the wagon careened toward Insorsil, Rhett laid out their fighting strategy. Even though he didn't allow his frustration to show on his face, Liss knew he must be losing his mind. He'd gone from commanding the most powerful army in all the lands to leading a handful of amateurs. And that was putting it politely.

After he'd finished trying to explain a tactical formation to Mari's brothers, which they clearly intended to ignore in favor of brute force, Rhett gave up. He sat down on the wooden floor next to Liss.

Leaning into her so only she could hear, he asked, "Liss, what's happening to you?"

She jerked back, surprised by the question.

"Two of my friends were captured by Jaikon's soldiers," she said. "I'm upset."

It was only when he pressed his hand to her forehead that she realized she was sweating despite the cold.

"Do you need a witchdoctor?" he asked.

Liss scoffed. "That's a great idea. The two most wanted criminals in Lagonia are just going to walk into Insorsil and ask for some potions. I'm sure the witchdoctor won't be tempted by whatever reward the Emperor has put on our heads."

Rhett gave her a steely look. "I am far more persuasive than Jaikon's jewels."

"Seriously, I'm fine," she told him. "Just a headache."

She had a strong suspicion about what was wrong with her, but she wasn't about to tell Rhett.

"Liss—"

"I said I'm fine."

"We're here," the Energizers called.

Liss pulled back the curtain on the small window and glanced out. They were right where she'd told the Energizer to bring them: behind the dragon stables. It put them just a few twisted back-alleys from Toil and Trouble.

No soldiers or Insorsiled swarmed their wagon, although she hadn't expected them to. There was nothing inherently attention-worthy about a wagon rolling into Insorsil. The Insorsiled weren't affected by opal contagion, so they still conducted business with the Extended.

Extorted them would have been a more apt description. Liss's mood soured further at the reminder of the gouged prices the Insorsiled charged her people simply because they could.

Even from her spot at the window, Liss could see posters plastered on every shop with her and Rhett's images. At least the pictures didn't offer their titles, otherwise everyone in the wagon would know Rhett wasn't just some nobody Lagonian. As bad as things were, Liss could only imagine how her people would react if they knew exactly who she'd brought into their hideout.

"The streets are too empty," Rhett said, staring out the window over her head.

Liss had made the same observation.

"They're all waiting at Toil and Trouble for us, I take it?"

"Mhm."

Rhett scanned their little group and sighed.

"We're going to be sitting ducks," he muttered.

"We would be if we used the main streets," Liss replied.

Rhett's expression turned intrigued. "Am I going to get to see the famous Opal Smoke at work?"

She winked at him before opening the wagon door and jumping over a pile of dragon dung.

When Rhett saw where they were, he raised an eyebrow at her.

"What?" she demanded. "Did you think every part of being a thief was glamorous?"

They were in a narrow alley behind the dragon stables, where even the grooms didn't venture.

Dragon urine and feces were tossed out of the stalls into this alley before being taken away by Insorsiled carts that required no driver. It stunk to high heaven, but the piles of manure made a kind of wall that kept them hidden from anyone walking on the cobbled streets.

Because of her thieving, Liss knew Insorsil better than most Insorsiled. She knew all the places where shops interconnected and the streets where Lagonia soldiers wouldn't consider setting foot.

This was one of those streets.

Liss led their group forward until the piles of dragon dung turned to bags of trash and rotting Insorsiled potions.

She felt a burst of pride at the sight of her mom, who moved as quickly and silently as Liss even with an arrow nocked in her bow. Rhett was on her other side, his dagger at the ready.

Romile came next, followed by Mari's brothers. Liss winced as their heavy footfalls just about screamed their presence to anyone who was bothering to listen. The men were all brawn and no subtlety.

"If you can't manage to breathe without snorting, then hold your breath," Rhett snapped at one of the brothers.

Liss glanced at Rhett, but his attention was swiveling from side to side, searching for any sign of an attack. She wondered if he was thinking about Stone, Wilsean, and Ciago and wishing he had them by his side.

Liss stopped at an unmarked wooden door and signaled that they'd arrived. Rhett and Nya stood at the ready on either side of the door.

When their little group was more or less assembled, Liss pushed open the door. It was unlocked and gave easily, just like Liss had known it would.

Liss moved into the familiar supply room on silent feet. She kept to the shadows of the towering stacks of beer kegs and dry goods that had always made for ideal hiding places.

So far, so good.

They all positioned themselves on either side of the swinging door that led out into the main bar. There was a sliver of frosted glass on the top part of the door, and Liss could see movement on the other side.

She clutched her butcher's knife. It wasn't ideal, but it was the sharpest weapon in the entire Extended camp aside from Rhett's dagger. He also had three throwing knives of dubious sharpness tucked inside his jacket. Liss wasn't optimistic about the weapons' chances when they came up against Lagonian armor, but she'd learned not to underestimate Rhett's skill, no matter how dull the weapon.

Nya pulled back the string of her bow.

Liss nodded to Rhett, and then she threw open the door.

CHAPTER 11

Rhett stepped behind the man who was too stupid to watch his own back. Under other circumstances, it would have irritated him that someone wearing Lagonian black and gold could be so careless. Now, he was grateful, because he knew that the man was one of Jaikon's hired mercenaries rather than a soldier Rhett had trained and fought beside.

Rhett sliced his dagger across the man's throat. He tossed the body forward, letting the dead weight make a path into the bar.

He glanced around, noting that even though the bar was full of people, there wasn't a single patron in the place.

Shouts erupted. Liss's butcher knife cleaved a man's face as he took a swing at her stomach. Nya loosed an arrow. It went through two soldiers, glanced off a metal plate nailed to the wall of the bar, and came back through three more. The five mercenaries sank to the ground without a sound.

Toil and Trouble was filled with soldiers.

Mari's Fighter brothers might be shit at sleuthing, but Rhett was grateful for them now. They bludgeoned men with their fists. A single one of their punches could cave in a person's skull. Their fists were even more lethal than Ciago's.

One of the brothers lifted two men off the ground—one in each hand. Then, he threw them through the window.

Glass shattered. People on the street outside screamed. More soldiers poured into the bar.

Everything was shouting and confusion. Rhett's own mind quieted in the way it did when he was singularly focused. He kept one eye on Liss as he cut a path through the soldiers, but she was holding her own. Rhett felt relief more than pride, although there was that, too.

He glanced around the room, wasting precious seconds to confirm he didn't know any of these soldiers. They all had that indefinable ugliness about them that told Rhett they'd been slavers before they donned Lagonia military fatigues.

It was against the law to employ slavers in any capacity, but Jaikon had clearly chosen to ignore that rule in favor of bolstering his army.

Rhett smiled. He rarely took pleasure in violence, but for the people who had tortured and enslaved Liss's people, he'd make an exception.

Rhett threw his knives, knowing they hit their targets without watching to see the soldiers fall. His dagger flashed in the candlelight of the bar.

He didn't think. He didn't have to. This was who he was, and he did his job well.

Two slavers ran toward him, their swords drawn. Before they got within slashing distance, their faces caught fire.

The men screamed and clawed at their skin. The Flamer strode forward. Fiery sparks shot from his raised hands. Three more slavers went through the shattered window, courtesy of the Fighter brothers. Liss yanked her butcher's knife out of a slaver's chest.

Their enemy had the advantage of numbers, but Rhett's people had abilities that went far beyond skill with a blade.

"Get the ones coming in," Rhett ordered Nya.

Wilsean would have done that without needing to be told. Ciago would have made the people he killed fall out of their path instead of into it, unlike Mari's brothers. The Fighters were strong beyond compare, but they lacked any kind of finesse.

Rhett's somber musings cost him. More soldiers had filtered into the bar, and by the looks of it, the Flamer was out of juice.

"Get his girl," a stocky mercenary called, grinning at Rhett as she pointed at Liss. "He'll come quietly once we start hurting her."

Rhett's mind went white.

For even speaking those words, Rhett went for her first. A throwing knife glanced off his forearm, but he didn't even feel it. This soldier had threatened Liss.

Rhett struck his dagger into her neck. Once. Twice. Three times.

Before she hit the ground, he turned to the others converging on Liss.

Five…six…seven soldiers fell by his hand. More sprung out of broom closets and from behind overturned tables. Nya shot them before they could even raise their weapons. Mari's brothers head-butted, punched, and elbowed a path through the soldiers.

Still, no matter how many they killed, more came.

When the Flamer and one of the brothers were too exhausted to wield their Extensions any longer, there was no one to replace them. Nya's arrows were almost gone. Liss was still fighting, but her moves were getting sluggish.

And still, Jaikon's soldiers kept coming.

The floor was sticky with blood and littered with corpses. Amid the chaos, Rhett caught the sound of whimpering from behind the bar.

Liss pulled her butcher's knife from a mercenary's back and turned to the bar, where a few orange curls were visible over the polished wood surface.

Knowing they had been seen, two soldiers stepped out from behind the bar. They used Spence and Mari as shields against Mari's brothers, who were roaring for the men's blood.

Spence's hands were tied in front of him, and his captor was being careful not to get close enough for the kid to use his Extension.

Mari's brothers were senseless with rage. So was Liss. They were on the other side of the bar from Rhett, separated by a dozen bloodthirsty soldiers. Liss and the brothers were so intent on reaching Spence and Mari that they didn't notice movement in the rafters.

Ropes dropped from the ceiling. More soldiers shimmied down the ropes, their knives clutched between their teeth.

"Liss, behind you!" Rhett yelled, bringing his dagger up to disarm and kill the two soldiers in front of him.

Nya's bow twanged, and her last arrow sliced through more of the men who were lined up and waiting to take on Rhett.

Not me, Rhett wanted to shout at her. *Protect your daughter!*

The mercenaries from the rafters surrounded Liss. She had taken down two more soldiers, but she was blocked in on all sides with nowhere to retreat. Rhett stumbled over dead bodies on the floor in his desperation to get to her.

Rhett jumped over an overturned table. He knocked out two of the men surrounding Liss by cracking their skulls together. Liss ducked under a blade that came at her face as Rhett forced his way into the circle.

He and Liss stood back-to-back, moving together as they parried two soldiers each. Rhett didn't lose his focus, even though he felt his energy flagging. Liss quivered against him from the strain of fighting so many. He needed to get her out of here.

"Get the kids," he told her. He held back the tide of mercenaries long enough for Liss and one of Mari's brothers to vault over the bar.

Liss dealt with the slavers, while Mari's brother grabbed the kids.

"Get them out the back," Rhett ordered, using his body and dagger to keep the horde of soldiers from overwhelming them.

There were too many, and he wouldn't be able to hold them off for long. He just needed to give Liss and the kids enough time to get out. He watched Nya leading them out of the bar, her bow poised with an arrow she'd pulled out of a man's chest.

A spray of blood flew through the air as another one of the slavers fell. Rhett spun away from another man he'd taken down. That was when he realized Liss was back beside him.

"Save it," she told him, slashing out with her butcher's knife. "I'm not leaving without you."

Rhett felt the first tendrils of panic begin to unfurl in his chest. Dozens of snarling men were waiting for them, and they were both spent. He could feel the newly-healed muscles and organs inside him straining to hold together.

There were too many to take down.

"We'll be rewarded for bringing you back to the Emperor," a slaver-turned-soldier gloated.

Of course, the man stayed far enough back to avoid Liss and Rhett's blades.

"The Emperor bought more of those invincibility pins from the Insorsil queen, and he's going to give them to us in payment for bringing you to him."

"Invincibility won't help you if you're already dead," Liss shot back, unintimidated by the man's threats.

Moving on instinct, Rhett pushed Liss back against the wall, using his body to shield her as an arrow came whistling toward them.

The arrow struck a soldier off to his side, who Rhett hadn't even seen because the man had been hidden by an overturned table. Another arrow followed the first. This one embedded itself in the neck of the slaver who had been baiting Liss. The man thudded to the ground.

That's when Rhett caught sight of the arrow's feathers. He huffed out a disbelieving breath.

The soldiers had stopped coming for him and Liss. They were falling so fast, only a handful of slavers now separated Rhett from the two people whose kills he recognized before he saw their faces.

His two best friends, Ciago and Wilsean, were fighting their way to Rhett from the street outside the bar.

"Feel free to jump in at any time," Ciago called to Rhett over the raucous sounds of battle.

Grinning, Rhett let go of Liss and gripped his dagger.

CHAPTER 12

few minutes ago, Liss had been sure she and Rhett would never be leaving this bar alive. Now, she stood back and watched as the three men sliced, shot, and carved their way through their enemies.

There was a terrible beauty to the way they fought. They moved around each other, ducking out of each other's way and guarding each other's backs without speaking a word. It was like a dance.

The bar was filled with dead soldiers. The smell of blood hung in the air. Liss and the men were covered with it. At the sight of entrails spilled across the bar's sawdust floor, Liss gagged.

Tables had been upended, windows broken, and a shelf of glowing Insorsiled alcohol had been smashed. Fluid dripped from the shattered bottles and mixed with the blood leaking across the floor.

Liss didn't feel sorry for the dead. They appeared to be mostly slavers in Lagonia uniforms. Liss had even less sympathy for slavers than for the Lagonians who had bought her people like they were nothing more than property.

Liss jumped at the sound of Rhett's dagger thunking down into the thick oak of the bar. He said something in a low voice, and then he and Ciago were hugging each other. After a few seconds, they released each other. Rhett and Wilsean clasped hands and patted each other's backs.

"Get over here, Lovely Liss," Ciago boomed in a voice that took over the whole bar.

She didn't hesitate, even though he was covered in blood. She let his muscular arms swallow her whole. For as brutal as he'd been while slaughtering a dozen men, Ciago's hold was gentle.

"You know I'm still madly in love with you, don't you?" Ciago asked, when he let her go.

Wilsean joined them, giving Liss a tired smile.

"Samara says hey," he told her.

Liss's heart leapt at the mention of her best friend and Wilsean's girlfriend.

"Is she okay?" Liss asked, worry gnawing at her insides. After what Samara and her sister had done to help Rhett, they were in as much danger as the rest of them.

"She's fine," Wilsean said, his smile fading.

Liss could sense the unspoken words *for now*. Worry and protectiveness radiated from Wilsean's soul, along with an undercurrent of love.

"Why did you come?" Rhett asked in his rough voice.

"Because if we hadn't, you and Liss would be dead," Wilsean pointed out.

"We came as soon as Stone told us what Jaikon was up to," Ciago added. "He would have come too, but he had another matter to take care of."

Ciago and Wilsean looked at each other. Discomfort, guilt, and anger radiated across their souls.

"But—" Rhett swallowed.

Liss didn't need to use her Extension to know what was bothering him. Ciago and Wilsean had killed Lagonia soldiers. That made them as much an enemy of the empire as Rhett and Liss.

Ciago shrugged his massive shoulders. "I hope you two have an extra room wherever you've been hiding out, otherwise we're all going to be getting very cozy." He winked at Liss.

"You can't," Rhett said.

"Sure we can." Ciago slung his huge arm across Liss's shoulders. "I'll cuddle with Liss, and you'll cuddle with Wilsean. It'll be a cuddle fest."

Rhett shook his head. "That's not what I meant." His normally-blank face was awash with the same guilt Liss was feeling. "Your families—"

"Are protected," Ciago said, clapping a hand on Rhett's shoulder. "Jaikon isn't powerful enough to take on the empire's wealthiest families. Our parents will be fine."

"But you can never go back." Rhett's voice was so low it was barely audible. "You've destroyed your reputations."

"I chose my duty over friendship once," Wilsean said, his expression as serious as Rhett's. "I won't make that mistake again."

Liss's throat burned as the three men exchanged a look so full of trust and understanding it made her chest ache.

Wilsean and Ciago's souls were full of a combination of guilt and honor. She knew they regretted how they'd done nothing when Stone arrested Rhett.

"Stone?" Rhett asked, clearly on the same train of thought as Liss.

"Trying to reign in the Emperor's crazy and keep the empire in one piece," Ciago said. "He single-handedly stopped several riots among the farmers and merchants when Jaikon raised taxes…again. He's dealing with other stuff right now, otherwise, like Wilsean said, he would have come."

"What stuff?" Rhett demanded.

Wilsean and Ciago exchanged a worried glance.

"Tell me."

Ciago let out a long sigh. "Jaikon sent every soldier he suspected of being loyal to you across the sea to attack the giants. He said if they returned before the giants had been conquered, he'd slaughter their families."

Liss saw horror emerge in Rhett's dark eyes. For a minute, they all just stared at each other.

Rhett sunk onto a bar stool.

"He sent all of them there to die."

Neither Wilsean nor Ciago argued.

Liss longed to say something to ease that deadened expression on Rhett's face. But if there were any words that could make this better, Liss didn't know them.

"Stone tried to stop it," Wilsean said in a subdued voice, "but Jaikon was set on punishing someone for your escape."

"How many?" Rhett asked, his tone flat and completely devoid of the emotions Liss knew were tearing him apart.

Ciago and Wilsean shifted on their feet, refusing to look at Rhett.

"How many?!" he thundered.

"A thousand," Ciago said, his voice hoarse. "He put Dannica in charge."

Grief flashed through Rhett's eyes before he turned away from all of them.

Liss had met Dannica when she first came to Lagonia. Dannica had loaned Liss one of her uniforms so she could blend in with the other Lagonians. Dannica was one of the few people Rhett trusted, and Liss had sensed the woman's loyalty and devotion to Rhett. She had also helped get Rhett out of Lagonia. Now, she was as good as dead.

The sea separating the two continents was rough and dangerous. It was likely that some of the boats that tried to cross those waters wouldn't even make it as far as the Giant Realm. The soldiers who did make it to the giants' harbor would be killed before they set foot on shore.

In the years of conflict between Lagonia and the Giant Realm, neither had ever been able to defeat the other. If the entire Lagonia army couldn't overpower the giants, a thousand soldiers certainly wouldn't be able to.

"I'm so sorry," Liss whispered, barely able to meet Rhett's gaze.

In a round-about way, this was her fault. If Rhett had known who and what she was, he never would have let himself fall in love with her. He never would have been forced to choose between her and his duty. The soldiers who loved him wouldn't have needed to go against their emperor to help Rhett.

"It's not your fault," Rhett told her. "This is Jaikon."

He slammed his fist into the wall, cracking the wood and splitting his knuckles. He didn't seem to notice.

"I'm going after them." Rhett unstuck his dagger from the bar and stood up.

"Don't be ridiculous," Wilsean said, at the same time Liss gasped, "You can't."

"How long ago did they leave?" Rhett asked, ignoring them.

"They left yesterday. But Rhett—"

"They're there because of me. I have to be there with them." Rhett's face was full of bleak determination.

Liss couldn't breathe.

"Dannica and the rest of them believe you're the leader Lagonia deserves," Wilsean argued. "They're willing to die for their belief in you. Don't spit on that kind of loyalty by getting yourself killed. None of them would thank you for it."

"What should I do?" Rhett whirled on all of them. "Stay in hiding while my soldiers get slaughtered?"

"No," Liss said, her voice breaking. "You free Lagonia of a tyrant."

"I can't abandon them." Rhett turned to her. His eyes pleaded with her to understand. "Liss, I just can't."

She had no words. She understood, because it was exactly how she would feel in his position.

"Maybe," she cleared her throat as she tried to gather her thoughts, "we could somehow get a message to them to hide on one of the abandoned islands until we take out Jaikon. The Emperor wouldn't know where they were, so their families wouldn't be in any more danger." She swallowed. "And then, as soon as we've defeated Jaikon, they can come back."

The men stared at her in thoughtful consideration for several seconds.

"Send me."

They all turned to Ciago. His face had gone ashen. There was no sign of his usual good-humored smile.

"Never," Rhett said, rejecting the idea. "You've already ruined your life for my sake. I'm not going to send you over there to die in my place."

"We all know you're going to be the one to defeat Jaikon," Ciago said. "Besides, there's a good chance I won't be able to track down our ships until we all reach the Giant Realm. Once we're there, I'll have a better chance of surviving than anyone else."

Rhett made a dismissive sound. Liss was distracted by the emotions pouring from Ciago's soul. There was hesitation and a dark fear she'd never sensed from him before.

Ciago sat down on one of the bar stools. It creaked and buckled under his weight.

"I don't know how to tell you this," Ciago began, keeping his eyes fixed on a blank spot on the wall.

Misery radiated off his soul, but he was determined. Several more seconds passed in silence.

"I'm part-giant," he blurted out.

With Ciago's size, it didn't seem like the biggest revelation of all time to Liss, but Wilsean's soul filled with shock. Rhett's face showed no emotion. Liss had no idea what he was thinking.

"You…what?" Wilsean stuttered.

Ciago dragged a hand down his stubbled cheek. "I—" he turned to Rhett. "Why don't you look surprised?"

"I already knew," Rhett replied.

Ciago's jaw dropped. "You did?"

Rhett nodded.

"How? My family *never* talks about it. To anyone."

"At the Battle of the Frozen Gate," Rhett said, pinning Ciago with his unblinking stare. "A giant was coming for us. You were fighting two of their humans, but I saw the giant look at you. It turned around and went to attack someone else, even though you were closest." He shrugged. "I figured it smelled giant blood in you."

"You've known for *two years*, and you never said anything?" Ciago asked. "Why?"

"Why would I?" Rhett countered. "It wasn't my business."

Wilsean let out a whistling breath.

"Of course, it was your business." Irritation flared on Ciago's soul. "You know the laws about bloodlines."

"What was I going to do?" Rhett asked. "Strip you of your titles? Send you and your family to the Giant Realm for having a sliver of giant blood?"

"Yes," Ciago said, still incredulous. "If anyone ever found out you knew, you would have been—"

"—on the run for my life?" Rhett gave his friend a grim smile.

Liss felt another wave of guilt. She had made sacrifices for Rhett too, but he'd given up everything that had ever mattered to him for her. She couldn't help but think his life would have been better if she'd tried harder to stay away from him from the beginning.

"Damn," Wilsean said, still shaking his head. "How did you keep that out of your family records?"

Liss remembered her mother telling her the wealthiest families in Lagonia kept detailed history books of their ancestry. If anyone had looked into Ciago's lineage….

"My great-great-grandparents paid an Insorsiled to—er—strike any mention of the giants from our records. There's no mention of it anywhere."

When no one said anything, Ciago continued, "If I encounter any giants along the way, maybe my giant blood will calm them down long enough for me to get away. I'll have a better chance of escaping than anyone else."

Rhett crossed his arms. "Just because they can smell your giant blood, it doesn't mean they won't still kill you." He gave his friend a hard look. "I won't let you do this."

"You can't go yourself," Ciago persisted. "Lagonia needs you."

"You heard what that slaver said," Liss added. "If the Insorsil queen gives Jaikon more of those invincibility pins, then things are only going to get more dangerous for anyone who goes against the Emperor. You'll be more help to your soldiers if you can convince Gatria to undo the magic of those pins."

The words were true, but Liss still felt selfish for trying to convince Rhett to stay on this side of the sea.

"This is a pointless conversation," Wilsean said, still looking at Ciago with a dazed expression on his face. "Even if you found a boat right now that could take you, you'd still be more than a day behind the army."

"Not necessarily," Liss said, hating herself a little at the thought of putting yet another one of her people in danger. Swallowing her hesitation, she looked at Rhett.

"An Energizer," he said, reading her thoughts.

She nodded.

Energizers were powerful. Even a weak one could get Ciago's boat across the stormy sea in half the time it would take the huge Lagonia ships.

"Let's get out of here first and continue this discussion once we're somewhere safe," Wilsean said, peering out one of the broken windows.

For several moments, no one spoke. Another terrible worry filled Liss's mind.

"What will happen to Samara when the Emperor finds out what you've done?" Liss asked Wilsean.

Wilsean and Samara didn't advertise their relationship, but they hadn't been as secretive as Liss and Rhett. If Jaikon wanted to get back at Wilsean, he might hurt Samara.

"She's safe because she's the courtiers' easiest source of Insorsiled goods," Wilsean said. "With the immunity flowers almost gone, merchants aren't traveling to Insorsil anymore. If anyone hurt Samara, the whole court would be up in arms."

His words were confident, but his soul was a tempest of worry.

"She can come to the Extended hideout with us," Liss said.

Wilsean shook his head. "She's safer away from me."

There was regret and determination on his soul.

Liss didn't have time to consider that more. Another question was bothering her.

"How did Jaikon know to send all of these soldiers here?" she asked, staring around at the ruined bar. Toil and Trouble had been her and the kids' most lucrative thieving spot for years.

Wilsean and Ciago both answered at the same time.

"Burk."

Liss's stomach turned over. It was the only explanation that made sense, and yet, Liss didn't want to believe it. Sacrificing her had been bad enough. But to put Spence, Mari, and Jema in harm's way—

"I'm going to kill him when we go back to free the slaves," Liss vowed.

She felt a little consoled when Wilsean and Ciago told her about Burk's new living conditions. Liss was still furious, though. Burk had given up the kids to Jaikon. He'd been willing to let them die, all so he could save his own pathetic hide.

She *would* kill that sniveling worm.

"Listen," Ciago said to Rhett. "Once Jaikon hears about this, he's going to send his invincible soldiers. We need to be gone long before then."

"How many more are we talking?" Liss asked, her stomach sinking even further.

"Twenty, so far," Wilsean replied. "But Jaikon has promised a pin for anyone who can prove their loyalty to him by slaughtering Extended." He gave her an apologetic look. "Half the empire is out hunting the caravans right now."

"We have to do something." Liss shook with fury.

"We will," Rhett promised, taking her hand. "We'll figure it out when we're back behind the ward."

"Um, Rhett." Wilsean exchanged a look with Ciago. A sense of discomfort filled his soul. "What's left of the flowers were too heavily guarded for us to get any more before we left. We each have enough immunity for a week, but beyond that—"

"I have enough for all of us," Rhett said without hesitation.

Liss bit her lip. *But for how long?* she wanted to ask.

The thought of Rhett giving away his flowers, even to his best friends, terrified her. When those flowers were gone, Rhett would be susceptible to opal contagion. He wouldn't be able to come near her or any of the Extended. And unlike the other Lagonians, he couldn't hide in the empire where he'd be safe from the contagion.

He'd be vulnerable…just like her father had been….

✳ ✳ ✳

They hurriedly divested the dead of as many weapons as the four of them could carry. None of them spoke. Liss could feel that Wilsean and Ciago's souls were as heavy as her own. For the first time, she was grateful for her pledge not to sort Rhett's soul. She didn't think she could handle the grief and despair she knew he must be feeling.

Liss led them out of the bar and back into the alley. She clutched the dagger she'd stolen off one of her victims.

Once they left the safety of what Liss and the kids referred to as *Dragon Dung Lane*, Liss peered around for any sign of Lagonia soldiers hiding in the surrounding buildings. Liss's mom, who was keeping watch from the wagon, signaled to her that the path was clear.

Still, Liss didn't breathe until they were all on the wagon.

"They're with us," Liss hurried to tell her mom, who was aiming an arrow at Wilsean and Ciago.

Nya gave the men a skeptical look, but she was too relieved that Liss was uninjured to ask any questions. She wrapped her arms around Liss in a fierce embrace.

Mari, who was sitting between her brothers, scooted off the bench and ran to Liss as Jema's parents powered up the wagon. The wooden axel creaked as the wheels began to spin. The view outside the window transformed into a blur of color as the Energizers sent the wagon into motion.

"I'm so sorry," Liss told Mari, wiping tears off the younger girl's opal cheeks.

She ignored Spence's protests and pulled him into the hug along with Mari. Neither of the kids were physically hurt, but their souls were shaken.

"I would have gotten us out, but they tied my hands," Spence mumbled.

"You did great," Liss assured them both, shuddering at the thought of what could have happened to them.

"They knew we were coming," Mari said, angry tears springing to her eyes. "How could they have known?"

"Burk told the Emperor."

Liss's hatred rose at the mere mention of their former caravan leader's name.

"That man is going to pay," Nya said, running her finger over the bloodied point of an arrow.

Liss's anger moved aside to make room for pride. She could hardly believe her mom was the one who had coolly shot arrow after arrow, taking down their enemies without hesitation. Liss smiled at her mom, hoping it would be enough to communicate all the things she couldn't say in front of a wagon-full of people.

"Hiya, kid." Ciago held out his gloved fist to Spence, who had escaped from Liss's hug and was now standing with his arms crossed.

After a brief pause, Spence reached out and bumped his fist against Ciago's.

Spence had as much reason to hate the Lagonians as any of the Extended, but Liss had seen his feelings toward the big Lagonian soften when they worked together to rescue Rhett. Spence would never admit it, but Liss felt Spence's pride when Ciago said, "You're a tough one, kid."

Ciago held out his hand to Mari. "You, too."

Liss would have expected the younger girl to balk, but she put her tiny hand into his without a moment's hesitation.

"You're Liss's friend, aren't you?" she asked.

"One of her very best," Ciago assured her.

Liss introduced everyone, and then sank down onto the floor, feeling all of her energy leave her at once. Rhett sat beside her. He brushed his thumb across a shallow cut on her cheek.

She didn't bother asking him if he was okay. She knew he wasn't. She also knew there was nothing she could say to ease his guilt and anger. He couldn't be with his soldiers, and that helplessness must be tearing him apart. She leaned into him and felt him relax against her, even though his expression stayed blank.

Liss's own mind was in a turmoil. Their task had seemed impossible before, when Jaikon was the only one with the Insorsiled pin. Now, there were twenty invincible soldiers, with more pins on the way.

One thing was becoming clear to Liss. If there was any hope of rescuing the Extended slaves, they'd need to convince the Insorsil queen to undo the magic of those pins, first. And that would mean haggling with a powerful, deadly witch who was notorious for killing anyone who went against her.

CHAPTER 13

Rhett spent the ride back to the Extended hideout in a haze of grief and bitterness. Jaikon had sent a thousand men and women on an impossible mission…all because of their loyalty to him.

Ciago had said those soldiers believed he was the leader Lagonia needed. They had chosen him over their own emperor. Now, they were paying for that misguided choice with their lives.

And what could Rhett offer them in exchange for their sacrifice?

He was an outcast from his own empire. He'd been stripped of his titles and was being hunted by every slaver on the continent. He couldn't defeat Jaikon…at least, not with his current invincibility.

"Stop beating yourself up," Ciago said quietly enough that no one else except Liss and Wilsean would hear him. "We all chose you over Jaikon for good reason."

Rhett felt his friend's words settle onto his shoulders. "I'm not the leader you think I am," he said. "I'm not—"

Ciago, Wilsean, and Liss all scoffed.

"Rhett, you've been leading the entire army for two years," Wilsean said. "You are exactly the leader we think you are."

"Let's take it one step at a time," Liss said, giving Rhett a worried glance.

"Good idea, Lovely Liss," Ciago boomed. He stretched like an enormous cat. "I'm actually looking forward to some time at sea. My assignments have been dull as tombs for the last week. *Collect taxes. Scare the poor peasants.* I'm ready for something with a bit more spice."

Rhett hated the idea of Ciago making a near-impossible journey across the deadly Brookgar Sea. And then there would be the even more impossible task of finding the Lagonia soldiers without the giants slaughtering him.

But he also couldn't abandon Liss to rescue the Extended slaves without him. He couldn't leave Wilsean and Stone to take down Jaikon.

"There's something else," Wilsean said. "If Ciago can find our soldiers—"

"When," Ciago corrected with all the confidence Rhett lacked. "*When* I find our soldiers."

Wilsean nodded. "I assume our plan is to combine forces with the Extended and take over the empire. But if we're going to fight together, the immunity is going to be a problem." He twisted the ring he wore around his index finger as his frown deepened. "Anyone with half a brain would rather die by the giants' mallets than from opal contagion."

No one spoke for several moments. Liss rubbed at her head as she squinted in thought.

"Then, we'll have to get more of the flowers," Liss said, interrupting the silence that had fallen. "We'll go to Insorsil and make a deal with the queen. I'm sure there's something we can give her that she wants."

The fierce determination on her face was one of the things Rhett would never get enough of.

"And if not?" Wilsean asked.

Liss lifted a shoulder. "Then, Rhett will do whatever it takes to make her hand over the flowers." She wound her arm through his. "After all, we wouldn't want him losing his hard-earned reputation."

✶ ✶ ✶

When their wagon rolled back into the Extended hideout, Rhett counted thirty more wagons parked along the edge of the field than had been there before. In spite of all his worries, he felt cause for optimism. If all of the caravans heeded his summons, and Ciago could return with a thousand of the best warriors in all of Lagonia, then they might actually have a chance.

If only he could divest Jaikon of his invincibility....

"I wonder what Extensions they have," Spence said as their wagon ground to a halt, "and whether they'll agree to be a part of our army."

"Oh, they'll agree," Liss told the boy. "I'll make sure of it."

"Beautiful, brilliant, and bad-ass," Ciago said to Liss, shaking his head in wonderment. "If you ever get tired of Commander Doom and Gloom, I just want you to know I'll be first in line."

Rhett didn't stop himself from scowling at his friend. He might still have reservations about Liss looking into his soul and seeing the darkness within, but one fact had emerged amid all of his misgivings. Rhett wanted Liss every bit as much as he had before he'd known the truth about her.

No, that wasn't right.

After everything they'd been through together...after everything they'd shared...he wanted her even more.

"I'll keep that offer in mind," Liss told Ciago with a tired smile.

"Not if I have anything to say about it." Rhett wrapped his arms around Liss and pressed a gentle kiss to her lips.

He would have done a whole lot more, but he could feel Nya's eyes on them. He forced himself to let Liss go. He caught a glimpse of her smile as she headed out of the wagon after the others.

They all gathered outside and assessed the newcomers.

"Two extra caravans aren't going to be enough," Liss said as they looked at the line of wagons.

"It's a start," Nya replied.

Liss's lips were pressed together in a tight line. Rhett understood her impatience. If the Extended huddled around their smoldering campfires were any indication, these newcomers weren't the warriors he and Liss had been hoping for. He could see the fear in their too-wide eyes. Their cheeks were sunken and their opal skin dull.

Desperation could be a useful tool to motivate, but these people were beyond desperate. They were beaten.

Or, maybe not, Rhett reflected, as the Extended caught sight of their Lagonian faces.

"Lagonian scum," a voice hissed.

Rhett turned to see an Extended man looking at them with murder in his eyes.

"Murderers! Slavers!" another woman yelled, pointing at their group.

"It's not what you think." Nya strode onto the field, holding up a placating hand. "These Lagonians just rescued two of our children. They are our allies."

Another woman, who must be one of the other caravan's leaders, stepped in front of the others.

"Let's all just calm down," the caravan leader told her people.

Nya gestured to Rhett, Wilsean, and Ciago to come closer. Rhett was amused to find that Mari's brothers flanked them, like they needed protection. Deciding to humor them, Rhett sheathed his dagger and went to join Nya.

He froze at the sound of Liss's gasp. It was a tiny sound, and one he shouldn't have been able to hear with all of the jeers coming from the growing mob.

He turned and saw a rope around Liss's neck.

Not a rope, he realized as he broke away from his group and went back for her. It was hair.

There was an Extended man standing beside her, and his hair was visibly lengthening as it wound itself around and around Liss's neck.

"I'm not Lagonian," Liss choked. "I'm one of you."

"Liars. All of you."

The burnt orange strands pulled tighter. Liss tried to break the hair, but it held fast. It continued to grow out of the man's head and twist around and around her neck.

"Take another step closer to me, and I'll kill her," the Extended man warned Rhett, stopping him mid-stride.

There was so much hair around Liss's neck that her skin was no longer visible.

Rhett locked down his emotions. He assessed his battlefield. He didn't look at his men, knowing they would react to whatever decision he made.

He moved.

He didn't go for Liss, which was what the man had been expecting. Rhett's dagger was at the other caravan leader's throat before anyone could blink.

Rhett used enough pressure that the caravan leader let out a hacking, choked noise as she tried to breathe. Everyone heard the sound in the tense stillness that had fallen. He turned a cold, merciless look on the man who was choking Liss. It was the dispassionate stare of an assassin who had killed dozens of Extended.

"Let her go, or your leader dies."

CHAPTER 14

Jaikon stared down at the gorgeous, naked woman sprawled out on his bed. Mireille was flawless. The black ringlets of her long hair splayed across the silk pillowcase. Her alabaster skin was without a single freckle or scar. She was one of his favorites.

It was a pity she was dead.

Jaikon adjusted her head so the angle of her neck looked less…broken.

He scowled at the beautiful, dead woman. Was it so much to ask to be able to pass a single hour without bad news?

It wasn't Mireille's fault. She'd simply been in his bed when he learned that Rhetteman and his bitch had eluded the mercenaries sent to hunt them.

As if in a mocking reminder of his plight, a jolt of pain shivered through Jaikon's right hand.

A frantic knock came at the outer door to the Emperor's chamber.

"Enter," Jaikon said.

Elouicia ran into the room. He was panting, and he was covered in fresh blood. There was even a smear of it across his lips. His gaze went to Mireille. He ran his tongue along his sharpened canines.

"What is it?" Jaikon demanded.

Elouicia tore his eyes away from the dead woman. "Your Majesty, the peasants are slaughtering each other. They've lost their minds."

Jaikon ground his teeth. The sheer incompetence of the people in his employ never ceased to astound him. "Then *make* them stop. We obviously can't have all our laborers dropping dead."

"We've arrested dozens of them," Elouicia said, flexing his Insorsiled claws. "I flogged ten of them to death in front of the others. It made no difference. They won't stop."

Jaikon was almost angry enough to drive his fist through the wall. He swore instead, which wasn't nearly as satisfying.

He'd thought it a brilliant strategy to dangle the limited number of invincibility pins over his subjects' heads and distribute them to the most loyal of his people. In theory, it had been a perfect idea. In reality, it was spurring the Lagonians to kill each other and make false accusations about their neighbors' loyalties.

Jaikon's soldiers didn't have time to run all over the countryside to deal with this madness. If word got out that Jaikon couldn't contain the lowest members of Lagonia society, it would make him appear weak.

He wouldn't tolerate appearing weak.

"Send more soldiers to suppress them," Jaikon bit out.

"There are no more soldiers, Your Majesty," Elouicia said.

"You're my Chief Assassin. Go assassinate."

Elouicia bowed low, but he didn't depart.

"Speak," Jaikon barked.

"The mercenaries are refusing to take the risk of tracking down the Extended unless they're provided with anti-contagion suits."

"I told Stone to give them the suits," Jaikon said, fury mounting by the second. He loathed pointless conversations and repeating himself. Today, it seemed, he was cursed to suffer both.

"Stone never did, and the suits are gone."

For several seconds, Jaikon couldn't see through the red veil of his anger.

"Send him to me," Jaikon said in a whisper. He flicked his good hand at the woman in his bed. "And toss this body over the cliff."

Elouicia hefted Mireille over one shoulder and departed. Jaikon thought he saw the crazed man run his tongue along the dead woman's neck.

Alone in his chamber, Jaikon stared at the ornate tapestry covering an entire wall. It had taken three Extended slaves to complete the tapestry, which depicted Jaikon's recent victory against the horde of giants that had attacked Lagonia's port.

Jaikon could feel his grip on his empire unraveling like the threads of the colorful tapestry. He was more powerful than ever before, and yet his hold on his own subjects was growing more tenuous by the day.

You have a plan, he reminded himself.

He'd already arranged for the rest of the pins to be delivered. He was flawlessly upholding his end of their bargain. Payment was brought to his Insorsil ally every Sunday without fail. Jaikon was spreading the rumors about the source of his new magic as he'd been instructed.

Soon, he would have the might to topple the Giant Realm. Those brutes would be weakened after their impending battle with the traitorous soldiers he'd sent across the sea. That would make it easier for Jaikon to defeat them.

Then, he'd turn his sights on Insorsil.

The Insorsiled had two great flaws. The first was their refusal to draft and train a real army. The second was their belief that old alliances and magic would keep them safe.

Nothing could be further from the truth.

Jaikon had confirmed his ally wouldn't be able to revoke the magic of the pins. There was nothing and no one who could stop him from taking that kingdom for his own.

Then, his subjects would understand the real meaning of power. The entire world would bend to his will. He wouldn't be just a man. He'd be a god.

"You sent for me, Majesty?"

Jaikon appraised his Master Interrogator. Stone didn't blink as he met his emperor's stare. There was no hint of challenge or fear. He simply waited.

"Where are the anti-contagion suits, and why didn't you give them to the mercenaries days ago?" Jaikon used the voice that made his fiercest soldiers quake. Again, Stone showed no reaction.

"I ordered all of the suits to be loaded onto the ships that went across the Brookgar Sea," Stone replied without hesitation.

"I see." Jaikon drew his sword out from its scabbard. He crossed the room…slowly.

Stone stood rigid and unyielding.

"And what use would anti-contagion suits be to an army on their way to the Giant Realm?" Jaikon asked.

"None, Majesty. I did it to prevent your hired mercenaries from being able to hunt the Extended once our flowers are gone. I believe that, if we simply implement the opal contagion protocols, thousands of lives will be saved."

Jaikon was struck speechless for a second. He felt a demonic grin spread across his face.

"Are you admitting to treason, Stone?"

"I am," the Master Interrogator replied.

The calm that filled Jaikon before he killed washed over him. He adjusted his grip on his sword, which still felt strange in his left hand. He watched the light from the room's chandelier play across his sharpened blade. He raised the sword.

Stone didn't flinch. He didn't so much as blink. The pompous traitor wasn't afraid.

The man's steadiness was more infuriating than when Jaikon's victims groveled. The calm veneer that came just before Jaikon killed was stripped away. An animal-like snarl began in his throat.

Without warning, Jaikon smashed the hilt of his sword across Stone's face.

Blood streamed. The Master Interrogator went down on his knees, and…smiled.

Rage turned Jaikon's insides to fire. And then, just as quickly, the anger transformed into a low simmer. His thoughts returned.

Jaikon wasn't a mindless barbarian like his Chief Assassin. He wasn't ruled by passion and loyalties or the ridiculous code Rhetteman lived by. His victories came because he was smarter than his opponents. He didn't just defeat his foes. He broke them.

Those of lesser minds didn't understand the distinction.

Stone was now an enemy of Lagonia. Since he clearly did not fear death or pain, Jaikon would simply need to find a more inventive means of punishment.

"Guards," Jaikon called.

Four men entered the Emperor's bedchamber at once.

"Bring our Master Interrogator down to the torture cage. Tell Elouicia to make him bleed, but not too much." He met Stone's unblinking stare. His smile widened. "And then, make a public announcement that Lagonia's former Master Interrogator will be executed in two days, along with every single one of the Extended slaves."

The wealthy slaveowners would be angered by the decree, but what did that matter? Jaikon was emperor. His word was law. The sooner his subjects came to heel, the longer they'd live.

The guards bowed. One of them clamped a pair of Insorsiled chains over Stone's wrists and ankles. Blood continued to gush from the wound across his forehead as the guards dragged him to the door.

"Oh, and one other thing."

The guards turned back, eagerly awaiting their order.

"Make sure news of these executions makes it to whichever rat hole Rhetteman and Opal Smoke are hiding in."

CHAPTER 15

The hair that was coiled around Liss's neck tightened until she couldn't even manage to gasp in a shallow breath. She felt each strand digging into her skin, as harsh and unyielding as wire. She'd never thought of hair as a weapon before, but this man's Extension was more useful for strangling than an Insorsiled noose.

For several tense moments, no one moved.

I wasn't lying, Liss wanted to shout at the Extended whose soul was filled with hatred and indecision. *I'm Extended!*

"I promise you, we will kill every person in your caravan before you finish with her," Rhett said, his voice so flat it sent a shudder through her in spite of her current predicament.

Ciago and Wilsean were both in her view. They had their weapons trained on other Extended nearby.

Stop! she wanted to beg all of them, but she was starting to see spots flicker across her vision.

Liss heard the twang of a bowstring. Then, the man strangling her began to howl. His hair fell into loose coils around Liss's neck. The Extended man bent down to grab hold of his leg, which was pierced straight through with one of Nya's arrows.

Liss yanked the hair off her neck. She threw the disgusting mass of hair back at its owner as the man continued to hop and clutch his leg.

"You could have hit Liss," Rhett snarled at Nya.

"No, I couldn't have," Nya replied calmly. "My Extension would never let me miss my target."

Rhett looked like he was seriously debating tearing her mother limb from limb. Instead, he came to Liss.

He made a low, furious sound as he inspected her neck. Her skin felt raw.

"You aren't going to let me kill him, are you?" Rhett asked, his voice as contained as his emotions.

Liss gave him a small smile and shook her head.

"This was all just a misunderstanding," the other caravan leader was saying. "There's been no harm done. Let's all just settle down."

"Let me make something very clear," Liss's mom said, coming to stand on Liss's other side.

"This is my daughter. She inherited her beauty from my Lagonian husband, and her soul sorting ability from me. If there are any who wish to deny that she is one of us, I promise you'll know what it feels like to be struck by a Huntress's arrow."

She turned to the other caravan leader, whose soul was filled with genuine distress and regret.

Nya continued, "I am the leader of this hideout, and thus, the leader of any Extended who seek sanctuary here. Is there anyone who would like to debate my claim?"

No one spoke.

Liss thought the conversation was over, but her mom wasn't finished.

"In payment for our protection, my new Lagonian friends will be needing the services of your best Energizer."

Liss's jaw slackened. She hadn't even realized her mom had been listening to Rhett and Ciago's conversation in the wagon.

The caravan leader's soul filled with confusion. "What do they want with my caravan's Energizer?" she asked.

"One of them needs to get across the Brookgar Sea, and quickly," Nya replied. "My Energizers have been worked to the bone as of late and have a young daughter. So, one of yours is going across the sea."

To Liss's amazement, the other caravan leader bowed her head in acknowledgement.

"Good." Nya flipped her bow across her back. "Then, I'd like to invite all of you to mingle while I go out to hunt supper."

Liss should let this entire unpleasant meeting come to an end. She should keep her mouth shut.

But she didn't appreciate the emotions flowing from the newcomers' souls. There was distrust, accusation, and contempt.

"I may not look like you, but I am Extended," Liss said, her voice carrying to the group that was starting to disperse. "And I have done more for our people than any of you."

Petty, but true.

The man who had strangled her let out a bark of harsh laughter.

"And what have you done for us, little Lagonian?" he sneered.

"I'm Opal Smoke."

Liss expected the gasps that rippled through the other Extended. What she hadn't expected were the reactions that followed.

"You're the reason why our people are going to be exterminated!" the other caravan leader shouted.

Hatred, fury, and blame rolled off the other Extended people's souls, along with fear. She even felt accusation on the souls of her own caravan members. Liss didn't understand.

"Are you people deranged, or just stupid?" Rhett asked the crowd. His voice was so laden with threat it was several moments before anyone responded.

When someone finally did speak, Liss silently groaned to hear Dolo's voice.

"Before the flower fields were burned, we were enslaved," the Flooder said. "But at least our people had a chance at surviving. Now, if we step outside of this ward, we'll be slaughtered. You're the reason why we're all dying."

Liss was shaking her head.

"That's not true." Her voice was a whisper.

"The next person who insults my daughter is getting an arrow through their skull," Nya said, her orange eyes flashing.

"And my dagger across their throat," Rhett said.

"And my sword to their gut," Ciago added.

Wilsean stepped forward. He didn't speak, but he held open his jacket, revealing the silver throwing knives strapped across his chest.

Her group's menacing faces and gleaming weapons were enough to make the crowd disperse. But even though everyone kept their heads down as they returned to their wagons, Liss was assaulted by the emotion pouring off them.

Hatred.

When they glanced back, the same emotion was in their eyes. They weren't looking at the Lagonian men, though. They were looking at her.

✳ ✳ ✳

The mood was tense, so Liss and the men took refuge in the abandoned cottage. Liss was desperate not to think about the way the other Extended were reacting to her. She'd thought telling them that she was the famed Extended spy would win them over to her.

She couldn't have been more wrong.

They saw her as the enemy.

No, she realized. She was worse than the enemy. They expected the Lagonians to betray them. But for an Extended—who didn't even have the decency to look Extended— to make their bleak lives worse, it was intolerable.

Liss had never felt like so much of an outsider among her own people.

When it was just the Lagonian men, Mari's brothers, the kids, and a roaring fire courtesy of Romile, her mood improved.

Rhett had gone with Liss's mom to hunt dinner and make arrangements with the Energizer for Ciago's voyage. A Clime Extended in Liss's caravan had sensed a storm heading toward the Brookgar Sea, so Ciago needed to leave as soon as possible.

The kids were still shaken from their ordeal, but they were recovering quickly. Ciago was teaching Spence and Mari's brothers a gambling game that seemed to involve a lot of shouting. At the same time, the guys were discussing Grub the giant, whom Liss and Spence had met in the Insorsiled forest. The question of why a giant would have come across the sea trying to sell furs was a mystery that continued to stump all of them.

Ciago was his exuberant self, joking and teasing everyone in hearing distance. His soul was unsettled, though. Liss was glad her mom had given Rhett the set of corresponders Burk had been hoarding in his wagon. At least this way, Rhett and Ciago would be able to communicate while Ciago was at sea. Liss hoped it would give Rhett some peace of mind if he could get in touch with Ciago whenever he wanted.

Mari was asking Wilsean all sorts of questions about Lagonia.

In spite of being the most beautiful Extended in their caravan, Mari wished desperately to look like the Uninfected. In the rare times she had gold to spare, she spent it on Insorsil illusion potions that made her look Lagonian.

It had always hurt Liss's soul to see the other girl long to change her beautiful opal skin and orange curls.

"Do you have a girlfriend?" Mari asked shyly.

Wilsean was good-looking and had a personality to match. Neither had escaped Mari's notice, it would seem.

"I have a Samara," Wilsean replied, dodging the question.

Liss rolled her eyes.

Wilsean and Samara were head over heels in love with each other. What Liss couldn't figure out was why they both tried to deny the truth of their own souls.

"Want to meet her?" Wilsean asked Mari, pulling a corresponder out of his pocket.

"You have a corresponder?" Spence asked, far more interested in that fact than the rest of the conversation.

"Samara is from Insorsil," Liss explained. Even though she was an Empty, Samara's siblings sent her all kinds of magical trinkets, which she in turn sold to the Lagonian gentry.

Wilsean held up the corresponder, which began to fill with smoke. Liss, who had been standing on the other side of the campfire, ran around to kneel beside Wilsean.

The smoke settled, and Samara emerged in the small glass sphere.

"Hey, beautiful," Wilsean said.

"Hi, handsome," she replied, her face breaking into a smile.

"Samara!" Liss called, stopping herself before she grabbed the corresponder out of Wilsean's hand.

"Liss!" Samara reached out a hand, like she wanted to touch Liss through the corresponder. "I miss you so much. Things haven't been the same without you."

"I miss you, too," Liss told her.

Liss had liked Samara from the moment they were introduced. Those feelings had only grown in the months Liss spent as a servant in the Lagonian palace. She hadn't realized until this moment how much she missed Samara.

"You're officially on Jaikon's shit list," Samara said.

Liss assumed that was to Wilsean, since she'd been on Jaikon's shit list for quite some time.

"I would have told you, but there wasn't time," Wilsean began, but Samara waved a hand.

"I'm proud of you," she told him. "I just want to know what our next step is."

"I'm going to Insorsil with Rhett and Liss," Wilsean said. "We're going to talk Gatria into undoing Jaikon's invincibility and giving us more immunity flowers. After that, we're coming back to set things right in the empire."

Samara nodded, like she'd been expecting this answer. She glanced around as though to make sure she was alone and then lowered her voice. "I'll hitch a ride out of Lagonia on one of the merchant coaches tonight. My brother can meet me with one of our family's Insorsiled bikes, which will get me to inner Insorsil by tomorrow."

"Absolutely not," Wilsean said, looking horrified.

Samara was an Empty, which meant she'd been exiled from Insorsil on her eighteenth birthday. Even though she still kept in touch with her siblings, she would be executed if anyone in Insorsil recognized her.

Samara rolled her eyes at Wilsean. "First, I don't recall needing your permission to go anywhere. Second, everything you're planning is going to end in complete disaster unless you have someone with magical knowledge to help you. I can get things that aren't even sold outside of Insorsil that will help us."

"And if someone sees you?" Wilsean countered. "I won't be able to protect you."

Liss understood Wilsean's fears, just like she understood Samara's determination.

"I don't remember asking for your protection, you big oaf," Samara said placidly. She narrowed her gaze at Wilsean through the sphere. "You also can't just waltz into the Insorsil castle and demand an audience with the queen. Fortunately for you, I happen to know all the court protocols that will keep you from getting your dumb Lagonian asses killed."

Liss tried not to let her hopes run away with her. She was starting to believe everything they were trying to do might really be possible.

Samara turned her attention on Liss, her frown transforming into a grin. "I'll meet you in Insorsil tomorrow at the western edge of the necromancy quarter."

Liss glanced at Wilsean, who was shaking his head and mouthing *no*.

She turned her attention back to the corresponder. It was a good meeting place—central, but in a part of town with lighter traffic.

"Eleven o'clock?" Liss asked, earning another glare from Wilsean.

"See you then," Samara replied.

"Samara, let's talk about this," Wilsean began.

She blew a kiss and disconnected. Her face disappeared, and the swirling smoke settled back down to the bottom of the corresponder.

Wilsean gripped the sphere in his hand. For a second, Liss thought he was going to throw it. His soul was furious. After several seconds, he slipped it back into his pocket, muttering something about his stubborn goddamn woman.

"Why don't you just admit you're in love with her?" Liss asked, interrupting a string of curses that was making Jema giggle.

It wasn't her business, but she was tired of seeing two people she cared about dancing around their real feelings.

Wilsean's gaze softened. "Samara is a servant and an Empty, and my family is—"

"Important?" Liss bristled on Samara's behalf. "Just because she wasn't born rich like you doesn't make her any less worthy."

"I know that," Wilsean said before Liss could thoroughly chew him out. "But if I was with her publicly, my family would disown me. I'd lose my right to serve in the Lagonia army and, when my father retires, I wouldn't be eligible to take his place as an advisor to the Emperor."

"You've already lost your position in Lagonia," Liss pointed out.

Wilsean nodded. "I can't go back to Lagonia so long as Jaikon is the Emperor, but if—when—he's dethroned, I'll be able to go back.

"If I married an outsider, I'd be stripped of my name and expelled from Lagonia."

"Do you have any idea how stupid that sounds?" Liss demanded.

Wilsean's shoulders straightened. "If I have any intentions of serving the new, more deserving Lagonia emperor, I need to obey the laws of my empire. Samara understands."

Liss wanted to be angry with Wilsean. She knew only too well what it was like to be a second-class citizen. At the same time, she understood that, in a way, Wilsean's hands were as tied as Samara's.

"I'm sorry," she told him, and she meant it.

"Me too." Wilsean turned away from her, but he couldn't hide the genuine pain and regret flooding his soul.

Another round of shouts and back-slapping pats came from the guys who were gambling on the other side of the room.

"I have a question," Spence said as he swept the other men's pebbles into his own pile of winnings.

Spence squinted at Ciago. "How does a giant and a human…you know…?"

Wilsean chuckled.

Ciago grimaced. "Some questions, kid, are better left unanswered."

She missed whatever Spence said next. Her soul jumped, and she turned to find Rhett standing in the cottage's doorway. She quickly clamped down on her Extension.

"Rhett!" Jema got up from the circle and ran toward him.

Liss watched in amusement as Rhett bent down to say something to Jema. The little girl waved her hands in excitement and pointed in the direction of her wagon. Rhett was carrying something, but Liss couldn't see what it was. Jema scampered off, gesturing for Rhett to follow her.

Rhett's heated gaze connected with Liss's. She saw a dozen emotions in his eyes that he usually kept buried inside before he turned to follow Jema.

Curious, Liss was about to see what they were up to when her mom filled the doorway to the cottage. She kicked snow off her boots before stepping inside. She looked tired but alive in a way she hadn't in as long as Liss had known her. Nya had her bow in one hand a quiver full of arrows in the other.

"Lagonian," Liss's mom called to Wilsean. There was a playful twinkle in her eyes Liss couldn't remember ever having seen. "I hear you fancy yourself quite the bowman."

"The best on the continent," Wilsean affirmed, grinning at Liss's mom.

"Want to test your skills against a real Huntress?"

A few minutes later, Liss found herself standing on the frozen field with the rest of the Extended. People gathered around the fires and held their bowls of venison stew as they watched the spectacle. Wilsean and Liss's mom made one impossible shot after another, teasing and heckling each other the whole time.

Liss forgot about whatever Rhett and Jema were up to. She stood by a roaring fire and watched her mother. The bow was like an extension of her arm, and with each shot she made, her smile grew. There was no hint of the frail, grief-stricken woman she'd been for most of Liss's life.

The crowd whooped when Liss's mom shot one of her arrows straight through Wilsean's while his was still hurtling through the air. Wilsean took an imaginary hat off his head and bowed low to Liss's mom, which brought out more cheers from the onlookers.

A Minstrel Extended had started a song that was so hauntingly beautiful it made Liss ache. A Molder Extended was carving blocks of ice into tiny centaurs, dragons, and castles. The details were so intricate that the carvings looked like they might burst into life at any moment.

Someone had brought out a bag of winternuts, which could only be purchased in Insorsil. Their earthy smell curled around all of them and had the added bonus of making the air feel less cold.

Liss smiled along with everyone else, but her mind was in too much turmoil for her to relax. There was nothing that could be done until they got to Insorsil the next day, but all of the uncertainties and unsolved puzzles were eating her alive.

Why would Queen Gatria give a potential enemy the magic of invincibility?

Did Insorsil have more of the immunity flowers, and would Liss be able to get her hands on them?

How much longer would Jaikon allow the Extended slaves to live, and how was Liss going to get them out of the empire without getting herself and everyone she loved killed?

Liss caught sight of Rhett's silhouette coming from the direction of Jema's wagon. The fading light threw his whole profile into shadows, which made him look like a work of art as he easily moved through the crowd toward her. Liss couldn't take her eyes off him.

Jema was jogging to keep up with him. She was carefully balancing a plate in her small hands, and her mouth was moving a mile a minute as she jabbered to Rhett.

"Rhett's a really bad cook," Jema announced when she was close enough to Liss to be heard over the other conversations. She held out the plate. When Liss caught sight of the concoction, her soul turned to mush.

On the center of the plate was a messy resemblance of Lagonia's famous golden cake, which was the most delicious food she'd ever tasted. She could see the effort that had gone into shaping the cake and smoothing the frosting, although the execution was endearingly pitiful.

"Where did you get all of the gold and sugar?" Liss asked, feeling guilty as she accepted the plate Jema was pushing into her hands.

"Rhett. Duh." Jema leaned closer and whispered, "I think he wants to kiss you."

Liss choked back a laugh. She peered up at Rhett, who was looking as awkward and out of his element as Jema was comfortable. He also had a smudge of flour on his cheek.

Her soul lurched with the need to see into his. When she held it back, a burst of pain surged through her head.

"I—I mean we," Rhett motioned to Jema, "thought you might want something to eat besides oatmeal."

"Thank you," she told them both, and she meant it.

She'd eaten a few slices of dry bread an hour ago, and her stomach was still protesting. Her insistent headache was making her feel queasy and unbalanced, and had stolen away her appetite. She wasn't sure she could handle the richness of cake, but Jema and Rhett were both watching her.

"Where did you get all the ingredients?" she asked Rhett.

"He *stole* them from Toil and Trouble," Jema cackled.

"I saw everything in the supply room when we were leaving the bar," Rhett explained, looking sheepish.

"I think I'm a bad influence on you," Liss said, unable to hide her grin.

She took a big bite of the cake.

"Mmm," she said appreciatively.

It was full of everything she loved…namely, sugar. If she'd been herself, she would have eaten the entire thing. Food just wasn't interesting her the way it usually did, though. She had to force herself to swallow the bite and take another.

"Best cake I've ever eaten," Liss said.

She took one more forkful before offering the plate to Jema.

"Go on," Liss encouraged when the little girl hesitated. Jema was the only person in the world who loved sweets more than Liss. After another few seconds, Jema couldn't hold out any longer. She started in on the cake, foregoing the fork and just using her small fingers.

"I'll be right back," Liss said, standing up.

She made it behind the nearest wagon before she threw up. Her throat was already burning from almost getting strangled, and her eyes watered as her stomach tossed and turned, rejecting the little bit of food she'd eaten. Her head pulsed even more fiercely.

Her hand was shaking when she wiped it across her mouth.

Liss straightened and took a step…and ran into an unmoving force.

"I'm getting a witchdoctor." Rhett's chest was rising and falling with the emotions he was keeping in check.

"No." She grabbed his arm.

The last thing she needed was Rhett risking slavers and soldiers just to go into Insorsil.

"Then, tell me what's wrong with you," Rhett ordered.

"Um, I wasn't aware there was something wrong with me," Liss said in a light tone.

"Don't lie to me." A storm of fury, or maybe even disgust, churned in his eyes. Without sorting his soul, Liss couldn't know for sure. The uncertainty made her chest ache.

They glared at each other for several seconds.

"I'm not going to watch you waste away," Rhett said. "Either tell me what I can do to fix this, or I'm going for a witchdoctor."

If Liss told him the truth, she'd have to go back to seeing Rhett flinch any time she came near him. As unpleasant as her symptoms were now, they were tolerable. Rhett's disdain for her wouldn't be.

"You may not remember, but I spent two weeks making sure you didn't die…again," Liss snapped. "There are a few other things on my mind, as I'm sure you can understand. Can you blame me for being a little peaked?"

She didn't give him a chance to respond before she stalked off, leaving Rhett and all his furious tension behind.

CHAPTER 16

Burk glanced at the smoky blue moonlight filtering through the window bars and into the squalid room. He smashed a roach with his bare foot and wondered how all of his carefully-laid plans had gone so far awry.

"I been readin' 'bout them smells, and I gots an idear 'bout what we can do ta freshen things up."

The others around the table nodded emphatically at the homeless man's idiotic statement.

Burk was head advisor on the Lagonia Council of Sewer Management. Over the last week, Jaikon had sent every one of the empire's rejects to serve *at Burk's command.* The other members of the "council" were passionate about their new roles, which infuriated Burk all the more.

The homeless man who stank worse than the sewers had insisted on being the council's secretary, despite the fact that he was illiterate. The degenerate old fool painstakingly printed gibberish on squares of toilet paper with a pencil nub at each meeting.

It sickened Burk that he should have to be party to such humiliations.

Being who he was, it was impossible for him to drown out the others' infuriating voices. Burk was certain Jaikon had ordered their meeting to be held *in the sewer* because it was a veritable echo chamber. Every sound bounced off the walls and filled Burk's ears until he was afraid he might go deaf.

Burk craned his head, trying to get a better view of the moon and the world beyond this filthy, rat-infested hell he'd somehow found himself in. As he did, he caught the faintest vibration of the Emperor's voice. It was coming from floors above. Layers of concrete, expensive granite, and plush carpeting separated them. Burk made an effort to tune out the drone of his fellow councilmembers—who were now discussing their preferred thickness of toilet paper—to single out the thread of the Emperor's voice.

Burk closed his eyes. He tuned out every sound except for the Emperor's voice.

Burk could tell the Emperor was speaking to someone on the other end of a corresponder, since the other voice was too muffled for even Burk to discern.

"…payment returned for an inferior product," Jaikon was saying. "…bitch mangled my hand."

Burk had seen the Emperor's crippled hand and wondered who had caused it.

"While I'm gratified to know that the pins now shield against all wounds, that doesn't account for your previous failure, Krozor," Jaikon said, his voice rising with his emotions.

Krozor. The name was unfamiliar to Burk, but he filed it away in his memory.

Jaikon continued, "If you had told me your first batch of pins would only protect against *mortal* wounds, I might still have two working hands."

He listened as the person on the other end of the corresponder spoke. Burk could sense the Emperor's impatience and mounting anger by the *thud thud thud* his footsteps were making as he paced across his room.

Burk could only imagine the finely-woven carpet cushioning his every step. Knowing the Emperor, it was spun with threads of real gold. Burk looked down at the slick stone beneath his own grime-covered feet and scowled.

"No, I most certainly won't remove the pin for a witchdoctor to heal my hand. That would make me vulnerable and weak, and I refuse to be either."

Jaikon listened for several beats.

"What good will numbing crystals do me?" he demanded. "I can't use my right hand!"

Burk winced as the glass corresponder hit a wall and shattered. It was like a drum reverberating in Burk's ears, and he almost missed it when

Jaikon muttered to himself, "Oh, I'll make you king of Insorsil. And then I'll force you right back into that basement rathole you crawled out of."

The Emperor's angry mutterings died down. All went quiet in that luxurious room that Burk could only dream about rather than experience for himself.

Burk sat back against his rickety seat, grimacing as a droplet of ambiguous moisture plopped down from the ceiling above.

All Burk had ever wanted was a small slice of the comfort and luxury to which all Lagonians were born into. Instead, what had he gotten? A dank cell and a yard full of literal shit. He had made a bargain with Jaikon in hopes of bettering his bleak situation. Instead, he'd made himself an enemy of his own people and unwittingly become little better than a prisoner of the Lagonia Emperor.

The source of Burk's problems suddenly became apparent. For as long as he could recall, he'd been taking care of others. As his caravan's leader, it had been up to him to safeguard the other Extended. He'd been so preoccupied with this task that he'd had little energy left over to take care of himself.

The Lagonia Emperor didn't concern himself with the needs of others. He looked out for himself. It was precisely what Burk should have been doing from the start.

Burk promised himself that, from this moment on, he'd do whatever it took to achieve the life he'd been so long deprived of.

The only problem was that he was still as stuck in his current position as he'd been a few minutes ago. If he returned to the caravan, his people would kill him. He'd already given the Emperor all of the information he had, and so Burk was left with nothing to bargain with. If he threatened to publicly expose what he'd learned from the Emperor's private conversation, Jaikon could torture him or allow someone outside of Lagonia to kill him. Burk's language in the contract had been woefully ambiguous on that point, as well.

Someone pushed back his chair, drawing Burk's attention back on the conversation taking place around him.

"Gotta get ready fer the banquet," one of the "councilmembers" said, groaning as he creaked to his feet. He picked up one of the horrendous tools Burk had learned were called "sweepers" and limped off to the sewer tunnels. "Gotta get ahead a things a'fore they get ahead a us," the man called back to the others, who eagerly grabbed their own sweepers and hurried to help.

Burk stroked a hand down his stubbled throat as he considered those words.

Get ahead of things before they get ahead of us.

Since Burk made his agreement with Jaikon, all he'd done was fall prey to the Emperor's machinations and allow himself to be the brunt of Jaikon's jokes. He'd allowed it to happen because, as the Emperor so frequently reminded him, what choice did he have?

Now, though, that was no longer the case.

Burk might have an unbreakable contract to tell Jaikon all he knew about the Extended, but the contract said nothing about him making agreements with others or even leaving the palace. He hadn't left before because he'd had nowhere else to go.

Now, he did.

Burk ran a hand through his greasy, tangled orange hair. He took the roll of toilet paper his "secretary" had been using to keep meeting notes and picked up the stub of pencil. He began to make a list of all the terms that would need to be included in his newest agreement. He wouldn't fall prey to ambiguous language again.

As he wrote, he considered his new suite of rooms, and how many personal attendants he would require. He felt certain there was no limit to what his newest ally would pay for the information he now possessed.

His leg began to bounce in his growing excitement. Anticipation sent heat prickling through his body.

If the Lagonia Emperor was powerful, there was another leader who was even more so. The Insorsil queen. And if Burk had heard correctly—and Burk *always* heard correctly—the Emperor was intending to murder her.

CHAPTER 17

Rhett lay on his pile of blankets and stared at the dark beams of the cottage's ceiling. Wilsean had been sleeping for more than an hour, but try as he might, Rhett couldn't get his mind to settle.

He reviewed everything he knew about the Insorsil queen in his head, creating a script for how he would negotiate with her.

Gatria was beloved by her people, and if Rhett offended her, he'd become an enemy of the entire kingdom.

Rhett was already being hunted by his own empire and on shaky ground with the Extended, to say the least. He decided he didn't need to add another group to the list of those who wanted him dead.

In his mind, he made a list of all the secret information about Jaikon and Lagonia he'd be willing to give Gatria in exchange for her cooperation. It went against his training and principles to share a single one of his empire's secrets with an outsider, but it couldn't be helped.

If he had Stone and Ciago with him, he wouldn't be worried. Stone would glare at the queen, Ciago would flatter her, and they'd walk out with everything they needed.

But Stone was in Lagonia, and Ciago was….

Ciago was on his way to the Giant Realm. Rhett had gone with him to the edge of the Insorsiled forest earlier in the night to see him and the Energizer off.

The Energizer had seemed competent enough and, unlike the other Extended in her caravan, wasn't terrified by the prospect of leaving her wagon.

Ciago had jewels and connections, so Rhett wasn't worried about his ability to commission a ship. It was what came after that had Rhett tossing and turning.

Now that Ciago was gone, Rhett thought of a dozen things he should have said before they parted. The heavy weight of the corresponder in his pocket gave him some comfort—at least he'd be able to communicate with Ciago. Not that he'd be able to do anything to help his friend if Ciago ran into any trouble.

When he ran into trouble.

Ciago's last words to him circled around in his mind now.

"Go win yourself a palace, Emperor."

It was too preposterous to even bear consideration. The last thing Rhett wanted was to be a politician of any kind. All he cared about was saving his soldiers and Liss's people. Then, he wanted to take her somewhere far away from this place and all of the people who might still be hunting them.

Foolish wishes.

His left hand rested on top of the deflated bag of flowers by his side. Ciago hadn't wanted to take any, but Rhett had insisted he take half of what was left. It was bad enough Ciago was crossing an unforgiving sea. Rhett wasn't going to let his best friend contract opal contagion from the only other crew member onboard his ship.

Rhett had counted the flowers he had left again. If he and Wilsean each took one a day, they had a little more than a week's worth. If he couldn't convince the queen to give him more….

Steel doesn't know love or despair. It can't be bent or broken. It needs no heart or warmth. I am steel.

Repeating the familiar refrain in his mind brought him some comfort. It kept him awake and free from his nightmares' clutches.

If he closed his eyes, he'd see Liss covered in blood, with Jaikon looming over her. He'd hear her screams….

Rhett got up and started dressing. He needed to go for a run to clear his mind.

"What's the matter?" Wilsean mumbled, gripping his bow even in his state of mostly-sleep.

"Nothing. Go back to sleep."

In two heartbeats, his friend was out cold again. Rhett slowly opened the door to the cabin to keep the sound from waking Wilsean. A biting wind swirled around as he stepped out into the soft, powdery snow that was beginning to fall.

He meant to head toward the path that led away from the hideout and deeper into the forest. Instead, his legs took him toward Liss's wagon almost against his will.

I'll just make sure she's alright, and then I'll leave, Rhett told himself, knowing Liss wouldn't appreciate him skulking around her wagon in the middle of the night. She already had that creep of a Flooder pining after her.

Rhett flipped up the collar of his jacket, but it did little to protect him from the wind that was whistling through the camp. He shivered, but the discomfort wasn't enough for him to turn back. He needed to know Liss was okay. Then, he could go to sleep.

Mari's brothers and several other Extended were hard at work constructing the barrier he'd described earlier. Most of the people in Liss's caravan were useless for fighting, but their artistry Extensions enabled them to bring the description Rhett had given them to life. He stopped to suggest a few alterations that would take advantage of the Extended Architect's skills. A Metalsmith also had some ideas about fortifying the structure, which Rhett agreed were useful improvements.

By the time they were finished, there would be a wall surrounding the entire compound that would be defensible. The Extended would just have to outlast the Lagonians' immunity, and then they would be free. This barrier would give them that chance. The issue of how to get enough food inside for a two-week siege was a problem he'd need to discuss with Liss's mother in the morning.

Even though all of the other wagons were dark, a light still burned in Liss's. He could see her shadow through the curtained window as she paced.

Why was she still awake?

As he watched her pace back and forth in front of the small window, Rhett's heartbeat quickened. In that moment, he no longer cared that she had deceived him.

The words Samara had told him when he'd been in the torture cage and hovering on the brink of death came back to him.

Whatever is between you and Liss, it's real.

He believed those words. Liss had lied, but not when it came to the way she felt about him. Her feelings were as deep and real as his, and he'd been a fool for ever doubting that much.

In that moment, he wanted more than just a glimpse of her shadow through a tiny window. Rhett considered knocking on her door. He even climbed the steps and raised his fist to the door before dropping it to his side. What would he tell her—that he was hallucinating and getting more obsessed with her safety by the minute?

Liss wouldn't tolerate being stifled by him.

Time to leave, he told himself.

He'd wanted to see that she was safe, and he had. And yet, he found himself unable to walk away. He sat down on the frozen ground, telling himself he'd wait for just a few more minutes.

Even with the snow collecting on his jacket and seeping into the layers below, his over-active mind found a peaceful kind of stasis. With his back to Liss's wagon, he'd be able to see anyone who approached.

She'll never know I was here, he told himself. He could just stay and make sure she was safe. With that thought calming him, he tipped his head back against the frosted wood of her wagon.

The door creaked open.

Rhett jerked to attention, sending the snow that had collected on his jacket spraying into the air.

Liss let out a startled cry and jumped back, her hand fumbling for a weapon in the dark.

"It's me," he said quickly.

Liss, clutching her heart, came out onto the narrow stoop of her wagon. She was barefoot.

"What the hell are you doing?" she demanded.

"Get back inside before you get frostbite," he countered, trying to stave off the inevitable humiliation when he had to admit why he was here.

"Not until you tell me why you're out here collecting snow when you have a dry cabin to sleep in."

This is what you get for being a paranoid idiot, Rhett told himself.

"I, um…." Rhett said, stuttering over an explanation he didn't have.

Liss put her hands on her hips. "If you're going to give me a heart attack, the least you can do is tell me why you fell asleep outside my wagon instead of coming in."

Rhett hadn't been asleep, but he didn't think now was the time to point that out. Instead, he said, "You're right. Can I come in?"

Giving him a quizzical look, Liss stepped back into the wagon, holding the door open for him.

He knocked his snow-caked boots on the steps before entering the warm kitchen. A fire burned in the small potbellied stove, which was enough to heat the entire wagon. The place smelled pleasantly of wood smoke.

Rhett pulled off his sodden jacket and shirt. He caught the towel Liss tossed to him and used it to mop the melting snow from his head.

"Why weren't you asleep?" Rhett asked.

"Why weren't *you*?" she shot back.

"Fair enough."

Rhett stepped out of his soaked pants. He looked up to see Liss staring at him, and he couldn't hide his grin. She quickly turned away, but not before he saw the flush that had crept down her neck.

"So, what now?" Liss asked, still not looking at him.

Something about standing in her wagon in nothing but his undershorts made Rhett realize that any hopes he had of salvaging his pride had gone out the window. So, he admitted, "I haven't been sleeping well."

She turned to face him.

"Are you upset about Ciago?"

Rhett gave her a nod. It wasn't a lie, it just wasn't the reason why the thought of falling asleep made him break out in a cold sweat.

"Is there anything I can do to make you feel better?" she asked, her expression guarded.

He was about to say no, but lying seemed like more effort than he could summon. So, he asked, "Can I stay with you tonight?"

She thought for only a moment before nodding.

Rhett finished drying himself off and then followed her into the bedroom, which was really just an extension of the main room that had been sectioned off with a sheet hung across the doorway.

He noted the narrow bed that occupied almost the whole of the small space. The lopsided wooden frame didn't look like it could handle them doing anything more than sleeping on top of it.

Too bad.

He left his dagger on top of the wicker chair, which was the only other piece of furniture in the room. He didn't like sleeping without it, but with the dreams he'd been having, he wouldn't risk accidently cutting Liss if he flailed around in his sleep.

Liss pulled off the sweater she was wearing, and it was Rhett's turn to look away before he started something he wouldn't be able to stop. That wasn't why he was here.

He climbed into bed, sighing when she scooted back to press her body against his.

"This was a good idea," Liss said in a sleepy voice.

Rhett slid his arm around her. He moved his bare legs close enough for Liss to warm her cold feet against them. He pressed his face into her sweet-smelling hair and felt himself falling into sleep.

CHAPTER 18

Liss woke to Rhett's body tensing around hers.

"No, no, no," he murmured, tightening his hold on her until it was painful.

"Rhett," she whispered.

His heart was racing against her back, and his sweat was soaking through her thin top. Rhett started to thrash. Liss had to scramble off the bed before she caught one of his flying fists.

He woke himself on a strangled shout. Liss saw him cut his hand through the air like he was slicing the blade of his dagger through an imaginary foe.

Rhett's eyes were wild when they met hers.

"Liss?" His chest heaved as he tried to catch his breath. The hand he held out toward her was shaking. "Did I hurt you?"

The look on his face was tortured.

Liss shook her head, too stunned for words. She knew what night terrors looked like. She'd woken Spence from his own on more than one occasion after his mother was murdered. It just never occurred to her that someone like Rhett could have them. Rhett didn't have fears.

Jaikon almost tortured him to death, she reminded herself. Even now, she couldn't let herself think about what he'd looked like when she rescued him. There had been more blood outside him than in. No wonder he was having nightmares.

"I'm sorry," Rhett said, his voice hoarse. "I thought if I was with you, it wouldn't happen. I should have warned you."

He started to move away from her, but Liss caught his hand. She felt shudders wracking his body as she tugged him back onto the bed.

"Jaikon?" Liss asked, kneading at the knotted muscles in his broad shoulders.

Rhett dipped his head in acknowledgement.

"He tried to kill you," Liss said, her voice coming out loud in the otherwise-silent wagon. "Anyone would be haunted by that kind of experience."

"No." He shook his head, unable to look at her. "That's not it."

Liss's hand stilled. "Then, what—?"

"I see him torturing you."

Another shudder rolled through his body.

"Me?"

Rhett almost died—*had* died for a few seconds—and he was having nightmares about her getting hurt?

"Every time I fall asleep, I see what he would have done to you. And I can't stop it."

Liss could hear in his voice what it cost him to admit this weakness to her.

"Jaikon can't get me here," Liss said, wanting to give him some comfort. She was having trouble processing how much Rhett valued her life over his own.

"I know," he said, without looking at her.

Liss didn't think he'd really even processed her words. So, she took his hand and put it over her beating heart. That got his attention.

"I'm safe," she told him. "I'm okay."

Rhett's trembling eased. He drew in a long, unsteady breath. When Liss let go of his hand, he kept it pressed over her heart. He leaned forward until their foreheads were just barely touching.

"Liss." He said her name like a prayer.

Before either of them could say anything else, there was a sharp rap at her wagon door. They both jumped. Rhett vaulted over the bed and grasped his dagger just as a voice called, "Liss? Rhett?"

Wilsean, covered in a light dusting of snow, came into the wagon. His corresponder was clutched in his hand.

"What is it?" Rhett demanded, all business. Any vulnerability he'd shown in the last few minutes was replaced by the icy calm he usually exuded.

In answer, Wilsean held up the corresponder. Samara's worried face filled the glass surface of the sphere.

"Jaikon just put an announcement out all over the empire," Samara said in a breathless voice. "Stone and all of the Extended slaves are being executed in two days."

CHAPTER 19

Ciago held onto the railing of the small ship as salt spray and wind blasted his face. The deck dipped and shuddered as another wave crashed over the bow.

He tried to shout encouragement to the Energizer, his only companion, but the furious wind ripped his voice away. He saw the woman straining as she fought to keep the boat moving forward.

They were close to shore. Before the storm, he'd seen the harbor filled with the giants' towering ships that had made him feel like he was riding on a child's toy. Now, though, his only view was of black clouds, raging water, and sea foam.

Even though they'd taken the same route the Lagonian ships would have sailed, and the Energizer had sped them along fast enough to overtake the other fleet, Ciago had seen no sign of his fellow soldiers.

Had the storm blown them off course?

He strained over the rudder, doing what he could to help the Energizer steer the ship.

His memories took him back two years, to the last time he'd been on this sea. The Lagonian fleet was making for the crummy island the giants had claimed and Jaikon wanted for the empire. It was the worst storm any of them had ever encountered, with waves over a hundred feet high. The water had looked like it was boiling with all of the white froth. The difference then was that he'd been on a Lagonia ship instead of this dinghy.

Ciago had been on deck, drawing in the sails and helping to secure everything down. Some fool had left a keg of beer loose, and the thing had blasted into Ciago as the ship lurched. He'd been tossed overboard before he could grab hold of the rigging. With the rain and waves, there was no way anyone would have noticed he'd gone overboard, and even if they had, it would have been suicide for anyone to come after him.

His last thought before he hit the water had been that a keg of beer was going to be what killed him. He'd be the butt of soldiers' jokes for generations to come.

And then his body had struck the icy waves.

One of the sails had torn off and wound around his body, and the canvas was dragging him down with the surf. Even for a swimmer as powerful as he, there was no fighting that tempest. He'd taken what he thought was his last breath of air, when he felt arms dragging him out of the depths of his watery grave.

Rhett was there, cutting through the tangled sail with his dagger while he fought against the current for both of them. Wilsean and Stone had somehow managed to toss them a rope and reel them both back on deck.

Rhett had saved two more soldiers from a similar fate during that voyage.

Ciago was pulled out of his musings of the past as a wave crashed over the boat. He spluttered as freezing salt water went into his mouth and nose.

"Remind me why I agreed to go on this accursed mission," he muttered to himself as he wrestled with the rudder.

The question was annoyingly easy to answer. Rhett was the reason why he'd put his family's reputation and his own life at risk. Ciago had become a traitor to his empire for the sake of his friend.

All of their sacrifices would be worth it once Rhett killed Jaikon and ascended to the throne.

But for Rhett to stand a chance, he was going to need allies. Ciago had to find these damned Lagonian ships before he accidentally crashed up on the giants' shores. Or drowned. As the storm grew fiercer, the latter seemed more and more likely.

As the small boat fought against fifty-foot waves, Ciago wondered when he had become so noble.

The Energizer screamed. Ciago wiped sea foam and sleet from his eyes just in time to see the enormous wave before it broke across the deck.

Water crashed through the glass panes protecting the small enclosure where the Energizer had been huddling. She was swept overboard along with the black water.

Ciago cursed. Then, he dove in after the woman.

The water was so cold it stole his breath away.

As tumultuous as the water had looked from the deck of their boat, it was worse when he was in it.

Move, he ordered himself.

"Where are you?" he shouted, getting a mouthful of salty water for his trouble.

He couldn't see the woman anywhere. All he saw was a wave towering over him. He dove before it broke on top of him.

The strength of the water sucked at his clothes, pulling him down. He dove again, forcing his eyes open against the swirling grit and saltwater, searching for some sign of the Energizer.

A flash of color sped through the black water. Another gurgled curse sent bubbles from his mouth.

A sinuous, red-scaled body cut through the water close enough to touch. Horns emerged from the frothing waves. A glassy yellow eye met his.

The sea serpent bared its fangs in a demonic grin.

The creature made Jaikon's golden dragon seem small and unthreatening in comparison.

Ciago swam. He knew he was worse than a fish wriggling on a line compared to this powerful creature, but his need to survive made him intent on doing something.

Ciago kicked and pumped his arms against the current. He rode another enormous wave, hoping it would drag him far enough from the serpent that the creature would lose interest in him. As the wave drew him higher, he still strained for some sign of the Energizer.

Not that he would be of any use to her now that a sea serpent was after him.

The wave pulled him back down. He took a deep breath and let the current suck him under.

He would have been more relieved at not seeing any sign of red scales if he wasn't completely fucked either way. He had no boat, and he was too exhausted to swim to shore, even if he'd been able to see it in this gale. He didn't even know which direction would bring him to land and which would bring him farther out to sea.

The massive red-scaled head burst out of the surf directly in front of him. The serpent displayed hundreds of snaggled teeth, each the size and sharpness of a sword's blade.

The creature's tail lashed the water. Ciago caught sight of his boat, which shattered into matchsticks beneath the serpent's tail.

It was a true testament to his current situation that his ruined boat was the least of his problems.

As a wave carried him higher, the serpent moved with him. It rose out of the water to keep him in its sight. In the distance, Ciago caught a glimpse of the docked giants' ships.

He was so close to land.

The serpent's yellow eyes glittered in anticipation. It opened its jaws to swallow him whole.

At least it's not a beer keg, Ciago thought as he stared into fathomless darkness.

CHAPTER 20

Stone and the Extended slaves had two days.

Two days.

Rhett's first thought was that he needed his army. *Now.*

"Get ready to leave for Insorsil as soon as it's light," he told Liss. "I'm going to call Ciago."

He tucked four immunity flowers into his jacket pocket before handing Liss the bag. He saw the look in her eyes when she took in the bag's shrunken contents. Her expression gutted him.

"Liss," he began, not knowing what he could say to make her feel better.

She straightened her shoulders. "I'll give these to Mari's brothers to guard while we're gone. Go call Ciago."

Her strength bolstered him.

Rhett closed his hand around the corresponder in his pocket. He hadn't tried to contact Ciago yet. He also hadn't felt the glass sphere heat in the way it would have if Ciago had been reaching out to him. As much as he'd wanted to talk to his friend and know that he was still alive, he hadn't wanted to bother Ciago if he was in the middle of something more important…like trying to survive. But he needed to talk to his friend now.

Their timeline had moved up. As soon as Ciago found the Lagonian fleet, Rhett wanted them sailing straight for Lagonia.

They were running out of time.

The reminder echoed in time with his every footstep.

Rhett knew such a public announcement was for his benefit. Jaikon wanted Rhett to come back to Lagonia.

Rhett entered the cottage and closed the door behind him. Wilsean was already inside, shouting at his own corresponder.

"Goddamn stubborn witch," Wilsean muttered, shoving the glass sphere back into his jacket.

"Samara isn't a witch," Rhett pointed out, pulling his corresponder out of his pocket.

White smoke began to swirl in the sphere at his touch. Rhett waited impatiently for the smoke to clear and Ciago to appear. The longer Ciago went without answering, the hotter the corresponder would become. Eventually, he'd have to answer.

If Ciago was too busy seducing that Energizer to notice his corresponder....

The smoke settled down to the bottom of the glass, but Ciago's face didn't take its place. Instead, the glass went dark.

"What the hell?" Wilsean murmured.

Rhett put both of his hands on the sphere and shook it. The white smoke swirled, but Ciago still didn't appear.

"Have you ever seen a corresponder do this?" Rhett asked. A bad feeling was creeping down his spine.

Shaking his head, Wilsean took his own corresponder back out. The smoke began to whirl.

"Unless you're calling to admit to being a pig-headed idiot, I'm hanging up," Samara's voice said as her face appeared in the corresponder.

Rhett and Wilsean exchanged a look.

"Samara, what does it mean if the person on the other end of the corresponder doesn't appear?" Rhett asked before she and Wilsean could start arguing.

"Did the smoke turn red after he didn't answer, or did it go black?" Samara asked.

"Black."

For a few seconds, Samara didn't say anything.

"Then, there are two possibilities," she said in a quiet voice. "The first is that the other half of the corresponder was destroyed. The other...."

She didn't need to finish that sentence.

All of the air was sucked out of his lungs at once. Rhett couldn't breathe. He slumped against the wall of the cottage, clutching his dark corresponder.

"Maybe he lost it," Wilsean said in a hoarse voice.

He couldn't look at Rhett. They both knew Ciago was anything but careless, and the corresponder had been their only means of communication. He wouldn't have let the thing out of his sight.

Rhett heard Wilsean speaking quietly to Samara but couldn't make sense of any of their words.

He'd sent Ciago on a hopeless mission. He'd sent one of his best friends to die.

Rhett threw the corresponder as hard as he could. It smashed through the wall of the cabin. A whistling sound filled the cottage as wind rushed in through the hole.

Stone was in the torture cage. Ciago was at the bottom of the Brookgar Sea.

Rhett had put all of this in motion. He'd made choices for himself, and now everyone he cared about was paying for them.

He drove his fist through the wall. The wooden boards splintered. He hit the wall again, and again. The old wood sliced through his knuckles, perversely giving him relief from the impossible pain that was tearing apart his insides.

He heard Wilsean shouting at him, but he didn't stop.

"Did you hear me?" Wilsean shoved him, hard. "We don't know that he's dead!"

Wilsean's eyes were too bright, and for some reason, that infuriated Rhett all the more.

He turned on Wilsean. His next punch was aimed at the other man's jaw. Wilsean blocked it with his forearm, returning with a blow that would have broken his shoulder if Rhett hadn't twisted out of the way.

He threw up his elbow, catching Wilsean in the chest.

Rhett was in this cottage, protected by a ward, while all around him, people were dying. *His* people. Because they thought he was a leader worth a damn.

Wilsean threw him to the ground. Rhett was back on his feet in an instant, charging at the other man. They went rolling across the cottage. He heard the wood crack but felt nothing as they barreled out into the snow.

Ciago was dead. Stone was going to be executed.

"This isn't your goddamn fault," Wilsean panted as they wrestled.

He was still talking, but Rhett couldn't hear a word over the screaming in his head.

Had Ciago drowned? Did the giants overwhelm him and feast on his lifeless body? Did one of Jaikon's invincible soldiers find him before he even boarded a boat?

"Rhett!"

Only one voice in the world could have pulled him out of the pit of despair that was dragging him under. He went motionless.

Cursing, Wilsean got to his feet. He swiped his hand across his lip, which was swollen and bleeding. He offered Rhett his hand. When Rhett made no move to take it, Wilsean grabbed his arm and yanked him to his feet.

"Ciago isn't dead," Wilsean said, giving Rhett a look that dared him to argue.

"Ciago…what?" Liss's eyes widened in horror. She had the corresponder Rhett had thrown in her hand. It was unbroken, in spite of the force with which he'd thrown it. Rhett couldn't look at her as he took the useless object and shoved it back into his pocket.

Wilsean said something to her. A few moments later, Liss wrapped her arms around Rhett. Somehow, even though she was so much smaller than he was, Rhett found himself leaning into her.

"We can't have you losing your shit right now," Wilsean said.

Rhett knew his friend was right, and that Wilsean was suffering as much as he was. It had been the three of them for as long as he could remember. They were brothers in every way that mattered. And now, one of them was gone.

Liss let him go and stepped back. There were unshed tears in her eyes, but her face was set in determination.

"I'm going to get some quick-heal," she said, eyeing Rhett's tattered knuckles. "And then we're going to Insorsil. We have a queen to intimidate."

142

CHAPTER 21

The wagon dropped Liss, Rhett, and Wilsean at the edge of the forest. A mile's walk along an abandoned path would bring them to the road that led into Insorsil.

Liss kept her hand in Rhett's bandaged one as they walked. They were all silent.

Liss didn't know how much more they could take. Ciago was dead. Stone and the Extended slaves were about to be executed. Rhett was almost out of flowers. And an unyielding queen and invincible army stood in the way of what they needed most.

Liss was having trouble thinking with all of the emotions that were coming at her.

She stopped walking.

"What is it?" Rhett asked, reaching for his dagger.

"Souls," she whispered. "Lots of them."

Wilsean nocked an arrow. Rhett signaled for them to each get behind a different tree. The clamor of emotions was growing in intensity. A few seconds went by, and then Liss heard the distinctive creak of wagon wheels.

Liss put up a hand to Rhett, who nodded in understanding.

She ducked back behind her tree as the first wagon in the caravan turned off the road. She wanted to rush out to greet them, but a thought held her back.

The Extended were already frightened enough. She didn't want them to see her Lagonian appearance and think they'd been lured into a trap. They'd either turn around and go right back the way they'd come or try to kill her.

She self-consciously put a hand to her throat, where that Extended man's hair had wrapped around it. She thought about Dolo's accusation about her feeling superior because she looked Uninfected. She remembered him saying she'd made things worse for her people by discovering the source of the Lagonians' immunity.

Liss shook away the unpleasant thoughts. None of that mattered. What mattered was that another caravan had come.

"This way, hurry, this way," a high-pitched voice called out. "Gotta get our honey. Mmm honey."

Liss caught sight of the fairies buzzing around the first wagon.

"Honey, honey, honey," another of the fairies sing-songed, rubbing his tiny stomach as he zipped in and out of the wagon's open window.

Another wagon appeared on the heels of the first. It was accompanied by more fairies, their squeaky voices chattering about honey.

Wagon after wagon passed. It was a big caravan. There were twenty-nine wagons, some of which were big enough to hold large families. Liss couldn't help but wonder what new Extensions these people had. There were some powerful Extended in the most recent caravan to come to the hideout. If there were more of the unusual, strong Extended, they'd become that much more formidable.

Rhett caught her eye from behind his tree and raised his eyebrows. Liss couldn't hold back a smile. She felt the tension inside her easing.

For years, she'd fantasized about the Extended coming together. It had been such a farfetched dream that she had never expected to see it happen. Now, for the first time, she thought her people might stand an actual chance.

It was only one more caravan, but it was one more than they'd had before. And if this caravan wasn't alone…if more were coming….

The moment the thought crossed her mind, another caravan came into sight. Their wagons barreled along the path, led by the chattering fairies. Another caravan appeared on its heels.

Liss's pulse picked up speed as wagon after wagon passed by. Her mind raced to the weeks and months ahead. They could fortify the ward that kept the Lagonians from discovering their hideout. Once the barricade wall was built, they'd have even more protection.

The abandoned farmland was expansive enough that, once spring came and the ground thawed, they could grow crops. They could build actual stay-in-one-place houses. They could do more than just survive.

They could live.

When the last wagon had disappeared along the path that led deeper into the forest, Liss stepped out from behind her tree.

"Shall we?" Wilsean asked, re-sheathing two throwing knives.

With the emotions from a hundred souls still swirling around in her mind, they continued on the road to Insorsil.

* * *

Liss had to force herself to focus when they reached the cluster of shops and taverns that marked the beginning of Insorsil. Her mind was so full of the new caravans that would be inside the ward by now—and the fact that they had less than two days to rescue hundreds of people from Lagonia— that she could barely keep her head on straight.

Liss led Rhett and Wilsean through a labyrinth of back alleys, interconnecting underground passageways, and still-closed shops with easily-picked locks. In this way, they avoided any mercenaries who might be on the lookout for them.

They were also dressed like Lagonian merchants, thanks to an Extended Tailor from the other caravan in the hideout. They all kept the hoods of their cloaks up and did their best to blend into the rest of the foot traffic as they made their way toward the necromancy quarter.

They skirted around warlocks selling foul-smelling brews that proclaimed to ward off death and evil spirits. They passed by witches holding crystal balls and magical staffs.

The shops that lined the street were mostly closed, since the necromancy quarter didn't become active until nighttime. Ominous music played from one of the shops, and an odorless purple smoke seeped out from under the door. Liss assumed the music and smoke were a poor attempt to make the place seem more legitimate. The shop also had a sign on the door that boasted the witches inside could contact any member of the dead…for only a pound of jewels.

They made it to the western edge of the quarter without incident. Liss led them into the abandoned alley between two closed shops where they'd agreed to meet Samara.

A woman with porcelain skin and Insorsil-long black hair leaned against the stone wall at the end of the alley.

"I could kill you," Wilsean growled, running for the woman.

Rhett reached for his dagger.

Wilsean pulled the woman into his arms, kissing her in a way that would have had Liss defending Samara's honor if she hadn't recognized the woman's soul.

The woman in Wilsean's arms looked nothing like Liss's best friend, but one glance into her soul left no room for doubt.

"It's Samara," she told Rhett, feeling a smile break out on her face.

Rhett had already put his dagger away. "I figured as much." He inclined his head at the couple, who were kissing like it had been months…rather than days…since they'd seen each other.

"Liss!"

Samara wriggled out of Wilsean's arms and ran to her. They collided, laughing and hugging each other. Samara kissed her on both cheeks before hugging a surprised-looking Rhett.

When she was surrounded by the rest of them, Samara took a sip from a flask in her pocket. She winced as she swallowed, and then the image before Liss's eyes rippled and shimmered as Samara's illusion fell away.

The porcelain-skinned, black-haired woman transformed into the real Samara. Her skin darkened to its usual honey-gold hue. Her long hair thickened and became white-blonde. Samara's face rounded out, and her irises changed from violet to amber.

Samara's soul was overflowing with love and affection, as well as an undercurrent of nervousness.

"Are you sure it's okay for you to be here?" Liss asked, looking around.

Samara rolled her eyes. "Don't you start, too. I already have a big bad protector I didn't ask for."

Wilsean looked like he wanted to either shout at Samara or start making out with her again. With the two of them, both were equally possible.

"My brother helped arrange a meeting with the queen for you and Rhett," Samara said. "Wilsean and I will see what we can figure out about the immunity flowers, just in case the brilliant Opal Smoke and terrifying Opal Slayer can't make Gatria hand them right over." She wrapped an arm around Liss's waist. "You and Rhett are going to be the esteemed Lord and Lady Jerriwein from Lagonia. You're a supremely wealthy merchant couple interested in purchasing a thousand pounds of jewels' worth of magic."

Liss hadn't realized until this moment how much she'd been missing Samara. Her friend's confidence was exactly what Liss needed, since all of her own seemed to have abandoned her.

"Stupid question, but are we sure Gatria is the one who gave Jaikon those pins?" Samara asked as they started to walk.

Rhett nodded. "A slaver said as much before I killed him."

"Besides, do you know of anyone in Insorsil with that kind of power besides the queen?" Wilsean asked.

Samara shook her head. "In that case, your best option will be to convince her to reclaim the magic, but if you can't, you'll have to…um…."

"Kill her?" Rhett asked without a hint of emotion.

Samara nodded.

"Killing an Insorsiled will immediately end any magic they have ongoing," she explained.

"I didn't know that," Wilsean said, looking impressed.

Samara gave him an annoyed look. "I know. No one outside of Insorsil knows that, which is one of *many* reasons why you need me."

Liss was a little taken aback by how easily Samara and the guys were talking about murdering a queen. On the other hand, they were all so desperate to get what they'd come for that no price seemed too steep or violent to pay.

Samara continued, "Killing Gatria needs to be your last resort. She has enspelled everyone in the kingdom into adoring her, and that kind of emotional influence won't wear off right away. If you move against her, you'll immediately become the enemy of every witch and warlock in Insorsil."

Rhett gave Samara a curt nod.

"You don't seem all that enamored with the queen," Wilsean pointed out.

Samara quirked her lip. "There are some advantages to being an Empty. Those kinds of spells don't work on me."

Samara handed a flask to Liss. Liss unscrewed the cap and gagged as a putrid brown smoke wafted out.

"It's a transfiguration spell instead of regular illusion," Samara explained as Liss pinched her nose and downed the foul drink. "They're my brother's specialty, and it'll be harder for the queen to detect since it's a much more complicated form of magic than illusion."

"I'll say," Liss gasped as she felt her nose grow larger. It didn't hurt, it was just weird.

She stumbled a little when her legs started to lengthen. Her stomach came out and her breasts shrunk. Out of the corner of her eye, she saw her hair turn thin and gray. She raised one of her new, pudgy hands and examined the fat ruby stone on her ring finger.

"She'll transform back, right?" Rhett asked, a note of anxiety in his voice.

"What's the matter?" Liss pouted. "This body isn't doing it for you?"

Rhett looked at her. It was weird to be staring at him from a different angle, now that she was half a foot taller than usual.

"Your body will always do it for me," he said, giving Liss one of his soul-deep stares.

Wilsean cleared his throat. Samara sighed appreciatively. Liss blushed.

"Now you," Samara said, handing another potion to Rhett.

Rhett tipped the flask in her direction and then downed it without the gagging and flinching Liss had needed.

Liss watched as he began to shrink. His huge, muscled frame turned into a completely unnoteworthy body. His defined arms turned to fat. His straight posture was forced into the hint of a stoop. A hairy beard sprouted across his cheeks, and a mop of curly hair sprung out of his shaved head. A matching ruby ring appeared on his ring finger.

"Nice," Wilsean said, patting Rhett's hairy cheek. "Very…um…Lagonian gentry of you."

"You would know," Rhett growled in return.

"You two need to get going," Samara said. "This spell will only last for half an hour before you start changing back."

Samara took two vials filled with a cloudy white potion out of her pocket. She gave one to Liss and one to Rhett.

"These will make you invisible if you need to make a quick getaway. They'll last for exactly one minute, so if you have to kill the queen, take these and run like hell.

"Now, Rhett, give Liss your dagger."

Liss almost laughed at the look that crossed Rhett's face.

"The queen will have you searched when you come into the throne room," Samara told Rhett. "But I'm betting she won't search Liss. The queen thinks it's barbaric that there are women soldiers in the Lagonia army. It won't occur to her that a rich merchant lady would be armed."

"You're brilliant," Liss told Samara, as Rhett reluctantly handed over his dagger. "You know that, right?"

Samara gave her an easy grin. "I know."

CHAPTER 22

It was the first time Samara had been back in Insorsil since she was officially declared an Empty and banished from the kingdom. That had been three years ago.

All contact between Empties and the Insorsiled was forbidden, and so she hadn't seen her family since her exile. Her parents, who took Insorsil laws much more seriously than any of their children, hadn't spoken to her since. Samara regularly kept in touch with her brother and sisters, but she missed seeing them terribly.

Samara's parents would be livid if they knew she was in Insorsil and coming to their house. Fortunately, their jobs as the queen's advisors kept them out of the house during the day. Even though Samara didn't have to worry about seeing them, it didn't make her any less nervous about being back in the kingdom.

She would never admit her worries to Wilsean, since he was squirrely enough about her being back here. So, she hid her nerves behind a stream of chatter about everything and nothing.

They both hunkered under the cloaks Liss had "borrowed" until they reached her childhood home. She'd given Liss and Rhett the last of the transfiguration potion from the care package her siblings had sent. As an Empty, Samara was banned from buying or using anything Insorsiled, so it wasn't like she could go to one of the dozen vendors in this neighborhood and purchase more. Of course, the more powerful Insorsiled just made their own potions in the first place.

Wilsean didn't say much, but he stayed close enough that their arms kept brushing. It helped ease her sense of discomfort about being back here.

"I don't understand why you'd risk your life to help a bunch of Lagonians," Wilsean muttered under his breath.

"Really?" Samara let sarcasm drip from her voice. "You have no idea what motivation I might have for wanting to make sure you don't get yourself killed?"

She wasn't normally a sarcastic person, but Wilsean brought out the worst in her.

Samara hadn't expected to feel any kind of loyalty to the Lagonians, who had only tolerated her presence in their empire because of her access to the magic they craved. And yet, they'd taken her in—albeit reluctantly—when her own countrymen had kicked her out.

Samara had worked her way up from a sweeper in the Lagonia grain mill to a servant in the palace. She'd started a side business of selling magical toys that weren't worth so much as a gold nugget in Insorsil. In Lagonia, though, they went for a veritable fortune. Since Queen Gatria severely limited the amount and types of magic that flowed out of the kingdom, there was always a surplus of Lagonians desperate for magic of any kind.

Thanks to her prosperous business, Samara had saved enough wealth that she could buy passage to any land on any continent. It had been her plan to leave Lagonia and travel the world. She wouldn't stop until she found a place where everyone was an outsider, which was the same as saying no one was.

At least, that had been the plan until an infuriating, sexy archer barged his way into her heart. Then, an Extended masquerading as an Empty found her way into Samara's life, and all her plans had gone to hell.

She and Wilsean continued to trade light-hearted barbs as they walked, but as they neared her old neighborhood, even his teasing couldn't distract her.

It was strange to feel homesick for a place and people who had discarded her. Still, her childhood had been a happy one and her family loving before it became clear she was an Empty and not just a late bloomer, as her parents had kept hoping.

Samara had known long before her parents that she didn't possess a single magical bone in her body. As a child and young teenager, she'd harbored the secret hope that, if she studied magical theory, she might be able to teach herself how to wield it.

She'd read every book in existence about magic. She learned the ins and outs of all kinds of spells and potions. While most Insorsiled used their powers without questioning where the energy came from, Samara knew every detail about how it all worked. She was probably one of the most knowledgeable experts on magical theory in existence.

Of course, all of her studying had been useless. If it was possible to teach oneself magic, then the Insorsiled wouldn't be the only ones casting spells.

On her eighteenth birthday, her parents had officially given up hope and, in accordance with Insorsil law, unceremoniously kicked her out of the kingdom.

That's the corner where they told me I could never return, she imagined herself telling Wilsean. Instead, she said, "My primary school is down the block. And there's the most controversial restaurant in the neighborhood." She pointed to the red-roofed building. "They make dumplings that can give you an orgasm. Literally. It's very popular with the teenagers."

Samara kept her voice light, even though it was getting harder to pretend like everything was okay.

Wilsean slipped his hand into hers as though he could sense what she was feeling. It was one of the many reasons why she wished things could be more between them. It wasn't possible, but sometimes in her more fanciful moments, she dreamed it could be.

By the time they reached the baby blue picket fence that marked her family's property, Samara was all but shaking with nerves.

The house had beautiful flowers climbing all along its façade. It was a simple spell and one that even the weakest witch in Insorsil could conjure. And yet, to Samara, it was just another reminder of what she couldn't do.

Pull it together, she ordered herself, trying to channel her fearless best friend. If Liss were here, she'd go charging right through the front door. So, after taking a steadying breath, that's what Samara did.

Before she could so much as call out, her siblings came bounding down the stairs. Samara found herself separated from Wilsean as they engulfed her. Her older brother, Ambrosius, lifted her off her feet while her younger sisters, Annabelinia, Lullianna, and Carilona swarmed Wilsean. To his credit, Wilsean had her sisters swooning within seconds.

All of her siblings were a year apart. Ambrosius was the oldest at twenty-two, and Carilona was the youngest at eighteen.

Without breaking their noisy chatter, they all went into the spacious parlor, which was supposed to be reserved for her parents' important guests. Her sisters unlocked the wine cabinet with the key their parents thought they'd cleverly hidden in an invisible box. Ambrosius had discovered the box when he was five.

Lullianna chatted easily with Wilsean as she rummaged through the wine cabinet. She and Wilsean had met when he helped smuggle her down to the torture cage to save Rhett's life. Even though she was only nineteen, she was already one of the most powerful witchdoctors in Insorsil.

Lullianna selected an expensive bottle of champagne. Ambrosius took out their parents' crystal goblets—also reserved for guests and potion-brewing—and poured.

Samara felt her heart expand at the sight of Wilsean, smiling and looking utterly at home as her siblings laughed and talked over each other.

"We couldn't get everything you asked for," Lullianna said, motioning to a satchel in the corner of the room.

"And I didn't have time to brew more transfiguration potions," Ambrosius added, giving the satchel a critical look. "They take a week to properly simmer."

Ambrosius was a transfiguration expert, and even the queen couldn't see past his disguises. It was why Samara wasn't worried about Liss and Rhett right now.

"It's more help than we would have had otherwise," Wilsean said.

"I'll pay you back for everything as soon as I can," Samara promised.

Her siblings scoffed.

"It's not like Mom and Dad let us spend our money on anything fun, so we may as well use it to help you," Annabelinia said with a long-suffering sigh.

"I don't know how we can ever thank you," Wilsean said.

"You already have by doing whatever you've been doing to make my sister's eyes sparkle like that," Ambrosius said. "I don't think I've ever seen her this happy."

Samara felt her cheeks heat. She looked away before Wilsean caught her eye and saw how deeply she cared for him. Things between them were already complicated enough.

As much as Samara wanted to hang out with her siblings and catch up on their lives, time was short. She put down her goblet and started going through all of the Insorsiled goods in the bag, re-organizing them and making a mental note of what else she'd need. The satchel wasn't nearly as full as she'd hoped. Still, as Wilsean had said, this would help.

As she went through the contents, they all discussed the issue that was foremost on her mind: the immunity flower.

"If there are any readily available in Insorsil, I haven't heard about it," Ambrosius said.

Samara figured as much. The flowers were too valuable to be sitting around in open markets. But that didn't mean there weren't more of them…somewhere. She had a couple of ideas about where to check.

"I was wondering," Samara said, turning to Lullianna, her witchdoctor-in-training sister. "If I could get one of the live flowers, could you find a way to enhance it and make it more powerful?"

"Like, so a Lagonian could eat a single flower and be immune for the rest of his life?" Lullianna asked.

Samara nodded.

Lullianna frowned. "With how much magic it must have taken to create the flowers in the first place, I doubt there's anyone strong enough to amplify their power any more. Besides, if that were possible, someone would have already figured it out."

Samara's hopes fell, but she told herself she could worry about that later. Right now, she needed to find more of the flowers, period.

First, they'd check the greenhouses where Insorsiled who specialized in earth magic grew all sorts of priceless plants. If they didn't find anything there, they'd try the black market. It wasn't a place upstanding Insorsiled citizens visited.

As luck would have it, she wasn't an upstanding Insorsiled citizen anymore.

"We'll be back in a little while," Samara told her siblings.

She slung the satchel over her shoulder and turned to Wilsean. "Care to take a walk?"

CHAPTER 23

Queen Gatria Melovina Iatheis drummed her inches-long nails on the armrest of her throne. She inhaled the heavy perfume given off by the tangle of winterthorns that climbed freely along the walls. She glanced down at the rows upon rows of white satin chairs filled with her adoring subjects.

Every one of these witches and warlocks would fight to the death to preserve her life. Of course, Gatria had used great reserves of her own magic to make her subjects idolize her.

But she wasn't able to take as much pleasure in the court proceedings as usual. The protection spell she'd woven earlier in the day had sucked her dry of every ounce of magical energy she possessed. It was extremely difficult to create a protection charm against other magical attacks, since a more powerful Insorsiled could unravel the spell if it wasn't potent enough. It was the most powerful magic she'd ever created, but it had been worth it.

When the filthy Extended man who spoke in whispers limped in, she'd nearly ordered his execution just for making her throne room smell like a sewer. When he began babbling about a murder plot, Gatria had been skeptical, but she'd allowed the man to speak his piece. After three-hundred years of life, true excitement was difficult to come by. So, she'd heard the man out.

She'd been distracted for the first part of the conversation by the man's little name—Burk. Gatria had never understood why the Extended chose such undignified names for themselves.

Honestly, how could those nomadic urchins expect the rest of the world to respect them, if they had no respect for themselves?

When Burk told her the name of the warlock who was supposedly planning her demise, Gatria's amusement had turned cold.

Krozor. As in Krozor Ragnor Mantis. The old warlock was a hermit, who lived in his basement hovel brewing potions that no one had any use for. Gatria simply hadn't believed it.

And yet, there'd been no conceivable reason why someone outside of Insorsil would know the recluse's name…unless everything the Extended man was saying was true.

Krozor had never come to a royal function or requested Gatria's magical assistance. The only reason the queen even knew his name was because of a controversial paper he'd published several years back.

It had detailed the warlock's perspective that Insorsil should refuse to trade with all non-magics. He argued that the Insorsiled were diluting their magic by selling it to those who could not produce it for themselves.

The argument had been too stupid to warrant a response from the queen. After all, without Lagonia's jewels, how would their kingdom survive?

Gatria didn't appreciate being at the pompous Lagonians' mercy any more than Krozor did, but there was nothing to be done about it. If the Insorsiled wanted their kingdom's wealth to continue to grow, they needed to sell their most valuable asset: their magic.

There were other Insorsiled who shared Krozor Ragnor Mantis's small-minded perspective. Gatria just hadn't imagined any of those miscreants felt strongly enough to try to assassinate her.

Fury had her magic sizzling inside her. She locked down on the emotion before she lost control.

The last time she'd let her temper get the best of her, she'd created a magical storm that had toppled several buildings and killed a dozen pixies.

After Burk had finished telling her everything he knew, Gatria had sent her guards straight to Krozor's hovel. Unsurprisingly, he hadn't been there. He hadn't been anywhere. So, she'd had no choice other than to guard herself against a possible attack from the warlock.

Creating the shield was costing her. She barely had enough energy to negotiate with the wealthy Lagonian couple now striding down the crimson carpet that stretched from the double doors to the dais where her throne sat.

The husband walked through the throne room with single-minded intent. The wife surveyed the lofty space, taking in the elegant architecture and sumptuous decorations. The woman tilted her head back to squint into the winter sun shining down through the glass tiles of the domed ceiling. She took in the enormous crystal chandelier, which hung suspended in mid-air by a dozen different levitation spells. The sunlight's reflection off every crystal globe of the chandelier made it look like diamonds danced across the crimson-and-white checkered floor.

It was an impressive sight for anyone, but must be downright awe-inspiring for the un-Insorsiled couple. The thought made Gatria sit a little straighter.

"Search the lord for weapons," she ordered one of her guards.

As the guard patted down the lord—who didn't look fit enough to wield a weapon even if he possessed one—Gatria scanned the crowd of her eager, doting subjects. Even with the hundreds of people piled into the throne room, her gaze caught on a single face.

Krozor Ragnor Mantis.

She started. *When had the man appeared? How hadn't she noticed him before?*

The stooped warlock who was wearing a dirty brown robe, stared back at her. He had a monocle over one eye, which he likely thought made him appear esteemed and scholarly.

To think that Krozor, who had apparently never heard of nose hair-trimming spells and wasn't even dignified enough to grow a proper beard, intended to unseat her….

Gatria fought a very unfamiliar urge to squirm. In the first time in as long as she could remember, Gatria didn't know what to do. Her own magic was too wrapped up in her protection charm for her to be able to summon a killing spell.

She could order her guards to execute the warlock, but if it turned out he was more powerful than he'd led everyone to believe, then Gatria could risk embarrassing herself in front of the entire court. Her subjects would see she was too weak to step in and finish the job, and that would be enough for the more powerful members of her court to begin resisting the manipulative hold she had on all of them.

Her protection spell would shield her against any magical attack, and her guards would protect her in the unlikely case of a physical attack. Not that Krozor looked capable of attempting murder of the non-magical variety. Therefore, Gatria embraced the only choice she had. She smiled, relaxed, and waited.

The guard who searched the lord nodded and stepped back into position against the wall. Gatria signaled for the couple to come forward.

There was something familiar about the lord's confident gait. But she would stake her centuries-long life that she'd never before seen this short, plain Lagonian man and his even plainer wife.

She peered at the couple, looking for the telltale ripple of color that would hint at the usage of illusion magic.

She saw nothing to indicate that these people weren't who they appeared to be. Besides, it wasn't like these Lagonians would ever be able to come by an illusion potion strong enough to fool her. Gatria ensured only the weakest magic—immunity flowers aside—ever found its way out of the hands of her own people.

"Your Majesty." The lord bowed.

That deeply masculine voice sent a shiver of recognition through her, although she couldn't place it in her magic-depleted haze.

"Charmed to make your acquaintance," Gatria told the man in the voice she'd honed, perfected, and infused with magic over her many years of life. It terrified some and entranced others, but none were unaffected.

Except for the man now standing before her.

How very strange.

The lord must either be heartless or utterly besotted with his ugly wife.

"I hear you have a business proposal for me," Gatria told the lord, although she couldn't immediately tell which member of this couple held the power. The secret looks they exchanged were impossible for her to discern. If the whole of her energy hadn't been spent on the protection spell, she'd be able to tease out the couple's interests and motivations with a glance.

A hot bath and a night's rest would replenish all of her strength, but until then, she was almost as useless as an Empty.

The thought sent another jolt of anger through her. She shifted on her throne, wrestling for control over the emotion before it cracked her protection spell. All the while, she felt Krozor Ragnor Mantis's beady eyes on her.

"First, we would like to purchase more of the opal contagion immunity from you," the lord said in his gruff voice. "Second, we want you to remove the magic of the invincibility pins you sold to Jaikon."

Gatria jerked to attention.

Burk had told her about the Lagonia Emperor's supposed invincibility, of course. She'd assumed Burk had been mistaken. There were a number of temporary strength spells that a weakling such as Burk might confuse with true invincibility.

Gatria was the most powerful of all the Insorsiled, and even she didn't have the skill needed to generate that kind of magic.

There was something about the grim expression on this lord's face that made the queen hesitate. Whatever he had seen or heard, he believed what he was saying. He believed Emperor Jaikon was invincible.

Impossible.

Gatria glared at the Lagonian man with her silver eyes.

Her gaze held no inherent magic, and yet, she had turned men mad with want or fear…or perhaps both…with this stare.

The lord didn't blink.

Recognition tickled at her consciousness, but again, she couldn't place him. Perhaps he was illusioned, after all. If she was at her full strength, she'd be able to rip away any magic clinging to the pudgy Lagonian pair. In her current state, though, she could not. She'd have to bide her time and wait for any spell they were under to wear off.

"Immunity flowers and invincibility," Gatria crooned, inclining her head and waiting for the tittering of her subjects to die down.

"Yes," the lord said.

Gatria's mind spun. She was traversing unfamiliar ground.

She couldn't admit that she'd had nothing to do with providing the Emperor with invincibility magic—and thus, was powerless to remove it—since that would mean admitting to her entire kingdom there was an Insorsiled stronger than she.

Gatria had gifted Jaikon, Sr. with the flowers to make him beholden to Insorsil. He would have used his army to win the Giant Realm for her. Eventually, he would have enslaved himself and his people to her will. If only he'd lived, Lagonia might already be within her grasp. Decades of amusing the former emperor with magical baubles and carefully laying the seeds to stealthily take over the empire had been wiped away by one murderous stroke.

Gatria's anger began to mount.

"Fist, there are no more flowers," she lied. She gave the couple a benevolent smile that should have made them shudder, although neither of them reacted. "Second, I will not be bullied into *removing* my magic from anywhere."

She gave her audience a conspiratorial wink.

"She's lying to us about something," the woman told her husband. "I'm not sure about what, though."

"You don't know a thing about me, little wench," Gatria hissed. To the lord, she said, "My agreement to provide the immunity flowers ended when your previous emperor was murdered. Your people will never see another flower from me."

Applause rang out through the cavernous room.

"She's also afraid and insecure," the wife continued.

"Silence her," Gatria ordered a guard beside her, flicking one of her long nails in the woman's direction. Gatria yawned, as though it was beneath her to summon the spell that would bind the woman's tongue when, in fact, Gatria was too weak to manage it herself.

The lord stood protectively in front of his wife.

"Touch her, and you'll never hear what I'm willing to give you in exchange for helping us," he said as the guard stepped forward to do his queen's bidding.

The Insorsiled crowd began to murmur. They didn't like impudent Lagonians giving their queen orders. Neither did she.

Gatria felt a moment of satisfaction when the wife tried to speak and could not.

The lord looked at his wife, his face awash in concern.

"What did your guard do to her?" he demanded.

There was real fear in his eyes. *Interesting.* Gatria didn't think that kind of devotion existed between Lagonian spouses.

"It's a simple silencing spell that will wear off in time," she replied, yawning again.

The lord gave her an unblinking stare that chilled her to her bones. In all of her long years, she could only recall one man who returned her gaze without emotion. It was the same man with the husky, masculine voice she'd known she recognized.

Rhetteman Loniger.

Gatria stared at the chubby, unassuming man now staring her down. And who was the woman? Could it be Opal Smoke, the Extended to whom the frigid former-assassin had purportedly given his heart?

It didn't matter. Lagonia's Chief Assassin was standing before her, and she was too magic-starved to deal with such a threat.

"Seize him!" she shrieked.

CHAPTER 24

L iss's lips were sealed shut. No matter how much she strained, she couldn't form a word.

She began to panic. The guards were converging on Rhett, who was weaponless.

She pulled out the dagger concealed in her cloak and tossed it to Rhett, who had already climbed the steps up to the throne. He caught it without looking away from the queen. In one swift motion, he pressed the blade of the dagger to Gatria's throat.

"Come any closer to either one of us, and I'll kill your queen," Rhett called out in a low voice that somehow managed to cut through all the other sounds in the room.

"I can kill your Infected woman with barely a thought," Gatria hissed.

She's lying! Liss wanted to yell. Guards were now blocking her so she couldn't even get Rhett's attention by waving her arms.

"You know who I am, witch," Rhett said in a deadly voice. "You've heard what I'm capable of when it's nothing personal. What do you think I'll do when it is personal?"

Liss felt nervousness shiver through the queen's soul.

"I want to make a deal with you," Rhett told the queen. "I know about Jaikon's plans to take over Insorsil. I have more information than you could dream of, and I'll share it with you if you give us what we need."

The queen cocked her head, like she was considering his proposal. Everyone else in the court waited with baited breath.

"I'll make you a deal, Opal Slayer." The queen's mouth quirked into an amused smile. "I'll take away the Emperor's invincibility. But to give you the power to slaughter your greatest enemy, you must pay me in the blood of your greatest love."

Deceit flashed through the queen's soul. Liss fought against the spell that was keeping her silent, but it was useless.

"I'll cut out my own heart before I spill even a drop of her blood," Rhett said, his voice calm and unyielding. "I promise that the information I have to trade will be of more value to you than either of our lives."

The guards and everyone else in the throne room stayed motionless, waiting for the queen's orders. When Liss tried to move to get Rhett's attention, the guards surrounded her more tightly.

The queen hesitated. Her soul was full of a nervous kind of fear. At first, Liss just assumed it was because of the blade at her throat. But as she watched the queen, Liss realized her attention wasn't on the dagger. Her silver eyes kept going to someone in the crowd behind Liss. Whenever her eyes darted that way, the fear in her soul flared.

"Take away Jaikon's invincibility and give us more of the opal flowers, and I'll tell you everything I know about how Jaikon plans to take over Insorsil," Rhett said.

"No deal," the queen replied breezily.

Rhett brought the blade of his dagger flush against the queen's pale neck. The guards surged forward.

As everyone stared, Rhett began to grow taller. When Liss looked down at herself, she saw that her round stomach was retracting.

Their transfigurations were wearing off.

She needed to get to Rhett. She needed to tell him everything the queen was saying was a lie. She needed her voice.

Liss forced herself to calm down and think. *Deal with today's problems now, and tomorrow's problems later.*

Solving in-the-moment crises was Liss's specialty.

She remembered Samara saying that killing an Insorsiled would make their magic die with them. If she could kill the guard who had put this spell on her, she'd be able to help Rhett again.

Liss took a tentative step toward the guard. Since his—and all of the other guards'—attention was on Rhett and the queen, no one noticed her. She was being ignored.

She took another step closer to the guard, and then another.

"I'll give you a potion that will bestow a long life on your firstborn," Gatria said, the whole of her fear now fixed on Rhett.

Again, Liss felt deception sweep across Gatria's soul.

Liss was right behind the guard now. Her practiced thief's eye caught the outline of a blade on his left hip in addition to the sword in his right hand. Liss began inching aside the man's crimson cloak to gain access to the weapon.

Slowly, she warned herself, as Gatria continued making ridiculous promises to Rhett.

Liss's hand closed around the handle of the knife.

"If you kill me, you'll never get more of the immunity flowers," Gatria said. "They're kept in a place only I can access."

Liss froze. The deception across the queen's soul didn't come.

Gatria was telling the truth.

Liss yanked the knife free. The guard spun around to face her, swiping his sword at her throat. She ducked.

"I've had enough of your snake tongue," Rhett said.

Liss screamed, but the sound never made it past her sealed lips.

Gatria is telling the truth!

Liss struck out with the knife, using a blocking maneuver Rhett had taught her months ago. The guard gave her a puzzled look.

"You're a girl," he said.

They were the last words he ever spoke.

Liss impaled the man on his own blade. Her lips sprang free.

"Rhett, don't—"

Blood arced through air as Rhett sliced his dagger across Gatria's throat.

CHAPTER 25

The queen slumped in her throne. She was dead.

The room went dead quiet for a single heartbeat. Then, it erupted into sound.

"Murderer!"

"Lagonian traitors!"

"Get them!"

The raucous shouts brought more witches and warlocks running into the throne room. Guards' feet pounded across the marble floor.

Thanks to the images plastered all over the kingdom, every Insorsiled knew Rhett and Liss's faces. There would be no way to easily lose themselves in the crush of people swarming the throne room. They were going to have to fight their way out.

At the way the throne room was filling up, it wouldn't be long before everyone in Insorsil was after them.

Rhett jumped back down the steps. He saw the knife in Liss's hand and fresh blood—not hers—staining her sleeve.

That's my girl.

"Potion," Liss yelled to him, tipping her own vial into her mouth as he fought his way through the guards separating them.

He downed his own invisibility potion just as a mob surrounded them.

Rhett fumbled around until he found her hand.

"Follow me," she said, her voice barely audible over the roar of the mob.

She steered him through gaps in the crowd that were there one moment and gone the next. Rhett counted down the seconds in his head as he and

Liss raced for the exit. Samara had said they'd have a minute before the spell wore off and all hell broke loose. They had to get out of here before that happened.

They were free of the main part of the crowd and sprinting across the checkered floor. They kept their hands locked together as they skirted around guards who slashed their swords across nothing but air.

Rhett's heart lifted. The queen was dead, which meant that her magic had died with her.

More importantly, the queen's death meant that Jaikon was vulnerable again.

Rhett remembered the stickiness of his father's blood as he mopped the throne room floor on his hands and knees. He remembered Jaikon ordering Rhett to hand over his own shirt so Jaikon could replace his bloodstained one. He remembered the way Jaikon had looked at Liss as he promised to make her suffer before she died.

I'm coming for you, brother, Rhett thought.

Ten seconds. Nine.

They were almost out of the throne room when Liss stopped short.

"What are you doing?" Rhett demanded in a harsh whisper.

Six. Five.

"Son of a bitch, I'm going to kill you!" Liss screamed.

Rhett was too stunned to stop her when she let go of his hand. He couldn't see her, but the part of him that was always attuned to her could sense she had disappeared back into the crowd. Rhett's heart lurched into his throat.

Where did she go? What was she doing?

Everywhere, Insorsiled were brandishing deadly magic. Bursts of light had begun zinging through the air. An explosion of fiery sparks came close enough for Rhett to feel their heat.

Damnit.

He had to find Liss. They had to get out before—

Rhett's heart stopped when his eyes caught on movement at the center of the mob. Liss was slipping through gaps in the bloodthirsty crowd. And she was no longer invisible.

CHAPTER 26

Wilsean knew they needed to leave, but he couldn't stand to pull Samara away from her siblings. Every one of them could be arrested if she was found here, so he had been expecting coldness and reticence from Samara's family.

His expectations couldn't have been more wrong. Samara's siblings were concerned about her being caught and punished, but that hadn't stopped them from surrounding her.

But that was who Samara was. She drew everyone around her to the light and warmth she exuded without even trying.

Wilsean would never have admitted it before, but he had been nervous about meeting Samara's siblings. He didn't have any of his own, since the Lagonian elite made a point of only having a single heir to consolidate wealth. After an hour with Samara's brother and sisters, all of his worries had fallen away. He felt more at home in this house than he ever had in his own parents' stiff company.

He loved the sound of Samara's laughter and the way her amber eyes sparkled when she was happy. He loved that Samara's siblings thought *he* brought out that sparkle.

He stood in the foyer of her family's house now, trading jokes with Ambrosius while Samara gave her sisters a final hug. He heard her youngest sister whisper, "Are you *sure* he doesn't have any brothers?" and couldn't keep a grin off his face.

Ambrosius gave his sister a hug. "Let us know if you need anything. We'll keep checking the greenhouse in case any of the flowers show up." He looked down at Samara. "And take care of yourself."

Samara kissed her big brother on the cheek, and then, hurrying to wipe a tear from her eye, nodded to Wilsean that she was ready.

Before either of them could reach for the knob, the door opened. Two older people Wilsean recognized from the paintings scattered around the house stepped inside.

They all froze.

"Why are you home so early?" Ambrosius asked, a nervous muscle ticking in his jaw. His shocked expression mirrored his sisters'.

Wilsean tensed. Samara, who was standing on Wilsean's other side, wasn't immediately in her parents' line of sight. Her mother's face was red and puffy. It looked like she'd been crying.

"Queen Gatria is dead," their father said in a hoarse voice. "The court is in shambles." The warlock stopped talking as his attention caught on Wilsean.

"Who—"

He cut himself off mid-question as Samara stepped forward.

Samara looked at her parents, and they looked at her. It seemed to Wilsean that time had stopped. No one spoke or moved. On instinct, his hand twitched for one of the knives in his jacket pockets, but he forced himself to stay where he was.

"Hi," Samara said, her voice timid in a way Wilsean had never heard it before.

Wilsean glanced at her, keeping the older couple in his view at the same time. He stiffened at her expression.

Samara was afraid of her own parents.

"She'll get us all killed," her mother cried, clutching at her husband's arm."

"I'm sorry," Samara began.

"Get. Out." Her father's face turned from ghost-white to scarlet. "Now!"

Wilsean had never felt anger like the kind now twisting his insides into knots.

"I'm sorry," Samara said again. She seemed to grow smaller as she moved to slink past her parents, like she had something to be ashamed of.

Wilsean couldn't stand it. He held Samara's arm to keep her from taking another step.

"You will *not* speak to her that way." He used the same voice as Stone right before he interrogated a suspect.

Wilsean's towering height was intimidating enough, but the look on his face drew the couple's attention away from Samara and onto him.

"Who the hell are you?" Samara's mother demanded.

Wilsean considered his answer as he continued his stare-down with Samara's parents. He knew most Insorsiled were different from Samara in that they valued family lineage. They also appreciated wealth and status.

"My family is the wealthiest and most influential in Lagonia," he said in that same, threatening tone.

If Ciago were here, he would have been quick to point out that his family's net worth surpassed Wilsean's a generation ago. Wilsean felt a sharp pang at the thought of his friend, but he pushed it away.

"My family controls half of Lagonia and as much of the wealth that travels from there to here."

It was a bit of an exaggeration, but only a bit.

"I also happen to be the best bowman in all of Lagonia."

He twined his fingers through Samara's and stepped toward her parents.

"More importantly than any of that, I'm Samara's boyfriend."

He'd never said that word before, and yet, it came out sounding more right than any single word should.

"And has your girlfriend told you she's an Empty?" Samara's father asked, giving his daughter a look full of disgust.

"Let's just go," Samara said, tugging on his hand.

Wilsean stayed where he was. "Do you think I give a damn about that?" He wanted to shout, but he knew from growing up under Stone's tutelage that quiet could be more threatening. And he wanted to threaten the people who were hurting Samara. "I wouldn't want her to be anything other than who she is."

He had never spoken truer words.

"If you don't leave right now, we'll make you," Samara's mother said, drawing a staff out from the pocket of her cloak. "I won't let you put my family in danger."

This time, Wilsean didn't stop himself from drawing two knives from his jacket.

"Whoa, whoa, whoa," Lullianna said, putting up her hands.

Wilsean didn't know if it was in preparation of doing magic or if she was just trying to calm everyone. He disregarded her. His attention was fixed on the threat before him.

"I promise you, my knives are faster than any spell you can cast," Wilsean told the couple.

"We're leaving." Samara grabbed his arm and pulled him to the door. Silent tears were tracking down her cheeks.

"I'm letting you live out of respect for Samara and her siblings," Wilsean told her parents. "But in exchange for your lives, we're taking your bikes."

Wilsean had glimpsed them out the window. They were top-of-the-line Insorsiled bikes equipped with flying capacity. The bikes would serve their purposes nicely if his suspicions about the mayhem his best friend had stirred up were accurate.

"We can't give an Insorsiled bike to an Empty," Samara's father said, aghast. "It's illegal."

"And we're going to need you to enable their flying capacity," Wilsean added as though the man hadn't spoken. He brandished one of his knives in the direction of Samara's mother. "Now."

The couple's wide-eyed stares went from Wilsean with his knives to their children. Wilsean would never harm Samara's siblings, but he let the couple fear that he would.

With a little sob, Samara's mother started for the door. Her father, whose face was now beaded with sweat, gave Wilsean a terrified look before following her.

Wilsean stalked out behind Samara's parents. He wrapped a possessive arm around Samara while her parents muttered the necessary incantations. Insorsiled bikes could be driven by anyone, but their flying capacity required a magical jump-start from a witch or warlock.

When her parents were finished, Wilsean turned to Samara for confirmation. She couldn't create the magic herself, but she knew when it was done properly. Samara gave him a short nod.

"Never come back here," her mother shouted. "Do you hear me? Never!"

"I won't forget the way you treated her," Wilsean told the couple as Samara climbed onto one of the bikes. "You made a very powerful enemy today."

Samara's family was silent as he walked past his own bike to Samara's. He could see her trembling, even though her face was frozen in a determined expression. He leaned over the handlebars and kissed her. Then, he spoke three words he'd never uttered before in his life…words he'd known he felt for Samara for months but hadn't said out loud. Words he'd rejected because of the complications and impossibilities that would come with them. The way Samara had come here and braved her parents' hatred gave him the courage he'd been lacking.

"I love you."

Samara's lips parted in surprise. Wilsean strode back to his own bike, a swagger in his step. He settled himself on the seat and twisted the handle. The bike started to rise.

CHAPTER 27

The throne room was bursting with Insorsiled. They were screaming, crying, and waving their staffs. One second, Liss was scanning the throne room for a hidden exit or servant's passageway. The next, she caught sight of a familiar opal-skinned face. She almost didn't notice him, because his skin and hair were so coated with filth he was barely recognizable. But the slimy familiarity of his soul had her heading for him before her brain had even registered who it was.

Burk.

"Son of a bitch, I'm going to kill you!"

Liss wrenched herself out of Rhett's grip.

"Go," she shouted at Rhett as she ran.

Burk had destroyed the field of flowers that protected Rhett and his friends from opal contagion. He had been willing to sacrifice her life for a goddamned room in the palace. He had told Jaikon where to find the kids on Liss's thieving crew.

Right now, she didn't care if the Insorsiled fried her alive…as long as she killed Burk first.

He ran for the far end of the throne room. She chased after him, using her stolen knife to part the crowd. She ducked underneath spells that zoomed past her as she raced for her target.

Burk reached the far wall. He was cornered with nowhere to go.

Got you, Liss thought with satisfaction. She tightened her hold on her weapons.

Two warlocks came at Liss, blocking her access to Burk. They raised their staffs. She had to roll to avoid the sparks of red and blue flying at her.

She slashed with the knife. She didn't care if the blade connected or not. All she wanted was to get these idiots out of the way.

The warlocks parted just in time for her to see Burk throw back the contents of a small flask. He smiled at Liss. She lunged for him.

Her fingers closed on empty air.

She looked around, confused. And then movement on the ground caught her attention. A beetle with opal-colored wings crawled out from beneath the dirty cloak Burk had been wearing.

She pounced, tearing through the cloak with her knife.

The beetle's opal wings twitched as the insect scuttled across a crimson floor tile. She slammed the blade of the knife down. It missed the beetle by centimeters.

Liss swung her knife again. The creature's wings fluttered as it hopped out of the way. She scrambled across the floor as she reached for him. The beetle slipped through a miniscule crack in the wall.

"No!" She beat her hands against the wall. She tried to drive her blade through it but came up against solid stone.

"Liss, come on!"

Rhett grabbed her arm.

"I told you to go," she yelled at him, her voice barely audible over the roar of the crowd shouting for vengeance for their queen.

"You did," he agreed, pulling her with him.

"I have to go after him—I have to—"

She kicked at the baseboards and tried to rip apart the wall with her bare hands.

Rhett picked her up and tossed her over his shoulder. He ran back in the opposite direction.

"I'll kill you!" she screeched at the top of her lungs, hoping with every inch of her soul it would make Burk permanently deaf.

Liss was too furious to process the fact that she had led Rhett back here, and there was now a wall of furious Insorsiled blocking their exit.

Rhett stopped moving, because there was nowhere else for him to go. They were surrounded.

He put her down. They each gripped their weapons, standing side-by-side. She ducked beneath two purple curses zinging their way.

A tremendous crash cut through all the other sounds. The ceiling, which was glass, shattered. Two Insorsiled bikes fell through the air. The first bike hit the enormous chandelier.

The crystal structure wobbled, and then the entire thing hurtled downward.

Shards of glass sliced through the room. Rhett turned into her, using his body to protect hers. Everyone was screaming. Slabs of glass ceiling and strands of crystals hit the marble floor and scattered.

Hordes of Insorsiled raced for the exit. It was madness.

"Rhett, Liss!"

Rhett moved, and Liss caught sight of Wilsean and Samara on the two Insorsiled bikes now idling in the middle of the room.

Rhett was bleeding, but it didn't stop him from taking her hand and pulling her to the bikes. Liss leapt on behind Samara. Wilsean's bike careened around until it was close enough for Rhett to jump on.

Liss held onto her friend's waist as the bike started to lift into the air.

Samara jerked the bike to the side as a green shimmer flew at them. The curse hit the wall, blasting a hole through the stone.

Fire and color shot at them as the Insorsiled below tried to bring down the bikes.

Samara and Wilsean steered the bikes higher as they weaved around the spells. They burst through the hole in the ceiling.

The curses didn't seem to be able to follow them. The colorful sparks hit some kind of transparent barrier and started ricocheting back to the ones who had cast the spells.

Liss whooped as the bikes soared into the dark sky, leaving the fireworks of death spells far below them.

CHAPTER 28

They flew the bikes into the Insorsiled forest, a mile's walk from the Extended hideout. Rhett made sure Liss wasn't hurt and assured her all of his wounds were superficial. Then, he helped Wilsean bury the bikes where they wouldn't be found. They were all edgy from their close call.

"Shit, Rhett." Wilsean huffed out a nervous laugh. "You're now the enemy of the two most powerful realms in the world."

"It couldn't be helped." Rhett shoved a pile of leaves over their buried bikes. "Gatria refused to remove the magic of the pins."

"So, you can kill Jaikon now?" Wilsean asked.

Rhett nodded. He knew he should feel more elated by the prospect, but he couldn't stop thinking about their other unsolved problem.

"There are no more flowers," he told the others.

Wilsean grimaced. "Samara and I went to the Insorsil greenhouses and the black market. I made it clear we had jewels to spare, but there wasn't a single flower to be had."

"I'm so sorry," Samara told Liss.

When Liss looked at Rhett, there was pain and uncertainty in her gaze.

"Um." She swallowed.

"What is it?" Rhett asked.

Her blue eyes were watering when she looked up at him. "You know how the queen said we'd never get another flower if you killed her?"

Rhett nodded. The queen had told him one lie after another when she realized her life was about to end.

Liss swallowed again. When she spoke, her voice was so soft he almost missed her words.

"I couldn't tell you because of that silencing spell, but Gatria was telling the truth."

"What?" Rhett demanded.

A single tear tracked down Liss's cheek. "I don't know anything more than that. She was lying about everything else she said, but that one thing was true."

Rhett exhaled. "You're telling me that there was a way to get more flowers, but now that she's dead—"

"Yes," Liss whispered.

A cold knot of dread formed in the pit of his stomach.

Rhett thought back to what the queen had said. He'd seen the panic in her eyes and had believed she was saying anything she could think of to spare her life. She'd made promises about long life and said something about his firstborn. It had all been nonsense. Or so he'd thought....

"Wait a second." Samara lifted a hand, breaking through his horror. "What exactly did the queen say?"

Rhett's heart thundered in his chest.

"She said if I killed her, I'd never get more of the immunity flowers, since they were kept somewhere only she could access." He nearly choked as he repeated the queen's words.

He'd had a chance to get more flowers and lost it?

Liss looked heartbroken. Wilsean groaned and buried his face in his hands. Rhett couldn't move.

"Interesting," Samara said.

"What?" the rest of them asked at once.

She looked at Wilsean and smiled. "We were looking in the wrong place."

A tentative grin spread across Wilsean's face.

"Explain," Rhett said.

"The queen told you that there were more immunity flowers, but you'd never get them without her," Samara said.

"Right." Rhett wondered why she looked so smug. The queen was dead.

"There's only one explanation that fits."

Samara told them there was an underground cavern beneath the castle where the queen kept her most treasured possessions. It was warded, enspelled, and had more curses protecting it than Samara could even guess.

"If we can get inside, we'll find whatever is left of the flowers," Samara said. "Guaranteed."

"But none of us can so much as cast a spell, let alone undo one," Wilsean pointed out.

Rhett's short-lived optimism faded. There were about a thousand other problems with getting inside the most highly-guarded place in all of Insorsil, but Rhett couldn't bring himself to point them out. The look of hope on Liss's face twisted his insides.

"I need to think more about it," Samara said, "but I have some ideas about how we might be able to get in and out with the flowers…and our lives."

Rhett didn't see fit to mention how unpromising that sounded.

"We'll go to Lagonia and free everyone first, since that's more urgent," Samara continued. "Once Stone and the slaves are safe, we can figure out how to steal back the flowers."

"Now, you're speaking my language," Liss said.

The sun was setting as they headed back to the hideout. They had little more than twenty-four hours before Stone and the Extended slaves would be executed, and Rhett's mind was consumed with the best way to do everything they needed to accomplish.

"We'll need to split up," Wilsean said, his thinking following the same line as Rhett's.

"Liss can take a group of Extended to get the slaves out," Rhett said. "Wilsean, you can get Stone. I'll take care of Jaikon."

"You need someone to watch your back with Jaikon," Wilsean argued. "He'll still be surrounded by guards, even if they're all mortal again."

Out of habit, Rhett turned to his right, before remembering Ciago wasn't beside him. Ciago would never be beside him again.

Steel doesn't know love or despair. It can't be bent or broken. It needs no heart or warmth. I am steel.

Rhett drew in a shallow breath.

"We'll just have to get Stone first and then go for Jaikon together," Wilsean said. He shrugged, but Rhett knew his friend well enough to read the tension in every one of his muscles.

They wouldn't talk about the loss they shared, but it hung between them like a hangman's noose.

* * *

The buzz of tree fairy wings filled the forest as they neared the ward. The creatures' bellies were swollen with honey, and there was a dazed expression in their eyes. Guilt stuttered inside Rhett at the sight.

He hadn't exactly mentioned to anyone that honey was a slow-acting poison that would eventually kill the fairies if they kept consuming it.

This was a war, of sorts, and if Rhett didn't use the few tools at his disposal, the people who were his to protect would die. In a perfect world, there would be no innocent casualties in the battle between Rhett and his half-brother. But no one needed to tell Rhett there was no such thing as a perfect world.

The ward rippled as they passed through. They all stopped short as the newly-constructed barricade loomed in front of them.

The barrier was made out of wood and stone. It rose up twenty feet and ringed the entire field. Rhett marveled at the structure, which would have taken hundreds of Lagonians months to build. The Extended had managed the same task in a day.

"How in the world did they build this so fast?" Wilsean murmured.

"Extended Archis and Arts," Liss said, grinning. She was bouncing on the balls of her feet as she stared up at the wall. "Jaikon's people are going to take one look at this and wet themselves."

Rhett didn't share all of her enthusiasm, but he had to admit it was an impressive sight.

The outer wall was smooth enough that no one was going to be able to climb it. Rhett saw the Extended had taken his advice about setting patrols on top of the wall's walkway. Extended marched back and forth with

Lagonian weapons clutched in their hands. Even from the ground, Rhett could tell he'd have to show them how to actually use the weapons, but still, they made an intimidating scene.

If nothing else, it would be enough to dissuade the slavers from getting inside the walls before the flowers ran out. After the flowers were gone, no Lagonian would be able to come near this place.

Rhett tried not to think about how he would be included in that group.

"Hiya, Liss," one of the Fighter brothers called down from the wall.

Liss grinned up at him. "This is amazing."

"You think so now, just wait until you get inside."

Liss didn't need any more encouragement. She ran for the armored door that led into the compound.

An unfamiliar Extended man stepped in front of the door before Liss could reach for the handle.

"No Lagonians inside the hideout," the man said.

"Let me put it this way," Liss replied. "Either let us in, or I'll cut out your eyeballs one by one."

She drew her knife out of her cloak and held it up so the setting sun glinted off the steel blade.

"She'll do it, too," Mari's brother called good-naturedly down from his perch on top of the wall. "You better let them in."

Liss humphed in satisfaction as the opal-skinned man moved aside. There was a creaking sound, and then the heavy wooden door began to rise.

"Pleasure doing business with you," Liss called to the man in a friendly voice before stepping inside.

"You're sexy when you threaten people," Rhett told her as they walked through the short tunnel within the barricade.

Liss gave him one of those dimpled grins that made his heart go double-time.

They stepped out of the dim tunnel and onto the open field.

"Wow," Samara breathed.

"Well shit," Wilsean said.

Liss laughed in disbelief.

They all just stared.

The hideout looked nothing like the way they'd left it. Instead of three caravans' worth of wagons, there was now more than twenty. Rhett took a quick count. There were two-hundred wagons in all. The army commander side of Rhett was pleased to see the way the wagons had been lined up along the edge of the barricade in neat rows.

"We did it," Liss said. Tears slid down her cheeks as she pressed her clasped hands to her heart.

Gathering all of the Extended was just the first step of many in what would be an arduous fight for survival. Still, even Rhett's cynicism was pushed to the background at the sight of Liss's elation. He stood beside her as they took in the scene before them.

Rhett had never seen so many Extended in one place. Their opal skin transformed the bleak landscape. The brilliant hues gleamed in the setting winter sun and reflected off the bits of ice embedded in the dirt. Everything seemed to shimmer. Everywhere Rhett looked there was color. And sound.

Almost two-thousand Extended could certainly make a racket. Some of them stayed huddled around their wagons, looking afraid and out of place, but most were milling around. Two Flamers had a bonfire going, and groups of Extended were talking.

Everything was organized chaos. Some of the Extended had set up tents. Rhett caught sight of a massive tarp that was being used to protect all of the food supplies that were being organized and inventoried by a man whose arms moved with such speed they were a blur.

Somehow, even though the ground was frozen, a garden was in full bloom. Only a day had passed since they'd last been here, and yet, full-grown tomatoes and squashes were burgeoning in patches of ground that had been cleared of snow. Fat, round cabbages dotted the field in alternating bursts of green and purple. Scruffy carrot tops blew in the harsh wind but didn't wither.

The only explanation was a Green Thumb. They were extremely rare and were one of the few Extensions Jaikon had never deemed a threat to Lagonia. Thus, Rhett had never needed to kill them.

A small sparring arena had been set up, where the Extended were taking turns practicing with their newly-acquired weapons. Their form was terrible, but their enthusiasm was admirable. It looked like Spence was leading the training exercises, showing off a few moves he'd clearly picked up from Ciago.

Rhett's heart lurched at the reminder of his friend.

Liss turned to him and took both of his hands in hers. Hope shone in her eyes as she looked up at him.

"We're going to survive," she said. "We're going to turn the Extended into the most powerful army the world has ever seen. We'll defeat Jaikon and kill every one of his slavers. We'll live in actual houses and eat golden cake every day for the rest of our lives."

Liss's joy was infectious. When she spun around in a circle, Rhett caught her around the waist and lifted her up. Liss wrapped her legs around him as he angled his face to kiss her.

"Lissy!"

Jema, the little girl who had helped him bake a golden cake for Liss, came bounding toward them.

Reluctantly, Rhett lowered Liss back to the ground, just in time for the little girl to latch onto Liss like a barnacle.

"All the caravans came," Jema chattered.

Liss took the little girl's hands, and for several seconds, the two of them jumped up and down as they laughed and hugged each other.

"Come on," Jema said, tugging on Liss's hand. "Your mom will want to see you."

Rhett, Wilsean, and Samara fell into step as they headed for the cottage. Rhett noticed the building had been repaired since his brawl with Wilsean the day before.

It appeared that all of the leaders had gathered inside the cottage.

As soon as Liss's mother saw them, she said something to the other leaders before excusing herself and coming to join them. Rhett took note of the hostile stares his group got from the others inside the cottage. He exchanged a look with Wilsean, who nodded. They didn't draw their weapons, but Rhett kept vigilant in case any of the Extended tried anything.

"I can't believe this," Liss said as her mother wrapped her arms around her.

"You did this, my darling," Nya told her. "I couldn't be prouder of you."

Liss smiled at her mother, but Rhett could tell she was distracted.

"Where are Mari's other brothers?" she asked, looking around. "Rhett needs his flowers back."

Rhett felt a pang at the worried expression on Liss's face.

When one of the brothers came with the bag of flowers, Rhett tried to keep Liss from looking inside as he unzipped it and handed a flower to Wilsean before taking one for himself.

"Where are the rest?" Liss demanded, shoving Rhett's arm out of the way to peer into the bag.

"This is all there is," he told her.

"There can't be more than a week's worth here. Did someone take the rest? Do they think this is some kind of joke?"

Rhett took Liss's hand before she stormed off to threaten some poor Fighter.

"Liss, this is all there is."

He could feel her pulse beating a frantic rhythm against her wrist.

"It's going to be okay," he said, trying to calm her down.

"I'm going to figure this out," Samara said, putting a hand on Liss's shoulder. "I promise, I won't let anything happen to our guys."

She wrapped her arms around Liss, so Liss couldn't see her worry and uncertainty. Rhett saw it all. He knew Samara had no idea how to replicate the magic of the flowers.

Rhett's thoughts turned to the empire that would soon be vulnerable once their own store of the immunity ran out. Would Jaikon close down the borders to Lagonia as their father had done during the last outbreak of opal contagion, or would he allow the contagion in to drive fear into his subjects? It was just the kind of sick power play Jaikon would use to further manipulate and control his people.

"We're going to Lagonia tomorrow," Rhett told Nya. "We'll need a team of Extended who can help us get the slaves out of the empire."

"It'd be great if we could get the other caravans' Energizers to help," Liss added. "The more wagons we have, the faster we'll be able to get all the slaves out."

"And if there are any Extended who can help disguise our wagons, we'll need them, too," Wilsean said. "It'll help keep us out of sight until we want to be seen."

Rhett nodded in agreement.

Nya looked troubled.

"What's wrong?" Liss asked her mother.

"Gathering everyone in one place has strained the caravans enough." Her gaze flicked to the other leaders, who were staring at them with suspicion. "It won't be easy recruiting people to go right into the lion's den."

"Try telling them their efforts will save their own people," Rhett said, more harshly than he meant to.

"I'll do my best," Nya replied acidly, "but your people have taught mine how to cower and hide. You can't expect us to become warriors overnight."

"Time is the one thing we don't have," he reminded her.

"Give me until dawn to find a team," Nya said.

Rhett didn't want to wait that long, but he could tell from the expression on Nya's face that he didn't have a choice. He gave her a curt nod. Liss gave him a look, so he added a gruff, "thank you."

Rhett didn't let his frustration show. He understood the Extended people's fears, but if they wanted all of the slaves to walk out of Lagonia alive, some of them were going to need to step up.

"Don't let Spence and Mari find out what we're planning," Liss told her mom, her voice full of anxiety. "They'll want to come, and it's too dangerous."

"I agree," her mom replied, sighing.

Nya gave a pointed look to the leaders standing in the center of the cottage.

"I'm afraid you might have lost your quiet place to sleep," she said. "But I'm sure we can rearrange some wagons to make extra space."

"Don't worry." Samara patted her full bag. "I have an Insorsiled tent."

"Oh, right then." Nya frowned a little as her gaze slid from Liss to Rhett.

Rhett went stock-still, wondering whether Liss would alleviate her mother's concerns by saying she planned to sleep in her wagon. When Liss didn't say anything, Rhett's heart stuttered back into motion.

"Have everyone you can gather ready to go before dawn," Rhett told Nya. "I'll brief everyone on the way."

CHAPTER 29

H ey, Lagonians," someone called.

Liss felt the anger churning on the soul before she turned to see a small woman coming out of the cottage toward them.

"I want to know why you're really here," the woman said, staring up at Rhett and Wilsean with a fearful but determined expression on her face. "And before you start spouting your lies, you should know I'm a Truthseer."

Rhett went very still. Liss tensed. She'd never actually met a Truthseer before, since the Emperor had labeled them as dangerous, and there were as few of them left as Soul Sorters.

Liss kept walking until a row of wagons blocked their group from any prying eyes. If they were going to be forced into a conversation with a Truthseer, at least they could limit the number of observers.

"Tell me why you're here," the Truthseer said, following them between two wagons.

"I'm going to help you protect yourselves against the Lagonia soldiers who are hunting you," Rhett replied. His voice was slightly stilted, like the words were being dragged out of him.

"And why should we trust a man who would so easily give up the secrets of his countrymen?" the Truthseer asked.

Rhett went motionless in the way he did when a maelstrom of emotions was raging in his soul.

Liss understood the Extended woman's fears. Months ago, Liss had the same distrust. But that had been before she'd snuck into Lagonia and everything she believed about the world had turned upside down.

"Our motivations are our own," Rhett told the woman. "But I will tell you that we have no intention of harming your people."

"A Lagonian speaking the truth," the woman murmured. "How unusual."

Liss didn't like the too-knowing look she was giving Rhett.

"The correct response is *thank you for giving us a chance*," Liss said, her voice as cold and threatening as she could make it. "You wouldn't have come here if you thought you could manage surviving without us."

"Us?" The woman gave Liss a look full of judgment and loathing.

"Yes, I look Lagonian, and yes, I'm Extended," Liss snapped.

The Truthseer glowered at Liss. "You're the one who brought all this new misery on us by destroying Lagonia's immunity."

Burk destroyed the immunity, Liss wanted to shout. But she found she couldn't say the words.

"I made it possible for Burk to burn all of the flowers," she said, speaking the words in a stiff monotone.

As soon as the words were out, she recoiled. It was an ugly truth, and one she hadn't fully understood until she was forced to speak the words out loud.

She glared at the Truthseer.

"Liss didn't destroy Lagonia's immunity, and it isn't her fault slavers are hunting your people now," Samara said. Her cheeks were flushed with the righteous anger churning in her soul. "She was willing to sacrifice everything for you, so I'll thank you to keep your rude and unwelcome thoughts to yourself."

Wilsean nodded in agreement. Rhett put his arm—the one that wasn't holding his dagger—around her.

"You look familiar for some reason," the Truthseer said to Rhett. "Who are you, really?"

"He used to be a Lagonia soldier," Liss cut in before anyone else could speak. "You've probably seen his Wanted picture next to mine in Insorsil."

It was a partial truth, so Liss hoped it would satisfy the woman who was becoming more irritating by the second. This was starting to feel like an interrogation.

"I was Lagonia's Chief Assassin," Rhett said, taking a halting step closer to the Truthseer.

"Rhett," Wilsean said in a warning tone.

Rhett took another step toward the Truthseer, and Liss noticed that his gaze had gone unfocused.

"I'm the Viper. Caravan Butcher. Opal Slayer."

Liss gasped.

As soon as the words were out, Rhett staggered back, like the ground had been ripped out under his feet. Wilsean put a hand on his shoulder to steady him.

"You—you!" The Truthseer clutched a hand to her heart.

"Lower your voice," Liss ordered, looking around wildly to see if anyone else had heard Rhett's confession.

"You were the one who came into my sister's wagon in the middle of the night and slit her throat. You left her husband a widower and her daughter motherless!"

"Yes," Rhett said, his voice and face devoid of emotion.

His gaze sharpened as he sucked in a breath.

"I—" he looked at Liss.

Liss didn't know what to say.

"Murderer," the Truthseer choked out. "Monster!"

She rushed at Rhett, her fingers reaching like claws. Rhett stayed still, making no move to defend himself.

Wilsean was the one who wrapped his arms around the woman and pulled her back. He restricted her movement in a way that was almost gentle.

"I'll kill you!" she raged. "All of you! I'll—"

Wilsean pressed his hand over her mouth before she drew the attention of everyone in the hideout. The woman jerked and fought, her soul a tempest of fury and hatred.

Liss looked at the others, who seemed as dumbstruck and helpless as she felt. Liss was being yanked in two opposite directions. She felt like she'd either tear apart or go insane.

Deal with today's problems now, and tomorrow's problems later, she ordered herself.

Liss reached into her cloak and drew out her knife. She had no idea what she was doing. She had no long-term plan. All she knew was that she had to silence this woman before anyone else discovered Rhett's identity.

Liss's hand shook only a little as she held the weapon up to the Truthseer's throat.

"You're not going to tell anyone who he is," she told the other woman, who had stopped struggling against Wilsean. "Because if you do, I'm going to kill you."

Liss didn't know how many people in this camp had friends or relatives who had been killed by Opal Slayer. If they knew he was walking among them, Liss had no idea what would happen.

She had no intention of finding out.

Rhett and Samara flanked her, making it clear that an attack on one of them was an attack on all of them. Wilsean let go of the woman and rested a hand on the knives strapped beneath his jacket.

"Go ahead and ask me if I'm lying," Liss challenged the Truthseer.

This was Rhett's life they were talking about. Liss wasn't messing around, even if she knew she'd hate herself for it after.

Liss waited until she felt resignation on the woman's soul before she lowered the dagger.

"I've known a few like you in my time, but none as bad as you," the Truthseer told Liss, her voice quavering with emotion. "You pander to them because you want them to accept you. You beg for the scraps of their attention. You betray your own kind in the hopes that they will one day accept you."

The Truthseer stepped closer. "And yet, they never will. All you'll ever be is an outsider looking in."

Liss couldn't breathe.

"You say Liss is pandering to us," Rhett said in his rough voice, "and yet, here we are in her hideout. If anything, I'd say we're pandering to her."

Liss felt her chest compress with gratitude for his words.

"Don't talk to me, Viper," the Truthseer said in a hoarse whisper. "Don't you dare even look at me."

Rhett lifted a shoulder, looking bored. "Then, don't insult Liss."

The Truthseer stalked away, but not before Liss caught the words *traitor* and *shameful.*

Liss felt her cheeks heat in anger and confusion. She wanted to call the Truthseer back and insist on explaining herself. The trouble was, her explanation wouldn't exonerate her. It would damn her further.

"Come on." Samara slung her arm around Liss's shoulders. "Let's go get cleaned up and have some dinner. When you get a look at the Insorsiled tent I brought, you're all going to be pandering to *me.*"

CHAPTER 30

They chose a spot on the far edge of the camp near a group of parked wagons. Samara took the tent out of the silk bag and dropped it onto the ground. Unrolled, the flattened tent was a couple of feet wide and a few more in length.

Liss knew about Insorsiled tents, but she'd only ever seen the inside of the one Rhett traveled with. It was amazingly spacious for a one-person tent, but it wouldn't be big enough for the four of them.

They all watched as Samara pulled out a small tube filled with silver sparkles. She uncorked the tube, overturned it on the flattened tent, and waited.

There was a soft hissing sound as the tent puffed up. It grew tall enough that Liss could probably squeeze herself inside…if she didn't have any desire to move or breathe. And she was the smallest one in their group.

Samara unzipped the flap and crawled in.

"After you," Rhett said.

Still uncertain, Liss got down on her hands and knees and ducked under the flap. She expected to get a mouthful of Samara's feet. Instead, the ceiling opened up into a narrow, but tall, room. It was wood on all sides except for a brass door that was cracked open. Liss pushed open the door just as Rhett crawled through the flap behind her.

Liss stood on the threshold and stared.

"Holy—"

"Told you," Samara giggled.

Liss was standing in a common room that was bigger than the whole of her wagon. Soft white lights were strung along the solid wood walls. There was a long, L-shaped couch and large, intricately-patterned rugs covering the wooden floor. A round table sat in the center of the common area, with four cushioned seats positioned around it.

The common room had two closed doors on opposite ends and opened up into a spacious kitchen.

Inside the kitchen, there was a large stove, ice box, and bowls overflowing with fresh fruits and vegetables. A pot was already simmering on the stove and perfuming the tent with the smell of a hearty meat stew. Something baking inside the oven was wafting cinnamon and nutmeg into the air. Even with her weakened appetite, Liss's mouth couldn't help but water.

"So, are you ready to start pandering?" Samara asked, winking at Liss.

Still awestruck, Liss nodded her head up and down.

"This is really nice, Samara," Rhett said in a serious voice.

Really nice didn't begin to cover it.

"Can I live here forever?" Liss asked.

Samara laughed, clearly not understanding that Liss was dead serious.

The ceiling of the tent had been Insorsiled to look like a clear night sky. A crescent moon hung over the table, and constellations peppered the rest of the ceiling.

"Dibs on the master bedroom, suckers," Wilsean called, opening one of the doors off the common room and motioning Samara inside.

"Let's all get cleaned up and then have some dinner before we call it a night," Samara said. She glared at Wilsean as he grabbed her butt on her way into the room.

"I guess this one's ours," Rhett said, opening the other door and waiting for her to go first.

"I guess it is." Liss's pulse sped up.

There was something very adult about sharing a bedroom with Rhett. They'd slept in each other's beds before, but this somehow felt different. More deliberate, or something.

Liss stepped inside the bedroom and gasped. Even Rhett's grim expression softened.

The room was spacious, with a large bed dominating the center of the room. A cream silk canopy hung over the bed. Colorful rugs, vases full of fresh flowers, and glass bowls with pyramids of oranges were scattered around the room. The whole wall opposite the bed provided a clear view of a winter wonderland, even though Liss knew the actual view behind that wall was a rickety old wagon. A merry fire crackled in the grate, and a chandelier with burning candles hung from the ceiling.

A large washroom adjoined the bedroom. Liss took one look at the clawfoot tub, which was already filled with steaming, soapy suds, and squealed in delight.

Rhett stood in the doorway, seeming more interested in looking at her than their opulent surroundings.

"How is this even possible?" Liss asked, going back into the main room, where the candlelight had dimmed and soft music had begun to play from a source she couldn't identify.

Rhett shrugged, but there was a twinkle of amusement in his eyes. "Magic."

Liss found a medicine chest in the washroom that had all sorts of Insorsiled lotions and healing crystals.

"Get cleaned up so we can see where you're hurt," Liss said, squinting at a label on a blue glass bottle and trying not to notice that Rhett was stripping out of his dirty, bloody clothes.

She heard his soft chuckle when she tossed a fluffy towel behind her in Rhett's general direction.

As Rhett moved past her, his bare chest brushed against her arm. She studiously ignored him as her soul gave a painful lurch.

Liss backtracked out of the washroom as she continued her exploration. Her next discovery was a door hidden behind a velvet curtain. It was a closet that was big enough to walk into.

"There are clothes in here, and they look like our sizes," Liss called to Rhett.

She found something that was too beautiful to be pajamas but too comfy to be a dress. It was a deep maroon color and made out of a thin velvet material. She could tell it would show off her body without being too revealing, which was always a challenge with her curves. She pulled it off the hanger to change into after she bathed.

Rhett emerged from the washroom, clean and with his dozens of cuts on full display. Some of them were still bleeding.

Liss didn't have a single scratch on her, because Rhett had used his own body to shield hers when that glass ceiling crashed in.

"I'm so sorry," she said, her eyes taking in all the cuts.

This wouldn't have happened if she hadn't gone after Burk…if Rhett hadn't needed to chase after her.

"They're everywhere," Rhett said, a smile threatening at the corner of his lips. "I can't possibly reach all of them myself, and I'm desperate for some quick-heal. Did I mention the cuts are everywhere?"

Liss felt a grin spread over her face.

"Whiny little thing, aren't you?" she asked.

"I think there might even be one—"

As Rhett started pulling off his towel, Liss ran into the washroom, laughing. "Let me clean up, and then we'll see what we can do about these horrible wounds of yours," she called out from behind the washroom door.

As Liss stripped out of her filthy clothes, she noticed with interest that the tub had cleaned itself and was in the process of refilling. Earlier, the suds had smelled like fresh citrus. This time, they smelled like summer flowers.

Liss stayed in the tub until her skin turned pruney and Rhett was complaining from the other room. She put on the maroon dress, which fit her even better than she'd thought it would. She couldn't stop herself from spinning around in front of the full-length mirror, admiring the way the fabric clung to her curves.

By the time she made it to the main room, Rhett was stretched out on the quilt wearing only a pair of loose black pants. His eyes swept over her from bottom to top, slowly. His heated gaze rested on hers. Rhett gave her a real smile—something that was as beautiful as it was rare.

Liss grabbed the quick-heal and went to sit on the bed behind Rhett where he wouldn't be able to see how flustered she was.

She rubbed the quick-heal onto his cuts, watching as they closed up before her eyes and sunk back into the map of scars covering his body. She didn't think she'd ever get used to the marks branded into his skin. Even though Stone was in the torture cage and would be executed tomorrow if they didn't stop it, she still hated him for what he'd done to Rhett.

From the tenseness of his muscles beneath her hands, Liss could tell Rhett's mind was elsewhere, too.

"You know, I don't think Ciago is dead," Liss told him.

Feeling him tense even more, she added, "And no, I didn't sort your soul to know that was what you were thinking."

"What makes you think he's alive?" Rhett asked, his voice coming out even rougher than usual. "Can you…sense his soul?"

"It doesn't work over distances, so no," Liss replied. She moved around to put the salve on his chest.

"Then, how do you know?"

Rhett's dark eyes were fixed on her.

"I know because Ciago wouldn't want to let you down," she said.

"I don't think he died intentionally," Rhett said, a bite of sarcasm to his words. Then, he sighed. "I'm sorry. I know you're just trying to make me feel better."

She was, but she also believed her own words.

"Don't underestimate a thief's instincts," she told him, earning a small smile.

She finished with the cuts on his chest and pushed up onto her knees to reach the ones on his neck and face. Rhett went very still. He didn't blink or even seem to breathe as her fingers moved over the rough stubble along his throat.

For her part, Liss felt her soul heat in a flurry of emotions. She had to concentrate on ignoring her Extension, which was reaching for Rhett's soul.

She watched the gash at the corner of his lip heal. Then, unable to stop herself, she leaned in and kissed that same place.

Rhett moved so fast she didn't have time to take a breath before he'd flipped her onto her back on the bed. He caged her body with his as he bent to take her mouth in a kiss that set her aflame.

Liss wrapped her legs around his back, drawing him closer. Rhett used one hand to keep his body propped over hers, while the other cupped her face. Rhett's clean, citrusy scent washed over her as their tongues and bodies tangled together. She was intoxicated by the smell, the feel, the taste of him.

When his hips ground against hers, they both moaned. She made a sound of protest when his mouth left hers, until she realized he was pushing aside the fabric of her dress. She gripped his shoulders as his tongue swirled around the peak of her breast.

She lost all ability to think as Rhett kissed his way down her torso, pulling her dress down as he went.

"I need you, Liss," Rhett murmured, his words vibrating against her stomach.

A pulsing ache had begun in Liss's head. She ignored it. A trail of liquid heat followed everywhere Rhett's lips and hands touched. She ran her fingertips over his scarred back as she gave in to his caresses. She turned into the pillow to muffle her cries as his hand slid up her thigh.

She shoved away her need to sort his soul as her control unraveled.

Pain exploded in her head.

"Stop," she gasped.

Black spots gathered in her vision as her head spun. If she wasn't already lying down, she would have fallen.

"Did I hurt you?"

Rhett's face wavered in and out of her focus. A surge of nausea rose up into her throat as Rhett's hand pressed against her sweaty forehead.

"Need space," she managed.

The pain got more bearable once he was no longer touching her, but he was still too close.

"Liss, what's wrong? Talk to me."

Liss tried to pull her dress back into place. Her hands…her whole body…was trembling too much to manage it. So, with the gentlest touch, Rhett did it for her.

"Please," she whispered. "Don't touch me."

A mixture of hurt and worry churned in his eyes as Rhett backed away from her. Their harsh breathing was the only sound in the room.

"It's my Extension," Liss said when she'd caught her breath.

Rhett's brow furrowed. "I don't understand."

"The more my soul feels, the harder it gets to resist sorting yours." Her heart was still racing. "It…hurts not knowing what you're feeling."

"You don't need to look as far as my soul to know what I'm thinking," Rhett said in a low voice. "You know how badly I want you."

Liss wasn't sure how to explain something she was only beginning to understand herself. Suppressing one's Extension wasn't a natural state of being for her people. When she'd done it the past with her mom, it had only been for short bursts. Rhett alone made her crave the kind of closeness only her Extension could bring.

"That's not what I meant. It's taking a physical toll on me not to use my Extension."

Rhett's whole body stilled in the way it did when his emotions were strongest.

"Is that what's been wrong with you?" he asked.

Liss nodded. Even that small motion made the room spin.

A look of horror flashed across Rhett's face. "I didn't realize. Why didn't you tell me?"

Because I couldn't stand the sight of the man I love flinching every time I looked at him….

"Because I wanted you to trust me again," Liss said, unable to look at Rhett as she made this admission. "I knew if I told you, you'd insist I use my Extension."

"Damn right I would."

"But then you'd look at me like I'm some kind of freak."

"I didn't—I don't—" Rhett dug his fingers into his temples before pinning her with his stare. "Do it right now."

Liss saw him brace himself, like he was preparing for a fierce wind to come and sweep him away. Or for a blade to slice into his skin.

Irritation stirred to life in her soul.

"No." She crossed her arms and glared at him. "You don't get to dictate when I use my Extension. I'm not one of your soldiers to command, Rhett."

He winced, and Liss felt a stab of guilt for reminding him that he no longer had an army. Because he'd given all of it up for her.

Before she could apologize, Rhett snapped, "I'm not watching you make yourself sick when there's an easy solution."

"You weren't so concerned before this got in the way of sleeping with me," she shot back.

It was an unfair accusation, but she didn't care. It was easier to be angry with him than admit to herself how much it mattered that he couldn't come to terms with her Extension.

"I didn't know this was the problem, because you didn't tell me!"

They glared at each other.

Liss blew out a frustrated breath. "I can't do this halfway thing we're doing. I want you to want all of me, with no reservations."

Rhett stared at her for a long moment as his chest continued to rise and fall.

"I'm not sure—" he began.

"I know." Liss didn't want to hear him say the words out loud. She couldn't bear the truth…that Rhett hated and feared the thing that made her who she was. Even now, her head throbbed at being so near to him without using her Extension. It felt wrong.

"Sort my soul. Please," Rhett said, gentling his tone. "I can't stand seeing you like this."

"And I can't stand knowing that I repulse you," she shot back.

"You don't repulse me," he said, aghast. "Just because I don't want you in my head like that—"

"This is who I am, Rhett." She threw up her hands.

"I know. I told you I'd get used to it. I just—"

"I'm not an itchy sweater. I don't want you *getting used to me*."

"That isn't what I meant," he growled. "Stop twisting my words around."

Rhett got up and paced across the room. When he came back to the bed, his expression had softened.

"If not for you, then do this for me."

Rhett reached up and ran his fingers through her hair, combing the strands back from her face. Goosebumps covered her skin as his fingers brushed against the nape of her neck.

Her desire to look into his soul was growing stronger by the second, but she resisted.

"I wouldn't want you to break your rules for my sake," she said, unconsciously leaning into his touch.

"I've broken all of my rules for you," Rhett told her. He leaned closer. "And I'll never be sorry for it."

Liss's heart jumped at those words.

"You're really okay with it?" she asked, still uncertain.

"Yes." He took her hand and kissed her palm.

Slowly, as though afraid Rhett might change his mind, Liss lowered the walls she'd forced between their souls.

His emotions hit her with such a tidal wave of force the breath was knocked out of her. After so many days of silence, the deluge of emotions was almost too much for her to stand. It was pleasure and pain in equal measures. Her chest expanded with the strength of emotions pulsing from each of their souls. It was too much.

Rhett's arms came around her, and she realized she was shaking.

"Are you alright?"

His voice came from far away as emotion after emotion crashed against her senses. Love, frustration, desire, anger, *disgust*.

Liss sucked in a breath. Rhett was disgusted…with her…with what she was. She had known it before, but feeling the emotion on his soul, and with so much strength it was eclipsing the others, was more than she could bear.

"Rhett, Liss, I'm starving out here," Wilsean called. "Move it or lose it."

Liss jumped up from the bed, ignoring the wave of dizziness and tears threatening.

"Wait," Rhett said.

She was out the door before he could stop her.

CHAPTER 31

Rhett had hoped that sorting his soul would make everything that had been wrong with Liss disappear. She had eaten close to a normal-sized dinner, which he'd felt more relief about than he cared to admit, but she was quieter than usual.

To be fair, though, none of them had talked much. If Ciago had been with them, there would have been laughter, bawdy jokes, and probably at least a couple of half-dressed Extended women prancing in and out of Ciago's room. His absence hung heavily over him and Wilsean, and they were all preoccupied with what the next day would bring.

They'd planned as much as it was possible to plan for something with so many unknowns. All that was left to do was wait out the night and see what kind of force Nya would have for them in the morning.

Rhett looked at Liss, who was fast asleep on the bed beside him. He should have said something to her after dinner. But he'd been too overcome with disgust at himself to find the words to begin apologizing. He had been the one to make her sick, because he'd doggedly insisted on privacy from the one person who should have access to his every thought and emotion.

He'd hurt her, and it made him hate himself.

Even though he could use the rest, he stayed awake. It was the only way to hold back the nightmares about Liss's torture. He didn't need those images making him freeze and lose his chance of killing Jaikon.

Now that Gatria and her magic were gone, there was no question about who would be victorious in hand-to-hand combat when he and Jaikon faced each other. Without his invincibility, Jaikon was just a man with adequate swordsmanship skills. Their father had had good reason for naming Rhett the Chief Assassin over his legitimate heir.

Rhett had never been desperate for the feel of blood running down his dagger and coating his bare hands. He'd never wanted to see the light drain from a person's eyes. Until now.

As he stared into the dying embers of the fire, Rhett rolled his corresponder around on his palm. He watched the white smoke rise to the surface, swirl around as it searched for its other half, and then settle back down in empty defeat. Every time the smoke settled, Rhett felt a piece of himself chip away.

Liss breathed out a soft sigh and turned over in her sleep. Without waking, she reached for him. He let the corresponder fall onto the blanket so he could wrap his hand around hers. She nestled closer and leaned her head against his chest. Rhett marveled at how, even as she slept, she put the broken pieces of his soul back together.

✳ ✳ ✳

It was still dark when they locked up the tent and made their way to the wagon that was waiting for them and already humming with the Energizer's power. An Extended Tailor had outfitted it to look more like a grocer's cart, although the disguise wouldn't hold up if someone inspected the vehicle closely.

The wagon was easily twice the size of Liss's, but it still was just one wagon.

"Where are the others?" Rhett asked Nya, who was standing in the wagon's doorway.

Nya had two full quivers strapped across her back, and Rhett had to admit she looked every bit as lethal as Wilsean.

"We'll only be needing a single wagon," she replied.

"Hundreds of slaves won't fit into a single wagon," Rhett said, annoyed at having to point out something so obvious.

"That's what I'm for," said an Extended girl who looked like she was a few years younger than Rhett.

The girl gave Rhett a hostile look as she said, "I can turn everyone pixie-sized by touching them." She gave the wagon a critical look. "It won't be the most comfortable ride back, but everyone will fit."

Since Rhett wasn't interested in the girl demonstrating her Extension on him, he turned toward the thick, soupy fog that was wafting out of the wagon. It filled the air and shielded the wagon in cloud of mist.

An Extended woman with spiky orange hair came out of the wagon. Fog billowed from her fingertips. She parted her lips, and more fog poured out of her open mouth.

The fog rose, thickened, and expanded. Unless someone looked closely, it would appear as though a low-hanging mist was blowing in. Anyone curious enough to investigate the wagon would have to come within killing range to get a good look at the vehicle.

Controlling any aspect of the weather required a great deal of power. Rhett was gratified to think that there might be more Extended like this girl who had slipped past Jaikon's notice.

"Where's the rest of our team?" Rhett asked.

It was too quiet for there to be enough other people waiting inside the wagon.

Nya gave him an inscrutable look, and then motioned to whoever else was inside the wagon.

Four Extended straggled out to join the Shrinker and Fogmaker. Rhett recognized one of them as Jema's father, the Energizer who was powering the wagon. He didn't know the other three.

He waited for more people to come out of the wagon, but no one else emerged. Six Extended stood in front of him. That was all.

Rhett looked at Liss, whose eyes were wide as she peered around the tiny group, looking for the rest of a team Rhett knew wasn't coming.

"Mom—" Liss began.

"I said we needed a team," Rhett grated out. "Unless one of their Extensions involves an ability to make more of themselves, then this isn't going to be good enough."

"They're the only ones who would come," Nya said, giving her daughter an apologetic look. "I asked everyone. I've been trying to convince the other caravan leaders all night." She gave them a tired shrug. "No one else is willing to leave the hideout."

Rhett saw fatigue written into the lines of Nya's face. Her orange eyes were dull, although she was trying not to let Liss see her exhaustion.

For several seconds, no one spoke.

"Mari's brothers wanted to come, but then the camp would be left without any Fighters," Nya continued. "And with so many Extended in the hideout, I can't leave it unprotected."

"What about Fighters in the other caravans?" Wilsean asked.

Nya rubbed at the back of her neck. "There are no other Fighters. The ones from my own caravan are all that's left since Opal Slayer started hunting them."

Liss looked like she was trying to catch her breath. Wilsean raised an eyebrow at Rhett.

"Well, then, what are their Extensions?" Rhett asked, channeling Stone's inner stoniness so he didn't succumb to the remorse and shame that had no business being in his head right now.

"I—I'm an Aromatic," the first man stuttered. His nose wiggled…whether it was an unconscious twitch or part of his Extension, Rhett didn't know. He was a small man with a bald patch on his head. His opal skin shimmered as nervous sweat beaded and darkened his stringy orange hair.

The Aromatic fumbled the Lagonian sword in his hands and dropped it, almost impaling his foot in the process. He yelped.

"Oh hell," Wilsean muttered.

Samara cleared her throat. Liss was staring slack-jawed at the pathetic man. Rhett seethed quietly.

"You can…smell things?" Liss asked the Aromatic.

The man's nose wiggled.

"We're n-not like p-people with Extended hearing. We're b-better."

"Can you smell someone to death?" Rhett bit out. He couldn't help himself.

Liss kicked him. "You're not helping," she whispered.

"Nothing's going to help him," Rhett muttered back.

The Aromatic put his trembling hands on his hips. "Smell is the r-richest sense. I can tease out the scent of a person."

As the man's excitement and pride in his ability increased, his stutter fell away.

"I can tell what you ate for dinner and who you slept with." His gaze moved from Samara and Wilsean to Liss and Rhett, as though to prove his point. "I can also make people think they're smelling things they aren't."

The air around them filled with the heavy scent of melted chocolate.

"Yummy," Samara said, sniffing the air.

Wilsean smacked a hand to his forehead. Rhett resisted the urge to punch the man.

"And what's your Extension?" he demanded to the elderly man beside the Aromatic.

"I'm an Air Extended." The man gave Rhett a defiant look, as though daring him to question the usefulness of his Extension. "And the only reason I'm coming is because my sister is imprisoned in Lagonia. I want to make it clear she is the *only* reason I'm coming. I'm not a do-gooder by nature."

"Noted," Rhett ground out.

"Are you like a Wind Extended?" Liss asked hopefully.

Rhett had never heard of an Air Extended, but he knew Winds could manipulate air currents. If the man had that ability, he might be able to fly the group of Extended slaves right out of Lagonia.

"My sister is a Wind Extended." He gave Liss a disgusted look. "I'm an *Air* Extended."

"Meaning?" Rhett demanded. They didn't have time for this nonsense.

"I can manipulate the chemical components of the air. I could suck out the oxygen from your bodies and kill all of you here and now. Or, I could infuse the air with so much carbon monoxide you'd all choke yourselves."

"Okay, that's useful," Wilsean said.

Rhett nodded.

"So glad you think so," the Air Extended bit back.

"You already know Jema's father," Nya broke in quickly. "He's going to power the wagon."

"And you?" Liss asked the last woman.

She looked about the same age as Nya, although it was difficult to tell in the dark and fog. Her frizzy orange hair was pulled into dozens of tight braids, and she had a scar that crossed her face and went all the way down her throat. Whatever had happened, the woman was lucky to be alive.

Rhett wondered who had done that to her. Had it been a slaver or one of his own soldiers? He wasn't sure he wanted to know.

"It's wonderful to meet you," the woman said, smiling at each of them, including Rhett and Wilsean. "My name is Keela, and I'm a Green Thumb."

"Are you the one who's making those crops grow in the field?" Liss asked, taking the hand the woman—Keela—held out to her.

"I am," Keela replied with an enthusiastic nod.

"You can't by any chance, um—" Liss chewed on her bottom lip. She glanced at the rest of the Extended before asking the Green Thumb, "Can you grow more of the opal contagion immunity flowers?"

"Oh." Keela gave Liss an apologetic look. "I'm afraid not. Those flowers are made from magic, and I only control plant life that is made naturally from the earth." Her expression brightened. "But I am quite skilled at cultivating foodstuffs, as you might have noticed from my vegetable gardens."

Wonderful. If anyone got hungry on the way, she could grow them a potato....

"Let's go," Rhett said before he lost his mind completely. "We'll work out how not to get everyone killed on the way."

CHAPTER 32

As their wagon hurtled along the road to Lagonia, Liss tried to ignore the way her stomach felt like a barrel of wriggling worms had gotten loose inside. Rhett and Wilsean looked as calm as statues. Liss was irritated to know their composure went soul-deep.

The rest of their group was as nervous as she was.

After Rhett finished telling everyone what their role would be, they all went silent. Everyone knew how high the stakes were. Hundreds of lives depended on them. If they failed, there wouldn't be a second chance.

"Stop the wagon," Rhett ordered.

Liss looked out the window, expecting to see nothing but murky fog. Instead, she saw the air ahead of them was clear. The Golden Bridge had just come into sight. Liss could make out the hundred archers standing on the bridge.

"My Extension isn't working," the Fogmaker said, looking both puzzled and alarmed.

"We're getting close to the border," Samara said in a quiet voice. "The Insorsil weather charm that protects Lagonia must be resistant to your Extension."

"Well that's just great." The Air crossed his arms and gave Liss a sullen look, like this new development was somehow her fault.

"What do we do now?" Liss's mom asked. "A few more feet will bring us into range. My aim's better than anyone on that bridge, but even I can't take down a hundred soldiers."

Without the extra cover of the fog, the Tailor's modifications to the wagon wouldn't be enough to fool the archers.

Liss saw the first sign of hesitation on Rhett as he exchanged a look with Wilsean.

The archers on the bridge weren't slavers or hired mercenaries. They were Lagonia soldiers, and Rhett wouldn't want to hurt them. But as soon as their wagon came into their view, he wouldn't have a choice.

"Ready your weapons," Rhett ordered Wilsean and Nya.

"Allow me." The Air smiled, but there was nothing pleasant about the emotions sweeping through his soul.

The man reached out his hand and then snapped it closed, like he was grabbing something invisible out of the air. From her vantage point at the window, Liss saw the archers on the bridge begin to drop. They clutched their throats and writhed on the ground.

"What are you doing to them?" Liss asked, aghast.

"Stole the air right from their lungs," the Air said with a self-satisfied smile. "They'll be dead in five minutes."

Liss didn't have time to blink before Rhett's blade was at the man's throat.

"Stop it," Rhett grated out. "Now."

The Air sucked in a breath. His orange-rimmed eyes emitted a fierce glow as he stared from Rhett to Wilsean.

Rhett's pupils dilated and all the color drained from his face. He clutched his throat. Wilsean doubled over as he began to choke, too.

Rhett raised his dagger even as he tried to breathe, but the Air darted behind the other Extended. Rhett's dagger clattered onto the floorboards as he sank down onto his knees.

"Let them go!" Samara cried.

Liss saw the Air's soul was full of loathing and a black sort of anticipation as he watched the men try to draw in a breath.

Pushing aside her own terror and fury, Liss shoved through the other Extended until she'd reached the man's side. In his ear, she said, "Let them go…let all of them go…or I'll make sure your sister never leaves Lagonia alive."

Hatred pulsed in the man's soul, but Liss didn't care.

Rhett and Wilsean both gasped in a breath. The archers on the bridge began to struggle to their feet.

"I'm holding you personally responsible for their well-being," Liss told the Air, motioning to Rhett and Wilsean. "If they don't come back in as good condition as I left them, your sister is going to be the one who pays the price. Do you understand?"

She would never let the Air's sister die, but this man wasn't a Soul Sorter. She kept a look of fierce resolve on her face and watched as a helpless acceptance warred with the hatred in the Extended man's soul.

"You are a disgrace to your own people," he snarled at Liss, as Rhett and Wilsean regained their breath. "You're foul. When you die at their hands, every Extended will look on and smile."

The man's searing hatred made her feel like all of the oxygen had been squeezed out of her lungs, too. She wanted to argue, but her own soul pulsed with uncertainty and guilt. She had threatened one of her own people to protect Lagonians.

"I c-can make them g-get out of our way," the Aromatic said, breaking the tension. "Without k-killing them," he added.

He went to the window. He stared out at the archers.

Rhett gave Liss a skeptical look and gripped his dagger. Wilsean readied one of his knives.

"Give him a minute," Liss said, not knowing what she expected this nervous Aromatic to accomplish that would be of any use.

A few seconds passed. The archers began to abandon their posts and run to either side of the bridge. They leaned over the railing as they vomited into the water below.

Rhett motioned to the Energizer to keep going. Even though their wagon was no longer shielded by the fog, not a single one of the archers looked their way when they reached the bridge. The soldiers were too busy puking over the railing to take a second glance at what appeared to be a grocery cart.

Liss's own stomach flipped at the sound of a hundred people hurling their guts up.

"How did you do that?" Liss breathed once they were safely on the other side of the bridge.

The Aromatic gave her a shy smile.

"A combination of spoiled cheese, d-dragon piss, and rotting corpses."

"Well, I'll be damned," Wilsean said, shaking his head.

"Oh, and d-dirty socks."

"Thank you," Liss told the Aromatic. She meant it. Not only had the Aromatic saved Rhett from needing to kill soldiers he cared about, but the alarm bell hadn't been sounded, which would buy them more time. The closer they could get to the palace before anyone realized they were in Lagonia, the better.

As soon as they were on the Lagonia side of the bridge, Liss felt the drastic shift in temperature. There was no longer an icy wind whistling through the wagon. Now, a soft breeze that smelled like sun and salt spray wrapped around her. Everyone else in the wagon was already shedding their jackets.

The weather was just another reminder of all the ways Lagonians were privileged over Liss's own people. The Lagonians lived a life of luxury, while the Extended starved and froze on a snowy plain. Disgust rolled through Liss.

Dawn was just beginning to creep over the horizon as the wagon rolled down the gem-studded cobble street. Since most Lagonians slept until noon, the only other people out and about at this hour had business of their own. No one gave their wagon a second glance.

Rhett directed Jema's father to stop the wagon near the abandoned training field where Liss and Rhett used to spend their mornings together. When Liss glanced at Rhett, she found him already looking back at her. He gave her a secret smile that made her insides warm.

"Air, you're with Wilsean and me," Rhett told the Extended man, who was muttering to himself about spoiled Lagonians. "You," Rhett pointed at the Energizer, "stay in the wagon and be ready to get everyone out. The rest of you will help Liss free the slaves. Any questions?"

No one spoke.

Discomfort wormed its way through Liss. This was what they'd discussed, but she wasn't happy about the idea of splitting off from Rhett.

Still, she knew it was the only plan that made sense. The longer they were here, the more chances they'd be giving their enemies to kill them. They needed to get in, do their thing, and get out.

While Samara and Wilsean were locked together in a tight embrace, Rhett led Liss into a quiet corner.

"Promise me you'll be careful," he said.

Liss managed a short laugh. "You're going to face down the Emperor and his fiercest guards, and you're worried about me?"

Rhett's immediate *yes* came without a trace of humor.

Liss took a deep breath. She forced herself to channel some of Rhett's outward calm.

"I'll see you in a couple of hours," she told him.

Rhett leaned down until their faces were only inches apart.

"You and I have unfinished business," he said in his husky voice. "I'm not going anywhere until things are right between us. And then, I'm definitely not going anywhere."

Liss gave him a nod.

"I want you to know I'm telling you the truth," Rhett told her.

She gave him a questioning look.

"Do it," he said.

So, she looked into his soul. She saw a burning hatred, which she knew was for Jaikon. She saw an even stronger love. *For her.* There was also determination and conviction. The only emotions that didn't seem to be in his soul were fear and uncertainty.

"Okay," she said, feeling oddly calmed by everything she saw inside him.

"Promise me one other thing," he said, brushing his thumb across her cheek. Worry flooded his soul.

"What?" Liss breathed.

"Even if you finish with the slaves before I get back, don't come looking for me. If I see you in the same room as Jaikon, I—"

Rhett cut himself off. He looked away from her.

When he turned back, there was a tortured expression on his usually-impassive face. "I can kill Jaikon and his men, but not if I'm imagining all the things they'll do if they get their hands on you. Please, just let me do this."

Liss gave him a shaky nod. "Okay."

Rhett exhaled in relief, clearly feeling a lessening of tension even as hers ratcheted up.

"Thank you."

He pressed a kiss to her forehead, and then he turned to take the flask of transfiguration potion Samara was holding out.

In the space of seconds, Rhett's appearance transformed just enough that he was no longer recognizable as himself. His nose was too big, his shoulders too narrow, and his hair too long. His black clothes turned into the black-and-gold regalia of the Lagonia guard.

Wilsean and the Air shared the other flask—the last of Samara's stock of magic potions. They both became variations of generic-looking Lagonia soldiers. Samara had said it would only last for fifteen minutes, but at least it would get them into the palace without turning too many heads.

Liss hoped.

"I wish I had more to give you," Samara said, fretting with the buckle on the satchel.

"We're going to be fine," Wilsean said, drawing her in for another kiss.

"And no detours to try and get more of the flowers," Rhett warned, looking right at Liss. "They're too heavily guarded, even for you. It's not worth the risk."

Liss nodded.

"Get going," Samara urged the men.

Rhett, Wilsean, and the Air jumped out of the wagon and headed for the palace.

Samara had said the Extended slaves were being kept in a pen—like animals awaiting slaughter—on the main training field. That was a mile away from the palace and nearly as far from where the wagon was parked.

"Everyone ready?" Liss asked, hoping her voice sounded steadier than she felt.

"Ready as we'll ever be," Samara answered.

"Ready." Liss's mom nocked an arrow and angled it out the wagon's open window.

Liss nodded to Jema's dad, whose opal skin glistened with sweat. He was used to working beside his wife, who had stayed back at the hideout with their daughter. Liss sensed a heaviness on the man's soul, like he was fighting off sleep.

Samara and Keela, the Green Thumb, stood next to Liss's mom as they looked out at the road. The Aromatic—who had said he was just called Arom when Liss had asked—sat on the wooden bench, rocking a little as he muttered to himself. The Fogmaker and Shrinker kept to themselves. After making it clear their help would only go as far as what they could accomplish from inside the wagon, they retreated to one of the other rooms and refused to talk to anyone except each other.

Jema's father slowed the wagon's pace so they wouldn't attract attention from the few soldiers who were out and about.

Their first test came when they heard the sound of raucous laughter. They had just reached Lagonia's historic quarter, where a group of men were playing a game—darts, by the looks of it. As the wagon came closer, Liss could tell they were slavers-turned-soldiers. The men were passing a pipe back and forth, which was likely the cause of their browned and rotting teeth. She tensed, tightening her grip on her knife.

"Hold your fire," Liss murmured to her mom.

As much as it grated on her to pass by these abominable men without killing them, they couldn't afford to draw that kind of attention to themselves. Not yet, anyway. For now, they were just a regular grocery wagon making their morning deliveries.

Nothing unusual to see here.

The men were so close to the wagon Liss could hear their conversation without straining.

"Not so handsome now, is you?" one of the slavers chuckled as he pulled darts out of an image tacked on the wall of the house of worship.

As the wagon passed the building, Liss got a good look at the poster. It was riddled with dart points but still recognizable.

It was a drawing, done in almost perfect likeness, of Rhett. Bold words printed beneath the image read: *Wanted. Former Chief Assassin Rhetteman Loniger, for treason and consorting with the enemy.*

Liss turned away from the slavers in disgust, only to realize that her mother was staring out the window. Her expression was twisted in horror.

"Lagonia's Chief Assassin?" Nya turned, and Liss recoiled at the emotions pouring from her soul. She'd never seen so much anger in her mother before.

"Mom," Liss began, and then stopped. What could she say?

"I allowed the Caravan Butcher into my wagon? Into our hideout?!"

"Ey, what're you shoutin' about so early in the morn'?" one of the slavers called. He reached for his weapon as he craned his neck to see into the wagon.

"Keep your voice down," Liss whispered to her mom.

The slaver marched closer.

"Go a little faster," Liss told Jema's father.

"Boys, somethin' funny about this here wagon."

The other slavers drew their weapons and joined the first.

"W-what do we do?" the Aromatic whispered. "I tried, but they d-don't mind bad smells."

"Not to worry," Keela said.

The Green Thumb lifted her hand, and a second later, the first slaver tripped on a root that had sprung up between the jewel-studded cobbles. The slaver sprawled onto the road face-first. His companions roared with laughter.

Still mocking their companion, the others came for the wagon. One tripped over a new upturned root. Another let out an un-slaver-like squeal when a rosebush on the side of the road struck out a thorny arm. The branch lashed the slaver across his face before retracting back inside itself.

"Them plants are bewitched!" the slaver yelled.

"I'm so sorry," Keela whispered as another slaver started hacking at the rosebush.

Liss assumed she was apologizing to the rosebush and not the slaver.

Keela's hand darted out. A root emerged from the ground and latched onto the man's ankles.

He howled.

He tried to run, but the vine held fast. The slaver fell to the ground.

Their wagon passed by just as more vines started curling around the man's wrists.

"Well done," Samara told the Green Thumb as their wagon picked up speed.

"Thank you, dear," Keela replied. She wiped sweat from her brow and glared out the window in the slavers' direction.

Liss sighed in relief.

Liss's mom grabbed her shoulder hard enough to hurt. "You didn't tell me Rhett was Opal Slayer!" There was a wild look in her eyes that Liss didn't recognize.

"Can we talk about this later?" Liss asked.

"Oh, you can guarantee we will," her mom replied.

Still glaring at Liss, Nya shot two arrows out the window in a motion so fast it was a blur. The slavers were too far away for any normal person to reach their target.

Liss saw four of the slavers fall dead as they writhed against their plant bindings.

"Go faster," Nya commanded the Energizer. "We're freeing our people and then getting out of here."

Liss tried to gather her scattered wits as the training field came into view. Her nerves turned to fury as she caught sight of the imprisoned slaves.

She thought she'd been prepared to see so many of her people crowded into one place. Too late, she realized nothing could have prepared her for this. There weren't hundreds of slaves; there were thousands. Liss realized she hadn't had a clue about how many Extended slaves were in the empire until this moment.

"Will you be able to fit all of these people in the wagon?" Samara asked the Shrinker, who was staring out the window as hatred rolled across her soul.

"Like I said before," the Shrinker replied. "It won't be pretty, but everyone'll fit."

The slaves were packed so tightly into the pen they couldn't even sit down. Their opal faces blurred together until it looked like there was a rainbow lake in the middle of the field.

The stench of feces and unwashed bodies assailed Liss's nose. Everyone in the wagon started to gag.

"I can fix that," Arom said with a shy smile.

A breeze wafted through the wagon, and with it, Liss caught the scent of freshly-baked sugar plum pie. She knew it wasn't real, and yet, it didn't stop her mouth from watering.

"You really do have the most amazing Extension," Keela told the man.

Arom's soul filled with pride even as he ducked his head in embarrassment.

"Look at all of those guards," Samara said, biting her nail as she peered out the window.

The guards surrounded the pen at ten-foot intervals. They each had a sword at their hip and probably half a dozen other weapons hidden beneath their dragonhide jackets. Liss peered into the souls of the nearest guards. They were vigilant, tense, and full of loathing.

Wonderful.

Even though there were enough slaves to overpower the guards, Liss could see that these Extended were too beaten and broken to try anything. Besides, even if they escaped, there was nowhere for them to go. The kingdom was surrounded by the mountains and sea, and the only direct way out of the empire was across the Golden Bridge.

Liss's soul ached as all of the slaves' hopelessness washed over her.

"I can make you small so you won't be noticed," the Shrinker offered. "Of course, then you'd be too tiny to do anything, and you'd probably break your neck just getting out of the wagon."

"Thanks anyway," Liss told her dryly before turning to Arom.

"Do whatever you have to do to cause a commotion," she told him. "I have to get close enough to look at the padlocks."

The Aromatic closed his eyes. Deep concentration radiated off his soul.

"Ho-ly hell."

The guard closest to the road covered her nose with the collar of her shirt. She gave the man standing nearest to her an accusatory look. "Your fart's a lethal weapon."

The other guard's face reddened. "That wasn't me, it was him." He pointed to the next guard down the line.

"Don't blame me, just because something crawled up your ass and died," the man retorted.

"He did it *again.*"

"It wasn't me, it was her!"

Liss heard the sound of weapons being drawn from their scabbards amid the arguing, which was getting louder and involving more of the soldiers by the second.

"*I* didn't eat a sack of onions like someone here clearly did."

"I told you all that milk would turn your insides rotten."

"Who on this shift just shat themselves?"

Liss couldn't believe what she was witnessing. The guards were about to come to blows…over a fart. She looked at Arom, whose eyes were bright with mischief.

While the guards continued to shout accusations and threats about the fart perpetrator, Liss studied the pen. The iron fence was wrapped with Insorsiled barbs. Liss had encountered the nasty little things on many of her thieving expeditions. She knew from personal experience that if they so much as grazed a person's skin, the barbs dug into flesh and festered.

Pushing down her fury and disgust, Liss forced herself to focus. There were four padlocks on the only part of the pen that wasn't covered in the barbs. The locks were complicated and beyond the skill of a common thief.

Fortunately, Liss wasn't a common thief.

"Once I get the pen unlocked, the guards are going to come after us," Liss told the others. "We're going to need to need to move fast."

"I'll take care of any guards who get too close," Nya said, running a hand down her bow.

"I can help with that," Keela offered.

"Alright," Liss said. "Arom, keep everyone busy until I get these padlocks open. Samara, you're in charge of getting everyone to the Shrinker without causing a stampede."

"Got it," Samara said, giving Liss a nod.

Liss took a deep breath and flexed her muscles. Then, she jumped out of the wagon.

CHAPTER 33

Burk sat on his rickety chair with the ambiguous fluid dripping down the stone walls. The same tiresome crowd was debating smell mitigation and solid waste removal.

He'd been so close to having it all…again.

The queen had signed his agreement. He'd even glimpsed the sumptuous rooms that would have been his as soon as that warlock, Krozor Ragnor Mantis, proved the veracity of Burk's claims by trying and failing to murder the queen.

Burk had been so close.

And then the disgraced Chief Assassin—who turned out to be the man Liss had betrayed her own people for—had killed the queen.

"How do you's feel 'bout collectin' them sewage worms to leave out for the birds?"

Burk met the gaze of the homeless man who had directed the question at him.

"Negatively," Burk replied.

The homeless man screwed up his dirty face, whispering the word back to himself as he tried to puzzle out its meaning.

Burk stared up at the green, jelly-like substance growing on the stone ceiling. His hearing picked up a myriad of shouting voices that must be coming from the training field he knew was above and to the west of the sewer. There was shouting, which even at this distance, hurt Burk's ears.

Among the unfamiliar voices, his practiced ears caught two voices he recognized.

What were Liss and Nya doing here? Had they been captured?

Perhaps Emperor Jaikon would allow him to watch their execution. He would love to see that even more than he longed for a bath.

Burk craned his head, trying to tease out their individual words amid the guards' shouting and the drone of the idiots surrounding his table.

Liss was blathering on about locks and hurrying. Burk got the idea they were trying to free the slaves, who were perhaps the only Extended in a more pitiful situation than himself. He reached for the bell hanging on the side of the wall—the one he'd been directed to use whenever a new and potentially useful thought occurred to him about the Extended. Because of the stipulations of the contract he'd signed with Jaikon, he'd had to humiliate himself by ringing the bell more than once these last weeks.

He hesitated before he yanked on the rope. From the tenor of the guards' shouts, he was sure the Emperor was already aware that a prison break was in motion. The contract didn't compel him to tell the Emperor something he already knew. Thus, Burk didn't need to say anything about the slaves.

As much as he wanted Liss and Nya to fail, he felt a distant sort of wish the slaves could escape. The Extended were still his people, even if he no longer had a caravan to call his own. He hated the Lagonians with every bone in his body, but the only ill will he felt toward his own people was reserved for Liss, who had landed him in his current position.

It would be a special sort of justice for the arrogant Emperor if the slaves got free right under his nose. Jaikon had been so intent on making a spectacle of their deaths that he'd been waiting to execute them until the last possible second.

Burk listened as Nya told a hysterical slave, "The far western edge of the Insorsiled forest, right before the tree fairy realm. It's warded. I promise you'll be safe."

A suspicion began to tickle Burk's nerves. His filthy hand inched toward the rope of its own volition.

"No," he groaned, fighting against the unconscious gesture.

Burk felt a straining inside him. He smelled ink and tasted it on his tongue. He felt ink tendrils wrap around his throat as the bargain he'd made with the Emperor came back to hold him to its provisions.

If Burk didn't tell the Emperor what he knew, he'd die for failing to uphold his part of the bargain. If he met the terms of the contract, all of the Extended would be in jeopardy. The small haven they'd built for themselves, which had been driving the Lagonians crazy for weeks, would be revealed. He would cause the deaths of thousands of his own people.

How many Extended risked their lives to come and rescue me? Burk asked himself as the Insorsiled ink continued to wind through his insides, curling around his throat and squeezing his heart.

Not one.

Should Burk give up his life, as pathetic as it was, to save others who had turned a blind eye to his suffering?

The ink was flooding his lungs. He choked on a substance he couldn't see but could feel in every crevice of his being.

You sacrificed everything for your caravan, he thought as he took a panicked, stifled breath. *The only one you owe loyalty to is yourself.*

Pain shot through Burk's chest. Clawing at his own throat with one hand, he grasped the rope dangling on the wall in his other. He gave it a mighty tug.

Even as the chime of the heavy bell made his ears ache, he felt the Insorsiled ink release him. It slithered away, back into whatever hidden place where it waited to claim him.

Burk was still gasping in putrid air when Jaikon's disgusting second-in-command loomed in the open doorway.

The man didn't speak. Instead, he grinned, displaying his horrid fangs.

The words were dragged out of Burk by a force he couldn't resist. If he wanted to live. Despite his despicable existence, living had become everything to Burk. It was all he had left.

He met the assassin's predatory gaze.

"Tell the Emperor I know where the Extended hideout is."

CHAPTER 34

Rhett led Wilsean and the Air through basement tunnels and narrow passages that snaked through the palace's walls. These spaces had been built in case an emergency ever required the Emperor to be ferreted out of the palace. Only a handful of people knew they existed.

Their Insorsiled appearances had worn off soon after they'd made it into the palace. The next time they showed their faces, they'd be recognizable as themselves. Any move they made would have to count.

He pushed down his fear when the alarm bells started to clang. He'd known this would happen as soon as the guards realized the slave pen was under attack. This was part of the plan.

Rhett kept his mind focused on his task, refusing to allow it to wander to Liss and to worry if she was alright. Liss knew what she was doing. He had his own job to do now.

He stopped when he reached the right door. He peered through a notch in the wood and looked into the corridor that led to the torture cage. As he expected, the Emperor was taking no chances with this prisoner. The corridor was filled with guards. Some of them were ones Rhett knew personally, and others were slavers wearing Lagonia livery.

His pulse sped up at the sight of Stone in the torture cage. Even with twenty-five guards separating them, Rhett could see his mentor was lying on the ground. He wasn't moving. It took all of Rhett's self-restraint to keep from barging in right then and there.

Stone wasn't likely to thank him if he botched the rescue by getting himself and Wilsean killed.

Steel doesn't know love or despair. It can't be bent or broken. It needs no heart or warmth. I am steel.

Rhett ducked back into the previous tunnel. It passed through the walls of the imperial library, which was empty more often than not.

"Is there anything you can do to get us past the guards without causing a fuss?" he whispered to the Air.

It was time for the Extended man to stop grumbling and pull his weight.

"There are too many people for me to control their individual air flow, but I can flood the whole place with carbon monoxide," the Air replied. "They'll be unconscious in a few minutes. As long as you can hold your breath long enough to get the prisoner out, you'll be okay."

"Can you make sure it won't kill anyone breathing the air?" Rhett asked.

The Air shook his head, looking more than a little pleased by the idea of Lagonians dying from carbon monoxide poisoning.

"The whole point of being down here is to get the prisoner out alive," Wilsean hissed at the Extended man.

Looking sulky, the Air released a long-suffering sigh. "I suppose I could infuse the air with nitrogen. It won't kill anyone, but it'll make them disoriented."

Rhett and Wilsean exchanged a look.

"That'll work," Rhett told the man.

Rhett led the Air back to the hidden panel that would bring them into the corridor that led to the torture cage. The Extended man stood on his toes until his mouth was level with the hole in the wall. Then, he blew out a breath into the corridor.

For several seconds, nothing happened. Then, the silent watchfulness in the corridor transformed.

First, there was giggling. A couple of the bigger guards just passed out. The rest stumbled around like they were drunk. Others were chattering nonsensically.

"You know what I just learned?" one guard slurred. She opened and closed her mouth several times like it was unfamiliar to her. "You're a boyyy." She poked another guard in the chest.

He looked down at himself. His eyes widened. "I am?"

When the first guard nodded, the man whooped and ran to the other end of the corridor. He knocked at least three people to the ground as he shouted, "I'm a boy! I'm a boy!"

Wilsean pushed Rhett aside. Covering his mouth with his hands to muffle the sound, he called through the chink in the wood, "There's a spoo-ky ghost in the torture cage. Run away. Run away!"

Shrieks and giggles filled the corridor as the guards fled. More than one was undressing as they ran for no discernible reason. Within seconds, the corridor was clear.

Rhett shook his head before taking a deep breath and pushing open the door. He ran to the torture cage, hearing Wilsean on his heels.

He bent to the lock. He used his dagger and pure brute force to break the lock open. He made a mental note to ask Liss to show him how to pick a lock properly later. It seemed like it would be a skill worth having.

"It's clean," the Air announced just as Rhett got the lock open. "You can breathe again."

Rhett inhaled a small breath, not fully trusting the Extended man.

Rhett let himself into the cage. Stone, who was lying on his side and facing the opposite wall, let out a groan. The sound was music to Rhett's ears. Stone might be in bad shape, but he was alive.

"Fuck off," Stone said, his words clipped like he was speaking through a broken jaw.

"Nice to see you too," Rhett replied.

Stone's body jerked, and then he was turning to look at Rhett.

Rhett winced. His mentor didn't just look injured; he looked like he'd aged a decade.

Rhett's guilt moved aside for anger. Jaikon had tortured Stone for the sole purpose of luring Rhett here.

"Damnit, Rhett," Stone rasped. "This is exactly what Jaikon wanted."

"Don't worry." Rhett bent down to lift Stone. "We have a plan."

Stone was a bloody mess, but his arms and legs were intact enough for him to stand on his own two feet. Rhett looked at his mentor and former guardian with respect. The man was tough as nails.

"Jaikon sent a thousand of your people across the sea," Stone said in a hoarse voice. "I tried to stop him."

"I know."

Rhett forced himself to maintain the emotionless façade Stone had instilled in him. He would never be able to make Jaikon suffer the way his soldiers would when they died by the giants' hands…if they ever made it to shore at all….

He was putting an end to all of this today, he reminded himself. Jaikon wouldn't be able to punish anyone else. He'd never lay a finger on Liss.

"I'm sorry," Stone rasped. "Rhett, I'm sorry. I should have realized how much you cared about Opal Smoke. I should have known you'd be stubborn enough to die for her."

"Wonder who taught him that stubbornness?" Wilsean mused.

Rhett was grateful for Wilsean, because his own chest had started to tighten. In twenty years, Stone had never apologized to anyone. Rhett least of all.

"I'm sorry I forced you all to choose between duty and friendship," Rhett said roughly, as unpracticed at apologies as his mentor.

He would make the same choice again and again, but he regretted the position it put his soldiers in.

"I would have done the same for Prescill," Stone said.

Mentioning his murdered wife was something else Stone never did.

Stone pulled Rhett to him. It was such a strange gesture coming from Stone that Rhett didn't at first understand what was happening. Once he did, Rhett returned the other man's embrace.

"This is beautiful, gentlemen," Wilsean said once he and Stone had let go of each other. He wiped a fake tear from his cheek. "But perhaps we should make some moves?"

Rhett slung one of Stone's arms over his shoulder, and Wilsean took the other.

"Where are you taking me?" Stone asked.

"There's a wagon," Rhett told his mentor. "It's going to bring you to the Extended hideout."

"And where are you going to be?" Stone demanded.

"I'm going to kill Jaikon."

"He's invincible," Stone said. "You know that."

"Not anymore."

Rhett and Wilsean filled Stone in as they wound their way through the tunnels that would bring them back outside.

As soon as he'd finished talking, Stone said, "Turn around."

"What?"

"I'm coming with you."

"Stone, you're in no condition to be fighting," Wilsean observed.

"Don't tell me what I can and can't do," Stone snapped. "I'm no invalid. I said I could fight. So, let me fight."

It was just like Stone to jump into a battle after he'd spent days in the torture cage.

Rhett knew it would be pointless to argue. Already, his mentor was shoving Rhett and Wilsean off with a force that shouldn't be possible for someone in his condition.

"Stubborn prick," Wilsean muttered.

"You know it," Stone shot back.

In spite of everything, Rhett couldn't help but grin. Just as quickly, his smile faded when he realized why the gnawing emptiness in his chest hadn't closed even though Stone was safe.

As though reading Rhett's mind, Stone asked, "Where's Ciago?"

Neither Rhett nor Wilsean spoke. It was answer enough. Stone's expression darkened, but he said nothing.

"You're going to make a fine emperor."

Rhett looked around, confused, before he realized Stone was talking to him.

"You must have hit your head," he said. "I'm not becoming emperor."

Even saying the words *I* and *emperor* in the same sentence was too ridiculous to bear considering.

"Don't be a fool," Stone said. "Not only do you have imperial blood running through your veins, you have your people's love. You're the *only* one they'll accept as their emperor."

In spite of the urgency of their situation, Rhett stopped walking. He looked from Stone to Wilsean.

"He's right," Wilsean said. "There were all sorts of secret meetings after you escaped the torture cage and before everyone knew Jaikon was invincible. People want you as their emperor, Rhett."

"This is insane," Rhett muttered. "We can talk about how I'm *not* going to be emperor after Jaikon is dead."

He couldn't think about this now. *He wouldn't.*

They got to the end of the passageway that would lead out to one of the palace's main hallways. Rhett bent his head to look out through a crack in the wood.

Normally, at this time in the morning, all of the advisors and courtiers would still be sleeping. But with the alarm bells still ringing, the whole palace was awake. The hallway was flooded with half-dressed courtiers and hired soldiers.

"Do that nitrogen thing again," Rhett told the Air, cracking open the door.

The Air blew out a breath through the crack. They waited in silence for an eternity, which in reality was less than a minute. When Rhett heard giggling and general pandemonium, he took a deep breath, indicating for the others to do the same, and pushed into the hall.

Stone managed to keep up without assistance as they jogged toward the throne room. Even without their illusions, no one paid them any attention. The courtiers were somehow even more ridiculous when their lungs were filled with nitrogen. Rhett passed by two of the Emperor's advisors who were spitting champagne into each other's mouths. A slaver was crawling on all-fours and howling like a wolf. No one so much as looked at Rhett or his companions.

They didn't stop until they got to the double doors that led to the throne room.

"Clear," the Air announced.

They all sucked in a breath. Rhett drew his dagger. Wilsean handed over two of his throwing knives to Stone before nocking an arrow in his bow.

"Get going," Rhett whispered to Wilsean, who was lingering at the entrance to the secret passageway beside the throne room that led out of the palace.

Wilsean needed to get to the dragon stables and steal a ride out of here for all of them. Now that they were about to split up, Rhett could see the hesitation on his friend's face. He knew Wilsean didn't want to leave this fight.

"I can handle this," Rhett insisted. "*Go.*"

"I've got your back," Stone added. "And this Extended man doesn't seem completely useless."

Rhett waited until Wilsean disappeared into the passageway. Then, he threw open the throne room doors.

CHAPTER 35

L iss couldn't believe their haphazard plan was actually working. She'd picked the locks so quickly she was impressed by herself. Keela and Liss's mom were keeping the guards from getting near the pen or the wagon. Nya shot arrow after arrow at the Lagonians, felling them before they could get close enough to hurt any of the Extended. Keela pulled roots out from the ground and wound them around soldiers' ankles. The field was dotted with squirming men and women. They hacked at their living bindings, which stubbornly re-wound themselves as soon as they'd been cut free.

If their situation was less dire, Liss would have sat back and laughed at the whole ridiculous scene.

Liss and Samara ushered the slaves out of the pen and toward the wagon. Arom was using the intoxicating smell of freshly-baked bread to keep everyone calm but moving as fast as they could. As each person stepped into the wagon, the Shrinker made them small enough that everyone would be able to fit.

Many of the slaves were too weak and frightened to be helpful, but there were some who wanted revenge as much as they wanted freedom. A few Flamers worked together to set one of the guards on fire. Other Extended joined Nya and Keela, using their abilities to keep the growing number of Lagonian guards away from them. Another Shrinker appeared out of the pen, and she helped speed along the process of getting everyone into the wagon. Two more Energizers offered to help Jema's father get them out of the empire as soon as everyone was in the wagon.

It took what felt like forever to empty the pen and for all the slaves to be shrunk and stuffed into the wagon. Samara and Arom were each supporting stragglers who were too weak to stand without help.

It was almost too easy. Liss didn't trust anything that worked out this smoothly. And yet, they seemed to be in the clear. There was nothing the Lagonians could do to these former slaves now.

"Come on," Samara said, motioning to Liss and her mom after everyone else was inside the wagon.

Nya jumped onto the wagon's stoop with a fluid grace Liss still wasn't used to seeing in her mom. Then, Nya pulled Keela up.

"Liss?" Samara asked.

"I'm going to go get our guys more immunity flowers. I'll meet you all back at the hideout."

The look that crossed her mom's face was terrible, but Liss couldn't worry about that right now. There would be time for explanations and apologies later.

"Rhett told you not to," Samara said aghast.

Liss gave Samara a shrug. "Sometimes thieves lie."

* * *

Liss waited a few more minutes to make sure none of the guards tried to follow the wagon as it sped back across the field and toward the bridge.

It passed dozens of guards who were still wriggling in their leafy shackles. The Lagonians who were on their feet were too slow to chase the wagon. In seconds, it was out of sight.

Liss turned in the opposite direction, heading for the palace. Since all of the guards had been dispatched to chase down the wagon, no one tried to stop her.

She reached the palace without incident. And yet, she was growing more uncomfortable by the minute. She couldn't explain why; she just knew something was wrong.

After all her time as a thief, she'd learned to trust her instincts.

Liss clutched her knife as a group of courtiers squawking like chickens came running toward her. She didn't stop to ask questions. For all she knew, it was a new game they'd come up with to stave off the boredom that came with too much money and comfort.

By the time she reached the palace, she was sweating.

Liss used the servant's hallways when she could, and ran through the surprisingly empty main hallways when she couldn't. She headed straight for the secret pantry where the immunity flowers were kept.

She took a shortcut through the soldiers' quarters, since she happened to know that most of the palace's soldiers were still wrestling against vine shackles out on the training field.

Her thief's sixth sense started to tingle when she heard voices coming from the guard tower near the Emperor's private chambers.

Liss slunk along through the shadows, using marble busts of emperors long-dead to hide her as she crept closer.

"What I don't understand is why he wouldn't make them look more impressive," a male voice complained. "Gold? Really? At least add some black diamonds."

"The Emperor told me the Insorsiled can only bewitch metals," a different man replied. "Besides, you know those magic folk have no taste when it comes to jewelry."

There was silence, and Liss caught the flash of metal as one of the soldiers tossed something up and caught it again.

"Does it really work as good as everyone says it does?" the first voice asked.

"See for yourself."

The piece of metal was tossed again. Liss slipped closer until a life-sized, solid-gold replica of Jaikon hid her while giving her a view of the two soldiers. The one who had just caught the tiny gold pin clipped it onto his dragonhide jacket.

"I must be an idiot for letting you stab me," he chuckled as he let his sword fall to the ground and stood to face the other.

Liss's heart beat faster.

They don't know the invincibility magic has been destroyed.

News traveled quickly between Insorsil and Lagonia, and Liss didn't know how these soldiers had managed to stay ignorant about the fact that the queen was dead.

Maybe they knew she'd been killed, but they weren't aware that the magic would no longer work once its maker was dead....

Liss saw the other soldier grip his sword as he made a joke about spraying guts. He marched forward. The other one just stood there, smiling like the world's greatest fool.

She squeezed her eyes shut, unable to watch as the unsuspecting soldier was impaled on his friend's sword.

When no horrified cries or squelching sounds came, Liss cracked her eyes open. Both men were still standing, very much alive, and without any guts spraying anywhere. They were chuckling.

What the—?

"What'd I tell you?" The man with the sword jabbed the other one in the chest. Or, rather, he tried to. A translucent blue shield spread out from the tiny pin fastened to the soldier's jacket. It continued to pulse until the other soldier lowered his sword. Then, the light retreated back into itself.

The hair on the back of Liss's neck stood on end.

Gatria was dead, but the invincibility magic was intact.

That meant Rhett was walking into a room full of invincible people. And he was the only one who could be killed.

Liss's panic had a viselike grip on her chest. Had Rhett already discovered Jaikon was still invincible, or was he on his way to the throne room at this very moment, unsuspecting of what awaited him?

Liss wasn't going to wait to find out.

As much as she wanted to run straight to the throne room, she forced herself to stay where she was. It wouldn't do Rhett any good if she showed up just in time to die alongside him.

Liss tiptoed back until she was standing just inside a servant's stairwell. She closed the door partway, so there was room for her to hide in the shadows. Then, she started to cry.

"Help," she said in the most damsel-in-distress tone she could muster. "Oh, please. Someone help me."

"Did you hear that?" one of the soldiers asked.

"In here," she cried, an octave higher than her real voice. "I need someone *strong* to help me."

She was laying it on a little thick, but the men's souls were haughty enough that she knew they'd come running.

They did.

"You could get hurt! It's—horrible," she called as soon as their footsteps came close.

"Don't you worry, darlin'," the soldier assured her. "I'm invincible."

Liss smiled to herself.

Not for long.

CHAPTER 36

Rhett threw open the throne room doors. He took the right half of the guards. Stone took the left. The Air stood against the wall, his orange eyes moving back and forth across the rows of soldiers.

Rhett didn't hesitate. He crossed the room and slashed his blade across the first guard's throat.

For the first time since he'd become a Lagonia soldier at the age of sixteen, his dagger failed him. It didn't slice through flesh. Blood didn't spray. Instead, the sharpened blade came up against an impenetrable, shimmering blue shield. Rhett was launched backward.

He hit the ground and vaulted back to his feet.

He didn't understand. Gatria was dead. The magic should have died with her. Unless—

Applause echoed off the cavernous ceiling.

"You really are as predictable as ever, Rhetteman," said the voice Rhett hated most in the world. "How many times have I told you? All that's needed to control a man is to find his weakness. And I have found your weakness."

Jaikon got off his gold throne and sauntered down the steps. He held his bejeweled sword loosely in his unmangled left hand. "I knew you'd buy my little yarn about the magic belonging to Gatria, just like I knew you'd come back here to save your guardian."

Rhett's training kept him from reacting to Jaikon's words, even as his mind spun out of control. The magic hadn't been Gatria's?

Impossible.

And yet, there was no other explanation for what had happened when he tried to stab the guard.

Rhett took stock of the room. Every man and woman was wearing a tiny gold circlet on their chest. Were some of them fake?

Only one way to find out.

Stone had the same idea. They attacked the line of soldiers from opposite ends. The soldiers stayed in place, not even raising their weapons. Some of them laughed. Others just stared at Rhett with mild interest as he tried and failed to reach them. It took tremendous effort not to be thrust backward by the force of the magic protecting the soldiers. His muscles burned as he tried again and again to drive his dagger home. In minutes, he and Stone were both heaving from the effort of trying to break through the blue shields.

These soldiers were invincible.

Jaikon was laughing so uproariously that he was dabbing at his eyes with the corner of his embroidered sleeve.

"Isn't it wonderful?" Jaikon asked as his chuckles subsided. "My warlock ally finally figured out how to enhance the pins so the wearer is protected from all injuries, and not just mortal ones."

Through his murderous rage, Rhett saw the soldiers spread out around the throne room until they were stationed in front of each set of double doors. They blocked off any chance of escape.

"I really must thank you," Jaikon said, finally getting a hold of his mirth. "Now that you've gotten Gatria out of our way, the warlock who actually provided me with this magic will be able to ascend to the Insorsil throne."

Jaikon smiled as Rhett's insides curdled.

"Just think," the Emperor said in a soft voice. "The most powerful warlock is my ally, and because I duped you, he is now in my debt for effectively gifting him with the Insorsil throne. This invincibility is just the beginning of all he will give me."

Rhett thought back to every action…every wrong assumption…that had led him to murder the Insorsil queen.

He hadn't questioned that slaver who said the magic belonged to Gatria. It had made sense…the Insorsil queen was known to be the most powerful among her people. Rhett had believed she was the only one who could create such potent magic. She had looked him in the eye and taken credit for creating the pins.

She lied, a hard, unsympathetic voice said in his head.

Rhett stood in the center of the throne room, surrounded by invincible enemies.

He gripped his dagger, even though it was useless to him. The only people in this room who could be killed were him, Stone, and the Air Extended.

"Now, I have you right where I want you," Jaikon said, coming closer. "I'm going to kill Stone first. Then, I'll let everyone in this room see how the great Rhetteman Loniger falls." Jaikon lowered his voice, like he was sharing a secret. "It's very difficult to be a martyr when your bloody, rotting head is stuck on a spike." His mouth twitched into a grin as he stage-whispered, "It's very undignified, especially when the crows start going for the eyeballs."

"Jaikon, you may kill us, but that will never make you the leader this empire needs," Stone said. "Only Rhett could ever be that man."

"Enough, Stone," Rhett said.

He knew better than to ask for mercy for his mentor, but he didn't need to hear Stone singing his praises when he had led him straight to slaughter.

"Is there anything you can do?" Rhett asked the Air.

The Extended man shook his head. "I've been trying to pull oxygen out of their blood. It should kill them, but it's not working. As soon as I draw it out, it comes right back."

There was nowhere for Rhett to sink his blade. There was no one to turn his fury on.

"Fight me, you coward," Rhett commanded Jaikon in a last, desperate attempt to salvage this disaster. "If you're the emperor Lagonia deserves, prove it. Take off your pin and fight me. Prove to your soldiers you're stronger."

"I've already proven I'm stronger." Jaikon's ice blue eyes glittered dangerously. "I outsmarted the once-beloved and now disgraced Rhetteman

Loniger. I won. And now, I'm going to have my vengeance for a lifetime of injustices…."

The Emperor's voice trailed off as a shudder went through the entire room. Rhett felt a great sucking, like all the air was being yanked out. He turned to the Air, whose face was glistening with opal-colored sweat. He was inhaling, pulling the air inside himself rather than blowing it out.

Some of the soldiers around the room cried out as chunks of the ceiling collapsed on top of them.

Of course, even hundreds of pounds' worth of gold, cement, and drywall didn't hurt the soldiers. The concrete bounced off the soldiers' translucent blue shields. The chunks crashed across the granite floor.

"What are you doing?" Stone demanded.

"Vacuum," the Air said, his voice breathy. "Taking in all the air."

Rhett felt like he was being compressed along with the rest of the room. Everything inside him was being squeezed. He couldn't breathe.

The ceiling stopped falling long enough for the Air, Rhett, and Stone to catch their breath.

"What are you all standing around for?" Jaikon roared. "Kill the Extended!"

The Air sucked in another great breath. A chunk of stone burst out from the wall. It skittered across the floor and bounced off Jaikon's shield. The stone split apart.

The soldiers were swarming around Jaikon, leaving the main entrance to the throne room unguarded. Stone saw it too, and was making for the exit. Rhett started after him before hesitating. The Air stayed where he was.

"Go," the Extended man ordered between breaths. "Can't keep this up…for long."

Rhett shook his head. He wasn't going to leave this Extended man behind. Rhett didn't leave people behind.

"Save…sister," the Air gasped.

Another block of ceiling crashed down on top of Jaikon. The pieces burst apart, leaving the Emperor unharmed. Rhett had to dive to avoid being impaled by a jagged piece of concrete.

He rolled to his feet in time to see two soldiers converging on the Air.

"Watch out!" Rhett called.

Out of habit, he threw his dagger. It pinged off the closer soldier's neck without making a dent and spun across the floor.

The soldier grinned.

"No!"

There was nothing Rhett could do as the soldier plunged her sword into the Air.

The Extended man fell without a sound. The soldier shouted in triumph as she drew her blade back out.

Rhett stared at the droplets of blood staining the marble floor.

Rhett's first thought was that he was going to have to tell Liss he'd let one of her people die. That thought was eclipsed by the reminder that he wouldn't be telling Liss anything, because his head would be on a spike and his eyeballs would be feeding the crows.

The ceiling stopped falling. All the pressure that had been sucked out of the room rushed back to fill the void.

"Your turn, Stone," Jaikon said in a soft voice.

Rhett took one step toward his mentor. He froze. His gaze was drawn to a door that was being eased open. It wasn't one of the main doors that led out of the throne room. This one had been painted over and appeared to be part of the wall. It was the passage servants used to deliver wine and food to the Emperor while he held court.

He knew who would walk through the door before he saw her. Rhett stumbled back. He was drowning…or maybe suffocating.

No one else in the room had noticed her yet, but they would.

Go, he silently begged her.

Liss wasn't looking at him. She was flitting between chunks of cement and other debris littering the floor as she made her way across the throne room.

Rhett's mind went hazy.

He saw blood streaming down Liss's chest. He saw Jaikon laughing as he wrapped a hand around her hair and yanked back her head, bearing her throat for his blade. He saw her head on a spike.

His legs failed him. He sunk to the ground. Bits of cement and scattered jewels cut into his knees, but he didn't feel them. He knew Jaikon was coming for Stone, but he didn't see that either.

All he saw was Liss.

"Stand up," Stone murmured to Rhett.

With an effort, he did.

"I want you to know that my only regret is that I won't live long enough to see you sitting on that throne." Stone spoke loud enough for Jaikon to hear.

The Emperor's face reddened. He readied his sword to cut Stone down.

"Hey, Jaikon," Liss called. "How's your right hand feeling?"

Jaikon went rigid.

Somehow, Liss had made it all the way around the room so she was behind Rhett. She wrapped her arms around him. She rested her hand on his heart for a few seconds before letting him go and coming to stand at his side.

"You promised me," he said, misery taking hold.

Liss looked up and smiled, showing off her dimple. "I lied."

Rhett's heart was going to explode.

"Well, Stone just earned himself another few minutes of life," Jaikon said. "I'm going to play with your whore first."

Feeling and sensation flooded back through him.

Rhett pulled Liss behind him. He backed up until she was sandwiched between him and the wall. He couldn't save her, but maybe if he died first, Jaikon would get less pleasure out of torturing her.

"I'm going cut off your legs so you can watch what I do to her from your knees," Jaikon said. "It's where you've always belonged."

Jaikon's sword slashed through the air. The blade was perfectly aligned to slice Rhett's legs off. If he moved, he'd risk the sword cutting into Liss.

Rhett stayed where he was and let the blade come.

CHAPTER 37

It had never before occurred to Ciago that a castle made out of ice could be warm and comfortable. Well, warm might be an overstatement. But the thick ice walls blocked out the vicious wind, which was the worst part about this frozen tundra. His furs were so warm he'd already shed his top layer. A giant-sized goblet of mulled wine rested on the table made out of ice in front of him.

Everything was ice. His chair—which was far more comfortable than an ice chair should be—was ice. So was the chess board and its pieces on the table before him.

Aside from when he first arrived and the giants tried to bash his head in with a stone mallet the size of a grown woman, Ciago had few complaints. If only the wolves would leave, he'd really be in business.

White as the snow that covered the ground and as big as Ciago himself, the feral predators prowled through the ice castle. Their black eyes were the stuff of nightmares, and their fangs....

One of them was sitting in the corner now, watching him. It hadn't blinked once.

Ciago gave the beast a disinterested stare before returning his attention to the game board.

Nothing had gone according to plan. He hadn't found the Lagonian fleet before he washed up on shore. He hadn't been able to do anything he'd promised Rhett. Now, Ciago was just making things up as he went along, and trying to be patient while he waited for an opportunity to make his move.

Ciago gave the leader of the Giant Realm a devious smile as he moved his bishop into position.

"Checkmate," he announced.

Lady Winnowa Umbrog stared at the board and then up at him.

"No one has ever beaten me at chess before."

Ciago was starting to get used to the accent that had been almost incomprehensible to him when he first washed up on shore, more dead than alive. He still couldn't believe he was here now, alive and conversing with the most secretive leader of any land.

Ciago, and everyone else on his side of the sea, had been under the mistaken impression that the leader of this realm was a he-giant lord. Ciago had quickly been corrected.

There was no question about who the giants looked to as their leader.

Lady Umbrog had ebony skin that was a stark contrast to the polished ice wall at her back. Her wiry hair was cut almost as short as his own. Swirls and jagged line patterns had been shaved across her scalp. She was slightly larger and more muscled than Ciago. But compared to the giants standing at attention in every corner of the room, she was downright diminutive.

Ciago had been more than miffed to awaken from his hypothermic stupor to discover he was quite likely the smallest person on this entire continent. Even the fearsome humans who were native to this land were huge.

What she lacked in relative size, Lady Umbrog made up for in intelligence and cunning. Ciago suspected it was these traits that had helped her rise to the top of these ruthless people and maintain her position.

In the time he'd been here, Ciago had learned that Lady Umbrog was the daughter of a kindly giant woman and a ruthless human man who had grown up among the giants. Ciago had also learned that Lady Umbrog was a fierce and unyielding leader. The way of the giants was to crush the weak and hail the strong. If their leader showed even the slightest weakness, she would be pulled down from her ice throne and have her head bashed in with one of the enormous stone mallets the giants wielded instead of swords.

In his short time among them, Ciago had seen that punishment doled out twice.

"I've killed over less, you know," Lady Umbrog said, indicating the chess board.

"Nah." Ciago leaned back, grinning at the fearsome giant leader. "You need me for my wit and charming personality."

"Charming?" Lady Umbrog took a sip from her goblet to hide the smile threatening at the corner of her lips.

"And dashing good looks," Ciago added.

"I don't need another lover," the giant leader said.

"What do you need?" Ciago asked.

Lady Umbrog considered his question.

"There are no others in this land who are quick-minded enough to advise me. My giants follow orders, but they can't even make simple decisions on their own. I find myself desiring someone with whom I can discuss matters of grave import." She paused. Almost like she was speaking to herself, she added, "Perhaps, I desire a friend."

Ciago took the giant lady's hand in his and kissed her knuckles.

"I can be that," he said. He was almost surprised to find he meant it.

Ciago could imagine how isolating it must be for Lady Umbrog, an intelligent half-giant with everything to prove. Just today, she'd needed to talk a dozen giants out of going for a naked swim across the Brookgar Sea. Because *fun*.

The laws in this land were as harsh and unforgiving as the weather. Their general rule was to kill first and ask questions later. When he first washed up on shore, a giant as dumb as he was big—which was to say *very*—had almost bashed Ciago's water-logged head in with a mallet. Fortunately, Lady Umbrog had scented his giant blood, faint though it was, and ordered him to be brought to the ice castle.

Ciago still marveled at how he was alive at all. When he'd stared into the sea serpent's waiting maw, his life had flashed before his eyes. His last thought had been that he was failing his best friend.

That thought had been followed by irritation that Rhett's face should be the last one to go through his mind, rather than the three gorgeous women with whom he'd shared his final night in Lagonia. And then that thought had reminded him of the glass sphere weighing down his pocket.

In a desperate, last-ditch attempt to defend himself, Ciago had wrestled the corresponder free from his pocket. He'd thrown the corresponder into the sea serpent's mouth just as the beast widened its jaws to swallow him whole.

The corresponder must have gone straight down the creature's windpipe. The sea serpent had lurched, belched, and proceeded to make the most horrifying sounds Ciago had ever head. The beast had sunk back down into the depths, still writhing. Ciago didn't know if it had lived or died, but he had already prepared the tale of how he'd single-handedly slayed the monstrous sea serpent amid a frozen tempest. If that didn't get him laid when he got back to Lagonia, nothing would.

After dispatching the serpent, he'd begun to swim. He'd searched the foaming sea for any sign of the Energizer woman, but she was as lost to him as their boat.

He'd barely made it to shore himself. Since then, he'd been recovering from his near death and waiting for an opportunity to get off this sun-forsaken land. He needed to steal one of the giant's ships and get back out onto the sea, as unappealing as the whole business sounded. He needed to find the Lagonian fleet, if it still existed after that storm. He was hoping they'd gotten stranded on one of the islands between the two continents. Even now, they could be back on the sea, heading this way.

He had to get to them before they reached the shore and killed themselves on the giants' weapons. He had to get Rhett's army home.

"And what of you, Ciago the Wanderer?" Lady Umbrog asked. "What do you want?"

Wanderer. It was a name given to those who lived on this continent but didn't call the Giant Realm or its surrounding villages home.

"To be your friend, of course," he answered smoothly.

Lady Winnowa Umbrog sipped from her goblet as she regarded him.

"I find myself trusting you," she told Ciago, looking puzzled by the revelation. "I don't think I've trusted anyone since I was a giant lass."

Ciago took the hand she held out to him.

"I'm honored by your trust, Lady Umbrog," Ciago said, bowing his head over their clasped hands.

The giant leader smiled at him. "Call me Winny."

Ciago gave the giant leader his most charming smile.

"Hear that, Ulfrath?" Ciago asked, meeting the black eyes of the enormous white wolf sitting sentry beside the lady's ice chair. "Looks like you've got competition for your master's affection."

In a moment of pure fearlessness, Ciago reached out a hand to pat the wolf's paw.

He yanked his hand back just before it was bitten right off. The wolf slunk back into its corner with its hackles still raised and its teeth bared. And what teeth they were….

"Do not touch my dog, Ciago the Wanderer," Winny said, an amused half-smile on her face once again.

As Winny re-set the chess board, Ciago glared at Ulfrath and tried to still the impatient bounce of his leg.

"As soon as the storms calm, I will send more giants to the continent across the sea," Winny said, rolling a game piece around on her palm. "The spy I sent returned without success."

Ciago tried to keep a straight face. The words *giant* and *spy* didn't exactly mix in his mind.

"Are you referring to Grub?" Ciago asked, remembering the name Liss had said when she described the giant she'd encountered in the Insorsiled forest.

Winny raised a thick eyebrow. "You met him, then."

Ciago didn't bother correcting her.

"What is it you hope to gain across the sea, Lady?" he asked, measuring his words. He knew a single wrong step would have a human-sized mallet coming at his face. "Riches? Conquest?"

Instead of answering, Winny rose from her seat. For a woman of her size, her movements were graceful. Her fur cape billowed behind her as she swept through the icy chamber, motioning for Ciago to follow her.

The wind cut through their furs as they stepped out of the ice castle. For several minutes, the only sounds were the punishing wind and the snow crunching beneath their iron-studded boots. Ciago's gaze kept going to the shoreline and the moored giant ships. He needed to get on one of those boats. He had to get out of here and find his people.

For now, though, there was nothing he could do. Ulfrath and another white wolf stalked along on either side of him, and he was fairly certain they weren't there for his protection. Winny's giant guards, who were slow to speak and quick to kill, flanked her. They were massive, close to double Ciago's size. Ciago made a mental note not to give them cause to look twice at him.

If he was going to get out of here with a boat and his skull intact, he'd need to wait for the right opportunity.

Winny led him toward a cluster of smaller ice shelters that looked far less inviting than the castle.

Giants sat hunched over animal pelts as they tried to coax a fire to life in the ceaseless wind. Some of them gnawed on large, bleached bones. Others stared morosely out at the churning waves.

"My people are dying," Winny said.

Ciago frowned. The giants didn't have enemies on this side of the sea, since no one was strong enough to challenge them. Disease wasn't a problem, because—

"I thought the giants couldn't get opal contagion," he said.

"Giants, no. Our humans, yes," Winny replied. "But opal contagion is not what is killing us now."

As they walked among her people, Winny told Ciago about the misfortunes that had befallen their realm. Ciago was aware that animal hides had fallen out of style on his side of the sea, and that the once-coveted furs that had been regularly imported into Insorsil had effectively become worthless. What Ciago hadn't known was that animal furs were the only resource the Giant Realm possessed. The pelts the giants prepared and wove into fine garments used to bring in enough wealth to import all of the food, weapons, and supplies that couldn't be made in this barren wasteland. But when the income from their only export dried up, so did their means of subsisting in this land.

"We only wish to survive," Winny told Ciago. "But for giants to live, we must leave this land behind. For giants to live, humans must die."

"So that's what Grub was doing on our side of the sea?" Ciago asked, fitting the pieces together. "You sent him to find a piece of land where you could settle?"

"It was a foolish hope," Winny replied softly. "There are no unoccupied territories on your side of the sea that are large enough, and we do not have the strength to take the land by force."

Ciago stared at a giant lad who was gnawing on a strip of dried meat. The beginnings of a crazy idea entered his mind.

It was insane. Stone would give him that scornful look and mutter something about *fanciful thinking*. Wilsean would laugh in his face. Rhett would just do his brooding thing.

And yet....

"Hey, Winny," Ciago began.

The giant leader wasn't paying attention to him, though. A horde of giants were running toward them, with their enormous wolves bounding at their heels. The ground underfoot trembled with the force of their strides.

"Trouble," Winny called over her shoulder before going to meet her people. Ulfrath and the giant guards went with Winny.

For the first time since he'd arrived in the Giant Realm, Ciago was left alone.

He glanced at the group of giants, who were shouting and gesturing. None of them were paying attention to him.

He might not get another chance.

With one more glance over his shoulder, Ciago started walking away from the giants. He cut straight toward the harbor and the nice little ship he'd had his eye on for the last day. It would be difficult to manage alone, but not impossible.

He broke into a run.

Ciago heard shouting behind him. He didn't look back. He slipped on a patch of ice before righting himself and continued his mad dash for the water.

A white blur came out of nowhere and overtook him. Ciago skidded to a stop as he came face-to-face with a snarling white wolf. It was so huge its eyes were at the same level as Ciago's.

Ciago put up his hands in what he hoped was a submissive pose and started backing up.

Snarling at his back had him halting again. He turned to see two more white wolves, growling and spitting. Their heads were lowered like they were about to charge him.

The wolves surrounded him. They prowled in a circle, nose-to-tail, keeping Ciago locked in their center.

"Oh, good," Ciago said in relief as Winny and her retinue of giants approached. "I think it might be time to feed your wolves—"

The giants were grunting and gesticulating in his direction. He couldn't understand a word they were saying, but the way they shook their mallets in his direction defied the need for spoken language.

Lady Umbrog—Winny—gave Ciago a wounded look. Then, the wolves stopped their prowling long enough for two massive giants to enter the circle with Ciago. One grabbed Ciago's bicep. The other kicked his legs out.

Ciago's knees hit the frozen ground. The giants' guttural cries and flailing mallets were more than enough incentive to keep Ciago from trying to break their hold.

The wolves snarled. The giants roared. A group of them had begun chanting a war song Ciago recognized from the Giant War. It sent a shudder down his spine.

As they sang, the giants pounded their mallets against the frozen ground and beat their muscled chests.

With the giants, showing fear or vulnerability was as good as an invitation to get killed. So, Ciago did the only thing he could. He puffed out his chest and scowled up at the giant leader.

"Winny, what is this?" Ciago demanded.

At the use of that name, one of the giants dealt Ciago a crushing blow across the back of his head.

"No ally," it bellowed. "Kill with all the rest."

Ciago's head swam, but those words struck him as important.

All the rest.

"There was a strange scent on you when you arrived," Winny said, all traces of good humor gone. "My people couldn't identify it with the other smells of sea foam and storm clouds, but now, I understand."

Ciago found himself comprehending precisely how this giantess had become ruler of such a brutal people. When he'd played chess with her, the giant lady's human nature had shone through. Now, she was pure giant.

Ciago didn't need a translation for the word the giants spit out in time with their mallets striking against the frozen ground.

"Kill, kill, kill!"

Veritable craters were left behind with each stroke of their mallets. Ciago couldn't help but imagine what his body would look like after a single strike from one of those weapons.

"Lady Umbrog, I don't understand," Ciago began.

One of the guards grabbed Ciago by the back of his neck and forced his head to turn.

Through the gaps between the giants' slamming mallets and the wolves' bristling fur, Ciago caught sight of the fleet. The ships were battered and sea-torn, and yet, there was no mistaking the gold and black sails. A war horn rang out from the first ship.

"Lagonian." Winny spit out the word. Her giants and wolves growled in response.

"Listen to me," Ciago said. "It's not what you think."

"They are your soldiers, are they not?" The giant leader's voice was a dangerous hum amid the striking mallets and bared canine teeth.

"Yes, but—"

"You led them here to kill us."

"No." Ciago tried to get to his feet, but the guards kept him on his knees. "Please, let me explain."

"Prepare for battle," Lady Umbrog commanded the giants, who were already lining up along the frozen shore. They wielded enormous bows and arrows in addition to their mallets.

So many, Ciago thought dazedly as he stared at the enormous giant ships. The storm-torn Lagonian fleet wouldn't stand a chance against them.

Another horn cry echoed from the Lagonian ships. Ciago could see the glint of swords and shields as the soldiers prepared for a battle that wouldn't be a battle at all. It was going to be a massacre.

"Wait," Ciago pleaded as the giant lady accepted an enormous mallet.

The giants' war cry reached a fever pitch. He could barely hear above their chanting and chest-pounding. The first of their ships was already heading out to meet the Lagonian fleet. Soon, it would be joined by others.

"Prepare yourself, human," Lady Umbrog told Ciago. "You will be the first Lagonian to die."

CHAPTER 38

Rhett felt the whoosh of air as the blade sliced through the air. He felt it stutter as it came up against an impenetrable barrier. A blue light radiated out from his chest and filled the air around him with an unnatural warmth. Jaikon topple over backward, his black-and-gold robe flipping over his head.

"Guess you're not the only one who's invincible," Liss called out.

Rhett pushed aside the flap of his jacked and stared down at his chest. In the place where Liss had touched him was a gold circlet pinned to his shirt. He turned around to gape at her.

Liss winked.

A furious shout came from somewhere nearby, but Rhett was busy marveling at the fact that his legs were still intact.

"You bitch!" Jaikon screamed.

"And you're jealous," Liss shot back, as fearless as ever. "You've been jealous of Rhett your whole life. I can see it on your soul."

Rhett caught her hand and pulled her toward the servant's hallway, motioning for Stone to go ahead of them.

"You want everything Rhett has," Liss continued. "But you'll never get it."

Jaikon's face turned purple in his rage. Rhett used his own body to shield them from any attacks from the soldiers in the room.

"Seize them!" Jaikon shouted. "Kill them!"

"Go," he told Stone and Liss. "I'll hold them off."

Jaikon's sword crashed against Rhett's dagger.

Neither of them could harm the other, but it didn't stop them from circling each other. Rhett might not be able to kill the Emperor, but he could shame him in front of his invincible guards. He could show them what kind of man they'd chosen as their leader. He was so fixed on his opponent that it took him half a second too long to realize where the shadow stretching across the wall was coming from.

Elouicia loomed in the opening to the servant's hallway. He raised a spear with a wicked, barbed tip.

Parrying with Jaikon had brought Rhett to the other side of the throne room. He smashed his dagger against Jaikon's sword to drive him back. Then, he ran. He shouted himself hoarse as he sprinted.

Both Liss and Stone were busy with invincible guards who were trying to stop them.

As Rhett's dagger came up against another sword in his way, he glanced at Liss. His eyes passed over her one, twice. There was no gold circlet on her shirt.

Rhett's stomach plummeted. He'd assumed she had one for her herself. But as a sword drove straight for her and sliced her shoulder, no blue light erupted. No shield came up. Her sleeve tore and red blood blossomed.

Liss wasn't invincible.

Three men moved in, blocking Rhett's dash for Liss. He whipped his blade, frantic to get past them to reach her. The translucent shields made it impossible for him to make any headway, though. The blue light blasted him away rather than toward her.

A furious roar bellowed out of him.

The guard who had cut Liss got his arm around her neck. Her knife fell to the ground as he tightened his hold on her throat. She struggled, but the man who held her was easily twice her weight. He was also wearing dragonhide, so he didn't even feel it as she threw her elbows and stomped on his booted feet.

Rhett ripped the pin off his shirt. Liss's arms were pinned to her sides, so he threw the pin to Stone instead.

His mentor was closer to Liss than Rhett, but he wasn't close enough. *Too late. Too late.*

Stone reached up a hand to catch the tiny pin. Another soldier barreled into Stone, and the pin fell onto the floor. It slid across the marble and disappeared from sight.

Elouicia raised the spear in his hand.

"No!"

Elouicia smiled his wolf smile at Rhett, turning his body so his spear was aimed directly at Liss.

He threw the spear.

Rhett couldn't get to her. The spear's aim was true—Rhett could see that from where he stood. The gleaming point was going to cut straight into her heart. Liss was locked in place and could do nothing to protect herself.

He couldn't save her.

Through his panic, Rhett saw Stone shove one guard aside as he jumped into the air.

The spear impaled Stone's chest, in the exact same place it was supposed to strike Liss.

Rhett reached Stone just as he began to fall. The spear had gone straight through Stone's chest. The barbed point stuck out of his back.

Rhett caught Stone before he hit the ground.

The double doors to the throne room burst open beside them. Rhett had just enough presence of mind to see it was Silverbird, with Wilsean on her back, snorting and tossing her head.

Get Liss out of here, he wanted to tell Wilsean, but his throat wouldn't work. Blood was gushing around the wound in Stone's chest. Rhett's hands were covered with it.

Rhett lifted Stone in his arms, careful not to jostle the spear. The barbed point would do more damage if it got pulled back through Stone's chest. They needed a witchdoctor.

"Come on!" Wilsean yelled.

Dust fell from the rafters as a man with opal skin appeared out of nowhere. Dimly, Rhett recognized the man as the Runner he'd locked in the torture cage, whom Liss had broken free.

"I'll distract them," the Runner called, his legs moving so fast they were a blur. "You all get out of here."

Rhett saw the Runner racing around the guards, Jaikon, and Elouicia. He made a human tornado, blasting the guards and Jaikon across to the other side of the throne room through the sheer force of his speed.

Rhett lifted Stone up to Liss and Wilsean, who were already on Silverbird's back. Rhett climbed on last.

While the Runner was still racing around the invincibles, Rhett raised his dagger. He pointed it first at Elouicia and then at Jaikon. He let them see his promise of vengeance as Silverbird wheeled around and plowed back through the rubble.

CHAPTER 39

Rhett knelt on the frost-covered forest floor beside his dying mentor.

Silverbird, Wilsean, and Liss stood a short distance away. The only sound was Stone's ragged breathing.

Rhett wanted to scream at whatever turn of fate had caused this new horror. He wanted to beg his mentor to pull through this. If he thought it might change anything, he would have.

But he'd seen enough soldiers die to know Stone was beyond help.

"I'm sorry," Rhett said. His voice was so raw the words were barely audible.

"I'm not."

Stone's blood-tinged gaze slid to Liss, who was standing beside Silverbird with a horror-struck expression on her face.

Rhett understood what his mentor was telling him in that single glance. Stone had meant to give his life for Liss's, and he had no regrets. He'd sacrificed the only thing he had left to save the person Rhett cared about most.

There was an invisible noose around Rhett's neck that kept him from uttering a single word.

"Prescill would…have been…proud," Stone whispered.

His pained expression softened. Stone's hand found Rhett's. And then, his chest went still. He stopped shuddering. The wheezing sound from his lungs cut off.

From somewhere nearby, Liss gasped.

Rhett lowered his head until his forehead rested on Stone's still chest. The forest rang with his muffled, inhuman scream.

* * *

Rhett was numb. He heard Liss and Wilsean's comforting words without processing them. He felt Liss's hand in his, but even that wasn't enough to banish the bone-deep cold.

Rhett used his dagger and bare hands to claw a shallow grave in the frozen earth. Liss and Wilsean helped, the three of them working side-by-side in silence. The only sound was the scraping of their blades against rocks and ice, and Silverbird's snorts.

After Stone was in the ground, Rhett kneeled beside the freshly-turned earth. On the flat rock Wilsean had placed on top of the grave, Rhett carved the words Stone had taught him when he was a child. He wrote the words that had been true about Stone until the end.

Steel can't be bent or broken.

Once it had been etched onto the granite, Rhett had no more words left to say. So, he just sat there as dusk turned to dark.

Wilsean was the first one to break the silence.

"You know what Stone would be telling you to do right now," he said, putting a hand on Rhett's shoulder.

Rhett blinked through the haze of his grief.

What would Stone say?

He'd tell Rhett to stop mourning, for starters. He'd gripe that Rhett had his back to any enemy who might see fit to sneak up on him. He'd tell Rhett he was a fool for sitting in the forest instead of finding shelter from the cold. But after that?

Stone had believed Rhett would become the new emperor.

"There's a warlock in Insorsil who controls this invincibility magic," Rhett said. Every word took more energy than he had, but he forced them out. "I'm going to kill him, and then I'm going to kill Jaikon."

Wilsean nodded.

"And then, I'm going to become Lagonia's emperor."

CHAPTER 40

Liss stood next to Silverbird as Rhett grieved, feeling more useless than she ever had in her life. It shattered her soul to see Rhett in so much pain when she could do nothing to help him. Worse, the reason why Stone was in the ground now was because he'd sacrificed himself to save her.

Liss had hated Stone for the scars covering Rhett's chest and back, but she'd also understood there was a deep bond between the two of them. Now, that bond was shattered.

Wilsean got on Silverbird's back. The usually-placid dragon was stomping her feet and snorting to get Rhett's attention. Silverbird huffed in offense when she wasn't rewarded with any pets or gold nuggets.

"I need to get this dragon something to eat after that sprint," Wilsean said, since it was obvious Rhett wasn't ready to leave. "The hideout is only an hour's walk, so I'll see you back there."

"Do you want me to go with him?" Liss asked Rhett, her voice barely above a whisper.

She almost expected Rhett not to say anything at all. He'd been so silent for so long, she didn't think he was even aware of anything outside of his own mind.

"No," he said, catching her hand as she turned to leave. "Stay."

So, she did.

Liss waited until the sound of Silverbird tramping through the brush disappeared before she knelt by Rhett's side.

A cold breeze stirred through her jacket. Liss shivered. Their Insorsiled closet had picked out warm clothes for both of them before they left the tent, but the temperature was falling fast now that the sun was gone.

"You're cold." Rhett's gaze remained fixed on the new grave as he took off his own jacket and put it around her. Then, he drew her against him.

She didn't try to insist he keep the jacket for himself. She had seen the look on his face in the throne room when he thought she was going to die and he could do nothing to protect her. She'd brought his nightmare to life in those moments, even though she'd done it to save him.

"I'm sorry," she told him, even though she knew the words would never come close to mending what was broken inside him. "Rhett, I'm so sorry. I should have—"

Done something, she wanted to say. While she watched Rhett grieve over Stone, she'd thought of a hundred different ways she could have moved, acted, reacted…a hundred ways the outcome of their failed venture could have turned out differently.

Rhett looked at her. His eyes were bloodshot but dry. When he took her hands in his, she felt the frozen dirt and blood embedded in his palms.

"If it hadn't been for you, Stone and I would both be dead. You're the only reason I'm still here now."

His words rang with truth, but she couldn't help feeling like she'd failed him.

"I know you've never liked Stone because of the way he raised me," Rhett said, staring at the fresh mound of dirt. "But Stone was a father to me in every way that mattered."

"I know."

Tears burned Liss's eyes. She forced herself to speak the words that were sticking in her throat. She owed Rhett the truth.

"Stone had almost made it out of the throne room when he came back to take that spear. If it hadn't been for me, Stone would have been able to escape." Liss couldn't look at Rhett when she spoke the words. "If I'd done things differently, it would have been me instead of him—"

"Don't." Rhett's grip on her hands tightened. "Don't even say it," he rasped.

Liss bit her lip, trying to hold back the tide of emotions threatening to overwhelm her.

They were both silent for several minutes.

"Do you know why Stone did that?" Rhett asked, his voice a harsh whisper.

"He did it for you," Liss answered.

"Yes." Rhett put his hand on her cheek, turning her face so she had to look at him. "Stone is my family, but you—" He looked away. He swallowed before returning his piercing gaze to her. "Stone knew I couldn't live without you."

Liss recoiled.

"Don't say that." She started to pull away from him, but he tightened his hand around hers.

An old, familiar fear began to slither down her spine. She'd seen what happened to people who existed for the sake of another. Her father had died, and her mother had nearly done the same. Their souls had been so intertwined they had been willing to do anything…including sacrifice their own lives…for each other.

"You have to live," she choked, unable to hold back the tears that were now spilling down her cheeks. "That's what matters most."

Rhett shook his head. "I need you."

Liss wrenched her hand free from his. All she could think about was Rhett's diminishing supply of immunity flowers.

"We're going to get more contagion immunity," Rhett said, as though he could read her mind. "We're going to find a way into that underground cavern where the queen hid them. It's going to be fine."

Liss needed to distract herself from the way her hope swelled at Rhett's words.

"Even if, by some miracle, you get enough flowers to last you a lifetime, we don't have a future together," Liss said.

The words almost crushed her to say out loud, but they needed to be said. The chances that they could actually get into that cavern and find more of the immunity were slim-to-none. Rhett was just stubborn enough that he might choose to stay with her even once his flowers ran out.

She wouldn't let that happen. So, she gave him a reason for breaking things off that he wouldn't be able to argue with.

"The Truthseer was right," she said, digging her nails into her palms as she forced the words out. "I've been denying what I am for your sake, and I can't do it anymore. I can't love someone who's disgusted by my Extension."

It was Rhett's turn to recoil.

"How could you think *anything* about you disgusts me?"

She tapped her chest with a finger. "Soul Sorter, remember?"

"Then you're not a very good one," Rhett said. "I've never…not once…felt disgusted by you."

"You may not have realized it," Liss qualified. She didn't have the heart to argue with him. Not when the sight of him kneeling beside that grave was shattering her bit by bit. "But I saw disgust in your soul last night."

Had that really only been last night? It felt like a lifetime ago.

"Yeah. I felt it at myself, for making you ashamed of something that's a part of you."

Liss opened and closed her mouth without uttering a word. She felt the truth behind his words.

"I don't want you to ever resist sorting my soul again," Rhett said, as she continued to try and make sense of what he'd just told her. "I should never have told you to stay out."

Liss blinked. "But what about how you said your thoughts were the only things you've ever had for yourself?"

Rhett's gaze flicked to the mound of dirt beside them and then back to her.

"I think I got it wrong," he said carefully, like he was just working it out for himself. "It wasn't that you were invading my privacy that was bothering me. It was that you would see parts of me that I didn't want to think about myself, let alone have you see. I didn't want you to think less of me."

She understood what he was saying. It was exactly how she would feel if their positions were reversed.

"Aside from suppressing my Extension," she said, "what can I do to convince you that nothing I see in your soul could ever make me think less of you?"

"How about this." Rhett tucked a loose strand of hair behind her ear. "You sort my soul and tell me what you see. Then, I'll explain the reason behind the emotions so there aren't any more misunderstandings."

"I guess we could try that," Liss said, feeling a little bashful and flattered that he cared so much what she thought of him. "But that still doesn't change—"

"We're going to find more of the flowers," he interrupted her, knowing exactly where her mind had gone. "You aren't getting rid of me that easily."

Liss couldn't manage to hide her smile at that.

Rhett got to his feet and offered her his hand. He led her deeper into the forest, still near to Stone's grave but not right on top of it. There were two trees that had been drawn together because of all the snow weighing down their branches, and they formed a kind of tent that shielded them from the worst of the wind. Rhett ducked into the shelter and leaned back against the trunk. He pulled Liss against him so her body was flush against his.

"I'm ready," he said in a low voice that made her forget about the frozen ground beneath her.

"Okay." She took a shuddering breath, and then she let herself see into Rhett's soul.

Liss sucked in a breath at what she saw. Even for Rhett, the emotions were raging like a violent storm.

"That bad?" he asked, quirking his brow as he looked down at her.

"There's so much grief," she said in a quiet voice, feeling embarrassed at this strangely intimate sharing. "And anger."

Rhett nodded. "That second one is all for Jaikon and Elouicia."

Liss had figured as much, but it was nice to get confirmation for once. It often frustrated her to know what someone was feeling and have to guess at the source of those emotions. Most of the time she got it right, but at times, she was completely wrong.

Like when she'd assumed Rhett's disgust was directed at her.

"There's also love, which I think is even stronger than your anger and grief, although it's hard to tell for sure."

Rhett leaned down and kissed the top of her head. "Any idea who that emotion is for?"

Liss couldn't believe he was teasing her. After what happened with Stone, she had begun to think she'd never see him smile again. She felt her own lips curve up.

"Silverbird?" she guessed.

"Nope." Rhett brushed his lips across hers, making a warm tingle spread through her body.

"That stray dog that somehow managed to get through the ward and has been begging for scraps?"

"It's for you, Liss." He spoke the words against her lips. "It's all for you."

Liss tried to deepen the kiss, but he pulled back. His eyes smiled even though the rest of his expression was still serious.

"What else?" he asked.

Liss frowned. "There's also some wariness mixed in with your love."

The softness in Rhett's expression disappeared. Guilt entered his soul along with the other emotions.

"I trust you," Rhett began. "And I'm over…everything with you being Opal Smoke. It's just that I've had so much deception in my life. I think I need a little more time to get back to where I was before."

She wasn't sure Rhett would ever get back to where he'd been before. He'd put walls back up around his soul that wouldn't easily come down. If they came down at all.

"I also see honor and responsibility," she said, sifting through his emotions. "And trepidation."

Rhett nodded again. "I don't want to be emperor, but I think the best way to honor Stone's memory is to make Lagonia a place where he would have been proud to live."

It was such a nobly Rhett thing to say that Liss almost laughed.

"That's a lot of emotions." Rhett sighed as he tipped his head back against the trunk.

Liss smiled. "Tell me about it. I'm dizzy from just looking at them. I can't imagine what it must be like to feel so much." Liss hesitated, and then she admitted, "Your soul is what first drew me to you."

"Really?"

She nodded.

Rhett settled himself more comfortably against the tree, putting one arm around her shoulders and draping the other across her stomach.

"Now, do the same for your soul," he said, nuzzling her neck.

Liss gave him a startled look.

He raised his eyebrows. "Fair's fair, right?"

Liss had never teased apart the emotions in her own soul this way before. It felt…odd.

By the time she was finished, they were lying on the cold ground, tangled up in each other. In spite of everything that had passed between them, this sharing of their souls was somehow the most intimate thing they'd ever done.

Liss expected to feel awkward after telling Rhett her deepest emotions. Instead, she felt free in a way she never had before. There were no secrets or hesitations left between them.

Rhett got to his feet and offered her his hand.

"What are your feelings on spending the rest of our night in an Insorsiled tent instead of on the cold ground?"

Liss took his hand, letting him haul her to her very numb feet.

"Extremely positive."

CHAPTER 41

Rhett still grieved for Stone. He still ached from losing Ciago. He had to come to terms with the fact that he was going to fight for the right to rule Lagonia.

But tonight, he just wanted to take a bath…with Liss. And then, he was going to love her the way he should have every single night since she rescued him from the torture cage.

As soon as they stepped through the ward, though, Rhett knew something was wrong. He drew his dagger. Liss looked at him, and then she pulled out her own. They moved forward together, silent and tense.

No one was standing guard on top of the barricade. There was no sign of a struggle or forced entry. It was just…abandoned. Even the tunnel leading through the structure was devoid of people.

Liss grabbed his arm when they reached the closed door on the other side.

"I can sense a lot of people. My mom, and—" She tilted her head like she was listening. "Jema and Mari." She reached for the door to the camp. "They're scared and upset."

Rhett stepped through the door right behind Liss.

"It's him," someone called.

Mari's brothers fell on him.

Rhett had no idea what was going on, but he knew the brothers were Liss's friends. He dropped his dagger and allowed them to yank his wrists behind his back.

"You won't be needing this anymore," an Extended woman taunted, picking up Rhett's dagger and looping it through her own belt.

"Be careful you don't accidentally slice your hand off," Rhett told the woman, annoyed at the way she was handling his weapon.

Mari's brothers began winding thick ropes around his wrists.

"You're going to need a better knot if you expect to give me a challenge," Rhett told them. "And if you plan to keep my dragon tied up, you'd better have a trough of gold nuggets to feed her."

"Mom, what the hell?" Liss shouted, giving one of Mari's brothers a shove before marching over to her mother.

Rhett looked around, noticing all the Extended were gathered. They each held a Lagonian weapon, and they faced him like they were an army about to march into battle.

"You brought Opal Slayer into our hideout," Nya said to Liss.

Mari's brothers continued to loop ropes around Rhett until he was more mummy than prisoner.

Liss was shaking her head. "Mom, don't do this. Please."

"I'm sorry, Liss," Nya said. She looked like she meant it. "But I'm doing this to protect you as much as to save everyone else in the hideout. This man," she pointed at Rhett, "is the worst of them all."

Rhett didn't disagree with her. While he had saved a fair number of Extended since meeting Liss, that didn't make up for all the lives he'd taken before he started to care about more than his own survival.

Liss backed away from her mother and toward Rhett. She gripped her knife.

Rhett turned his head—the only part of him that wasn't bound up—and caught sight of two other figures who were similarly bound together. Anger made his pulse speed up when he realized it was Wilsean and Samara. The ropes had been wrapped around and around them, until only their heads were visible. They were both also gagged.

Liss pointed her knife at the brothers. Her hand was steady, but her expression was furious.

"Don't make me choose," Liss told the brothers. "I promise you won't like my decision."

"Liss, don't!"

Mari, her opal face streaked with tears, tried to get between Liss and her brothers.

"I saved the kid from slavers so you could use her against Liss?" Rhett bit out at Nya. His disgust for the woman grew to an all-time high.

He understood doing whatever was necessary to protect one's people. It was a sentiment he might have respected under different circumstances. But this was Liss's mother, and her first responsibility should have been to protect Liss. Now, the mob of Extended was inching toward her with the same murderous looks on their faces that they were giving him.

"You belong with your own people," Nya told Liss.

"*They* are my people." Liss motioned to Rhett, Wilsean, and Samara. "Now, let them go before I have to kill anyone." She stepped forward, brandishing her knife.

When the mob of Extended didn't back away, Liss gave them a blood-chilling smile.

"Did I mention that Opal Slayer is the one who trained me how to fight?"

"Every day for months," Rhett added. He swept a freezing gaze over the crowd. "She's as good as I am."

"And a whole lot angrier," Liss said.

"She's really willing to kill for him," a voice choked with hatred called out.

The speaker stepped forward, and Rhett saw it was the Truthseer.

"You can have the four of us as your allies or your enemies," Liss told the crowd, facing them as fearlessly as she had stood up to Jaikon.

Keela, the Green Thumb, hurried over to stand between Liss and the crowd of Extended.

"I think we might be acting too hastily," she cautioned. "We can't forget that these four young people rescued all of the Extended slaves in Lagonia. I saw it myself."

"So, what, do you expect us to bow down before them?" an Extended man demanded.

Keela lifted her chin. "I expect us to consider this rationally, and not to make decisions that could hurt, rather than help, our people."

She put her hands on her hips and glared at the crowd. "If we start killing out of hate, then that makes us no better than the ones who did the same to us."

Rhett thought Keela was giving him more kindness than he deserved, but he stayed silent.

For several long moments, no one spoke.

Nya said, "All of the caravan leaders come to the cottage." Nya pointed a finger at Liss. "You too."

"Untie them first." Liss planted her feet.

Long seconds passed while Nya debated what to do. Finally, she nodded.

"Let them go back to their tent, but don't let them leave," she told Mari's brothers.

It was monumentally stupid of the Extended to unbind him and Wilsean, but Rhett didn't tell them that.

"Are you okay?" Liss asked him anxiously, taking his hand and scowling at the rope burns on his wrists.

"We're going to go suffer in our tiny tent," Rhett told her in his most serious voice. "We'll probably freeze to death or die of starvation."

Liss's mouth twitched.

"I'll fix this," she whispered, and then she hurried to the cottage after the rest of the leaders.

Rhett, Wilsean, and Samara stayed silent until they'd crawled through the flap in their tent and bolted the brass door on the inside.

They all stood in the warm common room that smelled like pine and baking bread, and stared at each other.

"Well, I suppose we're going to stick around until Liss gets back," Wilsean said.

Rhett nodded. "You suppose correctly."

"I can think of worse places to be imprisoned," Samara said. She settled herself on the couch and sighed in contentment.

Wilsean sat beside her. Rhett perched on one of the chairs, feeling a little badly about getting his filth all over the white cushions.

Samara had fallen asleep in the crook of Wilsean's arm, and Rhett had just worked up the energy to go clean up, when a quiet thunk against the brass door startled all of them to their feet.

"What was that?" Samara asked.

Rhett went to the door with Wilsean on his heels. He reached back, and Wilsean put a throwing knife in his hand.

The Extended people's second mistake was assuming Wilsean's only weapon was his bow.

Rhett looked out the peep hole that appeared as soon as he felt himself wishing for one. When he peered out through the glass, he saw no one on the other side of the door.

The gentle thunk came again at the base of the door. Rhett eased open the door as he tightened his grip on the knife.

There was no one there.

He was about to shut the door and bolt it again when movement on the ground caught his attention. A small sphere the same color as the tent's polished wood floor rolled inside.

As Rhett watched, the sphere began to grow and morph. Samara let out a little yelp as the sphere turned into an opal-skinned child in a crouch.

"It's me," Jema said, popping to her feet.

"That's a cool Extension," Wilsean noted, putting his knives away.

Before Rhett could do anything to prepare himself, the little girl wrapped her arms around his legs and hugged him.

"Um." Rhett looked to the others for some indication of what he was supposed to do.

Samara giggled. Wilsean put up his hands and said, "Can't help you, man."

Rhett gave Jema an awkward pat on the back. She looked up at him, and Rhett's discomfort deepened when he realized she was crying.

"What's wrong?" he asked.

"I'm sorry they tied you up and yelled at you," she said, wiping her eyes on her sleeve.

Samara gave him a pointed stare that made it clear he was supposed to say something.

Damnit. Where was Liss?

"It's not your fault," Rhett said, squatting down so he was closer to Jema's height.

Jema's orange eyes widened. "Are you really who everyone's saying you are?"

The expression on her face begged him to say no.

"I am," he said, "but I swear I'll never hurt another one of your people. I want to help you."

"Because you're in love with Lissy?" Jema asked.

"Yes."

Jema thought about that for a minute. Then, seeming satisfied, she lowered her voice to a whisper. "I spied on the meeting in the cottage."

That got Rhett's attention.

"What did you hear?" he asked, trying to keep his voice gentle.

"They decided our people are going to war against yours. They're all going to attack Lagonia."

"The Extended were too scared to come to Lagonia to free their enslaved friends and family," Wilsean scoffed. "They're not going to war."

"But they were mostly scared of the Viper, and since he's here, they aren't as scared anymore," Jema said. "Besides, the freed slaves told everyone about how most of the good soldiers have been sent away. They're going to take over the empire and kill all the people like the Lagonians did to us."

Rhett, Wilsean, and Samara exchanged a horrified look.

"They can't," Samara breathed. "It's just civilians left in the empire."

"And Jaikon's invincibles," Wilsean added.

Rhett gripped the edge of the table. He'd armed the Extended. He'd given them weapons from his own empire. Now, they were going to turn those weapons on his people.

It was true he'd never had much use for the spoiled, gossip-mongering Lagonian gentry. But they were still his people to protect. The need to keep them safe…to defend them from harm…sang through his blood.

Jaikon could stop the untrained army of Extended, but he wouldn't. He'd let thousands of Lagonians and Extended die without a second thought.

Rhett had fought in enough battles to know there was never any real victory for the men and women on the ground.

He squeezed his eyes shut.

Rhett had always imagined he might someday die by an Extended person's hands, but he'd never expected this. He'd never expected the civilians in his empire to be threatened because of his violent past. Now, that was precisely what was going to happen.

And he'd been the one to mobilize the Extended and make them a united front. He'd handed them everything they needed to destroy his empire.

"Come on, Jema." Samara offered the little girl her hand. "Let's go in the kitchen and get you some candy."

"What are you going to do?" Wilsean asked, as soon as they were alone.

What could he do?

Under different circumstances, he and Wilsean would start slitting throats until their enemy was too terrified to do anything except scatter. But to do that would mean killing Liss's mother and friends, and he'd sworn he would never kill another Extended.

Rhett didn't want to murder people who were just trying to survive.

"I don't know," he said. It was the truth.

He needed Stone.

Banging came from the other side of the brass door.

"Rhett," an adolescent male voice called. "It's Spence and Mari. Let us in."

As soon as Wilsean unlocked the door, the two kids barged in. Their orange eyes were wild and their hair was wind-tossed.

Before anyone could speak, Spence pulled off the blanket he'd been wearing like a cloak to reveal Wilsean's bow strapped over his back. Mari opened her jacket and took out Rhett's dagger.

"How did you manage this?" Wilsean asked, taking his bow and petting it like it was a beloved child.

Rhett didn't stroke his dagger, but he felt more at ease the second it was back in his hand.

"We're thieves," Mari said, giving Rhett a sly grin that reminded him of Liss.

"Thank you," Rhett told the kids.

"We didn't do it for you." Spence scowled at him. "We did it for Liss."

"Fair enough," Rhett replied.

"Our people are going to war against yours," Mari said, shifting uneasily from foot to foot. "Liss and her mom are in Burk's wagon. They're shouting. I—I don't know if Liss is safe. Everyone is so mad at her—"

"You should have led with that," Rhett bit out, heading for the door.

"Rhett—"

"Stay here," he ordered Wilsean.

He gripped his dagger and left the tent.

Two quick thrusts of his elbow had the Fighters standing guard outside their tent in an unconscious heap. For as strong as they were, the Fighters were as susceptible to getting knocked out as anyone else.

Extended were everywhere. Rhett flitted from shadow to shadow the way he had as an assassin. Everyone was too wrapped up in their own conversations and pre-battle preparations to notice the slight rippling near a wagon's shadow.

It took only a few minutes for him to reach his destination. He wanted to barge right into Nya's wagon, but he forced himself to wait. If Rhett was going to start killing people to save Liss, he needed to make sure he had no other choice. Liss wouldn't forgive him otherwise.

Rhett melted into the shadows and waited. He tensed, readying for anything. He didn't care if Nya was Liss's mother. If she was putting Liss in danger, nothing would save her.

CHAPTER 42

Liss stared at her mother. It felt like she was looking at a stranger. She couldn't believe the change that had come over her mom since discovering Rhett was Opal Slayer.

"I know this is difficult for you, sweetheart," her mother said, "but he is going to die. And then, the rest of his people will follow. This is just the way it has to be. Our people before theirs."

A year ago, Liss would have wholeheartedly agreed.

"It's not that simple," she told her mom…again. "There are good and bad Lagonians, just like there are good and bad Extended. Keela was right. If you start slaughtering innocents, you'll be as bad as the worst of them."

"I'd hardly call the Caravan Butcher an innocent," her mother replied acidly.

Liss couldn't disagree, and yet, she would watch the whole world burn before she let anyone hurt Rhett.

Every argument she'd tried with the other caravan leaders had fallen on deaf ears. Now that she was alone with her mom, she tried a different angle.

"I thought you would understand," she said. "You fell in love with a Lagonian, too. Wouldn't you have done anything to protect him, just like I'm doing for Rhett?"

"Your father was a Lagonian merchant!" Nya shouted. "Don't you dare compare him to the likes of Opal Slayer."

Liss felt a twinge at those words. It had been so long since Liss thought of Rhett that way, she almost couldn't remember the hatred she'd felt when she first discovered who he was.

"Give him time," she begged her mom. "You'll see he's a good man. He was forced to do horrible things to survive, just like the rest of us."

Nya sighed. "Liss, you're not helping to convince the other caravans you're on their side. You need to get your priorities in order."

Red hot rage welled up from Liss's soul.

"Get my priorities straight?" she bit out. "I'm not sure you remember, but I'm the one who put my life on the line every day for *years* to steal from the Lagonians to help our caravan survive. I'm the one who went into the empire to figure out how to destroy their immunity."

I'm the one who gave up my childhood to care for you, Liss wanted to add, but she wasn't angry enough to be that cruel.

"That was all very noble, but—"

"Don't talk to me about priorities!" Liss couldn't keep her voice at a reasonable volume. "I sacrificed everything for our people. I love Rhett more than anyone else in the world, and I betrayed him for our people."

Nya winced. Liss felt hurt flare across her mother's soul.

Liss didn't try to take back what she'd said. It was the truth, and she was done trying to tiptoe around it.

"You can't imagine what it's like to look at the person you love and know they don't trust you anymore because of the lies you told them," Liss continued. "So don't you dare question my commitment to our people."

"I know how much you must be hurting," Nya said, gentling her voice.

For some reason, it angered Liss all the more.

Her mom continued, "But whatever rift has opened up between the two of you is for the best. There is no future for you with Opal Slayer."

Her mom's hypocrisy overwhelmed Liss. "And I'm guessing when everyone told you that you had no future with my dad, you told them what I'm about to tell you. That you can all go shove—"

"The other leaders will agree to letting him live out the rest of his life in prison," Nya said. "Be grateful for that, and let this ill-fated love go."

A cackling, deranged laugh bubbled up from Liss's throat.

"Let me get this straight," she said to her mom. "You're jealous because Rhett is alive and my dad is dead, and you're angry because you think my dad deserves to be alive but Rhett doesn't?"

Nya didn't say anything. A tear trickled down her opal cheek.

Her mom's voice wavered when she spoke. "I'm telling you to bury your feelings for this man if you ever want the Extended to accept you."

"I am Extended," Liss felt compelled to remind her mom.

She was relieved to feel the truth of those words in her soul. With the way the Extended had been treating her, she'd been growing less certain herself. "And I'm in love with Rhett. The last time I was forced to choose, I chose the Extended."

She looked her mother in the eye. "I won't make that same choice again."

"Then, I won't be able to protect you."

Nya's soul was overflowing with despair. Liss's was all rage.

She stormed out of the wagon, slamming the door behind her.

"Liss."

She spun around. Rhett stepped out from the wagon's shadow. He was almost invisible in his black clothes.

"How much of that did you hear?" she asked, wiping the tears from her eyes.

"I—I thought you might be in trouble." His soul was a confusion of emotions.

"So, all of it."

She was barely keeping herself together. She needed to be alone so she could collect her scattered thoughts.

"Take Wilsean and Samara and get out of here," Liss told him, trying to hold back the tide of her emotions. "I'll meet you—"

"Give me one minute," Rhett said, wrapping a hand around her wrist. His grip was gentle but unyielding. "Please."

She felt vulnerable and exposed…raw.

To her dismay, Rhett knelt on the frozen ground before her.

"What are you doing?" she demanded, aware of her mother standing in the doorway to the wagon. Nya held her bow, although Liss didn't see any arrows. Liss kept her body positioned between Rhett and her mom just in case.

"I've been such a fool." Rhett looked up at her. "I was so wrapped up in feeling betrayed by you, that I never stopped to think how I was the one who needed your forgiveness."

"What?" Liss tugged on his hand, but he stayed where he was.

"I should have refused the orders to kill your people. I knew it was wrong and that they were innocent, and I did it anyway."

Liss sucked in a breath. They both knew what would have happened if Rhett refused to carry out his emperor's orders.

"I know I can never make up for what I've done," Rhett said, "but I'm going to spend the rest of my life doing what I can to make amends. I want to be worthy of you."

Liss felt fresh tears spring to her eyes. He'd said those words to her before…that he wanted to be worthy of her. The last time he'd said them, though, he hadn't known who she was and what she'd done. Now, he knew it all.

Rhett wrapped his arms around her, leaning his head against her stomach. She felt so much shame on his soul that she couldn't take it.

"Rhett, get up," she murmured. "Please."

"Get your filthy Lagonian hands off my woman."

Liss turned. Dolo was leering at the two of them. His hands were suspiciously behind his back.

If he'd hoped to surprise Rhett with an attack, he was going to be sorely disappointed.

Rhett got to his feet in a single, fluid motion. His face and eyes were completely blank of all emotion as he towered over the Flooder. His dagger was in his hand, even though Liss had seen it taken away from him.

Liss scowled at the Flooder. "I knew you were an idiot, but I didn't know you were also delusional." She folded her arms. "I'm not *your woman.* The only thing of mine that belongs to you is my disdain."

Instead of retorting, Dolo smiled. His soul was full of malice and triumph as he revealed what he'd been hiding behind his back.

Rhett went motionless. A scream began in Liss's mind.

Dolo was holding the bag that contained Rhett's remaining supply of immunity flowers.

CHAPTER 43

Ciago was tired of stupid giants who beat their chests and waved their mallets around threateningly. He had always been a quick thinker in the heat of battle, and he wracked his brain for the best way to salvage this situation.

The first Lagonian ship had reached the harbor. Ciago recognized Dannica at the helm, her black braid blowing in the gale. She was one of Lagonia's best soldiers…and an excellent card player. Ciago would be damned if her talents were wasted by being crushed underneath a giant's mallet.

"Winny!" Ciago bellowed.

His voice cut through the giants' chest-pounding and war chants. They were all so surprised by his outburst that they paused their ruckus to stare at him.

The giant leader adjusted her grip on the mallet in her hands, lifting it as though to test its weight. Ciago swallowed.

"I can get you what you need. I can save your giants from starvation."

He didn't let his relief show on his face when the giant leader didn't immediately bash his head in.

"I'm listening," she said.

Ciago spoke slowly, making sure every word was laid down precisely right. He knew if he got any part of this insane plan of his wrong, he wouldn't get a second chance.

"You need food, jewels, and fertile land to sustain yourselves, right?"

At the giant leader's hesitant nod, he forged on.

"I can make sure you get all those things. I can also make sure no Lagonian ever spills another drop of giant blood."

The silence stretched, but Ciago forced himself to wait for the giant leader to speak.

"How?" Lady Umbrog finally asked.

At that moment, a chorus of war horns bellowed from the Lagonian fleet. Ciago looked up to see the archers assembling along the ships' railings.

He caught the scent of fire just before the archers nocked flame-tipped arrows. Hundreds of fiery pinpricks stood starkly against the black cloud background.

Ciago cursed.

He threw off the giant who was holding him. He leapt to his feet and began to run.

The snarl of wolves filled the air, and heavy footsteps pounded the ground behind him. Ciago didn't look back. He ran faster.

* * *

An hour later, Ciago stood on the frozen shore. The frothy waves spit up chunks of ice and swelled around the small rowboats scraping against the sand.

Ciago scanned the document he'd written with Insorsiled ink that had been on board one of the Lagonian ships. It wasn't perfect, but it was the best he could manage on short notice. He signed the bottom with a flourish. He dipped his family ring into the ink and pressed the seal beneath his signature.

Once it was done, he sighed in relief. For the moment, he couldn't think about the challenges that lay ahead. He was just grateful that he, and everyone else standing on this frozen shore, was still breathing. The rest of the Lagonians stood at attention on the shore. They were all vigilant, but every one of their weapons was sheathed.

"I can only guarantee these terms if my friend becomes the emperor," Ciago warned Winny. He'd learned his lesson about holding back information from the giant leader.

"He is going to be the emperor," Dannica said with confidence. "Rhett is unstoppable." To the giant leader, she added, "And he'll be more than fair in his dealings with you."

"I understand," Winny replied. She put her quill to the contract and signed her name beside Ciago's.

Ulfrath put his massive snout to the contract and took a deep sniff. Ciago was gratified to see that the wolf didn't snarl, which he took to mean the creature approved of the historic, impossible deal he'd just brokered.

The next order of business was to confirm that every Lagonian on this shore was, in fact, loyal to Rhett. It wouldn't do any of them any good to return to Lagonia, only to have half of their army turn on them and rush off to join the enemy.

Ciago needn't have worried. It turned out that being sent across the Brookgar Sea to die had soured even the most duty-bound to their current emperor. Every man and woman swore their allegiance to Rhett, with Ciago, Winny, and Dannica as their witnesses.

Ciago glanced between the decades-long enemies, who were now standing on the same shore without making any move to kill each other. It had been no small feat to broker a truce between the two enemies before flaming arrows or mallets began to fly. But, being the suave, smooth-talking son of a court advisor, Ciago had managed it.

Whatever role Rhett gave him in the new regime better be an important one, Ciago thought.

His self-satisfaction drained away as Dannica filled him in on what had been happening in the empire. He could only imagine how much trouble Rhett and Liss had stirred up by this point. The more Dannica talked, the more Ciago knew they didn't have any time to lose. They certainly didn't have two weeks to cross back over the Brookgar Sea, likely losing a number of their crew to storms along the way.

"Is there any faster way across the sea?" Ciago asked Winny, despairing even as the question left his mouth.

If there was a faster route, he would have heard about it long before now.

"There is," Winny said, surprising him. "A powerful Wind Extended lives in a settlement an hour from here by sleigh. She could get our entire fleet across the sea in a couple of hours."

"We have anti-contagion suits on board," Dannica said, anticipating Ciago's objection before he could voice it. "So, being around an Extended won't be a problem for all of us humans."

Ciago couldn't believe his ears. And since the giants were immune to the contagion, they wouldn't have to worry about the disease at all.

"There is only one problem," Winny said, raising a finger. "Her fees are...vast."

Ciago and Dannica exchanged a knowing look.

Dannica whistled to the crew still on board. There was movement on deck.

"If there's one thing Lagonians come equipped with," Ciago told Winny as the chests of jewels started being passed down to the shallows, "it's vast wealth."

Winny sucked in a breath at the sight of the enormous chests the soldiers were straining to lift.

"Our severance pay," Dannica murmured to Ciago, as chest after chest was lowered from the ships. "Our emperor's final gift to the soldiers who betrayed him."

"I always knew Jaikon would be useful for something," Ciago replied with a smirk.

As Ciago watched the giants' expressions cloud over, his optimism transformed. He wondered if he'd made a grave mistake.

"We could kill all of you and take your treasure," Winny said, confirming his fears. "So many jewels will keep us alive for many long years to come."

"That's true," Ciago said, holding up a hand as the soldiers around him reached for their weapons. This was a fight they wouldn't win. "But if you did that, you'd be stuck on this frozen tundra for the rest of your lives."

He paused, giving Winny time to envision that future before continuing.

"Your alternative is a plot of land in Lagonia, with the most powerful empire in the world as your ally. You'd have easy access to trade with Insorsil. You'd never have to cross this sea again unless you wanted to take an icy vacation."

Winny cocked her head at him, considering.

"Besides," Ciago continued, "if you kill me, you'll never have anyone to beat you in chess again."

"There is that," Winny mused.

Ciago didn't let his relief show as amusement curved Winny's lips.

Winny clapped her gloved hands together, and giants and wolves began swarming around her.

"Prepare my sleigh," Winny ordered her giants. To Dannica, she said, "Get your jewels ready. We're going to need them."

CHAPTER 44

Liss couldn't breathe. Dolo was holding Rhett's bag of flowers. Pure evil filled his soul.

"Don't you dare," Liss whispered.

She spun to Mari's brothers, who flanked the Flooder.

"How could you?" she demanded. They were her friends and her mom's most trusted guards.

"Nya told us to give them to Dolo," Mari's oldest brother told Liss.

She shook her head. If she was anything other than a Soul Sorter, she would have refused to believe him. Emotions didn't lie, though. Mari's brother was telling the truth.

Liss turned to find her mother, who was still standing on the porch of her wagon. Her eyes were apologetic, but hardness filled her soul.

"Give them back," Liss told the Flooder, giving him all of her attention.

Never breaking eye contact with her, Dolo unzipped the bag. He was clearly intending to make a spectacle of this for all of the Extended who had gathered around to watch.

"Dolo, please don't," she said, softening her voice and sidling up to him. She kept her disgust hidden at the way his soul churned with excitement when she begged.

Still staring at her, Dolo turned over the bag. All the dried flowers fluttered out. Gasping, Liss lunged forward.

"I'm sorry, Liss." Romile, Dolo's Flamer brother, stepped in front of her. His hands were sparking. "If you come any closer, I'll have to burn you."

Liss didn't care. Those were Rhett's flowers…and they were now floating away on a stream Dolo had pulled out of nowhere. She dove for the flowers as Romile's hands erupted in flames.

She felt the heat of the fire on her face before Rhett's arms came around her, pulling her back.

"Let me go!" She fought against him, but Rhett only held her tighter against him.

Liss was frantic. She couldn't let this happen. And yet, Rhett's arms were steel bands around her. He kept her in place as she was forced to watch the flowers disintegrate in the water Dolo was controlling.

She writhed against Rhett, cursing and shouting. He kept his hold on her until the Flamer's hands were no longer on fire and the flowers were gone.

The flowers were gone.

The stream was still trickling across the field, but the dried-up flowers had dissolved. Nothing remained of them, not even the opal shimmer of their petals.

The moment Rhett loosened his hold on her, Liss lunged at Dolo.

There were screams as she drew her knife, but before she could stick it somewhere the Flooder wouldn't be able to ignore, she started to gag.

Her chest spasmed. She dropped her weapon as she tried to breathe. She couldn't.

"What are you doing to her?" Rhett demanded, his voice coming from somewhere far away.

Liss tried to speak. All she managed was a wet cough. Each time she tried to inhale, she got another lungful of water. She heard it sloshing around inside her as she took one panicked, water-filled gasp after another.

Dolo, her terrified mind realized. He was doing this to her.

"I'm drowning her with the water in her own body," Dolo said.

Through her blurring vision, Liss sent a pleading glance to the spectators. No one moved.

No one was helping them, Liss's foggy brain realized. Another spasm wracked her chest as she collapsed.

"Take care of Opal Slayer," Dolo ordered someone else. "She's all mine."

Through her watery vision, Liss saw Rhett move. She saw the blade of his dagger flash. She heard screams as Dolo fell to the ground.

Liss gasped. Air, rather than water, flowed through her lungs. It hurt. Every breath was a searing pain through her chest.

"He killed my brother!" Romile's shrill cry rang out. "Get him!"

"Take them down," another voice cried. "Take them down!"

Liss didn't take the time to appreciate the fact that she was still alive. She grabbed her knife from where it had fallen and stood back-to-back with Rhett as they faced off against the entire camp of Extended.

"Liss, please," her mom begged, stepping out from the crowd and holding out her hands beseechingly. "We're your people. Not him. Come back to me."

"Opal Slayer spilled Extended blood…again!" a man in the crowd shouted. "Kill him. Kill them both!"

An arrow zoomed past Liss, lodging in the man's skull.

Silverbird, with Wilsean on her back, scattered the crowd from her path. The dragon snorted and pranced. Her claws carved divots into the frozen ground. Right now, she didn't look like the kindly dragon Liss knew her to be. Silverbird looked ferocious.

Wilsean kept his seat as the dragon continued to rear. His next arrow was poised. In spite of everything happening around them, only one thought filled Liss's mind.

"When did you take your last flower?" she asked Rhett, raising her voice to be heard over the angry shouts of the crowd around them.

When Rhett didn't answer, she turned her head to look at him.

"About twenty-five hours ago," he said, his voice hoarse. "I was going to take another one today…."

All the sounds surrounding them were drowned out by the furious drumming of Liss's heart against her ribcage. A single flower only lasted for a day. That meant that, for the last hour, Rhett hadn't been immune. He had no protection against the Extended surrounding them. He had no protection from her.

"You have to get out of here." Panic made it difficult to get the words out.

Every fear she'd ever had about becoming like her mother fled. She didn't care about any of that. All she cared about was that Rhett was safe.

They'd find a way to get more of the flowers…somehow. She'd find that underground cavern in Insorsil and steal a whole field of them. But until then, Rhett had to get out of here. He had to survive.

"Go," she told Rhett and Wilsean. "I'll hold them off. Just get out of here. Get out!"

Silverbird swiped a claw at an Extended who got close. The woman shrieked and fell back, blood welling through the slashed fabric of her shirt.

"Not without you," Rhett said, his back still to hers as the tide of Extended came ever nearer. "I'm not leaving you here."

"I'll be fine." She shoved him away from the crowd. "Go!"

"We gave her a chance to come back," one of the caravan leaders told Liss's mom. "She made her choice. Now, we're making ours."

Liss heard those words in a tiny, insignificant corner of her mind. It was the same place where she heard her mother pleading with her not to do this…to prove her loyalty to her own people by turning on the two Lagonians at her back.

Liss would deal with her mom and the rest of the Extended later. Right now, she needed to get Rhett and Wilsean out of here. Every second they were here, they faced a kind of danger far worse than any blade.

The Extended were closing in on them. Wilsean shot arrow after arrow into the crowd. It didn't help. They were enraged…crazed…fueled by Dolo's blood staining the frosty ground.

All Liss could think as the Extended raised their weapons—the ones Rhett had given them—was that their virus was mixing into the air Rhett was breathing.

It was her last thought before the Extended attacked, and the sharp ring of metal filled the clearing.

CHAPTER 45

J aikon leaned over the balustrade of the Sapphire Bridge and stared down at the army assembled below him. It wasn't a particularly large force, but what they lacked in numbers they made up for in invincibility. Jaikon smiled to himself.

"Majesty." Elouicia, out of breath from racing up the stairs to the bridge, bowed low.

"What is it?" Jaikon asked.

"The peasants are fighting among themselves. There have been fifteen casualties already, and there are bound to be more."

This was to be expected. Jaikon had announced that the last immunity flower had been consumed, and now, his subjects' panic was at an all-time high. He had distributed all of the pins to his most loyal followers, who were now assembled before him. The rest of Lagonia was realizing that they should have tried harder to win his favor.

Soon, Jaikon would have Insorsil in his grasp. He no longer had the time or inclination to concern himself with peasants. He'd have an entire kingdom of magic-wielders at his disposal.

But first, he had another small matter to put to rest.

"Tell the peasants I'm going to solve their problem," Jaikon told Elouicia. "Tell them they will come to know me as the emperor who slaughtered every Extended on the continent. Tell them that, by next week, the Extended will no longer exist on this side of the sea."

Jaikon turned to the beaten, filthy, and hopeless Extended man at his side. He gave Burk his most benevolent smile.

"You can't kill me," Burk whispered. "Our contract—"

"Yes, yes." Jaikon waved a dismissive hand.

"I can't kill you. But I imagine when I bring you to your people's hideout and tell them how I discovered their whereabouts, they will do the killing for me." Jaikon sniffed. "I wouldn't want to dirty my blade on you."

Burk's opal skin drained of color. Jaikon felt a twinge of regret. He'd miss having this man around. He rather enjoyed watching the arrogant fool's slow demise.

"It's a shame there will be none of your people left to remember your name," Jaikon said, stepping back before Burk's filthy hand came within grasping distance of his new dragonhide boots. "I will go down in history as the emperor who consolidated all of the great powers under one domain. You will be forgotten."

With that thought warming him, Jaikon turned back to the army anxiously awaiting his command. The gold circlets on their chests gleamed in the rising sun. The pins winked at him, like they were in on his joke. It was perhaps the most beautiful sight Jaikon had ever seen.

"Come, my loyal soldiers," Jaikon called down. "First, we march to annihilate the Extended."

His audience's roar of approval echoed back to him. The sound was glorious to his ears.

"Then, we go to conquer Insorsil," he continued. "From there, we need only reach out our hand and take whatever we wish."

More cheering and bowing.

"We are Lagonians, and we are invincible!"

Jaikon raised his sword in the air as cries of *Long live Emperor Jaikon!* filled the air.

CHAPTER 46

A tremendous howling filled the woods, the likes of which Rhett had never heard. It was loud enough to drown out the Extended crowd's shouts for his blood.

Silverbird roared in terror. The dragon thrashed until Wilsean was thrown from the saddle. Then, Silverbird bolted through the crowd of Extended, scattering them.

White beasts burst from the trees. They looked like wolves, only they were bigger than any creature Rhett had ever seen. They even dwarfed his dragon, who was senseless with fear as she raced away from the wolves' foaming mouths and bared fangs.

The Extended screamed as they tore into the trees. The creatures ignored them. It seemed to Rhett the wolves' feral eyes were pinned directly on his small group.

Rhett put himself between the beasts and Liss, even though these wolves were beyond even his skill. They were massive. He doubted his dagger could even pierce their flesh…if he could survive their snapping jaws long enough to get in a strike.

But even as Rhett wondered whether he would die before or after one of the beasts had swallowed him, a sharp whistle rang through the trees. The wolves, their hackles still raised and their massive fangs bared, began to circle Rhett, Liss, Wilsean, and Samara.

The wolves faced outward, growling at the few Extended who hadn't yet fled into the woods. That was enough to make the ones who still remained scatter.

"They're protecting us," Liss's breathless voice said from behind him.

That was what it seemed like to Rhett, too. He just didn't understand why.

"Good boy, Ulfrath," a familiar voice boomed. "Thank you for not eating my best friends."

Rhett thought he was hallucinating. It was the only explanation for how Ciago, wearing an anti-contagion suit, was standing at the edge of the field that was now surrounded by giants.

Liss shrieked with joy.

Rhett's hope and disbelief were suspended when Liss ran right underneath one of the wolves. She didn't even need to duck to avoid its hairy underside. Rhett breathed again when the wolf didn't gobble her up in a single bite.

When Ciago caught Liss and spun her around, Rhett knew this had to be real. He exchanged a look with Wilsean, and then they were running for Ciago, too.

"Ciago." It was the only word he could get out.

Ciago put Liss down. She backed up a few steps, giving Rhett a *go on* look.

"Ciago," he said again, stupidly.

Ciago grinned at him before inclining his head at the wolves, which were now whining and wagging their tails at the giants. "Now that's what I call an entrance."

"How—"

Apparently, Rhett was incapable of saying more than a single word.

All of the Extended except for Liss's mother had scattered into the Insorsiled forest. Nya, her bow in hand, stood with her back to the barricade. She looked from Liss to the mammoth wolves.

"Liss, come on," Nya said, her voice trembling with fear. "We have to go."

Liss shook her head and moved closer to Rhett. When Nya took a step toward them, one of the beasts growled at her.

Disappointment and grief flickered through Nya's eyes as she slipped through the door to the barricade and disappeared from sight.

Rhett tried to think of what he could say to erase the look on Liss's face, but he didn't have a chance.

"My friend, Liss!" a giant's voice boomed so loudly it shook the ground.

The giant used an enormous grappling hook to swing himself over the twenty-foot wall instead of crawling his way through the tunnel as the others must have. One stride brought him onto the field.

"Hiya, Grub," Liss called, craning her neck to grin up at the giant.

Rhett just about lost his mind when the giant squatted and tilted his head, so his eye—which was as big as Liss's entire head—was level with hers.

"It's great to see you," Liss told the giant, her dimple on full display. "What are you doing here?"

"Help new emperor," Grub the Giant replied.

Rhett rubbed his head, wondering if he'd fallen and knocked his brain around without realizing it.

Silverbird returned from the depths of the forest, looking half-sheepish and half-terrified as she pranced to Rhett's side. She eyed the wolves, who were sitting attentively by their giant masters' feet. The wolves' massive, pink tongues lolled out of their even more massive mouths.

"I know, I know," Ciago said, slinging a heavy arm across Rhett's shoulder. "My handsome face is a lot to take in when it wasn't expected. I would have warned you if I could."

Rhett whirled on his friend. "The corresponder," he managed, doubling the number of words he was now capable of uttering.

"Believe me, I have a good excuse for losing that corresponder," Ciago said, still grinning. "But I'm not giving you the abridged version. You're going to have to wait until there's wine, a hot meal, and an audience of at least a dozen women."

"We'll make it two-dozen," Wilsean promised, taking the hand Ciago offered him and pulling him into a back-slapping hug.

Rhett, finally managing to work himself out of his stupor, did the same. He was still gripping Ciago when the woods began to fill with color. Hundreds of regular-sized humans wearing yellow anti-contagion suits tromped onto the field.

Rhett choked on a laugh. Even with the suit covering her from head to foot, Rhett recognized Dannica out in front. He knew the others, too. They were all men and women he'd trained with and fought beside.

"May I proudly present…your army," Ciago announced, puffing out his chest and flourishing his hands. "And, may I also introduce you to the brilliant, terrifying, mallet-wielding leader of the Giant Realm, Lady Winnowa Umbrog."

The giantess held out a hand to Rhett. Still in a daze, he accepted a bone-crunching handshake from Lagonia's greatest enemy.

After Ciago introduced them to the giants flanking Lady Umbrog, Ciago leaned in to whisper to Rhett.

"I hope you weren't too attached to Lagonia's eastern farmlands," he said.

"Why not?"

Ciago gave him a sheepish grin. "Because you gave them to the giants."

Rhett raised an eyebrow. "I did?"

"You will," Ciago corrected. "As soon as you become emperor."

Rhett swallowed.

"I don't know what to say."

All he knew was that his friend was here, alive, and at his side. Liss and Wilsean were here, and so were the thousand men and women he had thought were lost.

"Say you'll be the leader we need," Ciago said. "Say you'll find a way to defeat Jaikon and take your place as our emperor."

Rhett looked at Liss, who was smiling at him.

"Thank you," he choked out. His gaze went from Ciago to the soldiers who were lined up in pristine rows that went back farther than he could see. "I just—thank you."

"Someone make a note that Rhett's going to need a speech-writer," Wilsean joked.

"All hail the future Lagonia emperor," Dannica called.

Then, she sank down on one knee, lowering her head in reverence.

"No." Rhett pulled Dannica to her feet, stopping the others before they followed her. "I serve all of you."

No matter his reluctance to take the Lagonian crown, that much would always be true.

CHAPTER 47

Rhett couldn't quite get used to being surrounded by giants and enormous wolves, especially when he tried to come to terms with the fact that both were there to help him. It was surreal.

"This was some seriously good timing," Wilsean told Ciago.

"You know me. I never miss a party," Ciago replied. He raised an eyebrow at Rhett. "You really do seem to have a knack for making enemies."

"How did the wolves know not to eat us?" Rhett asked, ignoring his friend's teasing.

"Ulfrath and his pack are *excellent* judges of character," Ciago said, giving the largest of the white wolves a pat on the leg. The beast turned to growl at him before a harsh command from Lady Umbrog had it slinking away. "Also, Winny," Ciago grinned at the leader of the Giant Realm, "ordered them to protect all of you."

The wolf that had just growled at Ciago turned its attention on Liss. Rhett tensed, but the beast didn't show its impressive fangs or raise its hackles. It licked her hand with its huge tongue.

"Did our time together mean nothing to you?" Ciago asked the wolf, giving it a wounded look.

Liss grinned.

Seeming to notice the Extended were no longer anywhere to be seen, Ciago looked around. "So, what did you do to piss all those Extended off?"

Rhett blew out a breath. "That's a story in itself," he said.

"Speaking of which," Liss said, her smile turning to worry, "do you have any more of the anti-contagion suits?"

"Why yes, we do." Ciago gave Liss another self-satisfied smile. He raised a hand, and a soldier came forward bearing two of the suits.

It was a man Rhett had often trained with, and who was one of the most loyal soldiers in the empire. Rhett was surprised to see the man here now.

Then again, Rhett thought wryly, he wouldn't have guessed he might find himself as the most wanted enemy of Lagonia, either. As he accepted one of the suits and started taking off his jacket, he looked at Liss.

Nothing had worked out the way he'd expected or planned, and yet, they were here and alive. They were together.

"Explain to me how you had all of these anti-contagion suits on board ships that weren't supposed to ever return to the empire," Rhett said as Wilsean stepped into his own suit.

Ciago smiled. Wilsean winced.

"Stone," Wilsean explained in a rough voice. "He was trying to get the Emperor to implement the opal contagion protocols in the empire before the flowers ran out. Instead, Jaikon wanted the slavers to take the suits and start tracking down the Extended. So, Stone had the suits put on the ships."

Ciago added, "By the time Jaikon figured out what had happened, the ships were already on their way to the Giant Realm."

Rhett's heart gave a painful lurch.

"What?" Ciago looked at him.

When he couldn't meet his friend's eyes, Ciago turned to Wilsean.

Wilsean was just as incapable of speaking.

"How?" Ciago whispered.

"He saved my life," Liss said in a tremulous voice.

Ciago let out a long breath. He looked away as he composed himself. "Then, he died well," he said, pressing a fist to his heart.

Rhett started pulling on the anti-contagion suit, telling himself there would be time to return to his grief later. Right now wasn't that time.

The suit was multi-layered, and it was a process to roll the thick fabric over his legs. At least it would buy him enough time to return to Insorsil and find more of the immunity flowers. The worst part of the whole ordeal would be not being able to touch Liss until he was fully immune again. That thought had him catching Liss's eye. He gave her a look that made her blush even as her dimple creased her cheek.

"Rhett?" Samara frowned at him. "Are you bleeding?"

Rhett looked down. A darkening streak was smeared across the sleeve of his yellow suit. It wasn't much, but he didn't remember anyone getting near enough with a weapon to injure him.

Ciago chuckled. "Don't tell me you let someone get the drop on you. Really, Rhett. You're getting soft."

Rhett felt a pulse of discomfort on his left forearm. He rolled up the sleeve of his shirt and stared.

He heard the gasps of others around him. His gaze was fixed on the ugly, oozing pustule on his forearm.

He pulled his eyes away from his arm to look at Liss. There was raw, unbridled panic in her blue eyes. Her lips were parted, but she seemed incapable of speaking.

No one said a word. They had all seen these blisters before and knew them for what they were. There were no other explanations, no possibilities that could salvage this situation.

Rhett had opal contagion.

He yanked his sleeve back down, ignoring the looks of horror and muted cries around him. All of his focus was on Liss.

No tears fell from her eyes. Her chest heaved the same way it had when the Flooder was drowning her. Her face had gone deathly pale, and her gaze was fixated on the spot on Rhett's arm where his sleeve now hid the pustule.

"Look at me." He took her face in his hands.

She was holding her breath, like that could prevent the disease from spreading.

They both knew it couldn't.

Rhett leaned down and kissed her. Liss's heart beat so fast against his own he was struck by her fragility…her mortality.

He almost laughed at the irony of that thought, when he was the one in the first stage of the contagion.

"Nothing is going to take you away from me." He held Liss with his gaze. "I won't let you go."

Liss let out a choked sob. The sound cut into him like a blade.

"Rhett." It was the only word she could manage to gasp out.

Her nails dug into his back as she clung to him. He leaned closer, resting his forehead against hers.

He ignored the growing panic of the men and women standing behind him as the news spread through their ranks.

Rhett has opal contagion.

Ciago and Wilsean were speaking in low, urgent tones. Dannica was saying something to the soldiers. Rhett ignored all of them as he focused on Liss.

Her whole body was shaking with silent sobs.

He wanted to tell her it was going to be okay. Instead, he said, "I told you I wasn't going anywhere. I'm not going to leave you."

As both of their gazes went to Rhett's arm, he knew that, no matter how much he wished it could be otherwise, his words were a lie.

There was only one enemy more impossible to defeat than Jaikon's invincible army.

Opal contagion.

THE END

* * *

Because reviews are so important for a book to be successful, please consider leaving a brief review on your favorite retailer if you enjoyed *Opal Slayer*. Many thanks!

* * *

Sign up for Stephanie Fazio's e-Newsletter to learn about upcoming books at:
https://StephanieFazio.com/subscribe/

Acknowledgements

Thank you to all of the wonderful people who helped with this book.

To Andrew Brodsky, Keith Tarrier, and Ellen Schaeffer. Thank you for being part of the team that made this book possible.

To Bob Brodsky, Rhoda Schneider, and the rest of my ARC team, for seeing new ways to bring my characters and stories to life.

To my amazing friends and family, who have supported me every step of the way.

To my readers. Thank you for giving me a reason to write.

To Andrew. Thank you for being you.

About the Author:

Stephanie Fazio is a fantasy author. She grew up in Syracuse, New York, and prior to writing full time, she worked in the fields of journalism, secondary education, and higher education. She has an undergraduate degree in English from Colgate University and a Master's degree in Reading, Writing, and Literacy from the University of Pennsylvania. Stephanie lives in Austin with her husband and crazy rescue dog. When she isn't writing, she's getting lost in parks, hosting taco nights, or ironically and miserably losing at word games, but having fun while she does it.

Connect with Stephanie Fazio:

Visit her Website: https://www.StephanieFazio.com
Sign up for her newsletter: https://StephanieFazio.com/subscribe/

Continue the Opal Contagion series

Book 3, *Opal Storm*
AVAILABLE JULY 2020!

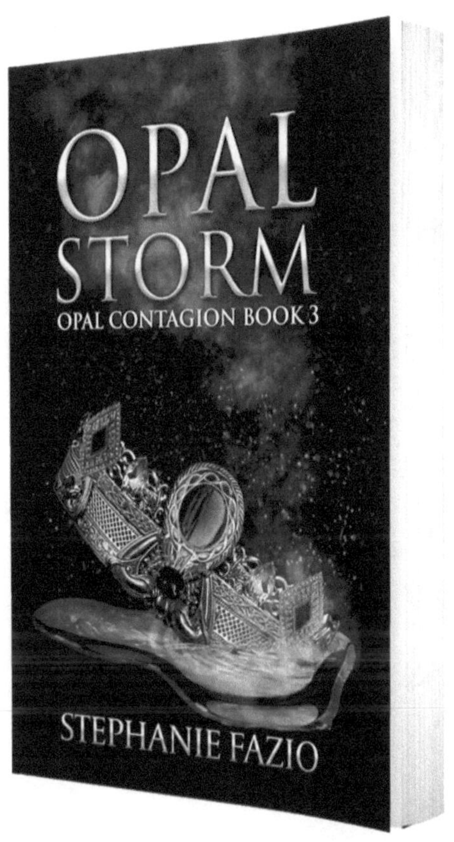

StephanieFazio.com

Discover other books by Stephanie Fazio

The Fount Series

The Prince's Chosen

The Forsaken's Choice

The Chosen Union

Bisecter Series

Bisecter

Halve Human

Dusker Dark

Captain Harkibel

Opal Contagion Series

Opal Smoke

Opal Slayer

Opal Storm

StephanieFazio.com

www.ingramcontent.com/pod-product-compliance
Lightning Source LLC
Chambersburg PA
CBHW051646180726
48284CB00006B/1887